# A Deadly Little List

Kay Stewart & Chris Bullock

**Library and Archives Canada Cataloguing in Publication**
Stewart, Kay L. (Kay Lanette), 1942-
A deadly little list / by Kay Stewart and Chris Bullock.

ISBN-13: 978-1-896300-95-5
ISBN-10: 1-896300-95-2

I. Bullock, Chris, 1945-  II. Title.

PS8637.T4946D42 2006       C813'.6       C2005-907685-2

Board editor: Lynne Van Luven
Cover and interior design: Ruth Linka
Cover image: Bonnie Moro
Author photo: Gary Ford

 Canada Council    Conseil des Arts
for the Arts       du Canada

 Canadian    Patrimoine
Heritage     canadien

 edmonton
arts
council

NeWest Press acknowledges the support of the Canada Council for the Arts and the Alberta Foundation for the Arts, and the Edmonton Arts Council for our publishing program. We also acknowledge the financial support of the Government of Canada through the Book Publishing Industry Development Program (BPIDP) for our publishing activities.

NeWest Press
201–8540–109 Street
Edmonton, Alberta  T6G 1E6
(780) 432-9427
www.newestpress.com

2  3  4  5  09  08  07  06

PRINTED AND BOUND IN CANADA

*In Memoriam*

*Norma Snow*

*Beloved sister and sister-in-law*

*1950–2005*

# Prologue
## Victoria, British Columbia
### Friday afternoon and evening, July 7

"Why do I have to interview the bloody cast?" Arthur Fairweather stood in the lobby of the Caprice Theatre grumbling at its owner, who was, not so incidentally, his ex-wife. "It's bad enough that I have to review *The Mikado* yet again. Sometimes I think you organize these things just to torture me, Thea."

"Reviewing is your job, in case you've forgotten. And what's wrong with *The Mikado*?" Thea yanked the rubber band out of her silky dark hair and redid her ponytail. Her truculent expression reminded Arthur of an old family photo he'd seen of her with her older brother, boxing gloves at the ready though she was a head shorter and many pounds lighter. He couldn't resist a jab or two.

"Gilbert and Sullivan are past their expiry date, that's what's wrong. People in Victoria want theatre that goes along with their sweet shops and retired colonels walking their golden retrievers, and you're pandering to them."

"You're the one who sounds like a retired colonel, and you're not forty yet."

"Tell me I'm wrong."

"You're wrong, Arthur. Victoria's a more complex place than you ever want to admit. Yes, it has its sweet shops and its British farces, but it also has nightclubs and rock music and experimental theatre, as you should know after two years here. Why do you stay if it's all too unsophisticated for you? You can save up your pennies and go back to England anytime you want to, you know."

"Who got me here in the first place?"

Thea's cellphone rang. As she unclipped it from the belt of her jeans, she said, "Arthur, I haven't got time for this. The cast is waiting for you. Go and do your interviews."

Still grumbling to himself, Arthur marched into the auditorium. On stage, a handful of actors were making a late lunch from trays of sandwiches, fruit, and cheese, the footlights casting their dark shadows upon the closed curtains behind them. Gathered around a bright blue music stand, laughing and talking, were three men. Two of the men—one slight and olive-complexioned, the other slightly taller and barrel-chested, with a greying hippy ponytail—were wearing identical grey T-shirts with some sort of logo; the third, a sandy-haired giant of a man in a black kimono, was the only person in costume. This, Arthur decided, must be the director.

"I'm Arthur Fairweather, from the *Victoria Post-Dispatch*," he announced. "I'm looking for Zachary Smith."

With a clown's exaggerated look of surprise, the man with the ponytail peered intently at his two companions, and then pointed a finger at himself. "You've found him."

When it became clear Smith didn't intend to budge, Arthur clambered onto the stage and settled himself on a wooden crate beside the music stand. He searched for what he hoped would be a safe opening question. "Why do you call yourselves—" he glanced at his notes, "—the Vesuvius Light Opera Company?"

"Why Vesuvius? Because when we sing—" Smith grabbed the blue music stand as though it were a microphone and boomed, in a parody of an operatic tenor, "It's volcanic!"

Startled, Arthur almost fell backward off his crate; the giant in the kimono reached out a hand and steadied him. Smith's laughter bounced around the theatre.

"Zach, don't be childish!" snapped a woman from stage right. She was sitting in a folding chair a little apart from the rest, a water bottle angled toward her throat.

"She who must be obeyed has spoken," said Smith, making a mock bow in the woman's direction with a fluid grace Arthur could only envy. When he turned back to Arthur, his voice and manner were flat, businesslike. "Vesuvius is the place we're from, at least most of us, on Salt Spring Island. Named for a British gunboat that explored these waters in the 1850s." Grinning impishly, Smith pointed to his chest. "Makes a great T-shirt for an opera company."

Sure enough, against the grey background, a black volcano rained musical notes on a sea of outstretched arms and upturned faces.

"But let me introduce the others," Smith said. He pointed to the sandy-haired giant. "First, our esteemed Mikado, my old buddy Larry Weston. Larry and I went all through school together. We would have ended up working in a cement plant like our dads, except for Vietnam. 'Nam saved us. Larry was a little slow, as usual. He went to war first. I came straight to Canada."

"The tortoise and the hare," the giant said, smiling as

at a joke he had heard many times before. The man looked more like a tank than a tortoise, Arthur thought, conscious of his own flabbiness beside Weston's broad-shouldered solidity. He had the look of desert about him, sun-bleached hair, sun-baked skin, a dryness beneath his genial manner, more suited to a Stetson and chaps than a kimono, Arthur thought.

Smith waved vaguely at the others. "Our incomparable stage manager, Emile Gaboune. My wife Carol, whom you've heard from." Arthur returned their silent nods. "And *The Mikado*'s young lovers, my son Hendrix and the enchanting Sandra Ohara." Hendrix waved without raising his head from his girlfriend's lap. The young Asian woman, who had been feeding Hendrix bits of sandwich, gave Arthur a bright and, he suspected, phony smile.

Smith bent to pick up the play script that had tumbled from the music stand. "I expected you earlier. The others are due back soon for the dress rehearsal."

Arthur decided to get to the point. "Tell me about your interpretation of the play. A few good quotes always help."

Smith gave him an appraising look. "For most directors, Gilbert and Sullivan are like a pair of old shoes: familiar, easy to wear, broken in. Polish the shoes up a bit, and you've got a production. It's easy to play Gilbert and Sullivan as worshipping British tradition and making fun of everyone else's. But *The Mikado* is much more compli-cated than that. I want to get under the surface, explore that complication."

"Can you give an example . . . ?" Arthur stopped short as a slender young woman came hurrying in from the wings, one hand clutching a long batik skirt, the other pushing a cloud of dark witch's hair back from her face.

"Hi Dad, sorry if I've held up the rehearsal," she said breathlessly, giving Zachary a quick peck on the cheek. The odour of sandalwood emanated from her garments, as though she were a shrine. "I just had to see Angelo. He's such a talented Tarot reader, and I was dying to know how the performances are going to work out. You don't mind, do you?"

Arthur, sensitive to the smell of incense, sneezed loudly. She shrank back. "Oh, hello."

"Lavender, this is Arthur Fairweather, the drama critic who makes rude mechanicals like ourselves quake in our boots. Our fate lies in his hands, not in Angelo's. And this," he said over his shoulder to Arthur while holding the girl appraisingly at arm's length, "is my daughter, Lavender. She can't sing, and she can't act, but otherwise she's a perfect Pitti-Sing." Father and daughter made faces at each other, laughing.

"Be kind to us, Mr. Fairweather," Lavender said, her thin hand pushing again at the halo of fine black hair that set off her intense green eyes. Her eyes widened, her lips quivered, her voice assumed a perfect Southern drawl. "We do so depend upon the kindness of strangers."

Arthur felt a sudden jolt in his blood, as if he had downed a fifth of Glenfiddich.

Dropping her pose, Lavender glanced around. "I'm not the last, I see. I'll change while I have the dressing room to myself." Then, her skirt spreading out behind her like peacock feathers, she dashed backstage, almost colliding with Carol Smith, who had risen from her chair.

"Lavender, watch where you're going!" Carol called after her. Although Carol's face was set in hard lines, she was only ten or twelve years older than Lavender, Arthur guessed. A second wife, then, for whom things were not going well?

"I still say we should have gone out to lunch like the others," Carol said, picking up a kaiser bun and dropping it again. "These sandwiches are oozing fat."

"And so are you, my sweet," said Smith, patting her well-rounded bottom. "But I shouldn't say that in front of our esteemed critic. You make a perfect Katisha, don't you?"

"You've trained me well," she said bitterly, spearing an olive and retreating to her chair.

Smith tucked the play script under his arm. "Look, I have to work out some blocking problems with Emile. Talk to the rest of the cast before we get started, if you want to."

Dismissed, Arthur was wondering whom to approach when Weston said, "Sandra has better credentials than the rest of us for doing *The Mikado*. Her background is Japanese."

"How do you feel about the Japanese stereotypes in the play?" Arthur asked Sandra, grateful to Weston for the opening.

"Sandra's marvelous at stereotypes," Carol threw in.

Ignoring her, Sandra drew a silky white scarf over her halter top. "Why should I care if some Englishman writing a hundred years ago put his characters in Japanese trappings? All that matters," she said, keeping her eyes on

Arthur's as she loosely knotted the scarf over her small breasts, "is to do the part well. Then you get asked to do other plays." Gazing down at the young man reclining in her lap, she added sternly, "That's how you build a career. That is, if you're not too lazy."

"There are other ways," Carol said. "If your father's a millionaire. Or you sleep with the right people."

"Lay off, Carol." Sitting up with a sigh, Hendrix Smith tucked his black Grateful Dead T-shirt into his tattered jeans and slipped on leather sandals. He looked much like his father must have in the sixties: the same long jaw, square chin, long dark ponytail. Yet he seemed to lack his father's restless energy. He was thinner, too, and had a row of tiny silver cuffs piercing one ear.

Turning to Arthur, Hendrix fingered the cuffs like worry beads. "Unlike Sandra, I'm not ambitious. I only take parts I like." If Hendrix was trying to portray himself as free and easy, Arthur was not convinced; he thought the director's son looked tired and preoccupied.

"You only take parts if they don't interfere with your social life." Zachary Smith, reappearing from backstage with a tape measure and a pencil, had caught his son's last statement. "However, you've taken on this one, and you need to be on time. You almost missed the ferry this morning."

Hendrix shrugged, reached for Sandra's hand. "So I'm slower than the March hare. I made it, didn't I? And right now I need a smoke."

Smith stared angrily at his son. "I want you in costume and ready to start in fifteen minutes."

Weston touched Arthur's arm. "You know how it is. Opening night jitters." His comment seemed to break the tension. Smith turned to scribble something in the play script, and Hendrix followed Sandra out of the auditorium.

"If you want something to write about," the big man went on, turning away from Arthur and holding his arms out chest high, "take a good look at this costume. We may be a small company, but that doesn't mean we do everything on the cheap."

"It's beautiful," Arthur said, examining the dragons, birds and cherry trees embroidered in gold on the sleeves and back.

"It was made for a Noh theatre company sometime in the late eighteenth century. You can't find craftsmanship like this anymore. Not that many people care these days. Zach would buy all the Company costumes at garage sales if he could. Isn't that right, Zach?"

"What?" Smith was kneeling on the stage, making some light chalk lines on its surface. "Showing off your treasures? How about doing something useful? Move these trays so I can finish the blocking—"

Weston dropped into a gunslinger pose, legs braced, hands at his hips as though about to draw a pair of Colt .45s. "You mess with my scenes, you're dead, podnuh," he said. The John Wayne imitation was perfect, but beneath the genial spoof, Arthur sensed a hard edge.

Smith gave a tight smile. "Compromise the dignity of our esteemed Mikado? I wouldn't dare." He poked his head around the curtain and shouted, "Ten minutes."

Arthur heard the sound of scuffling feet, then Lavender and another woman dressed as a schoolgirl peered round the curtain, laughed, and disappeared again.

Arthur was about to follow—surely he had time to ask Lavender a few quick questions—when the auditorium door banged open and the young lovers strolled down the aisle. Still no costumes. Arthur held his breath as Hendrix marched up to his father. Zachary Smith didn't even glance up. The young man put out a hand.

"I'm sorry we're not dressed yet, Dad. Blame it on my tobacco addiction."

Zachary Smith straightened up, ignoring the out-stretched hand, and glared at his son. "Your tobacco addiction." He looked as if he was going to say something scathing, but then, after a sideways glance at Arthur, seemed to change his mind. "Carol remembered to get your second kimono from the cleaners. It's hanging next to Rodney's."

Scowling, Hendrix dropped his arm and reached for Sandra's hand, and the two of them went backstage.

Larry Weston grasped Arthur's elbow. "I'll walk you out. I could do with some fresh air."

Arthur let himself be shepherded out. The sunlight was startling after the gloom of the auditorium, and he paused to let his eyes adjust. To be polite, he picked up where their conversation had left off.

"Do you like Noh theatre then? Not many people do, outside Japan." He didn't add that he himself found the stylized gestures and simple plots of this ritual theatre form extremely tedious.

"Not many people today like anything disciplined," Weston responded, setting off with long strides, oblivious to the curious stares of passersby. "I should know. I run fishing charters for rich jerks who haven't learned how to fish. Most of them couldn't catch their tails in a fishbowl. See that?" He held up a bandaged wrist. "Sucker hooked me on his first cast. And you know what's worse?" He gestured toward a group of teenagers playing hackysack across the street. "Young people used to learn a trade, enter a disciplined life. And what do they do now? Kick a limp ball around. Skateboard in malls. Bliss out. Melt down their eardrums. It's pathetic."

Arthur, hurrying to keep abreast, murmured something noncommittal.

"Anyway, there's no point in getting angry." Weston halted abruptly at the corner and gave Arthur a friendly clap on the shoulder. "I need to get back. I hope you enjoy our production. We're much more professional than you might think."

The big man turned and strode back down the street, his flapping kimono making him look like a large ungainly crow. Still, there was something in his slightly bowed legs that reminded Arthur of the cowboys in old Westerns. Crow or cowboy, the message was clear: Get out of town before sundown, if you know what's good for you.

.-. .-.

Over an early dinner, Arthur wondered about the currents of tension he had sensed in Zachary Smith's family.

A bad case of first night jitters could either ruin the performance or give it an exciting edginess. Speaking of excitement—Lavender was a beauty, and sensitive too, obviously. Her Blanche Dubois impersonation seemed specially put on for him. Maybe he would get the chance to talk to her after the performance.

The thought of Lavender was enough to propel Arthur at speed up the worn steps of the Caprice Theatre and into the foyer. Only a small crowd so far, but then he wasn't usually so early. He smoothed his damp, unruly hair, straightened his favourite summer jacket—when had it shrunk?—sucked in his gut, and adopted an expression of mild disdain. No sense in letting Thea see that he was excited about a new woman.

The door to the office opened and Thea emerged, wearing the 'little black dress' she always wore for first nights. As usual, something about her tall, lean figure encased in the delicate dress made her look frail and vulnerable, though Arthur knew she was actually as tough as nails. The smirk slid off his face.

"Arthur, you're early. Unbelievable!" Thea's high heels clicked toward him. She laid a cool hand against his sweaty forehead. "But you are hot and bothered. Why don't you take off that awful jacket?"

Heads turned as Arthur waved his arms to stir up a breeze, and he glared back. "I told you to sink a few quid into air conditioning," he grumbled.

"If dear old Aunt Agnes had left me another ten thousand dollars, I would have been happy to."

"You mean it was more important to replaster cherubs

and repair that bloody chandelier," said Arthur, knowing his comment would needle; Thea was proud of her restoration of the Caprice. Once Victoria's oldest theatre, it had been clumsily converted into a cinema, and then left unused for years. Now the oak floors shone again, and the heavily moulded ceiling, with its fresco of nymphs and fauns, was resplendent. The price, in Arthur's view, had been their marriage: Thea had worked eighteen-hour days while he, an unhappy stranger in a strange land, had tried to get his feet under him. An obstacle, an unexpected expense—that seemed to be her attitude toward his unhappiness. And finally, like the air conditioning, he'd been expendable.

Thea, her face set in that look of earnest concentration he knew so well, ignored his jibe. "How did the cast interviews go?"

Arthur was glad to drag his mind away from the past. "Now there's a soap opera for you. Eccentric father, wicked stepmother, ne'er-do-well son and his temperamental girlfriend. Enough drama there to keep the masses glued to the telly for years."

"You forgot the beautiful damsel, no doubt in distress."

Arthur tried not to blush. Thea had an unerring nose for sniffing out his fancies.

"How's the box office?" he asked.

"Fine. Well, not fine. But, it'll be okay if you give us a decent review. The Vesuvius Light Opera Company isn't a household name." Her look was half pleading, half defiant. "Your reviews are getting tougher and tougher,

Arthur. I know you're seeing more Gilbert and Sullivan than you want to. But please, be flexible. This is Victoria, not New York, not London."

The buzzer sounded and the crowd started to file through the ornate cherrywood doors into the theatre.

"Must go," Thea said, bending close to peck at his cheek. "Don't forget I'm picking you up at six tomorrow morning. My meeting's at eight, so we have to make the first ferry." Her perfume—Mystique, with its corny name but haunting aroma of pears and smoke—reminded Arthur of their first night together, at the George Hotel, off St. Peter's Square in Manchester. He was about to give her a quick hug, for luck, when she hurried off.

Arthur wandered down to his favourite seat next to the middle aisle. Her comment about being flexible bothered him. Hadn't he agreed to let Thea drag him from England to live on an island off the west coast of Canada? And hadn't he agreed just a week ago to let her drag him to Salt Spring Island—hardly bigger than a bathtub—to review its so-called Arts Festival, which she just happened to be running? Who was being flexible, and who inflexible? He sat down with a sigh.

Then the house lights dimmed, the curtains parted, and a small chorus clad in black tights and short black kimonos dashed across an ornate bridge and down into the auditorium, singing lustily.

So that was how Zachary Smith had solved the usual problem at the Caprice: its too-narrow stage. Arthur, admiring the director's ingenuity, pulled out his notepad and pencil. This was theatre, Arthur's passion, and he scribbled his notes furiously, all complaints forgotten. Then a blue eye winked at him in passing, and he almost dropped his pencil. Who could that be? Not the director's daughter, green-eyed Lavender. Or the snippy Japanese–Canadian girl playing Yum-Yum, surely her eyes were brown.

While Arthur was speculating, the chorus retreated to the stage and disappeared behind the bridge. Three men re-emerged, having shucked their black kimonos for more colourful garb. Nanki-Poo, the young lover played by Hendrix Smith, wore a lime-green kimono embroidered with musical notes, while Pooh-Bah and Pish-Tush, the two nobles interrogating him, were in leather vests and motorcycle boots. Bizarre! Good singing, though. Even Arthur, with his tin ear, could admire the way young Smith's hopeful light tenor dashed itself fruitlessly against the assured bass and baritone of the two Japanese nobles. Then snickers broke out among the audience. Ko-Ko, the Lord High Executioner, garbed in a convict's black-and-white striped T-shirt, was alternately cringing and brandishing a monstrous sword as he crossed the bridge singing "Taken to the County Jail." Arthur, joining in the laughter, found himself revising his judgment about the costuming. The last Ko-Ko he had seen (and he'd seen far too many) had sported a tennis racquet and a fake monocle. Zachary Smith's costume made sense: the victim as victimizer.

Now it was the victimizer's turn. As the chorus sang "Defer, defer / To the noble Lord High Executioner!" Ko-Ko walked along the line, swinging his sword aggressively

over the row of bowing heads. It was well-executed physi-
cal theatre.

Then the rhythm of bobbing heads became frayed.
The piano grew louder, seeking to impose its timing.
Even so, the last person in line was bowing too slowly.
Lime green kimono.

"Defer, defer—"

"Duck, you fool," Arthur shouted. The blade swung.
Hendrix Smith sank to his knees, blood pouring down his
face.

# Chapter 1
Salt Spring Island: Saturday, July 8

Constable Danutia Dranchuk sat scrunched up in the RCMP float plane, her face pressed to the window and her eyes squeezed shut, silently repeating the Lord's Prayer. She hated being strapped into this cramped space, suspended in nothingness. Milky blue air around her, grey-blue water below. A Prairie girl, she liked her feet on solid ground. Amen.

Breathe, she told herself. You can handle it. The boss's call has thrown you off balance, that's all. Sergeant Lewis hadn't exactly welcomed her to General Investigations in Victoria. The youngest member in Major Crimes and the only woman, she'd spent two months doing joe jobs for senior officers. "Learning the ropes," Sergeant Lewis called it, and there was plenty to learn. The RCMP provided police service for all of Vancouver Island and the Gulf Islands except Victoria, with local detachments handling routine matters and calling on General Investigations for more serious cases. Relieved to get away from Winnipeg, she had thrown herself into plainclothes work. But after two months, as she joked to her sister Alyne, "learning the ropes" felt more like being tied up in knots, unable to move an inch without Lewis's say-so.

Then this morning, on her first Saturday off, the chance she had been waiting for had finally come.

"I have a case for you," Sergeant Lewis had said. "A body's been discovered in a deserted cabin on Salt Spring, on property that's just been bought by David Ohara. You know who he is, don't you? Pacific Developments. Owns half of Victoria and the Gulf Islands. Apparently the dead man was working for him. Len Berwick—he's head of the local detachment, a good man—says it's suicide."

"Then why are you sending me?"

The muted tap-tap of Lewis's pencil warned Danutia to brace herself. "Problem is, the attending doctor insists the man's been murdered. Threatens to go to the media if we don't investigate." He paused, and the tapping died away. "Ohara doesn't want any bad publicity."

So that was it. Don't think for yourself, simply rubber stamp the suicide verdict and sweet talk the doctor into going along. "I hear you."

"Fine then." Lewis's manner became friendlier. "Sharma will take care of the technical stuff. He'll meet you at the Inner Harbour in half an hour. There's a float plane leaving for a drug recon."

"Shouldn't we take the Ident van?"

"You'd be all day, and I need Sharma back."

What about me? she wanted to ask, but the line went dead.

And now, like the throbbing of her own pulse, the plane's engines hummed, "no trust, no trust."

Suddenly the plane pitched and rolled. Danutia gasped and squeezed her eyes tighter, her ears straining to catch the engines' steady roar, as in childhood she had listened for her next heartbeat each time she dutifully recited, "If I should die before I wake . . ."

Deaths unexpected, unprepared for. Police work was

full of them. Car crashes, industrial accidents, drownings, drug overdoses, suicides, homicides. It was the death of her brother Andrew in an inexplicable motorcycle accident that had drawn her to police work in the first place. Surely, she had thought with an eighteen-year-old's certainty, if only the police had cared enough, worked hard enough, refused to give up, they could have told her and her grieving parents exactly what had happened, exactly who or what was to blame.

Ten years in the force had taught her better.

The engines cut back, and the plane descended, the pontoons touching down with a bump. From the seat behind, a large, warm hand patted her shoulder. "Sharma says you may open your eyes now."

Sheepishly Danutia met her Forensics partner's mild dark gaze. His long thin lips stretched into a grandfatherly smile beneath his bulbous nose. She loved his face, knobbly and richly textured like the oak carving with a secret compartment a friend had given her. She suspected Sharma too had his secrets.

Outside the plane window, a tranquil bay curved protectively around them. Sailboats tacked in a light breeze, and an open ferry crammed with cars and RVs chugged toward the shore. Tourists. The Gulf Islands depended on them as much as Victoria did. No wonder Ohara was anxious to avoid bad publicity.

Danutia pulled her map of Salt Spring from the backpack into which she had hurriedly dumped enough gear for the weekend. Since her mission was likely to be so short-lived, and Lewis hadn't indicated any further need of her, she had resolved to explore the island, get in some hiking.

The map showed Salt Spring, the largest of the southern Gulf Islands, stretching along the east coast of Vancouver Island like three oblong cookies that had melted and run together in the oven.

"There we are," Sharma said, pointing to the west side of the top cookie. "Vesuvius. Second largest village on Salt Spring."

Through the plane window Danutia saw no sign of the volcano-shaped mountain she assumed the place to be named for, only low green-clad hills rising behind the scattered houses of the village. As the plane bumped across the ferry's wake Danutia caught a glimpse of a large red-roofed building with dormer windows and brightly coloured hanging baskets.

"Dockside Inn," said Sharma. "Best beer on the island."

"How would you know?" Danutia asked, unbuckling her seat belt. "You don't drink."

Sharma chuckled. "You don't either, so you can't prove me wrong. Mind your head."

···· ····

As soon as they had unloaded Sharma's gear onto the floating dock, the pilot waved and the props whirred. Danutia's hair, short as it was, whipped into her eyes and face. Next time a buzz cut like Sharma's, she thought, watching a short, stocky man in uniform clamber down the stairs from the parking lot above.

"Berwick sent me." The breath came in quick pants from his round, red mouth. "Larocque," he added, with a wink at Sharma. "You know, The Rock. Strong. Hard."

Danutia shouldered her backpack and headed toward the stairs.

Larocque hurried along beside her. "You guys are wasting your time. The guy got drunk and shot himself, plain as day. I found the suicide note, for chrissake."

Danutia halted. "You didn't handle it, did you?"

Larocque stumbled to a stop beside her. "Look, I was just trying to figure out what was going on."

Her spirits rising, Danutia took the remaining stairs two at a time. If Berwick was as incompetent as his constable, she might be needed after all.

⋅•⋅  ⋅•⋅

Soon the police cruiser had left behind the straggling village with its fish and chip shop, decaying motel, and small white bungalows. The road cut inland and then swung back to follow the shoreline toward a densely-forested hill that Larocque identified as Mount Maxwell. Somewhere near its base was the deserted cabin where the body waited. Towering Douglas firs swallowed up the last houses and the road plunged toward the sea. Ahead, an unpaved parking lot held a dozen or so cars and trucks; on the narrow strip of beach below, a handful of children threw wet sand at each other or skipped rocks into the water.

Just short of the parking lot Larocque cut the wheel sharply to the left and the cruiser lurched toward a knot of people milling around a black wrought-iron gate. Above it, a white banner proclaimed "SAVE SALT SPRING HISTORY" in green letters shaped like plants and trees.

"That's them," he said, beeping his horn. "The tree huggers I was telling you about." Danutia had tried to follow his rambling account of the morning's events and given up, preferring to size up the situation for herself. He beeped again, the demonstrators reluctantly moved aside, a constable swung the gate open, and the cruiser passed into a cool tunnel of cedar and fir trees. After about half a kilometre, the narrow dirt track opened into a clearing where scattered arbutus trees raised twisted limbs to the sky, their reddish bark peeling like skin too long exposed to the sun. "Sunburn trees," Danutia had heard them called by First Nations people, and she could see why.

Larocque parked in the shade between a grey Mazda and a dusty Chevy Blazer. On the other side of the Mazda stood an ambulance, slow blues floating from its open doors. The driver was keeping time on the steering wheel, his buddy reading a newspaper. Neither glanced in Danutia's direction as she headed across the clearing.

On the far side of the clearing, the rear end of a blue pickup poked out from behind a weathered split-log cabin, the moss on its roof caked and brown. Two men waited on its narrow porch, the one in the white medical jacket half turned away, talking into a cellphone. The other, a lanky, balding man in khaki pants and shirt, watched her approach, his arms folded across his chest. Sergeant Berwick, she assumed. A sudden breeze came up, carrying a sweet stench like rotting meat. Why the hell couldn't they have moved away? Too used to the smell of death to notice, or too macho?

Behind her Larocque coughed and hesitated. She remembered the faint spots on his uniform, its sickly smell, and her stomach heaved.

Keep walking, she told herself. Two minutes, that's what they say, two minutes and you won't notice. Pretend it's a baby's dirty diaper, or a drunk's vomit. Unbidden, the words of the psalmist whispered in her ear: "Yea, though I walk through the valley of the shadow of death—"

A gust of wind blew away the next words, the comforting words.

⋅—⋅ ⋅—⋅

As soon as they had introduced themselves, Sharma set to work inside the cabin. Danutia regarded Dr. Edward Fidelman, a fidgety thirtysomething with reddish blond hair, hazel eyes, and a fox's sharp face. He was obviously still smarting from Berwick's referring to him as "Salt Spring's brilliant and therefore no doubt temporary" head of ER.

"What makes you think it wasn't suicide?" she asked.

Frowning, Fidelman shoved his hands in his jacket pockets and must have found a ballpoint pen in one, for an irritating click-click soon punctuated his reply.

"I spent three years as assistant to the LA medical examiner," he said, "and in that time I saw a lot of self-inflicted gunshot wounds. Most men—and it mostly is men—who commit suicide with a handgun shoot them-selves in the temple. A few stick the gun barrel between their teeth. They never hold the gun outside their mouth. In this case, it's obvious from the shattered teeth and jaw that the gun was held outside the mouth. Ergo, someone else pulled the trigger."

"That's all very well," said Berwick, unfolding his arms and making a circle with one thumb and forefinger, "but did you notice the size of that barrel? That's a 9 MM Glock. Maybe it wouldn't fit. The gunpowder residue around the mouth suggests contact. He could have rested the gun against his teeth."

"In that position? You must be joking."

"You forget. There's a suicide note."

"I still say the man was murdered," Fidelman shot back.

Danutia regarded the doctor, who was glaring at Berwick. Fidelman hadn't provided much evidence for his opinion. Too proud to let his judgment be challenged by a small town police officer? If so, what would happen if Danutia's investigation bore out Berwick's conclusion? Still puzzling about how to handle Fidelman, she turned to Berwick. "What do you make of it?"

He ran a hand over his bald spot, which was deeply tanned and liver-spotted. "From the looks of it, he'd been drinking. There's no evidence of a struggle. And the sui-cide note sounds genuine to me."

"You knew him?"

Berwick nodded.

"I'm sorry. Well enough to make a positive ID?"

"The name's Joe Bertolucci. The face is pretty messed up, but as you'll see, the tip of his right middle finger is missing. I asked him about it once. Fishing accident when he was a kid."

The porch creaked behind her as Sharma emerged from the cabin. "It's all yours," he said. "I'll take a look at the truck."

"Anything else you want to know? Berwick asked.

"Can't we get on with this?" Fidelman demanded. "I'm needed at the hospital."

Danutian nodded at the two men and stepped inside. Once more the smell assaulted her. She held her breath, waiting for her stomach to stop heaving and her eyes to adjust to the dim light. Then she donned latex gloves and flipped on her pocket tape recorder.

Methodically she detailed the contents of the room. On a folding table under the lone plastic-covered window stood a Coleman stove with a coffee pot on it, a lantern, an ancient manual typewriter with a piece of paper in it. The suicide note? She would come back to that.

To the left of the table, a cardboard box of dishes and utensils and a few cans of food. Inside a cookie tin, dry dog food, enough for a few days. No one had mentioned a dog. She looked around. Two empty aluminum pie plates sat on the floor in the far corner.

Sprawled in the middle of the floor, the body of a man.

To the right of the table, a folding chair with a paperback lying open, face down, in the seat. Patrick O'Brian, *Desolation Island*. A 20-litre water jug, almost full. A broom and a round plastic washing-up bowl. Against the back wall, an air mattress and sleeping bag, a small duffel bag containing two changes of clothes and another O'Brian, *The Fortune of War*. Everything neat and tidy.

She returned to the typewriter, eased the bar up with the eraser end of a pencil, and read the brief note: "My dearest Antonia, I can no longer bear the thought that I have failed you. This is all I've thought about since your mother and I seperated. I can't trust myself, it seems, and so I can never make things alright. Take care of your brother. Forgive me, for nothing is more precious to a father than the love of his children." Then slowly she read the note onto the tape, her voice breaking when she came to the last words.

She could delay no longer. At her feet lay the dark shape that had once been a man, his face a black hole below the staring eye sockets. The fingers of his right hand, bloated and discolored like an abandoned balloon, were curled around a thick-barreled handgun. Scattered around him were a Jamieson's bottle, almost empty; a video camera; a spent cartridge; a cellphone. Distress line. Reach out and touch someone. Everything except the camcorder was spattered with dried blood and gobbets of flesh.

This man, whose shattered body she had tried to ignore, had begun to take shape in her mind. He had a dog for a companion, a dog he was careful to provide for. What kind of dog, she wondered, thinking of the mongrel pup she had found wandering the country roads when she was six.

Hardly aware of what she was doing, she sketched a

quick cross over all that remained of a human life and stepped outside.

In the clearing Berwick and his men were bagging charred debris from the fire pit, as well as an assortment of cigarette butts, beer bottles, plastic wrappers, and used condoms, while Fidelman bantered with the ambulance men. Danutia noticed a narrow path leading northward, to the water, she supposed. She was about to follow it, away from the pervasive smell, away from Fidelman's sharp laugh and Berwick's laconic orders, when Sharma rounded the corner of the cabin.

She waited for him to join her. "Suicide or murder?"

"What do you think?" His deep brown eyes were calm under his heavy brows, his face unreadable. "It's your case."

"That's the problem. Berwick thinks it's suicide. Sergeant Lewis wants the case closed. I write suicide in my report and they'll both be happy. It would be so easy."

"But?"

"Some things don't fit. Like the dog. Why would a man planning suicide bring his dog?"

"Perhaps he intended to put the dog down as well. To keep him company in the next world."

"Then why bring so much dog food?"

Sharma gazed at her curiously. "You found Dr. Fidelman's argument convincing?"

"I wouldn't say that. It may not be common for someone to shoot himself in the mouth without ramming the gun down his throat, but it would be possible. And, as Berwick says, there's the suicide note." Feeling perspiration gather under her arms—heat or anxiety?—she retreated into the shade. "I can't recommend a full-scale murder investigation when there's no evidence to warrant it. But if I don't, think of the headlines. 'DOCTOR EXPOSES RCMP COVERUP.' Either way, Lewis will close the case and put me back on joe jobs."

Sharma put his palms together and nodded slightly. "As Krishnamurti says, 'Freedom from the desire for an answer is essential to the understanding of a problem.'"

Danutia frowned. "What's that supposed to mean?"

"The good Doctor Fidelman, Sergeant Berwick, Sergeant Lewis—they all want an answer, and you feel you must give them one. And so your understanding of the problem is clouded."

"Gee, that's a lot of help." She searched his face, seeking a path in its bumps and hollows.

A few minutes later, having found what she was searching for, Danutia was again standing on the cabin porch with Berwick and Fidelman while Sharma loaded his cases into Larocque's cruiser.

"At the moment," she said to Fidelman, "the manner of death seems inconclusive—"

"What do you mean, inconclusive?" he fumed, fumbling in his pockets. "That man was murdered."

"That remains to be determined," Danutia continued, trying to remain calm. "The autopsy won't be done until Monday, maybe Tuesday. Here's my proposal. If you withdraw your statements about murder until we have the autopsy results, I'll ask my superior, Sergeant Lewis, to allow me to investigate informally."

"And give the murderer time to destroy evidence?" Fidelman drew out a packet of cigarettes, then shoved them back in his pocket when Berwick shook his head. So that was another cause of the doctor's irritability, Danutia surmised—nicotine withdrawal, for which he no doubt blamed Berwick.

She continued calmly. "The man's been dead at least twenty-four hours, you said, perhaps as long as thirty-six. The murderer—if there was one—has had plenty of time, and opportunity, to destroy evidence. Not to mention the demonstrators, the ambulance attendants—"

"Don't forget the police," Berwick chipped in. "Larocque is sure to have mucked up something."

Danutia glanced at Berwick. She had taken an instant dislike to Constable Larocque, a type she'd had to deal with at the Academy and every posting since. Guys who called you a ball breaker if you didn't join them for a beer, and a 'crip' if they had to work with you, meanwhile rating the body parts of every woman they saw—nice ass, big boobs, thick ankles. Men who were careless with details because they knew all the answers at a glance. So it was too bad that Larocque was the first officer on the scene. Still, for Berwick to criticize one of his men publicly—.

She turned back to the doctor, who was again digging around in his pockets.

"Even you must have disturbed the scene while you were tending to your patient. And who could blame you," she said when he glared. "But think of the thrill-seekers who'll be prowling around if the media mention the word murder."

"You don't need the media for that," Fidelman said, cellophane crackling as he unwrapped a mint and popped it into his mouth. "I'll bet rumours are already flying."

Danutia thought of the demonstrators still hanging around the gate, the others who'd given their names and gone about their business. "We'll have to do what we can to stop them."

Fidelman's hazel eyes narrowed, and a hint of a sly grin played around the corners of his mouth. "If I agree, you'll investigate?"

"I'll do everything I would do if this were a murder investigation, except call it one."

Berwick spoke up. "You can't keep a murder investigation secret."

"I won't 'investigate' in any obvious way," Danutia said stiffly. "People will expect the police to ask questions. Larocque mentioned that you're short-handed because of the Arts Festival. You can say you requested assistance from General Investigations. Will you go along with that?"

Berwick pulled at his right earlobe. "If Lewis authorizes you to proceed, I have no choice."

"What about you, Dr. Fidelman?"

"It's a deal. If your chief buys it. If he doesn't—maybe the media will change his mind."

⁘⦁ ⦁⁘

A short while later Danutia sat with Berwick on the edge of the cabin porch, idly picking at the grass growing up between the boards. She watched the trees swallow

Larocque's cruiser with Sharma now beside him in the front seat, and then the ambulance with its body bag, bound for the float plane at Vesuvius. She wondered whether the dead man had been afraid of flying.

They were waiting for a tow truck. Sharma had suggested securing the Pacific Developments truck for a more thorough inspection. They could have left a constable behind, talked at the detachment office in Ganges, but here they were, as if by mutual consent. They could have moved under the trees, away from the lingering odour that seeped like fog through the cracks of the old cabin, but something held them there.

At last Danutia broke the silence.

"You said you knew the dead man. Tell me about him."

"Joe Bertolucci." Chewing thoughtfully on a grass stem, Berwick gazed through the trees toward the water, where in the distance the small car ferry from Vesuvius chugged toward the smoking pulp mill on the opposite shore.

"Until a few weeks ago, he was the bartender at the Dockside Inn. Good man, quiet but friendly. Tossed out drunks when he had to."

"Family?"

"An ex-wife and two kids in Vancouver. Antonia, the daughter the suicide note was addressed to, and a younger son. Joe never talked about them much."

"Have they been notified?"

"I'll take care of it. I was holding off until Headquarters decided how to handle this."

The wind shifted quarter, bringing a faint sweet scent

Danutia didn't recognize, almost covering the smell from the cabin. A sudden gust set the treetops swaying, and a loud crackling made Danutia jump.

"What was that? Deer?"

"Broom pods," said Berwick, pointing across the clearing to a fringe of spiky, dark-green bushes. "When it's hot like this, the pods explode. Haven't you heard them before? Sometimes they're so loud they sound like gunshots. When you're in the country, anyway."

"How can plants make so much noise?"

"Beats me."

Danutia shredded another grass stem. "Larocque's account of what happened this morning was pretty garbled. Can you lay it out for me?"

"From what I can piece together, David Ohara bought this property and hired Bertolucci as a security guard. Ohara's maintenance man, Bob Kelly, was supposed to bulldoze the cabin this morning. The demonstrators got wind of the plans and tried to stop him."

"Why would Ohara hire a security guard for land with nothing on it?"

"To you it may seem like there's 'nothing on it', but that's not the way a lot of islanders see it. The Bittancourt cabin is one of the oldest structures on the island. Save Salt Spring History—the group behind the demo—had applied for an injunction to stop the sale because of the land's 'historical and ecological value'. They were hoping to delay the bulldozer until a court injunction came through."

"Still, a security guard?"

Berwick shrugged. "There's been some vandalism here and at his house on Welbury Bay. We haven't found out who was responsible."

"You mean Ohara lives on Salt Spring?"

Berwick nodded. "His parents were market gardeners here before the war. He moved back about ten years ago."

"And the demonstrators?"

"My men have names and addresses for most of them. A few may have left before we got the blockade up."

"What about the guy who found the body?"

"Andy Johnson. Larocque got a brief statement from his wife Martha. Andy had gone up to the cabin to do some filming. When Martha heard the bulldozer coming, she went to look for him. Andy had fainted inside, near the body. She used the cellphone you saw to call 911. Dispatch sent out Larocque and an ambulance."

"So how did Fidelman get involved?" Danutia leaned over and plucked a dandelion growing beside the porch.

"He's Johnson's regular doctor. Martha insisted on Larocque calling him. Andy has a heart condition, and Martha was afraid he'd had an attack. After Andy was sent off to the hospital, Larocque figured he could get Fidelman to examine the body and sign the death certificate, have the case all wrapped up before he called me." Berwick glanced down at the dirt under his fingernails. "I was cultivating my garden, or more exactly, my grape vines. He should have called me sooner. He's had a few choice words from me over that one. Anyway, you know the conclusion Fidelman came to."

"What do you know about the Johnsons?"

"Craftspeople from down around Beaver Point. That's the south end of the island, near Fulford. Martha's a potter, Andy a woodturner, both in their sixties, I expect. Martha insisted on riding in the ambulance with Andy, so Larocque didn't get much from her. There's probably not much more they can tell you."

"Maybe not," Danutia said doubtfully, pulling yellow petals from the dandelion head. If this proved to be murder, the demonstrators would be logical suspects.

She threw away the bare dandelion stalk. "And the dog?"

"Joe had a border collie, used to wait for him outside the inn. Nobody's mentioned seeing it."

"That's strange. Collies are so loyal. Could you make some discreet inquiries? The vets, demonstrators, people who live out here. Just pass the word that you'd like to make sure the dog's taken care of." This business about the dog disturbed her, and she wasn't sure why.

In the distance a truck geared down for the sharp curve to the beach. Danutia slid off the porch and stood facing Berwick.

"You don't think this is a murder case, but still you secured the scene, got the names of all the demonstrators, didn't try to stop me snooping around until the autopsy. Why?"

Berwick rose and shook off the blades of grass clinging to his trousers. "What if I'm wrong?"

# Chapter 2
## Salt Spring: Saturday morning, July 8

Bleary-eyed and a bit hung over, Arthur stumbled down the foot passenger walkway at the Fulford ferry terminal. Thea had promised a lively village with lots of Arts Festival events; he saw nothing but a car park, a shop, a scattering of houses ready to slide off into the sea, and in the distance, an empty and mountainous island.

Glaring back at the passengers crowding on his heels, Arthur stepped aside to scan the car park for Thea's white Honda.

Someone tapped him on the shoulder and he whirled around. It was a skinny girl in torn black jeans and hooded sweatshirt. Tiny ribboned braids dangled to one side of her pale, scowling face. She could almost have been one of the mohawked and body-pierced youth swarming the streets of London or Manchester. Arthur reached into his pocket for spare change. The girl shook her head, sending her braids flying.

"Thea sent me," she said, heading toward an ancient station wagon with a grille like shark's teeth. Arthur stowed his gear on the back seat and climbed in.

For ten minutes or so they drove in silence through the kind of pastoral landscape Arthur was accustomed to ignoring. Small farms, country churches, pottery and woodworking studios. No big bustling city waited at the end of the road, just a dinky village with pretensions to culture.

In the meantime, he was stuck with this sullen teenager.

"Look at that church," he said. "I'll bet it's brown on the inside as well as the outside. Tomorrow it'll be full of dreary brown people singing dreary brown hymns."

The girl stared straight ahead, her braids bobbing, her fingers beating out a quiet tattoo in time to the barely audible radio. But Arthur caught a flicker of a smile.

Encouraged, he reached over and turned up the volume. "What's the group?"

"Silverchair. From Australia. They're really cool."

"So what do you do besides listen to the radio? Ever go to the theatre?"

"You're joking. That's my mom's thing. I wanna go to those concerts with light shows. There were fifteen trucks of equipment when Hell's Bones played at the Vancouver Coliseum last month. That's what my friend Danny said."

Arthur sat back, disappointed. His best memories from his own childhood were the Christmas pantos, the trips to Manchester with his mum to see touring musicals, the drama club at his grammar school. His first trip to London, to see *Jesus Christ Superstar* from high in the gods. Not so different from rock concerts, he had to admit.

Jolted back to the present when the girl braked hard, Arthur took in his surroundings. The street was jammed with cars, bicycles, skateboarders, tourists clutching ice creams and heavy parcels. This must be Ganges. The station wagon inched past a row of shops, an open-air market with gaily-striped tents, and a fire station with a square wooden tower, then pulled up across the road from a white clapboard building with green trim.

"That's where you're staying," the girl said. The Tidewater Inn looked like a colonial cousin of the seaside boarding houses where Arthur had spent miserable summer holidays. His room would have a brass bed, a marble-topped washstand, a chamber pot filled with dying ferns, and wallpaper striped like an old school tie. At least there was a restaurant and bar. Not that it would have any decent beer on tap.

He was retrieving his gear from the back when the girl pointed across the harbour. "You're supposed to meet Thea at the White Whale. Next to the marina. You can see the sign." When he turned to measure the distance with dubious eyes, she said, "Look, I've got to go."

"Sorry. Thanks for the ride." Arthur stood back, waiting for her to drive off. Instead she stared straight ahead, frowning, her face framed by the hood of the black sweatshirt. Reaching for his wallet, Arthur bent down to the open window. "Here, let me give you something."

She glanced at him, thin face serious beneath the multicoloured braids, and waved away the money. "My mom loves this island. She loves the history, all the old stuff. I think it sucks. I want to live someplace big." Gunning the engine, she drove off.

"Me too," Arthur said softly, watching Little Black Driving Hood disappear around a corner.

⋅—⋅ ⋅—⋅

Half an hour later, feet aching and head beginning to sizzle like a broiled grapefruit, Arthur spotted Thea among the throngs at the White Whale Marine Pub. Her dark hair was pulled back into the ponytail he detested; her omnipresent cellphone was clamped to her ear.

"Was this your idea of a joke?" he asked when she finally rang off. "Why didn't you have the girl drop me here?"

"Cindy. Her name's Cindy. Your beer should be warm enough to drink by now." She slid a pint across. "Sunshine, fresh air—do you good. Forgot your hat, I see—you look like a boiled lobster. Speaking of which, I've ordered you fish and chips. Now if you'd come over with me, as planned—"

"Your plan didn't include Hendrix Smith almost getting killed. That really threw me off. It took me four hours and a bottle of wine to do the review. No wonder I slept in."

"I did like the clever way you minimized the accident," Thea admitted. She peered at the newspaper folded on the table in front of her. "'A surprising bit of stage business that may not be repeated.' That was very generous of you, Arthur."

"Say no more." Arthur hid his pleasure at Thea's change of tone by taking a long swallow of beer.

"I also liked the way you talked about theme. What did you say? Here it is. 'Zachary Smith's original interpretation of the play puts Larry Weston's Mikado in conflict with Smith's own Ko-Ko, a sharply satiric view of modern man as lacking values, engaged in a quest to survive at any price. The subtlety of the production is that neither modern nor traditional values appear either wholly admirable or wholly despicable.' That's good, Arthur."

"Apart from the glitch, the production really was

impressive; it didn't hurt at all to write a good review. So now the Caprice can stagger on for a bit longer." Arthur drained his pint and signaled for another.

Thea raised her glass in a toast. "Here's to friendly reviewers." Then her face became serious again. "I must say, I hadn't expected Hendrix Smith to screw up. Remember the production of *West Side Story* I told you about, the one at my cousin's high school in Nanaimo? Hendrix was terrific in that."

"Peculiar, isn't it." Arthur took a long swallow from the new pint. Cold as a witch's tits, alas. "That accident keeps bothering me. Surely Smith could have done something—dropped the sword, changed the routine, whatever. He just kept swinging. I went backstage after the show to find out what had gone wrong, but Hendrix had disappeared, and everyone stonewalled me."

"That's the theatre for you. Was Hendrix all right this morning?"

"How should I know? You hung up before I could ask where the Smiths are staying."

"Sorry." Thea rummaged in her bag. "I have Lavender's Victoria number somewhere. I don't know about the rest of the family."

Arthur tried to keep his face noncommittal. "Lavender will do fine."

Thea stopped rummaging and eyed Arthur suspiciously. "Your review gives a lot of space to the 'too-often overlooked role of Pitti-Sing.' Isn't she a little young?"

Arthur blushed, even though Thea couldn't possibly know that, using his concern for Hendrix as an excuse, he'd knocked on Lavender's dressing room door after the performance and invited her to breakfast. Then he'd slept in and hadn't known where to call her to apologize. Aware of Thea's eyes on him, he said, "I mentioned Pitti-Sing in passing, along with several other minor roles."

Thea's cellphone buzzed ominously. As she picked it up, she shoved a festival program toward Arthur. "Have a look. I've marked the most important productions."

Arthur skimmed through the red-circled entries. A local history play, a children's entertainer, a harp concert. Surely she couldn't expect—

Thea put the phone down and reached for the program. "Quick, let's get you organized before Cassie phones again."

"So who's Cassie?"

"You know Cindy, the *Addams Family* wannabe who picked you up? Cassandra Wilson is her mother, and the writer/director of *Bullock's Folly*. I'm trying to get her to cut the Epilogue."

"*Bullock's Folly*. Isn't that one of the plays you want me to review?" Arthur reached to take the program back.

"Yes. The play's a centrepiece for the Festival because it deals with local issues. It's about an Englishman named Harry Bullock who arrived on Salt Spring in the 1890s. He bought hundreds of acres of land and set himself up as a country squire. Big house, boys from the local orphanage dressed in Eton suits waiting on his table, parlourmaids with white gloves. Imagine it! Anyway, Cassie portrays Bullock as Salt Spring's first land developer."

"So why do you want her to cut the Epilogue?"

"Because a man committed suicide—"

"Is the play that bad?"

Thea glared at him. "That isn't funny. The body was found early this morning at the old cabin where the Epilogue is set."

Arthur stuffed chips in his mouth. "So why cut? Sounds like good box office to me."

Thea sighed. "The land the cabin is on has just been bought by David Ohara, the guy who has been chopping down all the trees on the Gulf Islands to build golf courses. The problem is, he has also contributed half the money for the new Salt Spring Theatre—to advance his darling daughter's career."

"You mean he's Sandra Ohara's father?"

"None other." Thea's eyes travelled restlessly over the crowd. "I totally agree with Cassie's criticism of overdevelopment in the Islands, but now there's a death involved. . . . Anyway, I think we should back off, drop the Epilogue for now."

His fork poised mid-air, Arthur waited for Thea to meet his gaze. "Let me guess. Ohara is bankrolling the Festival as well, isn't he? No point in biting the hand, etcetera?"

Thea thrust the cellphone into her bag and pulled out a loose-leaf binder. "As you'll see, the play works fine without the Epilogue." She pushed back her chair. "Here's the script. Read it before the performance tonight, so you'll understand the issues. I have to go."

"Wait—you haven't given me Lavender's number."

"Call me at the office." Thea was on her way,

squeezing past a group of tourists in sailors' hats.

Knowing how busy Thea was, Arthur had no confidence he would ever catch her there. He would send flowers to the Caprice, with a note. And have Thea's box office manager read it? Think again. Maybe he'd stick around on Salt Spring until Lavender came back. There wasn't much theatre in Victoria at the moment. There wasn't much money in his bank account either, come to think of it. Now, if he could persuade the newspaper to cough up. Maybe he could write a story on this suicide?

Noticing that Thea had paused by the door to talk to someone, he stood up. "Thea, wait," he called. Heads turned to look at him, but he didn't care. "Why did that bloke kill himself?"

Several tables away a khaki-clad woman with a mop of blond curls looked up sharply from the file she was reading. Seeing her frown, Arthur pictured her blowing a whistle, giving orders—a camp director, perhaps. Attractive maybe, but not his type.

He glanced back at Thea. She shrugged impatiently, then disappeared into the sunlight.

# Chapter 3

"Why did that bloke kill himself?" an unmistakably British voice boomed out, quieting the lunchtime bustle at the White Whale.

Danutia glanced up from her copy of Larocque's report. A few tables away, a large man in a rumpled blue blazer was half-standing, staring at a dark-haired woman near the entrance, who shrugged her shoulders and hurried out. The man—a flabby Michael Caine, with curly, coppery hair, slightly bulbous nose, and thin upper lip—slumped back in his chair, frowning.

Was he talking about Bertolucci? Given the number of demonstrators, Danutia hadn't expected to keep the man's death a secret. But such a question in a public place—

The Brit rose from his table and set off toward the washrooms, leaving behind his jacket, a half-eaten order of fish and chips, and a stack of papers. Bertolucci file in hand, Danutia crossed to his table and paused there, as though searching for someone, then quickly scanned the papers spread out around his plate. An open Arts Festival program, a typescript of a play in a plastic cover, and there, beside his beer glass, a *Victoria Post-Dispatch* press pass. Keeping the story out of the media might be harder than she had thought. At least he hadn't mentioned murder.

When she returned to her table, her chicken burger had arrived; after saying a silent grace, she ate absentmindedly while she read and made notes. Larocque's report was short on details and badly written, covered with marginal queries and corrections in bold black writing she presumed to be Berwick's. The questions were good ones, but circling spelling errors? Not even Sergeant Lewis was so picky. Lewis had agreed to her proposal to stay and investigate on two conditions: no publicity and no pay. She was officially off duty this weekend, wasn't she? She wondered what would happen if the autopsy results confirmed that Bertolucci had been murdered. Would Lewis leave her on the case or give it to someone else, someone he trusted?

By the time she finished her fries, she had lists of questions to ask each of the people Berwick had agreed she could talk to.

1) Andy and/or Martha Johnson, still at the Lady Minto Hospital in Ganges, if they were in any condition to answer questions.

2) David Ohara, who lived at Welbury Bay, near the southeast tip of Ganges Harbour, and was expected to return from Victoria at any moment.

3) Bob Kelly, Ohara's maintenance foreman, who lived a few kilometres up the road from the cabin where the body was found.

4) Samuel Johnson, the manager of the Dockside Inn and Bertolucci's former employer.

Surely one of these people would tell her something useful. Whether Bertolucci had a reason to kill himself, for instance. Or whether someone else had a reason for wanting him dead.

43

Two hours later, after taking a wrong turn that landed her back in the snarl of traffic around the Ganges Saturday market, Danutia drove the detachment's unmarked Chevy Blazer into the Dockside Inn parking lot, now packed with cars.

So far she had found out nothing about the dead man, nothing at all.

Arming herself with a small bouquet from the gift shop, she had ventured into Andy Johnson's hospital room only to find him heavily sedated and his wife Martha, who reminded Danutia of her muscular Ukrainian aunts, in no mood to answer questions. Locked metal gates, incongruous underneath a yellow cedar archway, barred David Ohara's driveway; Danutia was forced to listen to the housekeeper's apologies over a static-ridden intercom. Mr. Ohara hadn't returned yet, and she didn't know how to get in touch with him, she fretted. Maybe his floatplane had gone down, he always insisted on flying himself when heaven knew he could hire a dozen pilots. A Dobermann on a long chain guarded Bob Kelly's empty place.

Why didn't she just give it up, go for a hike on Mount Maxwell?

From behind a stone wall that enclosed the Dockside's garden, came the shrieks of children. A yellow balloon drifted upwards, pursued by a young father, who caught the trailing string as the bright ball sailed into the trees. Triumphantly he disappeared with his booty.

Persistence pays, Danutia told herself, and went inside.

While a waiter went off to find the manager, Danutia stood at the bar along with half a dozen customers waiting for tables. The pub was divided into three or four small rooms, all of them full, as was the verandah Danutia had noticed from the float plane. Suddenly a bustle of activity swept through, as though someone had announced a game of musical chairs. When the hubbub subsided, the place was half empty and a man who looked like Alfred Hitchcock with bushy white hair stood at her elbow, fingering the gold watch chain that stretched across his striped burgundy vest.

"Charon calls, and the shades depart," he intoned, gesturing toward the ferry approaching the dock below. "Guaranteed turnover every hour. What more could a restaurant want? I know, I know, you aren't here to talk about the restaurant business," he said, "but first things first. Have you eaten? I'll have the kitchen send something to my office. Mussels? Very fresh. Or perhaps you're a vegetarian. We do a lovely fettuccine primavera."

Danutia refused, politely.

"A pity," he said, leading her behind the bar and into a large book-lined room, where he settled her into a leather armchair before seating himself behind the stately oak desk. A nameplate in flowing italic script read, Samuel Johnson, Ph.D. Beside it, a makeshift cardboard sign proclaimed, 'The doctor is in'. "Andy's my brother," the manager said, following her gaze. "Martha phoned after you left. Kind of you to take him flowers."

Danutia struggled not to blush. The flowers weren't exactly protocol, but small-town habits died hard. "Any change in his condition?"

"Oh, he'll be fine in a day or two. As I reminded

Martha, he rather enjoys his bouts of ill health. Now what can I do for you?"

"If you've talked to Martha Johnson, I presume you know that your brother discovered a body this morning. I must ask you not to discuss this matter with the media or anyone else. We haven't been able to contact the next of kin yet, but Sergeant Berwick has identified the man as someone who worked for you until recently. Joe Bertolucci."

"Joe?" The benevolent smile faded and Johnson reached for the Sherlock Holmes pipe held upright in a ceramic ashtray. Sucking noisily on the stem, he asked, "You don't mind, do you?"

She did, but didn't object. The name had obviously been a shock. Neither of the Johnsons had recognized the body it seemed. Little wonder considering the circumstances.

Johnson tamped more tobacco into the bowl and lit it. "I thought it must be a drifter who OD'd. You see them coming off the ferry: backpacks, scruffy jeans, and that dead look in their eyes, so you know they aren't here for the scenery." A thin wisp of apple-scented smoke spiralled upward. "But Joe now. I can't believe it. What happened?"

"That's what we're trying to determine," Danutia said, taking out her tape recorder. "There are some routine questions we try to answer in all cases of sudden death."

"And the fact that David Ohara owns the property is purely immaterial, I suppose?" Johnson asked, raising his bushy eyebrows.

A shrewd question and there was no good way to

46

answer it. If pressure from Ohara made her role more believable, so be it. She slipped a tape into the machine and recorded the identifying information.

"I understand that Joe Bertolucci worked as a bartender here, Mr. Johnson—Dr. Johnson—"

"Everybody calls me Doc."

"How long had he worked for you?"

Doc Johnson sent a smoke ring curling lazily upward, another. "It was a Bloomsday—that's June sixteenth, the day in which the events of James Joyce's *Ulysses* take place—it must be four or five years ago. I was having a little celebration, readings from Joyce and a few drinks and the like, and rushing around like Chicken Little because my bartender hadn't shown up, when this man stepped behind the bar and said, 'Looks like you could use some help.' Never saw him before in my life, and didn't really see him then, because he was in costume, like a lot of other people—eye patch, moustache, brilliantined hair. That's Joe there," Dr. Johnson said, pointing to a wall of framed photographs.

Women in turn of the century bathing suits or flapper dresses, men in Charlie Chaplin hats or white suits and spats. Danutia, who hadn't liked playing dress-up even as a child, wondered why adults deliberately made themselves look ridiculous. Finally she spotted a dark-haired, thin-faced man with an eye patch.

"Turned out Joe was an out-of-work actor friend of Zachary's—that's Zachary Smith, a local director—from Vancouver," Doc Johnson continued. "Anyway, he pulled beers and mixed drinks for five or six hours, smooth as you please, as though he knew at a glance where every-thing was. By the end of the evening, he had a job. Best bartender I ever had, and the only one who stayed more than a year or two." He sucked once more on the pipe and then returned it to the ashtray.

"When did he leave?"

Leaning forward on his elbows, his fingers steepled together, Doc Johnson pursed his lips. "The reason Joe was such a good bartender, you have to understand," he said after a moment, "was that he didn't drink himself. To be more accurate, he was on the wagon. Joe had lost everything—wife, kids, job, house, boat—because of his drinking, so Zach told me. All too common in the theatre world. He went into a treatment program, and when he came out, Zach gave him his old Airstream trailer and helped him find a bit of land to put it on, and he went to work for me. Usually after we closed I'd have a brandy, and Joe would have an espresso, and we'd chat about books for half an hour or so. Until this winter I never saw him take a drink.

"After Christmas it rained for three weeks solid, and Joe came down with a bad cold he couldn't seem to shake. That's when I first smelled alcohol on his breath. Third or fourth time, I asked him about it. Hot toddy for his cold, he said, nothing to worry about. But when the cough finally went away, the drinking didn't. A couple of months ago Joe started showing up a little late, dropping trays of glasses—the kinds of things that happen to every-one, only they never had with Joe. I didn't say anything, hoping he'd get the drinking under control again.

"Then it was Bloomsday again, June sixteenth. I didn't see what happened, but just before closing time Joe came in the office saying he quit. He'd lost his temper with a customer, and if he couldn't trust himself, he didn't expect anyone else to. Seems that one of our regulars, an obnoxious little bastard, had been yap-yap-yapping at Joe all evening. Finally Joe asked him to leave and hustled him out the door that leads down to the garden. The next thing Joe knew, the SOB was lying at the bottom of the stairs." Reaching for his pipe again, he added lightly, jokingly, but with pain in his eyes, "Maybe that's why Joe killed himself on Ohara's property. To make trouble for the weasly bastard."

"I don't understand the connection."

"The man was Bob Kelly. He's maintenance foreman for Ohara."

Danutia's ears pricked up. "Did Kelly press charges?"

"Threatened to. While Joe and I were here in the office, Kelly came thundering back up the stairs, demanding that Len arrest Joe. Len asked around, but no one had seen Joe push Kelly, or at least no one would admit it. So Len said that what he had seen was Kelly being drunk and disorderly." Doc Johnson banged the pipe against the ashtray, then reamed it out with a pipe cleaner.

"That shut Kelly up in a hurry. If he'd landed in jail, he would have lost his job. He would have brought dishonour to Ohara's most honourable business. At least Ohara claims it's honourable. A lot of folks on Salt Spring would disagree."

"Did you see Bertolucci after that night?"

"He came back the next morning for his cheque. Then

he seemed to disappear. I assumed he'd gone to Vancouver. His daughter was getting married."

"Did he seem anxious or depressed?"

"Do you mean did I have any idea he was planning to kill himself? Certainly not."

Danutia changed the subject. "According to our information, Bertolucci was working as a security guard for David Ohara."

"Why would he do that? He thought developers like Ohara were ruining the Gulf Islands."

"Maybe like the rest of us, he needed the money."

"Could be," Doc Johnson said doubtfully. "He seemed to be laying out a bundle for his daughter's wedding, all right." He brandished his pipe, sending ashes flying. "Look here, it just doesn't make sense. I can imagine almost anyone coming to a point where living seems too painful, but as I said, Joe was a conscientious worker. If he took on a job, he'd do it. So why would he suddenly decide to commit suicide?"

To deflect him from the obvious answer, she asked, "Is there anyone who might have known Bertolucci was working for Ohara?"

"Zachary Smith maybe, the director I mentioned. He's off-island though. The company's performing in Victoria this weekend." Putting the pipe down once again, he rummaged among the papers on his desk, then passed over an Arts Festival brochure. "That's Zachary," he said.

A mocking dead-white face winked at her over a black and white striped T-shirt.

Doc Johnson extracted a gold watch from his vest

pocket. "The time has come, the Walrus said, for the next onslaught of culture vultures and bargain hunters. Is there anything more I can help you with?"

Danutia clicked off the tape recorder. "Do you have a photograph of Bertolucci I could borrow? Preferably one where he isn't in costume."

The portly manager hunted among the prints on the wall. "Ah, here's the one I was looking for," he said. "His daughter took it last summer." He studied the photograph a moment before handing it over with a shake of his head.

In the photo Bertolucci was sitting on the pub's verandah. His thin face half-turned toward the camera, he reached down to stroke the border collie at his feet. The gesture was so full of love that Danutia could not believe this man had meant to die.

She put the photo in her backpack and rose to leave. "Have you seen Bertolucci's dog in the last few days?" When he said no, she asked him to get in touch with the detachment if the dog should turn up.

"One other thing," Danutia said. "I want to find out more about this altercation between Bertolucci and Kelly. You didn't mention the officer's last name."

Doc Johnson drew the office door shut behind them. "I assumed you knew. Berwick, Len Berwick. He made a very good Leopold Bloom that evening, by the way."

···· ···

Doc Johnson's bombshell ticked away inside Danutia while she hunted down Hillside Farm, the bed and breakfast Berwick had arranged for her near Vesuvius. It ticked louder as she stood under the hot shower, trying to remove the taint of death she felt clinging to her skin and hair. By the time she had driven back to Ganges and rung the after-hours bell several times, she was ready to explode.

"Why didn't you tell me about Bertolucci's run-in with Bob Kelly?" Danutia demanded when Berwick finally opened the door.

"I never discuss a case on an empty stomach," Berwick said, unruffled. He had changed into grey slacks and shirt, elegant in comparison to her Mountain Equipment Co-op hiking gear, the only extra clothes she'd brought. "I'll just finish running the last six names through PIRS and then I'll take you to dinner."

"Empty stomach or no, I want an answer," Danutia said, her hiking boots echoing on the wooden floor as she followed him into the stifling hot mailroom where a kaleidoscopic screensaver flashed and swirled.

Berwick logged in and the printer clattered as he downloaded a file. "The Police Information Retrieval System we have," he said, logging in. "A ceiling fan we don't. Go figure."

"About Kelly—"

The overhead light flickered, the screen blanked out, and the printer sputtered to a halt.

"Rats," Berwick said.

"You don't have to watch your language around me."

Berwick laughed and gestured toward the walls. "Rats. In there. Chewing up the wiring. In the old days the constable lived upstairs with his family. The rats and mice have been here ever since." Reaching behind the desk, he removed a panel and jiggled the exposed wires. The printer spat out a few more lines and stopped. He shut down the computer. "Time to eat."

As he steered her out the side door and into his pickup, she tried again. "About Kelly—"

"Later," he said.

So she gave up, for the moment. "Don't you get bored, working in such a small detachment?"

"Young guys like Larocque want more action, but it's a good place to end a career. We get maybe ten complaints a day. Vandalism, squabbles between neighbours. B&E's in the summer, when the transients come through. Occasional domestics, somebody getting loaded or having a bad trip. It's like being the town marshall after the gunfight at the OK Corral, if you know what I mean."

"No murders?" Danutia asked.

"Not in the five years I've been here. Restores your faith in human nature."

The Saturday market had closed down; cars no longer clogged the streets. Even so, there were few empty parking spaces in the cluster of shops at Mouat Square.

"Greek okay?" Berwick asked, ushering Danutia into a tiny blue and white restaurant before she had a chance to object. Steak, that's what she wanted, a good thick slab of Alberta beef.

Greeting Berwick like an old friend, the owner seated them on the patio overlooking Ganges harbour. "I'll send out a little something to get you started," Dimitrios said, handing them menus. A few feet away a large grill sent up mouthwatering smells of broiling meat. No steaks on the menu, though, so she settled for roast lamb. Moments later a platter heaped with pastry triangles, meatballs, and something that looked like onion rings appeared at their table, and with it a bottle of retsina.

Berwick offered to fill her glass.

"Alcohol gives me a headache," Danutia said. "Besides, if I remember rightly, the menu describes retsina as having an 'exhilarating resiny flavour'. Sounds like Pine-Sol to me."

Berwick laughed. "Let me tell you the legend of how retsina originated, and maybe it will sound more appealing.

"The Greeks and the Persians were always at war, as you no doubt know, looting and pillaging, raping women, getting drunk. The Persians were particularly fond of Greek wine sweetened with honey. So the next time the Persians invaded, the Greeks decided to protect their wine by opening up the huge clay storage jars and throwing in gobs of pine resin. You can imagine how awful the wine tasted to the Persians. But the Greeks found the new taste delightful. Or at least that's how the story goes. Maybe they were just grateful to have anything left to drink."

Not wanting to seem an enemy—not yet, at any rate—Danutia allowed Berwick to pour her an inch of retsina and took a cautious sip. Not as bad as she feared.

Deciding to bury her anger while they ate, Danutia let herself be drawn out when Berwick asked about her off-the-job passions. Hiking, she said. Hollywood musicals. Why? Because you couldn't forget for a minute that they were unreal. Even the sad ones, like *West Side Story*. So you didn't have to care about the characters, really. A relief, given the job.

By now they were sipping coffee—thick, sweet stuff that seemed all dregs. The last rays of the sun caught Berwick's bald spot, turning it pink and gold, like a distant hilltop. The patio lamps came on; the waiter lit the candle on their table.

"Speaking of the job," Danutia said, "Did you reach Bertolucci's family?"

"Yes and no." According to the address book he'd found in Bertolucci's trailer, the ex-wife lived in Richmond. The detachment there had sent a constable around to notify her, but she refused to have anything to do with claiming the body. "Mrs. Bertolucci said her daughter was away on her honeymoon and she didn't know how to reach her, because Antonia never tells her anything—"

"Sounds like my mother," Danutia put in.

"Antonia called me about an hour ago. Seems her brother Gino had her itinerary. She and her husband arrived in Victoria this afternoon after kayaking in the Broken Islands. Gino left a message at their hotel to get in touch with the RCMP. She'd just been to the morgue to make the formal identification."

"How did she sound?" Danutia asked.

"Shocked. Scared. But she pulled herself together like a trooper. They'll be over first thing tomorrow."

Danutia sipped her coffee, the bittersweet taste lingering at the back of her throat like medicine. After the school counsellor told her about her brother Andrew's motorcycle accident, she had calmly finished her Grade 12 math exam, then fallen ill with a mysterious fever that lasted six weeks. She wondered what lay ahead for Antonia.

"Nothing on the demonstrators so far but a couple of DWI's," Berwick was saying. "No news of the dog."

Danutia roused herself. "I asked Doc Johnson. He hasn't seen it. He did tell me about Bertolucci's run-in with Kelly a few weeks ago. Kelly was nowhere to be found this afternoon. Why didn't someone tell him to stay put?"

Berwick silently offered Danutia more retsina, emptied the bottle into his glass when she declined. "If I may remind you, Kelly's bulldozer—surrounded by angry protesters—was blocking access to the cabin. Larocque told him to get the hell out of the way. Not surprisingly, Kelly did just that. He'll be back."

"When? I want to talk to him."

"Monday or Tuesday. Ohara sent him to do some work on Hornby." A gull landed on the railing beside them, and Berwick shooed it away.

"How do you know? Did you talk to Ohara and forget to mention it?"

"No, my men checked the ferries. Kelly gabbed to one of the operators. Everything he does is all over the island in ten minutes."

And now he'll be spreading rumours up and down the coast, Danutia thought ruefully. Then another possibility occurred to her. "Is that how the demonstrators knew he was going to bulldoze the cabin? Maybe he set them up so someone would find the body. You have to admit, Kelly is the closest thing we have to a suspect."

"To have a suspect," Berwick said, emptying his glass, "you have to have a murder. Let's review the possibilities. One: accident. Two: suicide. Three: murder, accidental or premeditated."

"Fidelman ruled out accidental death, and I agree."

"But on what grounds? That no one 'accidentally' sticks a gun to his mouth and pulls the trigger. Except that they do—if they don't think the gun is loaded, or if they're playing Russian roulette, or if they're pissed out of their minds. They don't expect to die. That whiskey bottle was almost empty. If the autopsy shows a high level of blood alcohol, and there are no clear indications of foul play, the ME will rule accidental death, whatever Fidelman says."

Danutia shivered as a gust of cold wind blew off the water. The boats moored at the government docks clanked and rocked. "What about the suicide note?" she asked, her voice sharper than she intended.

"What about it? I'm the one who thinks it was suicide, not you. The guy's gone back to drinking, the whole cycle's starting over—he's lost his job, let his kids down again, probably neck-deep in debt over this wedding. He says to hell with it, writes the note, pulls the trigger. Classic suicide."

"While I was driving around this afternoon, I was trying to remember what I've read and heard about suicide. What about the fact there was no cadaveric spasm?

Bertolucci's right arm was lying by his side, with the fingers barely touching the gun. If he had shot himself, the muscles would have gone into spasm—"

"Not if the bullet hit the medulla—"

"Hold on, let me finish. The gun would still be held up to his mouth when he was found. I remember a case where it took three officers to pry the fingers loose."

"That does happen occasionally in suicides," Berwick conceded, "if death is absolutely instantaneous. But that's as far as you can take it. You can't claim that because there's no cadaveric spasm, it must be murder. That's one of the most elementary rules of logic." The candle guttered in the cool breeze. Berwick shoved back his chair. "You must be getting cold. Let's move inside."

Danutia thought longingly of the jacket in her backpack. "I'm fine," she said. "Dr. Fidelman—"

"Fidelman spent too long in LA. Everything's going to look like murder to him for a while."

"Okay, forget about Fidelman. The position is still wrong. If you're going to stick a gun in your mouth, you don't want to botch it. So you lie belly down on a bed or the floor or sit at a table, where you can prop your elbows on something. Bertolucci was on the floor, face up."

"You're arguing from what the textbooks say. In the real world, anything can happen."

"Let's get to your third possibility," she said. "Murder. A) Accidental. One of the environmentalists could have surprised Bertolucci while he was cleaning the gun. They struggled, the gun went off."

"No signs of a struggle."

"Or B) Premeditated murder. Someone with a grudge against Bertolucci—someone like Kelly, say—knows Bertolucci is in this isolated cabin. He kills Bertolucci. Makes it look like suicide, just in case the body is found. But he doesn't have to worry too much, because he knows in a couple of days the cabin will be smashed to smithereens, and the body with it. Then the demonstrators turn up, ruining his plans. So he skips out."

"Except, as even his own mother would tell you, Bob isn't clever enough to deceive anybody. We're left with suicide, I'm afraid." Berwick signalled for the bill.

A lemon-drop moon popped over the horizon, laying a wavering trail across the water. The boats rocked gently in their slips, silvered by moonlight. The patio had filled, the murmur of quiet conversation lapping around her like waves against the pilings. In a moment they would leave, and she would have lost her chance to make Berwick listen. From the next table she heard an American voice saying, "As I understand the problem," and she remembered Sharma's words from this morning: "Freedom from the desire for an answer is essential to the understanding of the problem." She had tried to argue with Berwick and it hadn't worked. So while he settled the bill, she put aside her need to pay for her own dinner, to prove herself his equal, and tried to open her mind. What was it about the circumstances of Bertolucci's death that had disturbed her?

When the waiter left, she spoke. "I admit the case looks most like suicide. And I admit the arguments about body position and such are weak. What really bothers me are the small things. From everything Doc Johnson said, Bertolucci sounds like a conscientious man. But a conscientious man doesn't accept a job, take along his dog, and then commit suicide. Those things just don't add up."

Berwick rose. He towered over her, his face lost in shadow. "Sometimes life's like that," he said. "As you'll learn."

# Chapter 4
Salt Spring: Sunday morning, July 9

"You could at least ask Norma why your review wasn't in today's paper." Thea's reproachful voice echoed down the dusty corridor of the not-quite-finished Salt Spring Theatre. At the top of a short flight of stairs she halted abruptly. "You did give *Bullock's Folly* a good review, didn't you?"

"I did my best," Arthur said, wishing he had stayed in bed with the Sunday papers. To deflect Thea's attention from the review he hadn't yet written, and didn't want to write, he added, "When are you going to show me the stage?"

"We're almost there." Thea led him down the stairs and through a side door into the dark auditorium. "No seats yet, as you can see, or maybe you can't. There should be a light switch here somewhere."

"Leave it." Putting his hand on Thea's shoulder, Arthur let the darkness and silence flow into him, washing away his irritation. Soon a different feeling emerged, a sense of hushed expectancy. "This theatre feels like a blank slate waiting to be written on," he said. "With each production new lines will be laid down over the old, and soon echoes will haunt the place like ghosts entreating our attention. Right now, there's a hungry silence. Can you feel it?"

For a moment Thea seemed caught up in his vision, and a warmth flowed between them, the warmth of two people sharing something they both loved. Then Thea moved away and switched on the light. The space looked naked, a proscenium stage in shining wood facing nothing but grey carpet sloping upward.

"The contractor has promised the lobby and auditorium will be ready for Friday night's opening of *The Mikado*, seats and all." She switched off the light and led him back to the lobby. "It will take another quarter of a million to finish all the workshops and the exhibition space." She poked him in the chest. "A fact you can stress in your article."

Arthur cut off an irritated retort. Although the news editor had turned down his idea of writing about the suicide, he'd talked the arts editor, Norma, into letting him write a series of reviews of the Salt Spring Festival. The selling point had been tomorrow's harp concert; the performer, Deirdre Summers, was one of Norma's favourites. He'd intended to devote the week to pursuing Lavender. He hadn't considered that staying on would put him at Thea's beck and call. Still, no point in being angry.

"If you expect me to ask readers for money, like one of these TV evangelists, you'll have to buy me a drink. Where's the bar?" he said, trying for a light tone. "Every theatre has to have a bar. Relief from bad acting and boring plays."

"You aren't referring to *Bullock's Folly*, are you?" Thea had on her don't-dodge-the-issue frown. Taking a tissue from her handbag, she dusted a corner of the bench beside the glass entrance doors and sat down. "I want the truth. What did you say about the play?"

Arthur sighed as he sat down. "Thea, it's worthy, but

it's so bloody traditional. Just kitchen sink school in historical drag."

Thea slapped her hand down on the bench. A puff of dust rose and settled. "The play is traditional. It is historical. I know these used to be swear words for us once. But there are real traditions, Arthur. There's real history. There's connecting with place."

"Playwrights need to connect with theatre as well. Hasn't this woman read or seen any drama since Ibsen?"

"Arthur, you're talking about theatre in London or theatre in New York. What about theatre right here? People come to Salt Spring and they see the gift shops and boutiques and golf courses and yachts in the harbour and think the Island's cute. I don't know much about Salt Spring's history, but from talking to Cassie I do know it has one. Indian tribes disemboweled each other over fishing rights. The first non-native settlers were blacks escaping from slavery. The first white woman in Fulford Harbour had to chase away a cougar about to attack her little girl. There's nothing cute about any of that."

"So what's your point?"

"I'm saying that a playwright who puts real history in her play, and uses it to make a political statement about the present, is doing something worthwhile."

"But she doesn't have to put it in an outdated theatrical form. What about using film noir or music hall or comedy show routines, like Joan Littlewood and David Hare?" Arthur stood up, shaking the bench. A beam of sunlight through the glass doors caught particles of dust swirling above their heads.

"So you want Cassie to write the kind of plays that were fashionable thirty years ago? And that's not being outdated?" Thea's frown deepened. "You're rigid, Arthur—rigid, rigid, rigid. You've set up an ideal of innovative theatre, and it's chiselled in stone. There are other ways of being innovative, you know."

"Such as?"

"What about Jerzy Grotowski putting on plays in the Polish forest, with no scripts and no props? Or Peter Brook touring African villages with simple plays about shoes and rain? That's the kind of theatre Cassie is aiming for, outreach theatre involved with people in the places they live." The toe of Thea's shoe traced circles on the dusty floor. "And if I'm lucky I'll get to stay on Salt Spring and work with her."

Arthur was startled. "Stay on Salt Spring?"

Before she could explain, her cellphone rang, and she stepped outside to take the call.

Watching Thea through glass doors smeared with construction mud, Arthur felt the heat of the argument rise again. It wasn't anger at Thea's ignorance. She knew modern theatre as well as he did, probably better. They'd met in Manchester when she was a visiting graduate student, doing thesis research on regional theatre. But she was wrong to call him rigid; she'd given up her ideals and he hadn't, that was the truth of the matter. He was rehearsing his rebuttal when he noticed Thea's shoulders slump and the corners of her mouth droop. He was reminded of the night they'd met, a cast party where, surrounded by a ring of British wits, she had given earnest, halting answers to their taunting questions until finally she'd lapsed into silence. Arthur had caught her eye, asked if she wanted a bite to eat at the corner pub. The kindness of strangers. He suddenly felt a sorrow over how things had turned out for them.

Thea stepped back inside. "That was Zachary Smith calling from Victoria. Remember I told you about the man who killed himself in the cabin? It turns out that he was a good friend of Zachary's. Zach has hatched a plan for a benefit performance of *The Mikado* to raise money for the man's kids. He wants me to arrange space for a rehearsal tomorrow and a performance Tuesday night. How I'm supposed to do this on a day's notice I don't know."

In Arthur's mind the violent events of the last two days merged into a vision of a bloodied Hendrix on the floor of a rustic cabin. He shook his head as though to dispel this image. "Why doesn't he turn the Friday opening into a benefit?"

"I suggested that, but he says there will be too many outsiders. He wants to do a performance just for Salt Spring people. A noble gesture, but I hope it doesn't ruin our audience for Friday."

Arthur's gloom lifted as an idea occurred to him. Why not review Tuesday's performance? The benefit angle was new, and a few more interviews at tomorrow's rehearsal could help him get closer to the mystery he sensed at the heart of the Vesuvius Company. Not to mention that he would have an excuse to talk to Lavender.

"Oh, by the way . . ." Thea's voice brought Arthur's wandering attention back to her. She was gazing through the glass doors at what would some day be a courtyard, now piles of dirt and clumps of weeds and a muddy patch where an abandoned hose lay in loose coils. "Lavender asked Zachary to pass on her apologies for sleeping in yesterday and missing breakfast with you. She'll be happy you're staying on, I'm sure."

"Yes, well." Arthur, relieved, excited and embarrassed, hurriedly changed the topic. "Speaking of staying on, what was that about moving to Salt Spring?"

Thea reached for the door. "I really don't have time to talk about it."

"Five minutes," Arthur said, taking her hand.

Thea's eyes measured his. "Okay, five minutes. Here's the deal. An anonymous benefactor is endowing a half-time position for an Artistic Director of the new theatre. In return, the theatre board has agreed to sponsor performances in small communities and schools on the Island, teach classes for kids, that sort of thing."

Arthur felt an empty space opening in front of him. "And you're going to apply?"

"Of course. Zachary already has, I'm told. I wish I wasn't competing against him."

"Because he lives here?"

"He lives here. He's already doing school productions. And he has skills I don't have."

"Smith strikes me as a difficult person to work with," Arthur said. "The board members will know that. But if you get the job, what about the Caprice? Down the drain?"

"Of course not. Half-time here, with an assured

income. Half-time there, trying to make ends meet. I could book most of the same productions for both venues. It would relieve some of the pressure." Thea glanced at her watch. "I'd better lock up. Sorry about that brunch I promised you."

So she wasn't planning a complete break. And she hadn't discovered that his review of *Bullock's Folly*—several of them, in fact—had perished under the Delete button. He would try again tonight.

Outside he said goodbye and paused to consult his Festival program while Thea, unsteady in high heels, edged her way down the steep hill toward town. She looked back, and seeing him watching, raised a hand to wave. The slam of a car door seemed to startle her, so that her arm remained in the air for a moment before she turned and resumed walking.

Arthur was startled too; the sound took him back to the dull thwock of the sword, Hendrix's fall. Thea would be competing against Zachary Smith for the position of Artistic Director. Irrational as it seemed, the prospect made Arthur uneasy.

# Chapter 5
## Salt Spring: Sunday, July 9

"Oregon grape. Made it myself," said Danutia's B&B hostess, setting a dish of jelly the colour of dried blood on the table. Mrs. Whitmore was as small and nondescript as a wren, brown polyester shirt and slacks, grey-brown hair twisted into a bun, thin lips sharpening when she spoke. "Shocking business about Joe Bertolucci, isn't it?"

Danutia kept her eyes on her bacon and eggs. So much for secrecy. She should have known. In the farming community where she grew up, gossip was as valuable as gold.

"Been dead a while, I understand." Mrs. Whitmore had been flitting from fridge to stove to table. Now she hovered beside Danutia's chair, coffee pot in hand. "That's what Doc said—in strictest confidence, you understand. I almost didn't go to choir practice last night because Ivy's in Victoria doing *The Mikado* and I don't like to drive at night by myself, but then another friend said she'd drive. So we stopped at the Dockside for our usual glass of sherry. Doc just put our drinks down and headed off without saying a word. 'You better be nice to me,' I told him, 'I got an RCMP officer staying.' That's when he said Joe was dead, and you'd been around to talk to him. He thought I should know, since you're staying here. But there, it's none of my business."

Refusing to be drawn, Danutia asked whether Mrs. Whitmore knew the whereabouts of Bertolucci's trailer.

Last night she had driven back and forth on the road between St. Mary Lake and Southey Point without ever finding the turning Berwick had described when he handed her the key.

"Poor man." Mrs. Whitmore topped up Danutia's coffee and leaned back against the counter, her small grey head cocked to one side. At rest she looked older, frailer. "We had a joke about that, you know. His place is just on the other side of the ridge from my back pasture, you see, but if you're driving you have to go all the way around Southey Point. He was always saying, 'When are you going to cut a road through your pasture?' and I'd say, 'You've got to wait 'til I die, like those greedy children of mine.'"

Danutia had had a restless night, waking with tense muscles and a headache. A walk was just what she needed. "Is there a trail?"

"Joe used to walk over for eggs and such every once in a while, so I dare say there's a path beyond the pasture, though I've never been on it. Mind the sheep droppings."

A short while later, Danutia picked her way across the pasture, clambered over the aging split-rail fence, and set off across a sunny meadow, singing "We're marching to Zion, beautiful beautiful Zion," until she heard the voice of her high-school track coach shouting orders inside her head. "Drop the shoulders! Vacuum the stomach!" A refugee from Eastern Europe, Milos never let his high-school athletes forget he had coached Olympic contenders. "Long your arms—higher, higher. Drop. Now side. Now front." The backpack made her movements awkward, but she could feel her cramped muscles relax. Crows cawed overhead, a raucous accompaniment to her strange gyrations. "Now throw the shoulder blades—up, down, up, down. Shake the dust."

Ashes to ashes, dust to dust. Bertolucci's body returning to the elements from which it was made.

After a little casting about she found a narrow trail leading into the woods, chilly and dank where the sun had not yet penetrated. As she ducked under a low-lying branch, a spider web clung to her face like thin threads of doubt. She had done her best to stand up for herself last night; still, Berwick had dismissed every point she raised. He didn't have to be so patronizing. Sharma never treated her that way.

The trail had narrowed without her noticing and now seemed to peter out where a massive Douglas fir, its deeply scored bark encrusted with moss, had toppled into a thicket of dead branches and struggling undergrowth. She would have to fight her way through.

She had almost made it when her right foot hit a slippery patch of moss and she pitched forward. Doubling over as Coach had taught her, she managed to protect her head and soft front from jagged branches and prickly vines but gasped as pain shot up her leg. After the first shock subsided she tested the ankle and brushed herself off. A slight sprain, nothing more. A short distance beyond the thicket a wider path came in from the left. "So, super sleuth, you must have missed a turning," she muttered. Then she yelled into the stillness around her, "How much I have to tell you, keep the mind on what you do!"

Before long she emerged into a shady clearing where chickadees flittered and chirped. A sleek white Camry stood beside a battered Dodge Dart and an ancient Airstream trailer. A young woman turned away from the padlocked trailer door and spoke to the man behind her, who cradled something wrapped in a beach towel. The newlyweds. Danutia hadn't expected to see them here.

"Mia's been hurt," the young woman said as Danutia approached. She had a dancer's build, long thin bones outlined against her black tank top and leggings. Her face was like her father's, thin, with high cheekbones and large, dark eyes, puffy from crying.

"Constable Dranchuk, RCMP," Danutia said, showing her card. "You must be Antonia Bertolucci. I'm so sorry about your father."

"It's Savarini now. Antonia Savarini." She fingered a thin silver cross lying against skin blotchy from the sun. "This is my husband, Marco."

As the young man shifted his bundle to shake hands, the dog yelped.

"We were going to call a vet," Antonia said, "but we couldn't get in. Where did the padlock come from? Papa never locked up."

"Police precaution," Danutia said. "Is he badly hurt?"

"She. Mia's a she," Antonia said.

"She crawled out from under the trailer when we drove up," Marco said. "There's dried blood all over. She must have wandered down to the highway and been hit by a car."

Antonia reached a tentative hand toward the dog's head. "Maybe she was looking for Papa."

Reluctant as she was to admit anyone into the trailer, Danutia couldn't let the dog suffer unnecessarily.

While Marco and Mia sat outside in the shade and Antonia tried to find a veterinarian open on Sundays, Danutia surveyed Bertolucci's living space. Though the trailer smelled of dust and mold, it was as neat and spare as a ship's cabin or a monastic cell. Nothing cluttered the tiny Formica counter or the tabletop that must have doubled as a desk, judging from the cardboard file drawers beside it. At the far end of the trailer, a blue cotton blanket was drawn tight across a built-in captain's bed, the two drawers below no doubt containing neatly folded clothes. The only sign of comfort was an overstuffed chair, its upholstery covered by a matching blue blanket. Next to the chair stood a low bookcase with a kerosene lamp on top.

Antonia hung up the phone. "Dr. Einarsson will see Mia right away. Do you need me for anything? The officer I talked to yesterday said there might be some questions."

"Let's meet at the RCMP detachment when you've finished with the vet."

"I'm not a criminal," Antonia said. "Do we have to meet there? How about the coffee bar on the main road in Ganges—the newish one across from the fire station?"

"That's fine," Danutia said. "At eleven?" Gently she added, "There may be some things here—some personal things, letters and such—that I need to examine."

Antonia clutched the tiny cross at the base of her throat. "Take what you need," she said. At the doorway she halted.

"Even if he didn't go to church, Papa was a good

Catholic," she said, her eyes filling with tears. "He would never have killed himself. It must have been an accident."

As she turned to go, Danutia murmured, too low for the young woman to hear, "It would be comforting to think so."

As soon as she heard the Camry's engine start up, Danutia dialed the vet. Dr. Roberta Einarsson readily agreed to take some blood and hair samples. Satisfied, Danutia phoned Berwick to arrange for a constable to be present. The dog had been at the cabin. Some of the blood might be Bertolucci's—or his assailant's.

Pulling on a pair of latex gloves, she resumed her inspection. Nothing of interest in the kitchen area. Nothing in the small closet except white shirts and black slacks and a raincoat with a zip-out lining. No liquor bottles anywhere, full or empty. No garbage of any kind, not even a scrap of paper. Bertolucci must have cleaned up thoroughly before he moved into Ohara's cabin.

In the bookcase, an unabridged dictionary, books on sailing, histories of the Mediterranean, poems and plays in Italian and English, arranged by subject matter and by author within each section. A handsome volume on the history of commedia dell'arte, inscribed, '*Con amore*, Antonia' and dated two Christmases ago, heavily annotated in a small, neat hand. Antonia must have known her father well. No books lying on tables or stacked upon the floor. At the cabin, she recalled, there was a paperback open, face down, the back cover curling at the bottom edge, as though it had been put aside for a moment. Another small detail that didn't fit.

She turned to the file drawers. A white plastic desk organizer on top held pens, paperclips, tape, glue, plain white paper, envelopes, and stamps in tidy compartments. She slipped a few sheets of paper into a plastic evidence bag. The lab would determine whether they matched the suicide note.

Using the eraser end of a pencil, she flicked through the neatly labeled hanging files in the top drawer. Bank statements, old tax returns. Receipts, including one from Sea Adventures in Victoria. So Bertolucci had paid, and paid handsomely, for his daughter's honeymoon. Otherwise he seemed to live frugally, investing much of his income in something called Funds for Social Change. She slipped the latest record of transactions, which showed a total of $19,538 invested in a handful of stocks, into another evidence bag.

The bottom drawer held the remains of Bertolucci's personal life. Theatre programs from his acting days in Vancouver. Photocopies of his children's report cards. Separate file folders for each of his correspondents, most of them in Italy. Two folders of his daughter's letters, a bulging one labeled 'Antonia 1989–1993', and a thin one of her recent letters. Danutia tucked all the letter files into her backpack.

She was running a hand through T-shirts and sweaters in a drawer beneath the bed when she hit something solid. Porcelain, but not smooth. She drew out a figurine and eyed it curiously. A pink and white Little Bo-Peep with golden ringlets escaping from under her bonnet, her crook resting on Danutia's thumb, stiff layers of petticoats pressing against Danutia's fingers.

Another present from, or for, Antonia? Danutia doubted it. Bertolucci's taste was too austere, his daughter too old for such an ornament. So how did Bertolucci come to have it, and why was it tucked away in a drawer?

Danutia set the figurine on the bookcase. One tiny porcelain hand shielding her eyes, Bo-Peep gazed into the distance, her blue eyes wide, searching for her lost sheep. Danutia followed her gaze and found herself contemplating the neatly made bed. Did Bertolucci have a lover? A spurned lover, perhaps, who knew he was at the cabin, knew enough to fake the suicide note. One moment Bo-Peep perched demurely on the bookcase; the next she disappeared into Danutia's backpack.

Love and money. The motives for murder, nine times out of ten. If Berwick didn't like Bob Kelly as a suspect, maybe she could turn up another candidate or two.

.•. .•.

The day was heating up as Danutia sat on the verandah of Jumpin' Java, sipping her second cappuccino and reading Antonia's recent letters to her father. They were scrawled in black ink on thin blue onionskin; a draft copy of Bertolucci's reply, with many crossings out, was paper clipped to each one.

From January through March Antonia had written every week or two, bursting with excitement about her cinematography course and her wedding plans. Only one letter from April, dashed off between exams. In May she was job hunting, and the wedding preparations were becoming a nightmare: her cousins sulking because she'd chosen a school friend as maid of honour, and her mother and aunts wrangling over the catering. Thank goodness, Antonia told her father over and over, he would be at the wedding to protect her from all the fussing and fighting. To these letters Bertolucci responded immediately, reassuring her of his love and support. Now and then his formal turns of phrase reminded Danutia of the suicide note.

A car honked. Danutia looked up to see Antonia sprinting across two lanes of slow-moving traffic, her puffy eyes hidden now behind dark sunglasses. She waved to Danutia as she came up the stairs and went inside to order.

Danutia hurriedly flicked through the last two letters with her pencil eraser, then slowed down as she realized the dates were out of order and there were no replies. Inconsequential details, perhaps, except that Bertolucci seemed obsessively methodical. She would have the two letters dusted for prints.

Antonia's next-to-last letter, dated June 13, ended with a now-familiar refrain: 'I'm counting on you, Papa. I'll never make it through all this craziness without you.'

Uneasy with the pressure Antonia seemed to be putting on her father, Danutia shifted in her chair, banging her still-throbbing ankle against the railing. "Shit," she muttered, bending down to rub it. It was her right ankle, of course, the one she had broken in her last pole-vaulting competition.

The bar was too high, and she knew it. She stood holding the pole, her palms suddenly sweaty. The referee raised his whistle. She tried to block out the noisy crowd and the flash of runners on the track, to draw her energy into a smooth curve sailing up and over.

"You can do it," she heard her father shout from the sidelines, the voice insistent as always. You can do three hours of chores a day and still make straight As. You can drive to school through a howling blizzard. You can enter every contest and win win win.

The official raised his whistle. Ready or not, she couldn't delay any longer.

She had cleared the bar knowing she would land badly, her timing off a fraction. The ankle had healed; she had never entered another competition.

Sometimes people crack under pressure.

Antonia banged her espresso down. "Those are my letters to Papa you're reading, aren't they?" she asked. "I must seem like a self-centred little bitch. Nothing but me-me-me. My plans, my hopes, my fears, my successes and failures, my half-baked ideas about Art and Film, with capital letters."

"How is Mia?" Danutia asked, laying aside the file folder.

"All right. At least she will be in a few days. Dr. Einarsson is keeping her for observation." Antonia stirred a packet of raw sugar into her coffee. "Marco's rented a kayak for a couple of hours. It's easier to talk about Papa without him. It bothers him when I cry."

"I know this time is difficult for you, but I need to ask you some questions. I gather from your letters that you visited your father after Christmas."

"Yes, I slipped away for a couple of days—told my mother I was going to Whistler, even packed my ski things—and brought Marco over. Papa's greatest fear was that he had ruined my life, that I would end up marrying 'an irresponsible alcoholic' like himself. So I wanted him to get to know Marco, to see that he's like the Papa I remember from before the drinking began—competent and considerate and good fun when he isn't taking things too seriously. And it worked. Papa borrowed a boat and took us sailing, and when we came back he looked ten years younger. That was the last time I saw him." Silent tears escaped from beneath Antonia's sunglasses.

Danutia passed over some tissues. Antonia wiped her eyes and blew her nose. "Your father wasn't at your wedding? What happened?"

Without her dark glasses Antonia looked younger, more vulnerable. Finally she said, "Mama kept saying he'd never go through with it, he was too much a coward, but he promised, and I believed him."

"His last letter to you in the file was dated June second. Did you hear from him after that?"

"The wedding was Friday, June twenty-fourth, as close as we could get to Midsummer Night. On the twenty-first I left a message saying I'd pick him up from the ferry if he would let me know when he was coming. When I didn't hear from him, I assumed he had already left and was staying with a friend in Vancouver. Then at the wedding—" she struggled to control her voice— "the cellist ran out of pieces to play and started the *Wedding March*. Afterwards . . ." Her thin fingers picked a tissue into smaller and smaller pieces. "On our way to the Broken Islands I tried calling the Smiths and Doc Johnson, but no one had seen him."

"Were you worried about him?"

Antonia grabbed her sunglasses and flung herself out of her chair. "I'm going to get a refill."

While she waited, Danutia tried to absorb this new information. According to Doc Johnson, Bertolucci had begun drinking after Christmas—after Antonia brought her fiancé to meet him. Danutia imagined him sitting in the tatty old chair as the wedding drew closer, reading Antonia's letters and reaching for the whiskey. Wanting to be the father Antonia needed, to face down the shame and humiliation of his drinking years. Dreading what might happen if he returned to 'all that craziness.' Perhaps Berwick was right after all. Perhaps the strain had been too much, and Bertolucci had fallen into a suicidal despair.

Beyond the shady verandah, heat waves shimmered off the pavement, off the cars crawling past like an endless stream of giant ants, pausing now and then as pedestrians darted across the road, then flowing on, south to Fulford, north to Vesuvius. Rap music drifted across from a group of teens hanging out in the park. Beyond the park, the harbour stretched into the distance, dotted with sailboats and small islands. There was nothing solid here, it seemed, even the land breaking into smaller and smaller fragments.

"Sorry," Antonia said, handing Danutia a warm blueberry muffin. "A peace offering."

"Thanks." Danutia buttered her muffin, waiting. Finally Antonia spoke.

"It wasn't the first time Papa had let me down. He'd forget to show up for birthday parties, school plays, stuff like that. Or he'd be too drunk to go. Like my high school grad dinner. While I was giving the toast to the wonderful parents who'd helped us achieve our goals, Papa was at home with his head in the toilet. But after rehab, he never cancelled a visit or missed one."

"Until the wedding," Danutia said.

"Until the wedding. Then I went off on my honeymoon. And now he's dead."

"At the trailer you said there must have been an accident," Danutia said, wiping butter from her fingers. "Did your father own a gun?"

"Only an old one, a souvenir from the Second World War. My grandfather claimed to have taken it away from a Nazi colonel. When Nano died, the gun went to Papa." She picked up her cup and set it down again. "Papa must have taken it to the cabin to protect himself, and it went off accidentally. They say old guns do that sometimes."

"Accidents do happen," Danutia agreed. She didn't mention that the gun in Bertolucci's hand was no war souvenir but a Glock, a semi-automatic popular on both sides of the law. "In this case, there was a suicide note. Didn't anyone tell you?"

"I must have been in shock. There was too much to take in."

Danutia chose her words carefully. "Because of the circumstances, we can't release your father's personal effects until after the autopsy. However, I read the note onto a tape yesterday. If you like, I can play the tape for you."

Antonia's fingers curled around the silver cross. "Yes please."

Danutia set up the tape recorder and fast-forwarded to where the note began. The taped voice sounded like a stranger's, flat and distant, until she stumbled over the last words: 'Forgive me, for nothing is more precious to a father than the love of his children.'

Antonia's face was so white that Danutia reached out to steady her.

The young woman shuddered and pushed Danutia's hand away. "Don't touch me. You think I pushed him until he couldn't take it any more. That I might as well have killed him myself."

Danutia avoided the dark eyes. "The autopsy should give us a clearer picture of exactly how your father died." At the word 'autopsy' Antonia shuddered again.

Danutia began to pack up. She wasn't likely to learn anything more from Antonia this morning. "Where can I get in touch with you?"

"The Watermill. Near Fulford. Papa booked it for us for a week."

Danutia's fingers touched the china shepherdess and she drew it out. "I found this figurine at the trailer," she said. "Do you know anything about it?"

Barely glancing at Bo-Peep, Antonia shook her head. There was no room in her conception of her father, Danutia surmised, for such an ornament. "My father was saying he was sorry about the wedding, that's all," the young woman said, replacing her dark shades. "He didn't kill himself. He wouldn't do that to Gino and me."

Lucky girl, to have such faith, Danutia thought as she headed up the side street where she'd parked the Blazer. Her years in the RCMP had taught her more than she wanted to know about what parents were capable of doing to their children.

# Chapter 6
Victoria: Monday afternoon, July 10

Abruptly Danutia stood up. Three guys from Drugs were walking toward the worn vinyl booth where she had found Sharma waiting after the autopsy. She handed over the two letters she'd asked Sharma to dust for prints and fished out a couple of twoonies for their coffee. "Let's get out of here," she said. "I need a walk."

Outside the coffee shop the midday heat blasted them. Danutia looked around uncertainly. She didn't want to head back to the General Investigations building, not yet. "Where to?"

"The Gorge is just a few blocks from here," Sharma said. "It will be cooler near the water."

They set off, silent at first. Danutia could feel Sharma's readiness to listen, but she couldn't talk, not yet. Slowing her hurried stride to Sharma's easy, relaxed pace, she tried to calm her breathing, to let go of the images haunting her.

They turned down a side street, its row of social agencies and failing shops mute testimony to the neighbourhood's slide toward poverty, and descended into an area of repair shops: auto repair, gun repair, more auto repair, sheet metal. No place for mending broken bodies, broken spirits.

Asphalt and concrete radiated heat back at them. Sharma paused to wipe his sweaty forehead with a handkerchief. "Who was on today?"

"Krahn." Krahn's pudgy white fingers wielding the scalpel and saw, his voice slow and fussy.

Sharma nodded. Not the best medical examiner, Danutia was aware, but not the worst either. "What did he say?"

Danutia tried to pull her thoughts together. "There's a scalp wound we missed Saturday, a tear about as long as my thumb, starting left of the midline and running diagonally toward the crown. The hair was matted with dried blood, so the wound was made before the shot that killed him."

"Did Krahn say what might have caused it?"

"No, you'd have thought he was being cross-examined by a defense attorney. Could Bertolucci have hit his head on something? Possibly. Could he have been hit by the proverbial blunt instrument? Possibly. Any sign of gunpowder? No. Does that rule out a bullet wound? No, not necessarily. Would Bertolucci have lost a lot of blood? Could have."

"I have seen suicides who botched the first shot and tried again. But Berwick says the man was right-handed. So the wound you describe is at the wrong angle."

"So there you have it. A healthy, white male in his forties with his brains blown out. For the details, we have to wait for the autopsy report." Her ankle began to throb and she halted in the shade of a gnarled pear tree to rub it.

"What's the matter?" Sharma asked.

"It's nothing. I twisted it yesterday."

"You should have told me," Sharma said. "We needn't have come so far."

His gentle concern pierced the defenses she had been trying so hard to maintain.

"You've been doing this for almost thirty years," she burst out. "How do you keep it from tearing you apart? Oh, I've seen autopsies before, Lewis made sure of that. I was so cool and professional, like I was memorizing everything for an exam. First the external damage. Then the Y incision and the organs removed in this order. Today I'm standing there looking down at the body and there's the finger with the missing tip, and I think, 'my God I know this man—' Not that I ever met him, but I've talked to his daughter, been in his home, read his letters. It's like he was a neighbour's distant relative, someone you may never meet, but whose life seems part of the fabric of the community. And there he is stretched out naked on this cold metal table, and I'm staring as his body is sliced open, his kidneys and liver removed and weighed like so many cuts of meat."

Sharma nodded slightly, his eyes dark in their heavy folds. "An autopsy is not pleasant. But come, we have reached the Gorge. I have something to show you."

They crossed the road to where a high chain link fence enclosed stack upon stack of crushed cans and bundled newspaper. Scraps of yellowing paper clung to the fence and a musty odour permeated the air. An orange crane, its driver invisible, moved back and forth over a mountain of garbage that blocked the view of the Gorge Waterway, a long inlet stretching northwards from Victoria's Inner Harbour.

The crane tore a chunk from the pile, lifted its prize high. Seagulls cried and wheeled.

"That's my son up there," Sharma said. "Like the

scavengers of Manila, he makes his living from what others no longer value."

Danutia's fingers grasped the chain link fence. "It's like the morgue," she said. "A dumping ground for everything that's used up and tossed aside."

"Why should we revere the dead body? In India, Parsis expose the dead in tall towers as food for the vultures. In the West, the dead are enclosed in metal caskets, as though they are not part of the cycles of nature. Which practice shows more respect for life?"

A float plane droning toward the Inner Harbour drew their eyes upward.

"Sometimes," Sharma said gently, "we may think our concern is for the dead, when really it is ourselves we fear for—that we will be exposed in all our vulnerability. And so our feelings cloud our ability to see."

Danutia pushed sweaty curls aside to massage her temples. "Lewis wants a report first thing in the morning so he can decide whether to continue the investigation. I don't know what to tell him."

The crane dropped its load. A breeze off the hidden waterway caught bits of paper and plastic and floated them toward the fence.

"So here you are again, striving after answers." Sharma stretched long brown fingers between the wires, captured a scrap of paper, and offered it to her.

It was newsprint, yellow and brittle with age, one side sports scores, the other the top half of a comic strip, balloon-shaped speeches cut off from the action below. In the last frame, some unseen character was yelling, "Help!"

Chuckling, he pressed his palms together. "When you open your mind, little scraps of truth will enter. Even I have some scraps for you."

"You do? Why didn't you tell me?"

Sharma looked at his watch. "On the way back," he said, and they set off. "First, I found many different prints. Most of them belong to the ambulance attendants, the good doctor Fidelman, or the bumbling constable, whose prints I took yesterday. There is a print I have not been able to identify, a smudged one, on many things in the cabin. It is also on the Glock. I spoke to Sergeant Berwick this afternoon. Fortunately, he has experience in taking fingerprints. He will collect specimens from the Johnsons and others who might have been in the cabin."

"He'll do it, and then point out that the prints don't mean anything."

"You find him difficult to work with?"

"Oh, he's sharp. You should have seen Larocque's report after Berwick finished with it. But he won't throw himself into the investigation. Pours cold water on everything I suggest, especially if it involves anyone on Salt Spring." Danutia paused at a curb and looked up at her companion. "I wish Lewis would send you back with me."

Sharma again took out his handkerchief and wiped the perspiration from his shining face and neck. "Krishnamurti says 'if you look to one person as your teacher, then you are lost and that person becomes your nightmare'." Refolding the handkerchief, he tucked it into his back pocket. "I do not wish to become your nightmare."

The moment's spell broken, Danutia laughed. "Then tell me what else you found."

"Bertolucci's prints, as you would expect, are on many things, including the Glock. Those prints are too clear for my liking."

"What do you mean?"

"I'll show you. See that beer can in the road? Hand it to me."

Danutia picked up the crumpled aluminum and held it out.

"You can drop it now," Sharma said. "Did you notice? You didn't clutch the can rigidly in your hand. You picked it up and then adjusted your grip. That's the way most of us handle objects. And so the prints are a little smudged. When the prints are too clear, I am suspicious."

Danutia could feel her headache recede as Sharma's words sank in. "The prints. The scalp wound. These little bits of evidence begin to add up to murder, don't they?"

⋅⊷⋅ ⋅⊶⋅

Ten minutes to four. Danutia was early for her appointment with David Ohara. Sitting in her cruiser across from his office, her fingers drumming lightly on the steering wheel, she considered the building and its owner. In elegant contrast to the neighbouring heritage houses, Pacific Developments occupied a sprawling olive-green cedar building behind a neatly trimmed juniper hedge. The yellow cedar gateway matched the one Danutia had seen at Ohara's home on Salt Spring, though without the newly-installed cardlock gate that had seemed so incongruous there. A curving flagstone path lined with stone lanterns led through a gravelled courtyard, where a gardener pursued stray leaves with a blower, to massive wooden doors. Narrow tinted windows on either side of the door mirrored the late afternoon sun.

Danutia didn't have much experience dealing with people with money, not legitimate money anyway, assuming Ohara's was. In the Alberta farming community where she grew up, money went into land and equipment: no one had enough cash to be giving themselves airs. Her postings to Fort McMurray and Winnipeg had taken her into seamy streets and flop houses, trailer parks and neat working class bungalows where parents wrung their hands over what was happening to their children. She was entering the territory of the rich and she was nervous. For the first time, she missed the authority of the uniform she'd given up on joining General Investigations.

She was not the bearer of good news. Ohara was eager to avoid publicity, and Lewis had led him to believe that the case would be closed. Now little scraps of evidence were pointing toward murder. Ohara, for all his money and power, was about to become part of the investigation.

Danutia slid out of the car. Two houses away, the quiet James Bay side street ended at Dallas Road, where a steady stream of traffic and a thin strip of beach separated Victoria from the choppy grey waters of the Pacific. In the distance a sailboat with bright yellow and blue sails ran for home under a lowering sky, miles and miles of ocean stretching out behind it all the way to Japan.

A somber young Asian man ushered her into a

cluttered L-shaped office with glass outer walls.

"Mr. Ohara is coming soon," he said, motioning her to take one of the ornate mahogany chairs grouped around a low table, where a lacquered tray held a white porcelain tea service and a black cafetiere.

Danutia remained standing. No point in conceding that advantage. Besides, she wasn't sure she could move without breaking something. Jade carvings, porcelain vases, silk fans, and ivory miniatures jostled for position atop the low cabinets lining the inner walls. In contrast, the walls were bare except for two pictures. One was a sketch of a young girl with a broken arm, the other a modernistic white-on-white canvas whose subject eluded her.

She was still puzzling over the strange painting when she sensed movement in the shorter arm of the room. A short, slender man, his image somewhat distorted by the two glass walls, had risen from a computer workstation and was approaching her. His hair was still a vigorous black, Danutia noted, his face unlined, head and hands large for his body. He bowed slightly, his greeting as formal as his dark suit and grey silk tie.

"Good afternoon, Constable." He pulled out a chair for her, then seated himself behind the tea service. "It is Constable, isn't it? I'm sure that's what you said on the phone yesterday."

"Dranchuk," she said, setting up her tape recorder. "Constable Dranchuk. I have a few questions to ask you about Joe Bertolucci."

Ohara's hand poised over the teapot as though the ritual of the tea ceremony clung to this simple business courtesy. "Would you join me in a cup of tea? Or perhaps you prefer coffee."

Danutia hesitated. She loathed tea. Still she had an obscure sense that it was not her preferences that mattered, but how she responded to Ohara's moves, as though they were playing chess.

"Coffee for you, I see," he said, pouring from the cafetiere. Then tea with a scent like roasting chestnuts for himself.

"On Saturday I too had questions. I was assured by your superior, Sergeant Lewis, that my concern was unnecessary. It seems that my unfortunate employee committed suicide."

"So it seemed. Until the autopsy today."

Carefully Ohara placed his teacup on the table. "An accident, then?"

Danutia took a deep breath. "It's possible that Bertolucci was murdered."

"Murder." Ohara turned his head away from Danutia and gazed through the patio doors into the garden beyond. His eyes seemed heavy with sorrow and a sense of betrayal, though perhaps it was only the sagging folds of the lids that made them seem so. "I did not think they would go so far."

Surprised, Danutia sat forward on her chair. She had expected him to object when she mentioned murder. "Who do you mean?"

"My enemies. The ones who sent hate mail. Tore down survey ribbons. Dumped manure on the driveway of my home. What is the silly name they call themselves—Save

Salt Spring History? They want to save a few trees, a few old buildings. They do not see that without an economic life, a cultural life, the island will die. They betray the place they seek to save. And so the past repeats itself."

"If you were expecting trouble on Saturday, why didn't you alert the RCMP?"

"When I reported these incidents, Constable Larocque took a great many notes, and that was the end of it. So I determined that I must protect my property myself. I hired a security guard. And now he's been murdered." Ohara's left eye began to twitch.

"May have been murdered. Tell me how you came to hire Joe Bertolucci."

"For more than two years I have been secretly negotiating to buy the Mount Erskine property from a German who was reluctant to sell—the timber is very valuable. A few months ago investment opportunities opened up for him in the former East Germany. So he contacted me. Before I was able to conclude the deal, my plans became known and opposition developed. The final papers were to be signed last week. I knew that if my opponents heard of this—and I could not guarantee they would not—there might be more trouble. So I hired Mr. Bertolucci."

"When was that?"

"Last Wednesday morning," Ohara said. He had found Bertolucci at his trailer and asked him to occupy the Bittancourt cabin for a few days, until the final papers were signed and the cabin razed. "At first he refused—it seems he too was opposed to my plans. Then I talked about the economic benefits a world-class resort would bring to the Island, and to people like him."

"You mean you offered him a lot of money," Danutia countered, thinking about Antonia's expensive honeymoon.

Ohara spread his hands wide. "What is little to one man may seem like much to another."

Slowly Danutia gathered the details of Ohara's arrangement. Since Bertolucci's car was out of commission, Kelly was to buy supplies for a week and deliver them and the Pacific Developments truck. Bertolucci was also to get Kelly's business cellphone so that he could notify Ohara—and the RCMP—in case of trouble. He was to tell no one about their agreement.

"Bertolucci was found holding an unregistered handgun," Danutia said. "Did you supply that as well?"

"I know nothing about a gun," Ohara said. "I do not believe in violence." He silently offered more coffee, which Danutia declined.

"Did you tell Bertolucci when the cabin was to be levelled?"

"I gave Mr. Kelly his instructions on Thursday. He was to inform Mr. Bertolucci."

"And did he?"

"That you will have to ask Mr. Kelly."

Danutia leaned forward. "What I still don't understand, Mr. Ohara, is why you hired Joe Bertolucci. As far as we've been able to determine, he had no experience as a security guard. He was an actor and bartender, and he'd been involved in an altercation with Kelly. Were you aware of that?"

"Of course. That's why I hired him."

Danutia sat back in her chair. "Would you explain that please."

Ohara's gaze shifted to the garden visible through the glass walls. Flagstones led to a wisteria-covered arbour. There, in a stone basin shaped like a lilypad, squatted a stone frog, its mouth gaping wide to receive water bubbling from a bamboo flume. "Let me tell you a story, Constable," he said, his voice relaxed now.

"Once there was a samurai who had a young servant with a taste for sake," Ohara said, his voice the sing-song of the storyteller. "The young man did something foolish which might have called down the wrath of his master. But the warrior smiled and said, 'Not my servant but the sake did it.' This generosity inspired the servant with such loyalty that when his master lay dying, he begged permission to follow him in death."

His parable finished, Ohara regarded Danutia with an air of self-satisfaction. "Mr. Kelly is like the young servant. Periodically he makes a public nuisance of himself. In a city, such behaviour might pass unnoticed. But not on a small island like Salt Spring. Mr. Kelly knows that every time he does something foolish, I hear about it. From my daughter, from a shopkeeper, from a business acquaintance. But like the samurai, I am generous. And so every time Mr. Kelly creates a nuisance, he redoubles his efforts on my behalf. And for his efforts I reward him well. Not so well that he becomes complacent, but well."

"And Bertolucci?" Danutia asked.

"I knew from my daughter that Mr. Bertolucci too

had shamed himself. Yet before he took to drink again, he was an excellent worker. Such a man is grateful for an opportunity to redeem himself. And so you see, two men, enemies of each other, but both determined to prove themselves to me, would more than earn their wages. I am certain it would have been so."

"But something went wrong," she said. "Joe Bertolucci is dead."

"To have enemies is a terrible thing."

There it was again, the note of bitterness, as though the enemies he referred to were not merely people with different views and different values, but something closer to the bone.

"You've mentioned you knew about Bertolucci through your daughter. Was she aware of your plans?"

"As I said before, I told no one. Assuredly not my daughter." He stood up, his left eye blinking rapidly. "And now if you will excuse me—"

Danutia gestured toward the portrait of the young girl. "Is that your daughter?"

"Sandra would never be so imprudent as to break her arm," Ohara said. "It would interfere with her career. That is a silkscreen print by the Japanese artist Tetsuya Noda, whose works I much admire. The one beside it—" he pointed to the mysterious white-on-white, now revealed as the faint outline of a man's dress shirt— "was a gift from my daughter. A reminder, perhaps, that in her eyes I am a stuffed shirt." A gold tooth winked as he smiled broadly, the indulgent father.

"Too contemporary for my taste," Ohara went on,

"but anything by Taeko Urae is a good investment. My wife runs a gallery—" he broke off as Danutia, having packed away the tape recorder, moved toward the door.

"But forgive me, you are not here to discuss Japanese art. Perhaps you find history more interesting. Do you see that picture beside you?"

The slender gold frame held two worn and creased pieces of paper.

"My parents' identity cards," Ohara said. "From the Second World War. When my father died, I found them in the bottom of his safety deposit box, wrapped in red silk and tied with a ribbon. Perhaps you, like many Canadians, are unaware of their significance. Those cards identified my parents, who had immigrated to the West Coast in the 1920s, as enemy aliens."

"There was a television program," Danutia said, remembering images of kimono-clad women and children living in makeshift shacks in the deep snow of interior BC.

Ohara glanced again at the wrinkled pieces of paper. "My family, and all the other Japanese families on the West Coast, were forced to abandon our homes by the RCMP—"

At the sudden venom in his voice, Danutia thought, If I were wearing a uniform, he'd spit on it.

"—my father left our home, all our prized possessions, in the safekeeping of our white neighbours, who had been our friends. They stole our belongings and vandalized our house, and the RCMP did nothing. Now the past repeats itself, and again I have enemies."

Enemy aliens, with their little bits of paper. Betrayed by their country, their appointed protectors, their friends and neighbours. Out of the ashes of this betrayal Ohara had forged himself a new identity as one of the most powerful men in British Columbia. Was his talk of enemies merely the paranoia of the powerful? Or were the threats real?

# Chapter 7
Salt Spring: Monday evening, July 10

The rehearsal wasn't over, Arthur discovered as he eased open the side door into the gym-turned-auditorium at Salt Spring Elementary School. For lack of any other space, *The Mikado* had been squeezed in between a children's matinee and the final performance of *Bullock's Folly*, an arrangement Zachary Smith was none too happy about, according to Thea.

Luckily, Arthur didn't have to face the director's displeasure just yet. Smith was alone on stage, his rich baritone booming out over the piano accompaniment. The tune was familiar, but the words were strange. "Scheming actresses, their talents up for grabs"? "Wily Orientals, with development in mind"? What was going on?

The cast members gathered around the piano must have known, for each line was greeted with a burst of laughter. A moment later, Arthur thought he knew too: Smith must have added local references to *The Mikado*'s famous 'I've got a Little List' song, Ko-Ko's catalogue of "society offenders . . . who never would be missed."

Not everyone was finding the new lines funny. Sandra Ohara and Hendrix Smith had moved away from the piano and were arguing in fierce whispers. As the song ended, Hendrix shrugged and rejoined the others; Sandra headed for the door beside the stage, with Larry Weston following her.

There was an uneasy silence. "Ten minutes," Zachary

Smith said, scribbling a few words onto the play script propped on the blue music stand. "Then we'll re-do the execution scene." As the group around the piano drifted away, Arthur looked in vain for Lavender's mass of fine dark hair then edged toward the director. "Could you spare a few minutes? I'd like to ask—"

He broke off as the door behind him banged open to admit a rotund man with the air of a dissolute country gentleman. Grizzled hair curling almost to his shoulders, reddened cheeks, heavy jowls, a brocade vest with a pocket watch. All he needed was a pack of dogs roiling around his feet. Instead of a riding whip, he brandished a roll of loose papers.

"Posters, my friend Zachary," he said, handing one over. Though his manner was jovial, his eyes were sad. Noticing Arthur, he shifted the bundle under his arm and put out his hand. "Samuel Johnson. Everyone calls me Doc, for obvious reasons. You must be Arthur Fairweather. Zachary mentioned you. Staying for the whole Festival, I hear."

"Everyone on Salt Spring seems to know what I'm doing almost as soon as I do."

Zachary Smith looked up from the poster. "What is it you want? Doc and I need to talk about publicity for the benefit."

"That's what I'm here about," Arthur said. "I'm planning to review the benefit performance, and I'd like to include something about its purpose, where to send contributions, that sort of thing."

"I have to try out some new business and have Cassie's

set back onstage by seven o'clock. I could give you half an hour after that." Zachary's voice was flat, the skin around his mouth and eyes tight as a drum.

"I have to be at a harp concert at seven," Arthur said ruefully. "Could I watch the last part of your rehearsal?"

"If you want."

Samuel Johnson handed Arthur a poster. "This will give you the basic information. And now," he said, turning toward Smith, "tell me what else I need to do."

Time to find Lavender, thought Arthur, a little guiltily, as he headed off in search of the dressing rooms. Thea had looked so vulnerable yesterday when she passed on Lavender's message, Thea in her gauzy dress and with her hair loose, the way he liked it.

The corridor he was walking down came to an abrupt dead end at a boys' washroom with a 'Closed for Cleaning' plaque outside. To his surprise, the washroom door opened and Pooh-Bah came out, adjusting his blue blazer. Rodney Coutt was his name, Arthur knew that, but the man's aristocratic face and Oxbridge accent made it easier to think of him as Pooh-Bah, the supercilious, bribe-taking Head of State.

The two men stared at each other in startled silence.

"It's . . . it's out of commission," said Coutt. "I just—ah—didn't notice the sign."

"It's the ladies' dressing room I'm after, like," Arthur responded in his broadest Manchester accent, enjoying an excuse to be rude to the upper classes.

Coutt gave directions and Arthur headed back the way he'd come. When he glanced back, a shorter, younger man stood behind Coutt, tucking a dark green work shirt into a pair of scuffed jeans.

Now that's odd, thought Arthur, but the thought vanished as he heard the murmur of women's voices from around the corner. He was about to knock at a door decorated with a hand-drawn female stick figure when he heard Lavender say, "I'm taking Antonia and her new husband out tonight. She's devastated. She idolized her father."

"Like someone else we know."

"Oh, Carol, give us a break, will you." A new voice. Must be the other schoolgirl, Peep-Bo.

Arthur let his hand drop. His infatuation had made him thoughtless. Lavender had more important things on her mind than the desires of an overweight, underemployed drama critic.

Arthur retreated to the gym. When he opened the door, angry voices spilled out.

"And I say to hell with the authorized D'Oyly Carte production, we're doing it my way," Smith declared, making a note on the script. Beside him on a little wooden cart stood a miniature guillotine about four feet high, its suspended blade gleaming.

"Zachary, the thing's dangerous. Why not use papier mâché?" Rodney Coutt, his hands clenching and unclenching, faced the director across the stage, while the stocky redhead who played Pish-Tush waited patiently beside him. Hendrix Smith, sprawled in a front-row chair, seemed to be enjoying the argument.

"You know I want my props to look realistic."

"And look what happened in Victoria." Coutt couldn't quite keep the 'I-told-you-so' out of his voice.

"That was Hendrix's fault. We'd done that number hundreds of times." Smith patted the top of the guillotine. "Emile and I have tested and retested the honourable Chopper. It's foolproof."

"What if you pulled the cord by mistake?"

"Look," Smith said, demonstrating, "there's a safety peg across the channel, so even if I pull the cord, it won't release."

Coutt gave an exaggerated sigh. "Well, let's get on with it. But it seems a lot of trouble."

"Rodney." The voice from the silver-haired woman at the piano was firm, the accent unmistakably working-class Midlands. "There's no need to make a fuss."

"Mother has spoken. Obviously the matter's settled." Coutt walked stiffly to stage right, took off his blazer, and rolled up his shirt sleeves.

"Here's how it goes." Smith stepped behind the music stand. "I say, 'Besides I don't see how a man can cut off his own head' and you say, 'A man might try.' Then you and Pish-Tush step up, one on each side, and force my head onto the block. You put the cord in my hand and step back, looking encouraging as you say that cutting a head half-off still shows compliance with the Imperial will. While you two talk, I seem to be thinking about it. Then I say, 'No. Pardon me, but there I am adamant,' and spring away."

He took up his position and nodded to the others. "Ready? Okay, let's take it from the point I get the Mikado's letter."

Then there came the kind of moment that Arthur lived for, the moment where theatre was created as he watched. Although Rodney might still be furious, he was as inventive as the other two in exploring the new piece of business. The three blocked out positions, tried their lines, changed the blocking and started again, creating almost a dance toward and away from the guillotine. At first amusing, toy-like, by the end of the scene the guillotine had become a brooding black presence. To Arthur there was something intensely right about this scene. It was as if he kept sensing a dark presence in the Company itself, and now that presence was right out there, in the middle of the stage, compelling everyone to look at it.

"Hey, Mr. Smith," called a rough voice behind him. Startled, Arthur turned to see the muscular young man he had glimpsed at the washroom; the janitor, Arthur guessed from the ring of keys at his waist. "I'm going off work now. Make sure all the doors are locked if you leave before Cassie Wilson gets here, will you?"

"We're about to wrap up for now, but I'll have to come back after Cassie's performance tonight. So don't worry if you see the lights on late."

The janitor raised a hand to pat an errant strand of hair back in place, revealing an expensive-looking gold watch on his left wrist. "That's fine, but when there's a lot of you staying late, people get tired and forget who's responsible for a security check."

"Don't worry, Dave," Smith said, squatting down on stage to erase a chalk mark. "It'll only be me and Hendrix here."

"Why me?" Hendrix asked.

"We have to rehearse Nanki-Poo's attempted suicide scene with the guillotine, and we don't have enough time now. You can surely find half an hour in your busy schedule."

Hendrix shrugged. "Maybe."

For a moment Zachary stood in front of his son, his hands on his hips, his eyes sharp and angry. Then his hands dropped to his sides and he walked away. "We'll talk later. We have to get Cassie's set ready."

Checking his own Timex, Arthur discovered it was quarter to seven. He could be on time for the harp concert, or he could grab a bite to eat and be a few minutes late. Either way, he'd have to hurry.

"I still have some questions about the benefit," he called. "Can I come back later too?"

"If you like," Smith said. "I'll be here until around eleven. Just bang on the side door."

As Arthur stepped outside, he heard someone whistling the tune to 'I've got a Little List' a little slowly, a little off-key. His footsteps, as he hurried down the hill, seemed to echo the rhythm eerily.

# Chapter 8

Decay. The cloying odour hit Danutia as soon as she opened the door to her Fairfield apartment. Images from the autopsy flooded through her, making her stomach heave. Ignoring the flashing light on her message machine, she stuffed drooping daisies into the garbage bag she hadn't thought to dispose of on Saturday and dropped it down the chute across the hall. Still the odour lingered. It must be the smell of Bertolucci's death, clinging to the clothes she had worn on Salt Spring and to the autopsy. Grabbing her laundry basket and soap powder, she headed for the basement.

When she returned, the message light was still blinking. It could wait five more minutes. She made coffee and slipped a frozen pizza into the microwave, then stepped onto the balcony where her baskets of purple and white petunias hung limp in the late afternoon sun. Thin strands of cloud had gathered in a light haze. Perhaps it would rain. More likely, tomorrow would be another hot, dry day. She longed for a prairie thunderstorm to break the tension in the air and in her body.

She didn't know what to make of David Ohara. By turns he had seemed an aggrieved man who both wanted and didn't want an investigation, a greedy man whose thirst to regain what was lost could never be slaked, a betrayed man whose twitching eye sought to reveal what the affable face would hide.

Betrayal. By whom?

Bob Kelly? A blabbermouth, by all accounts. Since Ohara could expect anything he said to Kelly to become public knowledge, he was unlikely to feel betrayed when it happened.

Bertolucci? What if he had discovered something crooked about Pacific Developments? Ohara had insisted he'd had no further communication with the man after hiring him. Would the cellphone record verify that? She would run a quiet check on the developer and his firm.

Who else? Ohara insisted he had told no one except Kelly about hiring Bertolucci, "most assuredly not my daughter." Did Sandra have connections to Save Salt Spring History? That would explain Ohara's ambivalence about the investigation. Yes, the daughter would bear looking into.

On the way to the kitchen for her pizza, Danutia again noticed the answering machine's insistent blink. Nine messages. An emergency with her folks? Guiltily she picked up a pencil and punched the Play button.

Nine messages in a flat prairie voice, familiar but unwelcome. "Hi honey, I'm in town for a conference and thought we might get together tonight." "I'll try you later." ". . . at noon"; ". . . later"; ". . . later"; ". . . later"; "from the airport"; until finally, "Maybe next time."

"There won't be a next time," she had told Dennis repeatedly in the weeks before she left Winnipeg, glad to be putting the Rockies between them.

How did he get my number, she wondered as she pulled the Aspirin bottle from its place over the kitchen sink and ran a glass of water. Bending over, she placed her forehead against the sink's cool stainless steel rim. She remembered Oma lying in her darkened living room with a dainty silver knife pressed to her forehead, Danutia sitting on the floor beside her, stroking her hand. When the cold and the Aspirin had numbed the pain, Danutia reheated her pizza and coffee and carried them to the balcony.

The phone was reassuringly silent. How long would it stay that way? Her number was unlisted; the detachment wouldn't give it out. So how did Dennis get it? Suddenly she knew. Her mother, anxious to have her married, to a doctor, even one old enough to be her father. Danutia hadn't told her mother why she had broken off with Dennis. She would have believed whatever story Dennis told her.

And Dennis was good with stories, Danutia remembered, picking off a bit of mushroom and munching it.

They had met one October night when Danutia brought the victim of a stabbing, a well-dressed man of about sixty, into Emergency. While Dennis dressed the gaping thigh wound, Danutia took the man's statement. Someone had jumped him when he stepped into an alley to light a cigarette, he claimed. Nothing was taken. He hadn't seen his assailant.

Danutia was skeptical. Half an hour earlier, she had seen the man enter a flophouse with Sally Cardinal, who didn't take any shit from her johns. He stuck to his story and so when the doctor finished with him, she had to let him go. He hobbled out, one hand resting protectively on his injured thigh.

"Too bad you couldn't throw the bastard in jail," Dennis

had said, handing her his card. Dr. Dennis Epp. "How about washing the bad taste out of your mouth with a cup of coffee?"

Her shift was long over, and the doctor seemed presentable enough—not tall but muscular, no paunch, salt-and-pepper hair receding but not gone, mild blue eyes in a face not yet heavily wrinkled. Still Danutia hesitated; something in his manner made her uneasy.

As though sensing her reservation, he held up his left hand. "Divorced," he said. "And I'm suggesting coffee, not marriage." Laughing at her misgivings, she accepted.

What intrigued him, Dennis told her over coffee, was not the injury—he had seen much worse—but that she, an attractive young woman, was "mixed up in it." She tried to point out that she was no more "mixed up in it" than he was—she was just doing her job. He pursed his lips and shook his head. He would love to pursue the topic but it was late and she was no doubt tired—dinner tomorrow, or if not tomorrow, soon?

For a couple of months they grabbed a quick lunch here, a hasty coffee there, whatever their schedules allowed. Danutia liked his witty conversation, his easy self-confidence, and especially his small attentions—a loaf of crusty Italian bread, a pot of basil, an old movie for her video collection. And, unlike younger men, Dennis did not seem threatened by her independence or her job. He insisted on hearing about the fights and stabbings and rapes Danutia was called upon to handle in Winnipeg's red-light district, responding to each story with the same sad smile. In return he regaled her with stories about his Mennonite upbringing.

When they finally moved to "my place or your place," Danutia was surprised to find her charming companion an inadequate lover.

"Don't give up on me," Dennis begged the first time it happened. "Believe me, I'm not always like this. But when your wife leaves you for another woman, it takes the starch out of you."

The memory of what came next brought a hot flush to her cheeks and a tightness to her head. One evening, after some other strategy had failed, her fingers had idly circled through the grey hairs on his chest while she talked about a case that was on her mind.

"There she was in the laundromat, a skinny kid, couldn't be more than eleven, curled up asleep in one of those white plastic lawn chairs. Nothing but a Mickey Mouse T-shirt on under this huge down jacket. Said her stepfather had raped her, so she waited 'til he was asleep and ran away. She wouldn't give me her name and address, and she hadn't been reported missing, so I took her to the hospital and then down to the Youth Emergency Shelter for the night. She didn't complain—she looked grim, like kids do when they're used to being ordered around by adults. But she kept biting her nails, and by the time I left one of her fingers was bleeding. There must be something more I could have done for her."

"Maybe there's something I can do for you," Dennis said huskily, shifting on top. "My motor's racing. Why don't you come for a ride." Pleased by her success, she relaxed into his practised movements. Afterwards she felt a twinge of guilt about using her work to titillate him.

But she didn't stop.

Then it was Valentine's Day, and by some miracle they were both off. "Let me surprise you," Dennis said. "A twenty-four-hour mini-vacation. You won't have to do a thing."

Lunch and snacks in their backpacks, they had spent the day cross-country skiing, the air crisp, the newly-fallen snow sliding away behind them as smooth as silk. It was snowing gently again as they headed back to the city in winter's early twilight. Dennis dropped Danutia at her apartment to shower and change, returning with a dozen red roses and a gourmet take-out dinner. Snowflakes clung to his bushy eyebrows, and she reached up to brush them away.

"Hold on," he said. "I have another surprise for you." A few minutes later he was back with a bulging sports bag.

"Oh lovely," she said, picking it up. "A new set of weights."

"Don't touch," Dennis replied, taking the bag from her and putting it in the hall closet with his gloves, overcoat, and boots. "Dinner first." So they ate in front of the gas fireplace, lingering over their hazelnut torte and coffee until Danutia couldn't stand the suspense any longer.

"What's in the bag?" she demanded, jumping up and heading for the hall.

Dennis caught her by the wrist. "Don't spoil it."

He fetched the bag and led Danutia into the bedroom. "Ms. Winnipeg RCMP is about to disappear, to be replaced by—but that would be telling. All you have to do is put yourself in the capable hands of Dr. Dennis Epp, your fairy godfather."

"Sounds like a line the infamous Dr. Crippen would have used."

"Never you mind. Close your eyes, and no peeking."

Dutifully Danutia closed her eyes—she prided herself on always playing by the rules—and tried to relax as Dennis stripped off her wool sweater and slacks, her bra and panties. Feeling foolish standing there in her red and green Argyll socks, like a Christmas tree being decorated, she said, "Hurry up, I'm cold."

Quickly Dennis slipped a soft cottony material over her head. She smiled. A nightgown, to replace the sensible flannel pyjamas Dennis laughed at. He wrapped her in her terry cloth dressing gown and guided her to a chair he must have moved from its accustomed place beside the mirror.

"I'm putting a towel around your shoulders," he said. "We don't want any makeup on your dressing gown."

Bottles and metal objects clinked. Danutia said, "I hope you remembered the anesthetic."

"Trust me," Dennis murmured in his best bedside manner. "I never hurt a patient unless I have to." He cupped her chin in his hand, turned her face this way and that. "Let's see now. Ah yes, of course. If you promise to keep your eyes shut," he said, his fingertips gently pressing her lids, "I'll do something I know you'll like." The hands retreated, then returned bearing a rich cream fragrant with apple blossoms; hands so tentative when they made love now moved confidently over her cheekbones, down her neck. "Now while that herbal cleanser works its magic, let's see about your makeup."

At first Danutia found his running commentary vaguely unsettling, as though a crowd of eager medical students were watching his every move. But soon she was floating in a reverie, his voice a soft rumble in her ear. While he applied foundation, blush, and eyeliner, she imagined herself being transformed from the practical, no-nonsense Danutia Dranchuk to the sleekly glamorous Grace Kelly of *High Society.*

"How about bangs?" he asked, clicking scissors near her ear. "I'm good at cutting people."

"No bangs," she said. "When I was about ten, my dad decided to save money by cutting my hair himself. He couldn't get my bangs straight. He snipped one side and then the other until there was nothing left but this little fringe across the top of my head. My classmates teased me for weeks."

"All right, no bangs," Dennis said mournfully, with a final slow click of the scissors. "Just a little touch-up with the curling iron."

Not Grace Kelly, then. Maybe the tousled Marilyn Monroe look. The wild comedy of *Some Like It Hot.* While the warm iron picked up and dropped the neat curls lying close to her head, scenes from the movie played themselves out on the curtain of her closed eyes.

At last Dennis removed the towel around her shoulders. "No peeking," he said, leading her across the room to where the mirror should be. "Now when I count to three, fling back the dressing gown and open your eyes."

"Like that 'Expose Yourself to Art' poster you gave me?" Danutia asked, smiling in anticipation.

"Exactly. One, two, three—"

As Danutia took in the figure in the mirror, her smile faded. A baby-doll face: fat, shiny blond curls; long dark eyelashes; rosy red cheeks above a pink rosebud mouth; skin smooth and creamy white. Below, not a sensuous nightgown but a Mickey Mouse T-shirt above the red and green stockings. Christmas gift. The little girl who was raped by her stepfather. The turn-on.

"Game's over," she said, pulling her dressing gown tight around her. "Get out."

After Dennis left, still protesting that she was blowing things out of proportion, Danutia had phoned her sister Alyne, now a psychotherapist with a flourishing practice in Calgary. Maybe the man was right. Maybe she was overreacting.

"Sounds to me like it's not you he's interested in, it's the women you deal with, women who've been victimized," her sister had said. "You have to watch out for those hard-working, high-achieving types. A lot of them like the sense of power they get from hurting people. Right now Dennis knows he's playing with his fantasies. But men like that often become extremely jealous, accuse their women of playing around, rough them up a bit to keep them in their place. As you should know." Her tone softened. "Sorry, sweetie. You asked for my professional opinion. I may be totally wrong about him. But take care. I don't want you to get hurt."

At the time it had been easy to blame Dennis for what had happened, to believe that pushing him out of her life would solve the problem. Now she wasn't so sure. Why was she attracted to older men in the first place? Dennis was the most unsettling, but there had been others. Even in her dealings with Berwick she was aware of a tingle, a girlish desire to please.

Danutia retreated inside, stacked her dirty dishes in the sink. She left messages for Fidelman and Berwick and then, hoping for a little human contact after she finished her reports, she dialed Sue O'Malley's number. The voice on the answering machine was that of the husband who moved out six months ago, fed up with being married to a cop. She rang the detachment. "O'Malley's on grave-yard," the dispatcher said.

Two hours later, having written up the autopsy and the interview with Ohara, she drafted a memo to Sergeant Lewis outlining the reasons for keeping the case open a few more days. She didn't send the memo, not yet. Maybe Berwick would phone back with new information.

She was pedaling her exercise bike and watching *Showboat* when the phone rang. Her palms went sweaty. It might be Berwick or Fidelman, but what if it was Dennis? At the third ring she reluctantly dismounted.

Call Display showed a BC area code. As the answering machine made its preliminary click, she picked up the receiver.

"What did you find out at the autopsy?" a clipped male voice asked. Berwick.

"Another head wound," she said, relieved. "Pretty messed up. So maybe there was a struggle."

"Did the examiner say it was murder?"

"No." Danutia thought she heard a sigh of satisfaction

from the other end of the line. "But he didn't rule it out. Did you get the prints to Sharma?"

"Late this afternoon. Sharma must have thought you were coming back tonight. He just faxed over some preliminary results. Nothing on those letters you gave him. Pretty much what you'd expect from the cabin—Martha Johnson's prints on the phone, things like that."

"What about the print on the gun, the one that wasn't Bertolucci's?"

"It was pretty badly smudged. Hard to get many points of comparison."

Danutia had the feeling Berwick was holding out on her again. "Whose prints came closest? Bob Kelly's?"

The silence between them stretched taut.

"So maybe you were wrong about Kelly," she said.

"The gun isn't registered. Even if we could prove it's Kelly's, there's no evidence he pulled the trigger."

There was no point in arguing over the phone. "I want to ask him some questions."

"I told him to be here at nine o'clock tomorrow morning. The early ferry gets in to Fulford at 7:35. I'll pick you up."

"Maybe there was a struggle, and he panicked."

Silence.

"I'll call Sergeant Lewis." As Danutia hung up, she remembered there was something she intended to ask Berwick. What was it? Ohara's daughter. But that was the merest speculation. Kelly had a motive for murder, and his fingerprint was on the gun.

# Chapter 9
## Salt Spring: Monday night, July 10

"Hey, mister, got any change?" The voice came from a huddle of teenagers smoking in an alley. Arthur ignored them as he hurried past, heading for the school gym.

It was 11:45. Would Smith still be there? He had probably finished his work with Hendrix and gone home. Or, worse, he might have waited, ready to blow up when Arthur stepped through the gym door.

At the bottom of Rainbow Road Arthur stopped to catch his breath. The trees along the sidewalk were sighing in the stiffening breeze, their shadows dancing before him. 'Listen to the wind and you will hear the rippling of the harp,' Deirdre Summers had said, 'for that is where the harp gets its music.'

They had been sitting in the Greek restaurant overlooking the government wharf, finishing a post-concert meal and bottle of wine. Deirdre had answered his questions about her career with wit and good humour, each fact embellished with several lively anecdotes.

"I've always hated that traditional stuff," Arthur had confessed as he poured the last of the wine. "You know, a bloke in a cloth cap singing endless verses about tinkers running off with fair ladies. But I liked your music."

"You obviously haven't found a tradition that speaks to you as the Celtic tradition speaks to me." Deirdre's smile lit up her plain, broad face. "It reminds me that I'm part of the chain of life, and that animals, plants, and even those rocks out there at the edge of the harbour are all part of the same chain. When I play and sing Celtic songs about nature and heroes, I enter their world, and join it to our world."

Deirdre's words made Arthur's English scepticism seem like a small airless room. He searched for a retort. "Heroism's an outdated concept."

"Let's try something." Standing up Deirdre beckoned Arthur to follow her onto the restaurant's waterfront patio, empty except for them. The patio umbrellas creaked and groaned in the cold wind blowing off the water.

Drawing her shawl closer, Deirdre said, "Listen," so quietly that Arthur had to strain to hear. "The wind is the music the god Dagda sends singing through the tree-tops and running across the water. They say the harp is a ladder to the next world, and in its playing you can sometimes hear messages from the world that we will all ascend to. These messages lead heroes to the path. They say each of us can be a hero if we listen for the sounds and follow our own path. Close your eyes and tell me what you hear."

For a moment Arthur allowed himself to ease open the door of his small airless room. Then he slammed it shut.

"What do I hear? Just someone harping on about the weather."

The moment the words were out of his mouth, Arthur regretted them. He turned to apologize, but Deirdre was looking at him with such intense sadness—sadness that seemed not for herself but for him—that the apology stuck in his throat. In a moment she was gone.

And now, with the trees rocking and moaning in the wind, Arthur had again, for a moment, that sense of the world's aliveness he'd felt on the restaurant patio. But then he heard himself saying, "Just someone harping on about the weather," and the thrashing trees lost their magic.

Shaking off his sense of loss, Arthur trudged up the hill. Only one car was parked in the school lot, an ancient MG with a vanity license plate announcing HENDRIX in bold blue letters. Smith must have gone home, leaving his son to finish up. Good. He would ask Hendrix to pass on his excuses for being late.

He went around the corner of the building to the gym's side door. Light shone through the high windows. Arthur knocked and knocked again. No reply. Hendrix must be backstage, or in one of the dressing rooms. He tried the door. It swung open, throwing him off balance.

After the soft sheen of moonlight and lamplight, he was dazzled by the high fluorescent lights shining through their protective cages and the stage lights glaring down.

"Hendrix?" he called, heading for the stage. The dining table and chairs for the first act of *Bullock's Folly* had been pushed near the stage steps, clearing centre stage. A jacket was thrown carelessly across a chair back. Near the far wings stood Zachary's bright blue music stand, empty.

"Anybody home?" Arthur mounted the steps and was making his way around the jumble of chairs when he noticed a dark shape half-hidden by the table and near it, a splotch of red. Hendrix must have dropped a can of paint. Under the bright stage lights, the pool of red was dark, flat, absorbing the light. Images of the Victoria performance flooded into Arthur's mind: the sword whistling over Hendrix's head, then the blade connecting and the trickle of blood on Hendrix's forehead.

Something lay beyond the pool of red.

He didn't want to look. He wanted to tiptoe back the way he had come, close the door behind him. The concert had run late. The interview had taken a long time. It was too late to come back.

His foot moved forward.

Beyond the table stood a black wooden frame. A silver blade gleamed. Between the frame and the blade, a bloody head. Hendrix's head, with its mop of dark hair.

Arthur grabbed for the nearest chairback to steady himself. The chair slid out from under him and he fell heavily, the stage shifting and the bright lights criss-crossing above him. Then all was blackness.

# Chapter 10
## Salt Spring: Tuesday morning, July 11

"How's Mia?" Danutia asked Berwick as they waited for their breakfasts at the Black Swan Inn. From the ferry, the low black-and-white building had looked like the country pubs in British movies, perfectly situated at the end of Fulford harbour. From closer up, the old building clearly needed a paint job inside and out. Not to mention better coffee, Danutia thought, as she took a sip of the dark brew the waitress had poured without asking.

"Still weak," Berwick said at last, "but the lacerations and broken ribs are mending. The vet doesn't think she was hit by a car. No road grit in the wounds. Kicked by heavy boots, more likely. I sent the hair samples to the lab in Vancouver."

"Trying to protect her master," Danutia said, remembering the photo.

Over greasy bacon and eggs Danutia reviewed what she had learned from the autopsy and from Ohara, and Berwick went over the prints that had been identified. He had also attempted to track down the people in Bertolucci's address book, several of whom were members of the Vesuvius Light Opera Company.

"I dropped in on a rehearsal yesterday afternoon," he said. "No one had talked to Bertolucci lately, and no one knew he was working for Ohara."

"Not even Smith? From what Doc Johnson said, I thought they were close friends."

"Zach said he'd been too busy with rehearsals to get in touch. He was trying to be matter of fact, but he seemed angry. My guess is Bertolucci had cut him off, like everybody else, and he was sore about it."

"What about women?" Danutia asked, thinking of Little Bo-Peep.

"No one, as far as Zach knew."

Danutia spread marmalade on anemic toast. "What about the other people in Bertolucci's address book?"

"Half a dozen people in Italy." The correspondents whose letters she had found in the dead man's files, Danutia surmised. "A Vancouver number for a Luigi, no last name. I tried it half a dozen times, kept getting the message machine."

"A suspicious mainlander, eh? How convenient." Danutia gave up on the toast.

"According to Zach, Luigi is a recent immigrant Joe met in detox. Joe visited him in Vancouver occasionally, and Luigi came to Salt Spring a time or two. Zach met him once, made some joke about a Mafia connection, and Joe told him to mind his own business. After that he didn't introduce Luigi to his Salt Spring friends."

"Anything to the Mafia connection?"

"I've asked the Vancouver police to check."

Danutia mentally reviewed the list and frowned. "No entry for Ohara? Or his daughter?"

"The numbers for Ohara's home and office and the cellphone were on a slip of paper in the book Joe was reading. Why do you ask?"

"Something Ohara said. When I asked whether he had

told anyone about his plans, he said, 'Most assuredly not my daughter'."

"Sandra's a member of Smith's company, and so she would have known Joe at least casually. But she seemed as surprised as everyone else that he was working for her father."

"What about alibis?"

"We're not officially investigating a murder, remember? Hold on—" he said when Danutia leaned forward, ready to argue. "I did establish that the cast was rehearsing until almost midnight Thursday. They left for Victoria together on the 6:20 ferry Friday morning."

Danutia pushed away the remains of her meal. "With several hours unaccounted for. Like Kelly's prints on the gun. Unless you want to argue they don't mean anything."

Berwick picked up the bill and slid out of the booth. "Kelly's got some explaining to do, I admit. But I'll bet you a good bottle of wine he didn't kill Bertolucci."

·– –·

The detachment was buzzing when they walked in shortly before nine, Larocque talking excitedly to the receptionist and a constable Danutia didn't recognize. Seeing them enter, the receptionist, who reminded Danutia of a giant buttercup, held up her hand in warning.

Larocque turned to Berwick. "Did you get my messages, Sarge? There was this accident—"

"Can it, Larocque," Berwick said. "There were more of your fingerprints in the Bittancourt cabin than there were

122

facts in your report. So we'll be spending the morning trying to plug the holes. In the meantime, you can write a report about this accident. All of it—who, what, when, where, why, how. In complete sentences. Spelled correctly. Then type it up, or get Betty to."

"But Sarge—"

"No buts. And don't disturb anyone else. If I hear one word from you before your report's finished, you'll be on extra duty all week."

"This accident—" The receptionist broke off, as though struggling with her own desire for a good gossip. "Alastair called about a statement for the *Gazette*."

"Not now, Betty. Tell him I'll have something for him by three o'clock. That will still make his deadline for the next issue."

As he headed toward the stairs, Danutia cleared her throat. "Any orders for me?"

Berwick turned back. "Sorry. I'm going to set up the interview room. You can wait in my office if you like."

She didn't like, she wanted to get on with it. She glanced at the notes she'd made after Berwick's call last night. Then, restless, she paced the floor, from the front reception counter, where Garth Brooks floated upward from a radio beside Betty's desk, past the duty desk, where a moustachioed constable was taking a statement from an angry American tourist, to the back, where Larocque struggled with his report, sighing and groaning. Danutia couldn't help feeling a bit sorry for the man, despite his sexism and incompetence. Berwick should have made his criticisms in private. Both men would be relieved when Larocque was transferred. About those messages last night—where was Berwick, she wondered, that he couldn't be reached?

The clock above the reception desk said 9:12. Bob Kelly was late. Berwick should have sent a squad car to pick him up.

She had reached the stairs when a man looking like an aging extra from *Grease* swaggered in. He was thin and wiry, not much taller than Danutia, with sleek black hair and close-set eyes. A ribbon of smoke curled upwards from the cigarette cupped in his right hand.

"Morning, Betty, how's my best girl?" He propped his elbows on the counter, scattering ash. "Say, did you hear about—"

Betty shook her head to silence him as Berwick clattered down the stairs.

The man took a drag from his cigarette. "So, how can I help the police with their inquiries?" he asked, giving Danutia the once-over, then winking broadly at Berwick. "This little lady looks like she could use some help. Know what I mean?"

Danutia stiffened.

"Stop being an asshole, Bob, and butt that out," Berwick said. "This is Constable Dranchuk from General Investigations, Victoria. She wants to ask you some questions. We'll talk upstairs. You know the way."

Danutia followed Kelly up the narrow stairs. The interview room, a drab beige with only a 'No Smoking' sign for decoration, was already uncomfortably warm. Danutia seated herself in the metal folding chair in front of the window, but there was no breeze. She could feel damp patches gathering under her armpits and around her waist.

Maybe it was nerves making her sweat. Kelly was her first murder suspect. She didn't want to screw up.

Smiling lazily, Kelly took the chair across from Danutia. He pulled out a lighter and packet of Craven A's and tossed them on the table. A cut on the back of his right hand had not quite healed. Leaning back in his chair, he propped one boot, worn but polished, on the opposite knee and let his arms rest loosely on his thighs. Nothing to hide, said his body language. But those eyes, that tense energy beneath the apparent calm, reminded Danutia of a ferret she and her nephew had seen prowling its cage.

Berwick entered with a tray of coffee things and set it on the scarred wooden table. While the other two helped themselves, he switched on the tape recorder and entered the date, time, their names and that of Robert Blaine Kelly. Then he nodded at Danutia. Her move.

Breathe, she told herself.

"Mr. Kelly," she said, "there are still some questions about Joe Bertolucci's death. We hope you can help us answer them. It's easier on the family when we can give them the facts."

"Yeah, sure." Kelly took out a cigarette. "You got an ashtray?"

"No smoking, Mr. Kelly. You can see the sign." Danutia stood up. "Now as far as we know, you were the last person to see Joe Bertolucci alive. You were also on the scene when his body was found. So we want you to tell us about your dealings with Bertolucci from the time Mr. Ohara hired him on Wednesday until the police arrived at the cabin on Saturday morning. Is that clear?"

"Look, I told The Rock everything I know." Kelly fiddled with the cigarette packet. "I need a smoke."

"On Saturday Constable Larocque was responding to what seemed like a suicide. Subsequent investigation has raised questions about that conclusion."

Kelly stared at the ceiling, as though she were a teacher lecturing him about missed assignments.

"Meaning, Mr. Kelly, that Joe Bertolucci may have been murdered."

Kelly's neck muscles tightened and his eyes flickered.

"If you want to call a lawyer, we can wait," Danutia said. "Or you can remain silent. I'm sure you know your rights."

Kelly straightened himself in his chair. "What do I need with a lawyer? I got nothing to hide. You took me by surprise, that's all." He grinned at Berwick with an attempt at his old bravado. "I'm always willing to help the police, ain't that right?"

The tape whirred and Danutia made notes while Kelly told his story. After Ohara had called Wednesday afternoon, he had knocked off work and bought supplies in Ganges. Then he picked Bertolucci up at his trailer. That was about seven. Kelly then drove to his house, where he turned the Pacific Developments truck and its cellphone over to Bertolucci.

"And that was the last time you saw him or talked to him?"

"Last time."

"Thank you, Mr. Kelly. Now could you tell us what you did from the time Bertolucci dropped you off on Wednesday evening 'til you set out for the Bittancourt cabin on Saturday morning."

"What for? You asking me for an alibi? Maybe I should call a lawyer after all."

Berwick reached for the switch on the tape recorder. Danutia gave a slight shake of her head.

"I'm just trying to get a picture of what happened," she said.

"Nothin' happened. Went to the pub, came home, went to sleep, got up—"

"Places and times, please, Mr. Kelly."

"Okay, Wednesday night, say around seven-thirty, stuck my dinner in the microwave, ate, left for the pub—that's the Dockside—around eight o'clock, had a few beers, came home around eleven, went to bed. That better? Thursday morning, up around seven, left around eight, worked all day at Ohara's place, stopped in the pub for a few beers around six—"

"You didn't go home first?"

"Nah, Marlene had another rehearsal, so I figured what the fuck. Where was I?" Kelly stretched and leaned back in his chair.

Danutia waited, her body still, her expression noncommittal. Nothing had been released about the time of death. By Fidelman's estimate, Bertolucci had been dead twenty-four to thirty-six hours when he examined the body Saturday morning. That meant the man had died between seven-thirty Thursday night and seven-thirty Friday morning.

"Oh yeah. Thursday evening. Went home around eleven, as usual. Friday I was up at Hornby all day, and Saturday—"

"Go back to Friday. Give us the details."

"What is this, Joe Blow's diary?"

Danutia folded her arms across her chest and waited.

"Okay, okay," he hurried on. "Up at six, without my morning poke—the wife's already gone. Caught the 7:30 ferry to Crofton, drove up to Hornby. Left there around five, then the eight o'clock ferry to Vesuvius. No point in coming home because the wife's in Victoria with this fuckin' play. So I stopped in at the pub, had a few more beers than usual maybe, staggered out at closing time or maybe a little later, fell into bed all by myself—now isn't that a shame?"

Danutia ignored him. She would come back later to his movements on Thursday and Friday. Finally Kelly continued, "Saturday, it's up with the chickens and onto my trusty Cat for a nice little game of pick-up sticks. And you know the rest."

"Thank you, Mr. Kelly. Now if we can just go back to Wednesday. These supplies you bought—do you have the receipts with you?"

Kelly shifted forward and the front chair legs thumped onto the floor. "I don't carry stuff like that around with me. Why would I?"

"What do you do with your receipts?"

"I don't know—shove them in the glove compartment of the truck, mostly, or in a kitchen drawer at home.

Then at the end of the month I gather them all up and give them to Mr. Ohara's accountant." He turned to Berwick. "Say, when am I going to get the PD truck back, anyway? My old pickup's racking up the miles."

"We're through with it," Berwick said. "You'll have to take it in for repairs. There's dirt and ashes in the gas tank." And Andy Johnson's fingerprints on the gas cap.

"Fuckin' bastards. Should have run my Cat over them while I had the chance."

"Back to the receipts, Mr. Kelly," Danutia said. "They weren't in the truck. It was clean as a whistle."

A hint of a frown flitted across Kelly's face, and he shifted in his chair. "Old Joe was complaining about the mess on the way over. He must have cleared it out. I noticed there'd been a fire in the pit. Maybe he burned the receipts."

"I doubt he would have burned anything that looked like business. Have a look for the receipts and bring them down. That will help us separate what belongs to Pacific Developments from Bertolucci's personal effects."

"Sure, no problem." Then casually, "There may be some other stuff mixed in there, stuff for my trip to Hornby. I do a lot of work off-island, and it's easier to get things here, all together, instead of making a lot of separate stops, you know what I mean? Like, Thrifty's and Home Hardware usually have all the stuff I need."

"I'm sure you will be able to explain any discrepancies to Mr. Ohara's satisfaction," Danutia said, standing up again. A slight breeze wafted in the open window, bringing the scent of roses.

"Did you mention to anyone that Bertolucci would be at the cabin?"

"I might have said something to Marlene, in confidence like, and then she blabbed it about. You know how women are."

Danutia let that one pass. "Did anyone see you and Bertolucci together?"

"Not as far's I know. The kids are visiting my folks in Courtenay, and Marlene was out, as usual." He tried to say it lightly, but the words were cold and bitter, like the coffee at Danutia's elbow.

"Mr. Ohara said he asked you to get in touch with Bertolucci on Thursday, to let him know when you'd be bulldozing the cabin. But you say you didn't talk to him after he dropped you off."

Picking up his cigarettes, Kelly turned the packet over and over, the word Craven appearing and disappearing. Finally he said, "You didn't ask whether I tried to contact the guy. I tried calling him Thursday night, four or five times, but the line was always busy."

"What time was that?"

"Between nine and ten, something like that."

"You didn't try again? Or drive out to see him? You had all day Friday."

"I was off-island Friday, remember." He drained his coffee, shifted in his chair, ran his fingers through his greased-back hair.

"Did anyone hear you making the calls?"

"Nah, I used the pay phone outside the pub. Didn't want anyone to overhear the plans, eh?"

"So you weren't in the pub between nine and ten."

Kelly scratched at the scab on his hand. "Look, I didn't say that, did I? I phoned, I had another beer, I phoned again, I took a piss, I phoned again."

"Were you concerned when you couldn't get through?"

"Why should I be? All I gotta do is show up on Saturday, tell him the plan. What do I care if he runs up the fucking phone bill talking to some broad."

"That's what you assumed, was it?"

"All alone in the middle of nowhere? That's sure what I'd be doing." He grinned, exposing a row of small, sharp teeth. The better to eat you with, my dear.

"What time did you leave the pub on Thursday night?"

"Look, I told you. Eleven, maybe later. I had a few beers, shot some pool, talked to my buddies. I wasn't punching a fuckin' time clock."

"Was your wife—Marlene, is that her name?—was she home when you arrived?"

"Sure. We had a beer, watched a little TV. Well now, I wouldn't exactly say we watched it—know what I mean? Kids are great, but they sure put a crimp in your sex life."

"The Bittancourt cabin isn't far from your place. You sure you didn't stop by?"

"And get my leg chewed off by that dog of his? No way."

"Why do you think the dog would have attacked you?"

"Didn't like me, did it? Used to take a lunge at me every time I went into the pub." He absentmindedly scratched the back of his hand.

"Your hand's bleeding," Berwick said. "What happened?"

The question seemed to throw Kelly off. "What?" he said, looking down. The scab had broken open and blood was oozing out. "Oh, that. Who knows. You work with your hands, they're always cut up. Fuckin' machines will get you every time."

"Hold on a minute, I'll get a bandage." Berwick went out, leaving the tape machine running.

"Backhoe jammed up a few days ago, that's probably when I got this cut." Grinning at Danutia, he reached for his top shirt button. "I could show you lots of scars."

"Cut that out, Bob," Berwick said as he re-entered the room. He stripped open a plastic bandage, laid it across the cut, and removed it. "Too small," he said, opening another. "There. You don't want to get blood on your clothes." He carefully slipped the unused bandage back inside its wrapper, nodded to Danutia, and returned to his chair.

Danutia took her cue. "Did Bertolucci's dog attack you?" she asked.

A shadow passed across Kelly's face. "Lots of times, like I said."

"I mean last week. At the trailer. Or later. At the cabin."

For a second his eyes, so close-set they looked cross-eyed, met hers. She waited for the lie. "I didn't say the dog attacked me. Just didn't like me, that's all."

"Was the dog around Saturday morning?"

"Nah, now you mention it." He stuffed his hands in his pockets. "Must have run off."

Danutia glanced at her notes. "One of the demonstrators says you were in the bar Thursday night, boasting that the 'SSHIT asses'—I understand that's your term for people involved with Save Salt Spring History—were in for a big surprise. 'They can take their fucking cabin and stick it up their asses,' you said. 'There'll be plenty of pieces for everybody.' Sounds like you were trying to stir up trouble."

"Why would I do that?" His eyes flicked from her to Berwick and back.

"Perhaps because you had a grudge against Joe Bertolucci."

"Me, a grudge? Me and Joe was good pals." He forced a grin. "Why, when he dropped me off, I invited him in for a beer, but he said he'd better set up his gear before dark."

Danutia caught a hint of amusement beneath Berwick's calm demeanor. No better friend than a dead enemy.

"The way I hear it," she said, "he shoved you down the stairs at the Dockside."

Kelly picked up his lighter, flicked it on and off. "That was just a little misunderstanding. I'd had a little too much to drink, and I slipped." He nodded toward Berwick. "Ask the Sergeant. He was there."

Danutia stood up and leaned forward across the table. "On Saturday," she said, "you told Constable Larocque you didn't know anything about the gun Bertolucci allegedly shot himself with. Do you own a 9 MM Glock, Mr. Kelly?"

Kelly shifted uneasily in his chair, revealing dark stains under his armpits.

"We know there's not one registered to you, but then

you don't have a Firearms License, do you? A lot of people don't bother with those formalities." She paused. "Illegal possession of a firearm is one thing. Murder is another."

"You accusing me of murder? I want a lawyer." Kelly snatched the cigarettes and lighter and stuffed them in his pocket.

"Settle down, Mr. Kelly. I'm not accusing you of anything. I just want to know why your prints are on the gun."

Berwick spoke up. "As you know, allowances are made for people who help the police with their inquiries."

The bait was laid. Co-operate and we'll forget about illegal possession. Don't co-operate and you'll face criminal charges, maybe lose your job, who knows what else. Kelly was a survivor; Danutia knew what he would choose.

"All right," he said, his eyes hard and bright. "The Glock's mine."

"Do you know how Bertolucci came to have it?"

"I keep it in the truck."

"Why do you carry a handgun?"

"I travel all up and down the islands for Ohara. There's some real loonies out there—squatters, you know, druggies growing themselves a little pot, people like that. I got to be prepared."

"Yet you left the gun in the truck when you turned it over to Bertolucci."

"Yeah, fuckin' stupid, that was." Kelly slicked back his hair, scratched his head, grinned disarmingly. "Guess he must have found it."

"If Joe Bertolucci had killed himself, that would be a

simple and logical explanation," Danutia said. "Why didn't you tell us sooner?"

"'Cause I didn't know how he'd killed himself, did I, until you started talking about the Glock. And the first thing you said was, Joe didn't kill himself, it was murder. Think I'm going to claim the gun after that? No way."

"When you realized the gun was still in the truck, did you try to get it back?"

"Like I told you," Kelly said. "I didn't see or talk to Joe after he dropped me at my place Wednesday night. Now can I go?"

Danutia hammered him for another half hour, but his story didn't change. Reluctantly she turned him loose.

⋅–⋅ ⋅–⋅

Danutia had just settled herself under the whirring ceiling fan in Berwick's office when Betty buzzed to say an urgent fax was coming through.

While Berwick collected the fax, Danutia had a look around his office. There was little enough to see. The only personal touch was a ceramic bowl filled with polished stones next to the telephone. No reassuring photos of wife and kids, though the sergeant was attractive enough, with his face all angles and crevices like a weathered boulder. And, as she had discovered, as hard to budge. Infuriatingly stubborn. Inclined to lecture. And with plenty to lecture about, she thought, surveying his well-stocked bookcase.

She had taken down a new book on DNA analysis when Berwick returned with a sheaf of papers in his hand and a frown on his face.

"Betty gave me Larocque's report just now, along with a piece of her mind," he said. "Seems there was a grisly accident after *The Mikado* rehearsal last night. Zachary Smith beheaded himself."

"What?" Danutia thought of the dead-white face on the Festival pamphlet, with its clownish eyes and lopsided grin. The grin hardening into a death rictus. "Is there any doubt it was an accident?"

"When I stopped by yesterday afternoon, Smith was trying a tricky bit of stage business with a miniature guillotine. I warned him about it, but he just laughed and said he needed something spectacular for the opening on Friday. Apparently the safety mechanism failed." Berwick absentmindedly rubbed the shaving nick on his throat. "Zach was always full of schemes. Like the Bloomsday party. His death will be a real blow to the community."

Danutia shifted uneasily. "Who found the body?"

"A Brit named Fairweather. Drama critic for the *Post-Dispatch*."

"He keeps popping up," Danutia said. "He was in the White Whale on Saturday, asking why someone committed suicide. Can you keep him away from my case?"

"I'll do my best." Berwick dropped one set of papers on his desk and handed Danutia the other. "In the meantime, we'd better see what Krahn has to say."

Danutia reached behind her to return the book on DNA analysis to the shelf.

Berwick must have noticed the title. "Looking for a new angle?"

"Wishing Kelly had jacked off over the body," she

responded. "Maybe you would be convinced by DNA."

Berwick smoothed his bald head like a cat preening. "Give me some credit, Constable. Why do you think I thoughtfully bandaged Kelly's hand this morning? The bandage that was too small is tucked away in an evidence bag. Not as sexy as semen, but the DNA's the same."

"You don't think Kelly's capable of murder."

Berwick shrugged. "No judge would accept that bandage as evidence, but if Mia's hair samples contain human blood, and it isn't Kelly's, we can stop wasting our time with him."

And if Krahn's report said what she expected it to, Danutia thought as she flipped to the conclusions, she could quit pussyfooting around and launch a full-scale investigation.

"I was right," she said, trying not to sound smug. "Krahn says singeing of the scalp indicates a bullet wound. Maybe there was a struggle after all."

"No gunpowder residue," Berwick said, skimming the page. "That fits. We only found one cartridge in the cabin, remember?"

"So the first shot was fired outside. Anything in the debris from the clearing?"

"Nothing obvious, as you know. I haven't had a report yet on the contents of the fire pit. The fire was recent, probably Joe cleaning up and burning the litter. You saw how neat the cabin was."

"We need someone to go over that area again," she said.

"I'll send McTavish," Berwick said, reaching for the phone. "He's thorough."

When he hung up, she said, "I want to have another talk with Kelly. He lied about the gun, I'm sure of it."

Berwick picked a white stone out of his bowl of polished rocks and leaned back, fingering it like a worry bead. "You talked to Kelly. You think he could have written the suicide note?"

Danutia leaned forward across the desk. "Kelly had a motive, and his fingerprint was on the gun. Why do you find it so hard to believe that he might be a murderer? When they're cornered, little weasels like that fight back."

"You scratch deep enough, Constable, almost everyone has some kind of motive for killing. Most folks don't do it. There's still no evidence that points to Kelly. Or to anyone else, for that matter."

"No snakes in this little bit of paradise?"

Berwick passed the white stone from one hand to the other, back and forth, then cradled it for a moment in his right hand. "This is a good place, with good people. Know what I want to do? Retire here and start a vineyard. I'll do it, too, in about two years. But for now I'm a cop. And I don't care about motive."

He replaced the stone. "And if you want to be a good homicide cop, you shouldn't either. There's plenty to dislike about Kelly, I'll grant you that. He's a sexist pig, a petty criminal who drinks too much, gets in scrapes, maybe cheats on his wife when he has the chance. That doesn't mean he's a murderer. All we can do is our job: ask questions, check alibis, wait for reports, keep looking for evidence."

Danutia jabbed at the papers in her hand. "The scalp wound—"

The phone rang. Berwick listened and said, "Show her in."

A moment later Antonia flew into the office brandishing a crumpled white envelope. "I told you my father didn't kill himself. This letter proves it." She was in black again, a sleeveless silk chemise with a short tight skirt. She would have a whole wardrobe of black, Danutia guessed, not for mourning, until now, but for the dramatic effect against her milk-white skin.

Berwick motioned for Antonia to take a seat. Perching on the edge of the chair, she smoothed the envelope with long, tense fingers. "Gino brought it," she said. "He's my little brother. He came over for the benefit tonight. But maybe you don't know about that—"

"They're going ahead with it?" Berwick cut in. "After what happened to Smith?"

Antonia nodded. "Lavender can't believe it either. But Carol says Zachary never cancelled a show, and she isn't going to start now. Horrible, isn't it."

Unsure whether Antonia meant Smith's death or Carol's decision, Danutia murmured, "Yes, of course. Horrible for you all."

"But that isn't what I came about." Antonia flipped the envelope right side up and held it out to Berwick. "There's the postmark: June seventeenth. And the forwarding address label: our new apartment. Papa must have sent it to my old place. It should have reached me days before the wedding."

Berwick's eyes narrowed to obsidian points as he examined the envelope. "And you think this proves your father didn't kill himself?"

"Of course he didn't," Antonia snapped. "I'll read you the letter." She drew out several sheets, closely written in black ink. "'My dearest daughter.'" She cleared her throat, started again. "'My dearest daughter'—I can't," she said, sinking back in the chair. "You'll have to read it."

Berwick took the outstretched pages. "'My dearest daughter. Since your mother and I separated, my most fervent prayer has been that you and your brother would be all right.'" Berwick hesitated—trying to decipher Bertolucci's handwriting, Danutia supposed—then continued.

As she listened to the letter, Danutia's heart grew heavy. It was much as she had supposed—the drinking, the doubts about his ability to cope with his ex-wife and her family—though Bertolucci was careful not to blame his daughter for pressuring him to come to the wedding. She glanced at the young woman who had gone still as stone, silent tears sliding down her cheeks. Danutia offered tissues, which were ignored.

"'And now,'" Berwick read, "'you want me to give you away to the man you hope to spend the rest of your life with. I know I can trust your love for me; I'm not sure I can trust myself. And so it seems that the best wedding present I can give you is my absence. You can be sure of this, my beloved daughter—whoever stands beside you in the flesh, I will be there in spirit.'"

Berwick's eyes, softer now, rested on Antonia. "Sounds like your father was trying to warn you," he said.

Antonia wiped her cheeks with the backs of her hands. "You didn't read the last sentence," she said. "On the back."

Berwick turned over the last page. "'PS Don't forget that after your honeymoon, I'm taking you and Marco for a glorious week of sailing.'"

"Does that sound like someone who's planning to kill himself?" Antonia demanded. "I checked. He booked a 32-foot sloop for this week, said he'd be in last Saturday to take it for a test run." Her voice faltered.

Last Saturday. That's when the body was found, Danutia thought, rotting in a deserted cabin.

Berwick examined parts of the letter again then passed it to Danutia. "Your father has a poetic way of expressing himself," he said. "And a fine italic hand. Were his letters always handwritten?"

"Always," said Antonia. "Not business letters, he typed those. But he said it was bad manners to type personal letters."

Wondering where Berwick's questions were leading, Danutia scanned the letter. Here and there she recognized turns of phrase she'd come across in the other letters she'd read, as well as in the suicide note. But the suicide note, addressed to this same beloved daughter, was typed. And Bertolucci's replies to Antonia's last two letters were missing.

"Was he also particular about spelling?" Berwick asked.

"Wasn't he! There's a family joke that the first time Gino said 'ma-ma', Papa said, 'Wonderful! How do you spell it?' Why do you ask?"

Berwick ignored her question. "Even reasonably good spellers have a word or two they habitually misspell. Mine's 'accommodate.' I can never remember whether it's one M or two. Did your father have words like that?"

Antonia shook her head. "We used to play spelling games in the car. If we could spell a word he couldn't, he'd buy us an ice cream. We never managed to trip him up. He always bought us an ice cream anyway."

Danutia had spotted them now, two words spelled correctly in the letter but misspelled in the suicide note. 'Separated'. 'All right'.

"Constable Dranchuk never believed your father killed himself," Berwick said. "I believed he had. This letter may prove me wrong."

Hallelujah! Relief flooded through Danutia like a river. With Berwick on her side, the investigation would get somewhere. Then her elation subsided. Two words. It wasn't her judgment he trusted. It was two words on a piece of paper.

# Chapter 11
Salt Spring: Tuesday, July 11

Thea took a last sip from her juice box. "So what happened?" she asked Arthur. They were sitting at a secluded picnic table beside a tiny inlet, the remnants of a silent lunch between them. Arthur was poking at the ground with a stick, creating a line of shallow holes close to his feet.

Hesitantly at first, then in a flood of words, Arthur told her about the unlocked door and the empty stage, about seeing the bloody head and falling.

"The next thing I knew, Hendrix was bending over and shaking me. I remember seeing his silver ear cuffs and thinking he must have been playing some stupid joke. So I glanced over at the guillotine to make sure. The head was still there, staring back at me. This time I could see the grey in the dark hair."

Water lapped softly against rock. In the distance, children shouted with excitement. Arthur felt himself shiver. His hands and feet were cold even in the warm sunshine, and his head ached dully.

"I still couldn't quite believe that Hendrix wasn't dead—I mean, after that accident in Victoria, and his car in the parking lot."

Thea leaned over and touched his arm. "The whole thing must have been horrible for Hendrix. And for you."

Arthur poked at the ground again. "That RCMP man—Laroche, Larocque, whatever his name was, something French—asked me the same questions over and over again. 'Why was I seeing Smith?' 'Why was I late?' I just kept telling him to bugger off, my head was hurting. Finally he said to come in this morning and sign a statement. Hendrix took me to the hospital, or I might have gone to sleep with a concussion and never woken up." He rubbed the bump on his head, hoping for a little more concern for his bodily ills than Thea was in the habit of showing.

"Look, Arthur, the bump on your head isn't the point, and you know it. Something is bothering you, or you wouldn't be trying to run away."

"What do you mean, running away? You heard the guy when you picked me up—I'm free to leave the island."

"Of course the police have no reason to keep you. Zachary's death was clearly an accident, and you've made your statement. But something is eating at you. I can see it in your face, I can hear it in your voice. And I want to know what it is."

Arthur beat a rapid tattoo on the picnic table with his stick. "While we were waiting in Emergency, Hendrix kept saying, 'If only I'd gone back on time.' I keep thinking the same thing. If I'd been there when I said I would, Smith might still be alive."

Thea gently removed the stick and laid her hands on top of his. "There's no way you could know that for sure, either of you. Accidents do happen."

"If it was an accident," he said.

"What do you mean? Zach wasn't the type to commit suicide."

"I wasn't thinking of suicide, but maybe you're right. My suspicions are probably rubbish. After all, I was wrong about who was dead."

"What suspicions?" Thea's brow was furrowed and her jaw set in her stubborn bulldog expression. She would never give up now. Arthur's anger boiled over.

"Stop grilling me. You said if I told you what happened last night, you'd take me to the ferry. I've told you. Now take me to the ferry."

"After you told me everything, I said. You're still holding back, holding back and running away. And I know what you do when you run from things." Thea tossed the leftover bits of cheese and sausage into the hamper. "You'll phone up the *Post-Dispatch* and tell them you're sick, you can't review any more of the Festival, and then you'll crawl into bed and pull the covers over your head for a week. Meanwhile I'll be here trying to deal with this mess. You aren't the only one affected by Zachary's death, you know."

"I'm going for a walk." Arthur strode off angrily. Her bloody reviews, that's all Thea was thinking about. She didn't care a tinker's damn about him. Sod it. He'd had enough. No more Arthur to the rescue. If that meant forgetting his suspicions about Zachary Smith's death, so be it.

It wasn't much, what he'd noticed before he fell. Just the empty music stand and, at the edge of the circle of blood, two half-moon shaped indentations, as if someone had been standing there. But remembering these details early this morning, on waking from a fitful sleep, he had wondered whether Zachary Smith's death was the simple accident it seemed. He would have mentioned his observations to Larocque if the constable had been the least bit interested. But he wasn't going to tell Thea. She would only accuse him again of running away.

Which was ridiculous. The stress of living in a strange country, of trying to get by on part-time work, of not having anyone he could count on—it was making him paranoid, that was all. How else to explain his initial suspicion that Hendrix was in danger, and now his suspicion that Zachary Smith had been murdered? Whatever Thea might say, he needed a few days away. Maybe if he promised to come back for the opening on Friday . . .

Arthur, who had been oblivious to his surroundings, tripped over knotted roots in the path and almost fell. When he recovered his balance, he paused to orient himself.

Ruckle Park had once been a homestead, and the former owners still farmed part of it, Thea had explained, as they drove in past wheat fields, small orchards, a large Victorian house and barn. There were no traces of farm life here by the seashore, only trees and rocks and ferns and, beyond them, the blue of sky and water. Floating on the air, the cries of children, more raucous now.

Arthur rounded the point onto a rocky slope. Half a dozen young boys stood near the water chanting, "Yellow skin, yellow skin, pee the bed that you lie in." Sunlight flashed on a stick rising and falling in time with the chant. Balancing precariously on the jagged rocks at the water's edge was a small Asian boy in navy blue shorts and striped T-shirt.

"Yellow skin, yellow skin, pee the bed that you lie in," the children yelled again. Again the stick came down, forcing the boy backward toward the beating waves.

Before Arthur knew what he was doing, he was thundering down the slope shouting "Stop that! Stop that, or I'll break your bloody necks." Startled faces turned toward him and then the boys scattered, running up the slope and into the trees.

"Do you need a hand?" Arthur called to the boy on the rocks. He was around nine or ten, Arthur guessed, but slender and short for his age, with a mop of black hair.

The boy shook his head and jumped, landing near Arthur's feet. Without thinking, Arthur clasped his arms to help him up. He was amazed by the boy's lightness. Stepping back out of Arthur's grip, the boy smiled up at him. "Thank you for helping."

"Shall I take you to your parents?" Arthur asked

The boy shook his head and set off along the shoreline, his feet light and sure on the rocky gravel.

Watching the small figure disappear around a sunlit boulder, Arthur felt a change happening in himself, an odd and unexpected shift in perception. He suddenly felt as light as the boy he had held for a moment, as sure about his next step. He turned and walked slowly back, enjoying the sunlight. He didn't know yet exactly what he would say to Thea, but it didn't matter. The words would come.

He found her standing at the water's edge, skipping stones. Not idly, to kill time, but putting her whole body into it, her weight shifting, her wrist snapping, her stance expectant as she counted the bounces, then bending to search for the next perfect stone. Being Thea.

Hearing him approach, she turned, her arm poised to throw.

"You don't have to threaten me," he said, stooping to pick up his stick again. With it he drew circles in the sand, great looping circles going nowhere. Then, obliterating all but the last circle, he smoothed a few inches, sketched two fainter arcs within its rim, and stepped into the indentations he'd made. "I'm staying."

⚬⚬ ⚬⚬

But was he? he wondered as the evening's benefit dragged on. How could he imagine some dark secret in this troupe of worn, tired-looking people? And to cap the evening, a long, tedious speech from David Ohara inviting the audience to contribute to a trust fund for the Bertolucci family established by—surprise, surprise—David Ohara.

Thea nudged him. "A nifty bit of public relations magic," she whispered. "A few thousand dollars for the Bertolucci trust fund, and—hey presto! No more opposition to his development scheme for the Bittancourt property."

"'Wily Orientals with development in mind . . .'" Arthur muttered.

"What's that?" Thea asked, bending closer.

"Oh, probably nothing. You reminded me of a line Smith was singing at the rehearsal Monday night—the local version of 'I've Got a Little List.' Something about 'wily Orientals'. Ohara seems to have a finger in a lot of Salt Spring pies."

"You can say that again. With last month's donation, he must have put up about a third of the money for the new theatre. Wish I'd had a father to buy me a theatre when I was eighteen."

"You think he's doing it just for Sandra?"

"All I know is what I've been told. When Sandra graduated from high school last year, she told her father she wasn't going to university, she was going to join the Vesuvius Light Opera Company, and when she had learned all that Zach could teach her, she would go to Hollywood and become a star. And shortly afterwards, the building fund, which had been limping along for several years, received a whopping great cheque from Ohara."

"The developer with a heart of gold. Sounds like a great angle for the fundraising piece," Arthur said, gazing around the gym where members of the cast, still in costume, were mingling with the audience. "Why don't I talk to Ohara—"

"Mr. Fairweather," Carol Smith broke in. Though she'd taken off Katisha's wig and vampire cloak and removed her stage makeup, she looked years older than she had only a few days ago. "I understand you discovered my husband's body last night. I'd very much like to talk to you."

"Yes, of course. And I want to offer my condolences. Is this a good time for you?"

"No, not now. There'll be a wake for Zach about eight tomorrow night at the Dockside Inn—nothing formal, just people who knew Zach saying a few words about him. I've asked Thea already. Can you come? I'm sure there will be a moment or two for us to talk."

"I'd be honoured. I may be late, though; I'm reviewing something beforehand."

"I'll book a taxi for you," Thea said. "I can drop you off at your hotel afterwards."

"Until tomorrow, then." Giving Arthur a tired smile, Carol sank into a chair and drew Thea down beside her.

Arthur spotted David Ohara on the far side of the gym and set off in pursuit. As he squeezed past knots of people still chatting in the aisle, he kept his eyes down to avoid the sudden silences and sidelong glances, and so almost missed Lavender, who seemed to be sleepwalking. The radiant breathlessness that had entranced him in Victoria had vanished like air let out of a balloon, leaving behind a limp body, dull eyes.

He stretched out a hand to attract her attention. "I'm sorry about your father."

"Yes. Thanks." Lavender looked around blankly. "Sorry, I just want to . . ." She gestured toward the door leading to the dressing rooms and drifted off.

Give it up, Arthur told himself. Go have a drink and forget about Lavender, forget about Thea and this bloody festival, forget about Norma and the pieces you're supposed to be writing. Forget about the grisly head grinning at you. His stomach lurched again at the thought. How could the actors walk back and forth on that stage tonight? They don't run away, Thea's voice whispered inside his head. Not like you.

All right, all right, he told the voice. I'll see what I can do to bring in the shekels.

Squaring his shoulders, Arthur headed again toward

the corner where David Ohara stood talking with Larry Weston. Even without his headdress, Weston towered over his companion. As Arthur approached, he heard Weston mention hara-kiri.

"Not another death, I hope." Arthur shook Weston's hand and nodded to Ohara.

Weston introduced them. "I was saying to David that according to samurai custom, I should follow my friend into death by committing hara-kiri."

"Larry and I have many conversations about matters Japanese, and we manage never to wholly agree." To Arthur's surprise, there was a faint smile on Ohara's face. "I think he overestimates the significance of hara-kiri in samurai culture. I myself think the samurai's obligations to the living were far more important, such as providing for the families of men who died in their service. But I know it is the warrior code which has caught my friend's imagination, and I know he has studied it deeply, so it is not for me to say he is wrong."

"Yes, I've studied the code. But I know I'm too cowardly for true hara-kiri," Weston said. "At least Zach's death was clean and quick. Hara-kiri is slow and painful. But, still, a death by accident is not a good death." He swallowed hard.

"You're assuming it was an accident?"

"Of course. Who could think anything else?" Weston's tone was sharp.

Arthur shook his head. This wasn't the time to share his speculations.

Swiping a hand across the trickles of sweat that ran

down his forehead, Weston said, "I have to get out of this costume. Did you want to talk to me?"

"Just to express my condolences," Arthur said. "I have a few questions to ask Mr. Ohara, if he's willing."

"I'll come back after I've changed," Weston said, and headed for the door to the dressing rooms.

Ohara stood waiting, his hands behind his back, not at all uncomfortable with the silence, as far as Arthur could tell. Unsure how to broach the subject of his support of Sandra's career, Arthur said, "Your daughter Sandra must have been deeply shocked by Smith's death."

"We were all shocked, Mr. Fairweather."

"Sandra had chosen to study under Smith, I hear. Are you pleased with the progress she has made?"

"Unfortunately, tonight was the first time I have seen her perform in a long while, and as you will understand, she was not at her best."

"From your generous contributions to the new theatre, I thought you must be an avid theatre-goer."

"I am no longer in school, Mr. Fairweather, and that is where the Vesuvius Company mainly performs. I trust that with the new theatre, I will have the pleasure of productions by local companies. As for my contributions—" he made a gesture of dismissal—"we who do not practise the arts must do our part to support them. In traditional Japanese culture, after all, the samurai were trained to be both warriors and poets."

Arthur tried to bring the conversation back to Sandra. "Do you think your daughter will stay on Salt Spring and act in the new theatre?"

Irritation flitted across Ohara's face. "Do you have any children, Mr. Fairweather?"

"None that I know of." Arthur hadn't meant to be flippant, but he was taken aback by the question.

"You will find it a most enlightening experience. As I said in my small speech tonight, I value both tradition and individual effort. I cannot fault my daughter's effort; she is working very hard to be successful. She will go wherever success leads, Mr. Fairweather, without concern for family ties or obligations." Ohara paused. "If that is enough to make me happy, then I will be happy."

Arthur felt puzzled. Thea had led him to believe the man was supporting the theatre out of affectionate concern for his daughter's future; Ohara's comments suggested a more ambiguous relationship between the two.

At a loss to know how to proceed, Arthur was relieved when Larry Weston reappeared in a short-sleeved shirt and jeans. A moment later Doc Johnson joined them, carrying his tuxedo jacket. His white dress shirt seemed immense. "What happened to Zach's song?" he asked Weston. "I really liked it."

Weston's broad forehead creased in a puzzled frown.

"You know, the new 'list' song. Zach showed it to me at the rehearsal yesterday. He was very proud of his sly digs. I don't remember any of the words, but I remember there was a dig at me. And one at you, Ohara, if I'm not mistaken."

"I heard nothing about myself in the play," said Ohara, looking alarmed at the idea.

"No, that's the point." Johnson loosened his maroon

bow tie with his middle finger. "Hendrix just sang the original, without any of Zach's new lyrics. It would have been a fitting memorial to our friend to leave his words in."

"Now that you mention it," Weston said, "Ivy asked Rodney about that song. Rodney said he didn't believe in messing around with the original script, even if Zach's version had been available."

"What did he mean by that?" asked Arthur, suddenly alert.

"I don't know," Weston said. "To be honest, after what happened last night, I'd barely have noticed if Hendrix had sung in Swahili."

There was a moment of silent agreement, and then the group broke up.

Arthur's thoughts were racing. He had almost convinced himself that there must be a rational explanation for the empty music stand. But if the script had disappeared, that was surely odd.

Looking around for Rodney Coutt in the rapidly emptying gym, Arthur caught a tall blonde staring fixedly at him. One of the morbidly curious, he assumed, then realized it was the khaki-clad woman he'd seen in the White Whale on Saturday, though tonight she was wearing a stylish green and gold silk blouse and tailored suit. The bald-headed man standing next to her was surely the RCMP officer Thea had pointed out to him earlier—Burton, no, Berwick. Suddenly he remembered the woman's table had been full of file folders. Maybe she was not a camp director but a policewoman.

Whatever she was, she was definitely not his type, but, embarrassed by her gaze, he tried a half-smile. When her expression didn't change, he realized that she was staring not at him but at someone behind him. Surreptitiously he turned his head. A few steps away stood the actress who played Peep-Bo, Marlene Kelly. Assuming the blonde was RCMP, why was she interested in Marlene? Were the police getting suspicious about Zachary Smith's death too? If so, that policewoman would find out nothing, clod-hopping all over the case. No, if there were secrets in the Vesuvius Light Opera Company, it was up to him, Arthur Fairweather, to winkle them out.

# Chapter 12
## Salt Spring: Wednesday, July 12

Danutia slowed the Blazer to a crawl. About a hundred metres ahead, a yellow bulldozer was parked just off the road, among an assortment of trucks and other vehicles. Bob Kelly's place. A clearing had been gouged out of the mountainside, and a new two-storey house, grey with blue trim, perched uneasily in its raw surroundings, half defiant, half apologetic, like a teenager wearing the wrong clothes. It was 6:23 AM; she was on her way to walk Andy and Martha Johnson through the events of last Saturday. On her way back she would follow up her hunch that Marlene Kelly was Bertolucci's Bo-Peep.

Danutia reset her trip odometer. It was a little earlier than Kelly would have left on Saturday morning, sunnier than she expected until she came to the bend, where the road turned to gravel and a tiny creek splashed down to the sea. Here Douglas firs crowded in and the air was heavy with dew and wisps of fog. At night the dark would press down like a heavy blanket. So much darker than on the prairies, where the high blue dome of the sky keeps its distance.

Then the blue waters of the strait opened out before her, streaked with pink and golden sunlight. The shore curved around on both sides, making a protected harbour. In the parking area sat an old green Dodge van, 'Wood 'N' Clay Things' painted on its side with more zeal than artistry.

156

Danutia was relieved to see it. Andy Johnson had been released from the hospital on Monday, and though Dr. Fidelman had pronounced him in no further danger, Martha had been reluctant to let him come, relenting only when Danutia stressed that the case was now being treated as murder, not suicide. Still, Martha might have changed her mind.

Slinging her backpack over her shoulder, Danutia set off toward the weathered log where the Johnsons sat holding hands and staring out to sea, Andy bundled into a heavy sweatshirt with the hood pulled up over his head. The tide was out; the creek tumbled onto the beach and spread out, threading through the pebbles and turning the bright-green algae squishy and smelly underfoot. Broken clamshells, the leavings of the crows quarreling in the trees, littered the mud flats stretching seaward a hundred metres or more.

The voice began as soon as she reached them, the slow, flat voice of someone trying to fix dream images as they crack and melt away.

"I was standing here," Andy said, too wrapped up in his experience for small civilities. "I wanted to show what a peaceful spot this is, the gulls floating on the waves, the waves lapping in to shore. And then the walk up the path—" He slumped forward, closed his eyes. He was pale, Danutia noted, the cut on his forehead still bandaged.

"Andy, are you sure you should be doing this?" Martha broke in.

"No, no, I'll be all right." Struggling to his feet, he plodded slowly toward the embankment. The gate across the trail, Danutia noted, was standing open. So much for keeping out thrill-seekers. Or vandals.

"I understand there was some vandalism here, and at Mr. Ohara's residence. It would help if we could establish whether those incidents had anything to do with the murder. Can you give us any help with that?"

"Definitely not," Martha said. "We started a letter-writing campaign to the Island Trust and to the newspapers, and got up a petition to have the cabin declared an historical site. We would never be part of anything underhanded."

Andy breathed raspily beside her, his eyes fixed on the path. Finally he said, "The survey ribbons. I took them down, as many as I could find."

"That had nothing to do with the man's death."

"Of course it didn't. That's why I'm telling her." Andy halted, a matchstick beside a big Douglas fir. They must have been about the same age, tree and man. "The garbage on his lawn, the graffiti at the golf club, that stuff was not my doing. And I don't think anyone else in Save Salt Spring History did it, either. But when I saw those red ribbons on this land I've hiked for thirty years, and thought about the trees being cut, and the birds and the deer going the way of the bears and the cougars—well, it made me sick. So I followed the survey tags for miles and took down every one I came to." He ran a hand up and down the heavily creased bark. "I'm not sorry, either."

A few minutes later they stepped into the clearing. The bright yellow police tape they'd stretched around the cabin porch lay in ribbons on the ground. It probably didn't matter, Danutia knew, the cabin had yielded all it had to tell. But still it seemed like a violation.

Andy slipped an arm around his wife's stout waist. "To you that old cabin may not seem like much," he said. "To Martha here it's a piece of family history. She's descended from old Estalon Bittancourt, you know, one of the first settlers on Salt Spring. Portuguese he was, from the Azores. Shipped out when he was a lad, and still a lad when he landed here in the early 1860s. Few years later he opened a general store right where the Dockside Inn parking lot is. Brought in merchandise from Victoria on his own sloop. Between his store and his stone quarry, old Estalon did all right for himself, though he didn't have much luck with coal mining. All that is well documented," he went on. "It's less well known that old Estalon had a brother, Manoel, who turns up in the early records and then disappears. It's only recently we discovered that Manoel built this cabin, and probably used the old rowboat down at the cove there—" he gestured toward the water— "to row goods from the steamers to the harbour before the first landing was built. Then he must have got the wanderlust—"

Martha pushed Andy's arm away. "She doesn't want to hear all this."

"But she needs to know what kind of group Save Salt Spring History is, and why we were out here protesting," Andy said. "We're not some bunch of wild-eyed Trotskyites out to destroy capitalism. We're trying to save our roots, that's all."

Obsessed with the past. First Ohara, and now Andy

Johnson. Danutia wanted to know about the present. "Tell me exactly what you did from the time you reached the clearing until you found the body."

As though relishing the task, Andy described his video-taping in minute detail: the path down to the cove, the old rowboat there, then the clearing, walking in a semi-circle around the front of the cabin.

"A Pacific Developments truck was parked behind the cabin," Danutia said. "Did you notice it?"

His eyes downcast, his face drawn and pale, he shook his head no though he must know his fingerprints were on the gas cap. A futile gesture, pouring sand into the tank, and a cowardly one, for which he'd found no lofty justification. No matter. His conscience would be punishment enough. With his heart condition, Andy would never have gone to the cabin if he had known a body was there, and if she had known, Martha would never have let him. Nothing so far suggested links between Bertolucci's death and the demonstrators, though Danutia still wondered how they had found out about Ohara's plans.

"I stepped onto the porch and opened the door." Andy's voice was again flat and slow. "It was dark inside, so I waited for my eyes to adjust. Then I turned on the camera and stepped in. I didn't look down until my foot hit something. When I saw what it was, I keeled over."

"Didn't you notice the smell?" Even now, a faint sickly sweet odour seeped through the cabin walls.

"Can't smell a thing. Or very little. I'm always burning the toast because I stick it in the oven and wander off. There was a little whiff of something, but I thought an animal had found its way in and died—a rat or something."

Danutia turned to his wife. "Where were you while your husband was filming?"

"I was at the gate, helping to put up the banner. When I heard the bulldozer, I came to get Andy. The smell was awful. I thought it was the vandals again, filling the cabin with garbage. The door was open, so I went barging in, saying, 'Andy, Kelly's coming,' or something like that, and then I saw—" She paused, her hands clenching and unclenching.

"Mrs. Johnson, it's very important for me to know exactly how the room looked and exactly what you did. Tell me as much as you can remember."

"I'm a potter," Martha said. "It's my hands that remember." Her grey eyes caught and held Danutia's. "I'll have to go inside."

"I can't do it, Martha." Andy had pulled back his hood, and wisps of hair fluttered in the light breeze. "It's my heart. It's beating very fast."

"You're getting overexcited, that's all. Take a digitalis, if it will make you feel better. There's a log to sit on under that tree. You can call me if you need me."

Danutia opened the cabin door and stepped inside. When she was in position, she called out, "Ready," and turned on the tape recorder.

She heard a thud on the porch, a few hurried footsteps, and then Martha's head appeared in the doorway. One hand held her nose pinched tight.

"Andy, Kelly's coming," Martha said, sounding like

someone with a bad cold. She glanced toward the floor, where chalk still outlined the position of the body, and then her head jerked back, her eyes widened, and her hand slipped down to stifle a gasp. Two steps and she was kneeling on the floor, one hand reaching as though to feel a forehead, the other searching for a pulse. Glancing up, she shuddered at the carnage around her. Then relief washed over her face. She stretched her right hand outward with fingers slightly curled, as women do when they've had their hands in biscuit dough, or clay. Picking up an imaginary cellphone, she punched buttons and held her cupped hand near her right ear.

"Martha Johnson here. I'm in the old Bittancourt cabin. Something terrible has happened—" She turned her head toward Danutia. "I'm sorry for what I said about Joe burning in hell."

A voice came faintly through the door. "Martha." And then again, with a rising note of panic. "Martha."

Martha remained still, a question in the grey eyes.

"That's enough for today," Danutia said. "Your husband needs you."

.-. .-.

When the Johnsons' van had disappeared up the road, Danutia stood looking out over the lapping waves that separated Salt Spring from Vancouver Island. The ferry chugged toward Vesuvius, hidden behind a point of land. "Charon calls," Danutia murmured, remembering her conversation with Doc Johnson. But who was Charon?

The ferry reminded her of Andy Johnson's story about

a rowboat at the cove below the cabin. She headed up the beach to check it out, wondering whether she had learned anything useful this morning. Nothing much, she decided. She could tell Ohara what had happened to the survey ribbons, but she probably wouldn't. Nothing in the re-enactment had suggested where the first shot could have come from, the one that had grazed Bertolucci's scalp. Still, she'd had to try.

Rounding a rocky point, she came to a cove with a few metres of sandy beach, shaded by arbutus and salal. Tucked against the cliff face was the weathered rowboat, any paint it might once have had long faded. Light shone through cracks between the boards. Was there any proof it had belonged to the Portuguese sailor? Perhaps these people were satisfied with a story about what might have happened. She needed the truth.

She searched for a way up the cliff. Not far from the rowboat she spied steps, worn or cut into the rock, almost hidden by the vegetation. As she headed toward the steps, the glint of sunlight off metal caught her eye. Clumps of seaweed, outcroppings of rock, scattered piles of drift-wood. Nothing more. She must have imagined it. Then, turning, she saw the light again, like the signals Alyne flashed from the hayloft when Danutia had been spanked and sent to her room: It's okay. I'm here. Again it disappeared. No point in searching. The source of the mysterious light, if she ever located it, would turn out to be a beer can washed in by the tide, or something equally irrelevant. Still, she couldn't give up.

There it was, a dull gleam in a pocket of water.

Something wedged in a crevice. A large stainless steel flashlight of the kind a mechanic might own. Poking a small stick through the handle, Danutia wiggled it free. Its few nicks and scratches were still shiny. There hadn't been a flashlight among Bertolucci's effects, but surely he would have needed one. Maybe Kelly had bought it along with the other supplies. If so, it would be itemized on the receipts Kelly still hadn't delivered. Danutia slid the flashlight into an evidence bag and tucked the bag into her backpack.

What could have brought Bertolucci down here at night? What would have made him drop his flashlight? When the answer came to her, she began scouring the beach for signs of blood.

．．— —．．

An hour later Danutia sat drinking cup after cup of coffee at Marlene Kelly's kitchen table. Marlene had confirmed most of Bob's account of his activities, though there were some discrepancies that would bear checking out. Now Marlene was telling the familiar story of marrying early and growing apart. I could be an old friend, Danutia thought. Or a new friend, the kind you're instantly attracted to and want to tell the most intimate details of your life. Except for the tape recorder between them. Except for the possibility that Marlene's husband had murdered Joe Bertolucci.

But the pull was there, in Marlene's round, friendly face with the upturned nose, her low confiding voice, the pull of the sister-bond, and Danutia felt herself responding. She was reminded of women she and Alyne had grown up with: intelligent, ambitious girls who let themselves be sidetracked by sweet-talking guys, and by their thirties had divorced or settled into a brisk discontent. With her solid, rounded body, sensible jean skirt and blouse, and thick ash-blonde hair pulled back into a clasp, Marlene seemed the typical suburban housewife. Only the bright red polish on her fingers and toes and the lively play of expression across her face suggested another side to her character.

"Bob thought the house would make me happy," Marlene was saying. "What else could I want? I had him, I had the kids, I didn't have to work—no wife of his would ever have to work." She made a face. "Even if she was dying to. I told him I didn't want a new house, and besides we didn't have the money. Never mind about the money, he said, Mr. Ohara would lend it to him, interest-free." Taking a final puff, she stubbed out the half-smoked cigarette and began absentmindedly chipping away at her nail polish.

Ohara didn't seem the type to lend his employees money. A story to check.

"I guess I should have put my foot down, but about that time a friend told me—" She cleared her throat. "The Vesuvius Light Opera Company was looking for an alto and someone suggested I try out." A tremor passed over her face and was gone. "Sorry. First Joe and then Zach—Zach Smith, the director—you must have heard how he died. I didn't think I'd make it through the performance last night. Zach could be a bastard to work with, but he believed in me, even when I didn't."

"The performance last night must have been difficult for all of you," Danutia said. "When I saw you in your Peep-Bo costume, I realized you might be able to tell me about something I found in Joe Bertolucci's trailer." She reached into her backpack and drew out the china shepherdess.

Marlene looked up and the blood drained from her cheeks. Abruptly she stood up. "More coffee? I'll put on a fresh pot."

"Were you romantically involved with Joe Bertolucci?"

Marlene returned to the table, her movements slower, more measured, as though she were walking over slippery ground. Her face was closed now, the confiding manner put aside. She's going to deny it, Danutia thought. But then Marlene surprised her.

"For a while," she said at last. "I'm not quite sure how it happened. Last winter I occasionally dropped into the pub with Bob while the boys were at soccer practice. I'd say hi and take a table, Bob would razz Joe while he waited for our drinks. And then one night I was feeling reckless. I caught Joe looking at me and I looked back. A few days later I drove up to his trailer, not really expecting anything, just curious about what might happen. Nothing much did, that time. We walked in the woods around there, drank coffee. After that I dropped in two or three times a week. It was easy, you know, with Joe working nights, and the boys in school, and Bob gone so much."

"And when you got the part of Peep-Bo, Joe gave you the china shepherdess."

"I couldn't very well bring it home, could I?" She stared at the nails of her left hand, now almost bare, and set to work on the other. A long, thin ribbon of red peeled away.

"And were you still lovers when he died?"

Two spots of red crept into her cheeks. "No."

So that's how it was, Danutia thought. She's not ashamed of betraying her marriage vows; she's ashamed that her lover left her. As I was ashamed, am ashamed, of what I became with Dennis.

"One morning early in June I dropped in to see Joe unexpectedly. Bad move," Marlene said. "It was one of those perfect days, you know? And I wanted to share it with him. It had rained during the night, and the sun was sparkling off the leaves, and there was a strong earthy, piney smell."

Danutia recognized the urge for a connection beyond the coupling of flesh.

"We were sitting outside the trailer, drinking coffee, when Mia came bounding up with her nose full of porcupine quills. Joe comforted her while I went inside to get some tweezers and disinfectant. As I was passing by, I noticed a sheet of paper on the desk. 'My dearest Marlene,' it said. You can guess the rest."

"Some of it, perhaps, but I'd like you to tell me."

"Must I?" Eyes resting thoughtfully on the china shepherdess, she lit another cigarette. "Antonia's wedding was tearing him to pieces. Not just getting through the ceremony. Thinking about his marriage and how it had fallen apart, what his drinking and his wife's bitterness had done to his kids."

Marlene took a quick puff, the smoke curling out of her nostrils like dragon fire. "He said he wanted more than an affair, but he wasn't willing to break up my marriage and see my kids suffer."

She would have sacrificed them in a flash, Danutia realized. Bertolucci wouldn't let her. Maybe Kelly wouldn't either.

"What I can't forgive him for," Marlene said, "is for being right." She ground her cigarette into the overflowing ashtray. Ashes and lipstick-stained butts flew everywhere. Before she could clear away the mess, the phone rang.

"Well good morning. How are my favourite guys?" she asked in the jolly, soothing tones of a loving mother. No trace of anger in her voice now, no hint of impatience—for this moment, at least, she was wholly theirs. A good mother, or a good actress? Danutia wondered, startled both by the intensity of Marlene's anger and the ease with which she hid it.

Danutia turned off the tape recorder and stepped into the living room, scanning it for whatever it could tell her about the Kellys. The boys' soccer trophies. Marlene's tennis trophies. Family photos. A snapshot caught her eye. Four men in camouflage gear, leaning on their rifles. Marlene on a stump at Kelly's feet, cigarette dangling from the corner of her mouth, theatrically caressing the rifle stock between his legs.

Hearing Marlene say goodbye, Danutia replaced the photograph and returned to the kitchen table. Marlene was adjusting the clasp in her hair.

Danutia pushed the button of the tape recorder. "You were telling me about finding the letter. Did you see Bertolucci after that?"

"Only once, and I didn't talk to him then. I made an excuse not to go to the Bloomsday party, so I missed my beloved husband making an ass of himself, though as you can imagine I heard about it. I was about to leave on Wednesday when I heard the truck drive up. Joe dropped Bob off and left again. I guess he went on to the cabin."

Kelly said she wasn't home. Was he mistaken? Or was one of them lying?

"Did Bob know that you and Joe were lovers?"

"No," she said, examining her nails. "I'm pretty sure he didn't. He's too self-centered to notice, if you know what I mean. If I was obviously happier, well then he'd been right about the house. If meals were a bit haphazard and the laundry not always done, well I was busy with rehearsals and he'd always said I needed a hobby." She looked appraisingly at Danutia. "There's no reason for him to find out, is there?"

Was she glossing over Bob's resentment of her involvement with the play, or was she too preoccupied to be aware of it? Perhaps she underestimated Bob, and he did know of her affair.

Was that why he picked the fight with Bertolucci?

"I'm investigating a murder," Danutia said. "I can't make any promises."

Marlene blanched. "I still can't believe he was murdered. Or that anyone could think Bob did it. He's so stupid. He should have had a lawyer with him yesterday.

I told him so, but he's mister bigshot, he thought he could handle it. When Bob told me Joe had committed suicide—"

Danutia's ears pricked up. "When was that?"

"Saturday morning, in Victoria. He came over as soon as the police let him go. He was shivery, like he was coming down with something. But he insisted he was fine, and so all through breakfast we talked about the kids, and the work he had to do on Hornby over the weekend. And then I said, 'I thought Ohara wanted you to knock down that old cabin this morning,' and his face crumpled and he started to shiver again and cry, right in the coffee shop. So I took him back to the room, and then he told me."

"What did he say, exactly?"

"'The bastard's dead—'" She hesitated, as though remembering she wasn't, after all, talking to a friend.

"Anything else?"

Marlene studied her nails intently. Only a few flecks of red clung to the cuticles. When she looked up at Danutia, her blue eyes were wide with panic, and her voice mimicked her husband's. "'The bastard's dead. Shot with my fuckin' gun.'"

Kelly had sworn he didn't know how Bertolucci had died until Danutia asked him about the Glock. "Those were his exact words?"

"Something like that. I wasn't really paying attention. 'Joe—shot—Joe—shot' kept flashing through my mind."

Behind those blue eyes Danutia sensed a cool intelligence that made her uneasy. It was as though the woman was trying out and discarding a series of roles:

Misunderstood Wife, Discarded Mistress, Loving Mother. Honest Witness who cannot tell a lie, even to save her husband. But perhaps it wasn't Bob who needed to be protected. "You've told me what you remember about your husband's movements on Thursday and Friday," she said. "Now tell me about your own. Start with noon Thursday."

"Mine? There's not much to tell. Thursday I had lunch at the country club with my tennis partner, Grace Evans, and then we played a couple of sets. Can you imagine me among the tennis crowd? Ohara gave us a membership, so I thought I might as well use it. The club has a good tennis coach. . . . Anyway, we had a drink afterwards, and then I dashed home, called the boys, made Bob a meal to put in the microwave, and drove into Ganges for a rehearsal. That was about seven. After the rehearsal I gave Ivy—that's Mrs. Coutt, our pianist—a ride home. Her son Rodney, who plays Pooh-Bah, had slipped out and left her stranded. I don't blame him, poor thing—she never lets him out of her sight. So I drove her home and made her a cup of tea. By the time I got home Bob was already asleep. He was still asleep the next morning when I left to catch the 6:20 ferry. I was in Victoria with the rest of the company until Monday morning."

Another discrepancy. According to Kelly, they had a few beers and made out in front of the television set. Why hadn't they tried to get their stories straight? Surely Marlene must have realized that she'd be questioned. Now Bob Kelly's alibi wasn't the only one Danutia would be checking.

Danutia rose from the Kellys' kitchen table. As she packed away Bo-Peep, her hand brushed the evidence bags from the beach. A flashlight, three salal leaves splattered with blood. And an angry lover. Not a bad morning's work after all.

What a day! Arthur took a great swig from his bowl of café latte, his jaw aching from gritting his teeth through the folksy humour of the children's matinee. It was late afternoon, and his table on the verandah of Jumpin' Java was shady and cool. There was a pleasant bustle and hum of people coming and going. If only he could relax, unwind, have a few beers. . . . But his laptop stared up at him like a guilty conscience. Norma hadn't been too pleased with the piece on Deirdre Summers he'd cobbled together yesterday. He'd have to do better with that fundraising article on the new theatre Thea kept bugging him about.

He should have written it first thing this morning, instead of struggling with his review of the benefit performance. By the time he'd decided to downplay its shortcomings in favour of a critical obituary of Zachary Smith, it was time to dash off to a Festival publicity meeting, then lunch and the children's matinee. So now he had two pieces to write, and he couldn't put them off until tonight—he'd promised Thea he'd catch *Peter's Political Puppet Theatre* and then meet her at the wake. Fortifying himself with another gulp of caffeine, he pulled out his laptop, raised the screen and punched the power button.

He was still staring at the blank screen when he heard a high-pitched voice call, "Hey Mr. Fairweather."

Arthur looked up and had a moment of panic. Three

burly young guys with dirty T-shirts and baggy trousers festooned with shiny chains had crowded around his table.

A young woman with spiked pink hair pushed her way through. "My mom says you wrote nice things about her play."

Arthur relaxed. "Hi Cindy. I'm glad she liked it." He congratulated himself again on his cleverness; he had side-stepped evaluating *Bullock's Folly* by focusing at great length on its historical background.

"Hey, Cindy says you were the guy who found the body," said the tallest of the young men, a solid, swarthy youth with bad teeth. "What was it like, man? I'll bet there was blood all over everything."

So that's my great attraction, Arthur thought. "Not so bad as that."

Looking disappointed, the swarthy youth stepped aside to light a cigarette. His ginger-haired companion dripped ash as he leaned over Arthur's computer. "You got that new version of *Deathwalk*?"

"No games at all. Sorry."

Cindy made a face as though to say don't blame me for my uncouth friends. "We gotta go, Mr. Fairweather. Keep cool, eh?" They shuffled off the verandah and spread across the sidewalk, forcing an old couple into passing in single file. Catching Arthur's gaze, the man shook his head in dismay at the lack of manners in young folks nowadays. Up yours, Arthur thought, shifting allegiance now that the teens were no longer in his face.

So where was I, he wondered, absent-mindedly brushing cigarette ash from the table onto his trousers. But his mind wouldn't focus on either of the two articles he needed to write; he couldn't shake the image of the pool of blood with its two slight indentations, the empty music stand, the missing play script. Slow down, Arthur told himself. You don't know for sure it's missing.

But what if it was? What if it turned out he was investigating a murder? Then he would have to draw up a list of suspects. Why not do that now, just in case? He opened a new file, typed in Suspects, and paused. Who goes on the list?

First, Hendrix Smith. Antagonism between father and son; no one willing to talk about it. The accident had made it seem that Hendrix was in some kind of danger from his father, but what if the opposite was true? The young man had seemed distressed at his father's death, but then, after all, he was an actor. What if he had committed the crime, and then waited, concealed, to 'arrive' just after Arthur kept his appointment with a dead man?

Who else? Rodney Coutt for sure. All that repressed anger when he and Smith were arguing about the guillotine.

Arthur glanced up; as if by magic, the supercilious Brit had materialized on the other side of the street.

"Rodney Coutt. Hello." Arthur shouted, waving him over. The tall figure hesitated and Arthur waved again. When he started across the road, Arthur hurriedly closed the Suspects file.

Soon Coutt stood at the bottom of the verandah, looking up. "Don't you know it's bad manners to yell at people?"

"Sorry," Arthur said, not caring in the least. "Could you come up here for five minutes? I'm writing a piece about the benefit performance, and I have a couple of questions to ask you."

Coutt looked at his watch and sighed, then walked up the steps and sat on the edge of a chair at Arthur's table, refusing coffee. "So, what do you want to know?"

"I was sorry that you didn't use Smith's new lyrics for Ko-Ko's 'list' song last night. That would have been a fitting tribute."

"We didn't have Zachary's play script. Not that it would have saved that performance. We were awful."

"You had a good excuse," said Arthur, his disdain for Coutt's Oxbridge accent softened by the man's honesty. But he persisted. "Didn't you look for the script?"

"No, why should I? I prefer the original words. You could ask my mother. She was asking about that song yesterday. Maybe she's put the script away somewhere. If so, it can stay there. Friday's production will be nothing but Gilbert and Sullivan." Coutt half-rose, but Arthur wasn't ready to let him go.

"I have one more question. More of a request, really. Because of the circumstances, I'm focusing my review on Zachary Smith's role as founder and director of the Vesuvius Company. Could give me some background on his work?"

Coutt glanced at his watch and sank back into his chair. "Five minutes, you said. Then I'm off." He was silent for a moment, his brow furrowed, his lips slightly pursed, as though he'd been asked to explain quantum theory to a puddingheaded three-year-old. Finally he said, "As you must know, there's not a very big market for serious contemporary plays in this part of the world. Zachary's technique was to make guerrilla sorties on plays that are popular, like the Gilbert and Sullivan operettas. He got a lot of mileage out of revamping the classical D'Oyly Carte productions."

"Revamping which you didn't like?"

"I've never seen the point of innovation for innovation's sake. There's enough wit in the lyrics of *The Mikado* or *The Pirates of Penzance* to carry a production. I don't want to speak ill of the dead, but Zachary wanted all the intelligence in the productions to be his; he was never open to the possibility that playwrights and lyricists might have some too."

"Was that why you were arguing with him on Monday night?"

"It wasn't me who was having the big argument with Zach. . . ." His voice tailed off as if he had only just realized what he was saying.

Trying to sound offhand, Arthur asked, "When was that?"

"Just after you left." Rodney Coutt again made as if to rise. "Anyway, I can't see how that's relevant."

Arthur had to think fast. "I had the sense in Victoria that provoking his actors was part of Smith's method as a director. On Monday night I got the impression he'd made you really angry. Now it seems you weren't the only one."

"Angry at Zachary?" Coutt seemed to need a moment

or two to digest this idea. "Listen, Mr. Fairweather: Zachary Smith and I disagreed from the moment I joined the Company. And yet two years later he made me Assistant Director. When all's said and done, I liked the excitement of his productions, and our artistic disagreements were never that important. Many times I've stayed into the early hours trying out one of Zach's hare-brained ideas."

Arthur saw an opening and took it. "That's another curious thing about Monday night. If there was more rehearsing to be done after *Bullock's Folly*, I would have expected Smith to ask the Assistant Director to come back as well. Kept the reins of power in his own hands, did he?"

"My job was finances and administration. Zach didn't need me after the Monday rehearsal, and I had other things to do."

"Other things?"

"Entirely my own business, Mr. Fairweather." Rodney Coutt stood up. "As acting director of the Company, I'm enough of a realist not to alienate the *Post-Dispatch* drama critic. So if you want me to answer more questions at another time, I'm willing, as long as they are about Zachary Smith and the Company." Radiating anger held tightly in check, Coutt turned and stalked down the steps.

Don't try that 'artistic disagreement' bit with me, mate, Arthur thought, watching Coutt's stiff back until he turned a corner. Not if you won't tell me where you were on Monday night.

# Chapter 14
Salt Spring: Wednesday afternoon, July 12

"Firearms report's in," Berwick said as he approached the back desk where Danutia had spent the afternoon making telephone calls. "Betty's making another copy."

Danutia nodded and stood up, rolling her head from side to side. "Telephone ear. And not much to show for it, either. That report had better give us some new leads."

As they neared the counter, Betty broke off her lip-synching rendition of "Stand by Your Man" to hold up ink-blackened hands. "You'll have to wait a few minutes. Another paper jam. If we don't get some new equipment soon, I'm quitting."

"That's what you said last year." Berwick ushered Danutia into his office. "If it wasn't for Betty, I'd need two more staff."

Danutia sat down. "Do you pay her as much as two staff?" Berwick looked startled. "I didn't think so."

Berwick changed the subject. "Anything on the mysterious Luigi?"

"Luigi Russomano, lives in a newish condo in east Vancouver," Danutia said, massaging her stiff neck. "No one answers the phone, no one's been at home the two times an officer stopped by. Not a high priority item for the Vancouver police, I'm afraid." Nor for her, she'd thought while she waited for some bored officer to dig out the file. Her talk with Marlene Kelly seemed to offer a more promising line of investigation. Still, the sooner she could cross Luigi off her list the better. "I've asked them to check with the neighbours and try to trace his car."

"Skipped the country, most likely."

"Still think the killer was an outsider?"

"Why not?" Berwick settled himself on the edge of the desk, his long legs uncomfortably close. If she let her hand drop, or stretched her toes, they would touch. She tucked her feet under her chair.

"Joe was a good guy," Berwick was saying, "but even good guys get mixed up in bad things. Where'd he get all the money he was lashing out for his daughter's honeymoon? Zach Smith joked about Luigi's Mafia connection. Maybe it wasn't a joke."

"Now who's talking motive, and one there's absolutely no evidence for?"

A tap on the door saved her from Berwick's rejoinder. Muttering about the ink stains that had spread from her fingers to her dress, Betty handed them each a copy of the firearms report and vanished again.

"I glanced through it earlier," Berwick said. "Take a look at the conclusions, last page."

The first item confirmed that the fatal bullet had been fired from the Glock.

"'Number two,'" Danutia read out loud. "'The pattern of gunpowder residues shows the gun was held approximately two to four inches from the victim's face.'" She glanced at Berwick. "Not against the teeth. So Fidelman was right."

"Looked like contact to me," Berwick said, rattling his pages. "Anyway, it's the last item that's important. See that? The Glock had been fired only once."

"But that can't be right," Danutia said, hunting through the report. "What about the scalp wound? Krahn says that's a gunshot wound."

"So it's a gunshot wound," Berwick said. "But it wasn't made by the Glock."

Frowning, Danutia dropped the report onto Berwick's desk and crossed to the narrow window. Gravel crunched and dust drifted in from a cruiser backing and turning in the parking lot. Beyond the detachment the hill fell off sharply, treetops and rooftops giving way to water glistening and coiling. The boats in the harbour, the shops clustering about, the cars darting to and fro seemed like fireflies, flickering for a moment and then gone. Like her case against Bob Kelly.

A liar, yes, a swaggering, swindling bully, yes, a man driven to murder by drink and rage, yes, she could imagine that. Kelly walking up and cold-bloodedly blowing out the brains of a wounded man? Here her imagination faltered.

So much for Danutia Dranchuk, super sleuth. Where to now?

Aware of Berwick's cool grey eyes waiting for her to proceed, she groped for an answer. The snapshot. She hadn't intended to say anything, not yet, she hadn't worked it all out, but she found the words emerging, cautiously, like steps on a high wire.

"We've been assuming—I've been assuming," she corrected herself as Berwick's eyebrows shot up, "that the murderer fired both shots from the Glock, and an accomplice wrote the suicide note. Maybe it wasn't like that. I saw a photograph. In the Kellys' living room. Bob's holding a rifle. The first shot could have been fired from the rifle." She hesitated. The sister-bond of kitchen table coffee. Then she gathered her courage and plunged on. "Marlene could have finished the job. With the Glock."

Berwick unfolded his long legs, removed himself from the desk, and dropped into the chair behind it. Selecting a glistening black stone from the ceramic bowl, he rubbed it thoughtfully. "So now you think Marlene is involved."

Danutia rose and began pacing the room. "I haven't had much luck verifying their statements. There are lots of little discrepancies, and no one can really vouch for their whereabouts at the time of the murder. Doc Johnson says Kelly was in the pub both nights, but couldn't pin down the times, and neither could the bartender. All the smokers, it seems, wander into the garden or down to the wharf during the evening, and no one pays any attention—"

"But—"

Danutia ignored him. "Marlene's alibi is no better. She says she drove the pianist, Mrs. Coutt, home on Thursday night. Mrs. Coutt says she's such a nervous wreck she can barely remember what happened this morning, much less last week. Then she went on about what a dear Marlene is, always giving her a ride when her son leaves her stranded, so if Marlene said Thursday had been one of those nights, that must be right. The prosecuting attorney would have a field day with her."

Danutia stopped, wondering whether her last comment was a mistake. They both knew that what went on in a courtroom often had little to do with finding the truth.

"Here's how it could have happened," she said. "Kelly's being forced to work with this guy who publicly humiliated him. Thursday night he calls and calls. He can't reach the bastard—maybe the phone isn't on. If there's any trouble on Saturday, Ohara will blame him. He's had a few to drink, and something clicks—the Bo-Peep he saw before Bertolucci whipped it into the drawer. He isn't as stupid as Marlene thinks he is. He puts two and two together. The guy's been screwing his wife.

"So he drives out to the cabin. He isn't thinking of murder, but he's had run-ins with the dog before, and so he takes his rifle. Bertolucci isn't in the cabin. He has put his book down and strolled to the cove. Kelly follows him there, and then something happens—maybe they argue about Marlene. Kelly fires and Joe falls, dropping his flashlight. Mia attacks, ripping open Kelly's hand, and he kicks the dog viciously."

Danutia stopped beside the bookcase, waiting for Kelly's next move to take shape in her mind's eye. "Kelly panics. He runs where he always runs, to Marlene. She tells Bob she'll take care of it. Bertolucci has dragged himself back to the cabin. Maybe he's unconscious, maybe not. Bob has told her the Glock is in the truck. She fakes the suicide, writes the note, and tries to obliterate the trail of blood from the beach. But she misses the flashlight, and she misses a few salal leaves."

Berwick flipped the black stone like a coin, over and

over, light glinting off its jagged edges. Obsidian, that's what it was, Danutia recalled, Native peoples made arrowheads and other tools out of it. It reminded her of Bible stories of people being stoned, of that horrible movie she'd seen in high school. *The Lottery*.

Berwick caught the stone in midair. "We still don't know whether it was Bob's blood on those samples from Mia, and we won't have the lab results on those leaves for a day or two. Time enough to question them when there's more to go on."

Danutia stood her ground. "I think this is the time. Kelly still hasn't brought in the receipts for the supplies. I can at least establish whether the flashlight was one he bought for Bertolucci, and check out the discrepancies in their stories. And I want to ask about the rifle."

"Both of them?"

Danutia shook her head. "Bob first. He's the one who'll break."

Berwick opened his hand. The black obsidian lay flat in his palm for a second, then he tossed it back into the bowl. "You're in charge," he said.

⋅⊷⋅ ⋅⊷⋅

The cruiser set the dog to barking. As they approached the house, Kelly jerked open the door. His starched white shirt was unbuttoned. Seeing Danutia he slicked back his hair, the bit player from *Grease* again. When Danutia asked about the receipts, he claimed he'd looked for them with no luck. From upstairs Marlene shouted, "Did you try the drawer?" Reluctantly he led them into the kitchen.

While he rummaged through a cabinet drawer stuffed with papers, Danutia slipped into the living room and pocketed the photograph. Berwick wouldn't approve, but she was tired of Kelly wasting their time with evasions and denials.

Berwick skimmed the receipts Kelly thrust toward him. "There's an item here we'd like you to identify for us, if you don't mind coming down to the station for a few minutes."

"Now?" Kelly asked as they headed back into the hall. Berwick nodded.

Kelly turned to shout up the stairs. "Honey, that cute RCMP officer you talked to this morning wants me to help them with their inquiries. I guess you'll have to drink to that prick Smith without me."

"You bastard!" The sound of breaking glass followed them out the door.

The flashlight was the one he'd bought at Mouat's, Kelly was sure of that. It was the only one with a glow-in-the-dark case. He'd joked with the cashier about it.

Danutia took him through his previous statement, focusing on the gaps and discrepancies.

At first Kelly denied everything. But, as Danutia confronted him with the phone company records, his story began to change. Whether she was any closer to the truth was another question, as she was ruefully aware.

Yeah, he still had the truck and phone at 5:32 PM Wednesday. Maybe he'd called home while he was buying supplies, to see if Marlene needed anything.

So somebody called the cellphone number Thursday

night. Maybe Joe had answered just as Bob hung up. Had they thought about that? Had they even checked the location of the phone?

Danutia realized she hadn't. She changed the subject. "Do you own a rifle, Mr. Kelly?"

He sat slumped in his chair, his hands hooked in his pockets, as wilted in the building's stale heat as his starched white shirt. After a long silence he said, "Never been much of a hunter."

Danutia pulled the photograph from her pocket and passed it over. "That's you in camouflage gear, holding a rifle, isn't it?"

Berwick stiffened and his finger shot out and turned the Off button on the tape machine. If he was expecting Kelly to object, he was disappointed.

Kelly took a quick look and handed back the photo. "That was years ago. Marlene didn't like me having guns around after the boys were born, thought they'd blow each other's brains out." He shifted uneasily, as though fearful he had conjured up the dead man.

"May I see that?" Berwick asked.

Danutia passed him the photograph. "So what happened to the rifle?"

Kelly's answer came fast, too fast. "Sold it to a guy I met in a bar in Comox, don't know his name."

The more she questioned him, the more evasive his replies became. Berwick was sitting back in his chair, his expression noncommittal. She could imagine what he must be thinking. Give it up.

She was about to when Kelly reached for his cigarettes.

The scab. Of course. She leaned across the table. "Tell us again how you hurt your hand."

Kelly shoved his hand into his pocket.

"Mia turned up, you know," she said. "With blood on her. We're waiting for the lab report. If a single drop of that blood is yours, we'll want to know why."

"I didn't kill the bastard," Kelly said, his black eyes suddenly hard and fierce. "No matter what the fuckin' blood report says."

Danutia kept him another half hour and then let him go.

While Berwick shut up for the night, Danutia wandered around the outer office, idly reading posters while her mind went over the case. An announcement of an upcoming photography exhibition caught her attention.

"The videotape," she said. "What happened to Andy Johnson's videotape?"

"It's in the evidence cabinet," Berwick said.

"Let's have a look."

Berwick's keys were out and his hand on the light switch. "Now?"

"Now," she said.

# Chapter 15
Salt Spring: Wednesday evening, July 12

By the time the cab dropped him at the Dockside Inn, Arthur was feeling pleasantly mellow. After suffering through twenty minutes of *Peter's Political Puppet Theatre*, he'd escaped by faking a coughing fit. Yet he didn't dare turn up at the wake so early—Thea would have had his head (or so he'd thought before quickly suppressing the image of Zachary Smith's bloody grin). So he'd sipped an inferior single-malt Scotch for an hour or so in the Tidewater's bar, its glum emptiness a striking contrast to the noise and light now pouring out of the Dockside.

Arthur paused in the doorway to scan the crowd. Right in front of him, Rodney Coutt, Carol Smith, and Larry Weston huddled round a small table covered in sheets of paper. The missing script? But no, only columns of numbers, too small for him to read. He coughed and Carol looked up. The fine lines around her eyes and mouth had been carved deeper since Smith's death.

"Oh, it's you," she said. "Thanks for coming, but I'm afraid I won't have time to talk tonight after all. Rodney insists on going over the books." The two men glanced up and nodded, Weston with a weary smile, Coutt with a frown. The two masks of drama.

"Perfectly understandable," Arthur said. "By the way, I've decided to focus my review of the benefit performance on your husband's career as a director. I'll talk to a few people, collect a bit of information, if you don't mind."

"Why should I mind? Actually, I have lots of material on Zachary you're welcome to use, and I still want to talk to you about—" she made a vague gesture. "You know. I could meet you early tomorrow morning for breakfast. You're staying at the Tidewater, aren't you? The Blue Moon vegetarian cafe is just a block from there. Or do you have to have a steak first thing?"

Arthur, tempted to say that sleep was what he most fancied first thing in the day, agreed on the Blue Moon at nine o'clock.

Exhausted by the effort to be polite to a woman he didn't much like, he backed away, only to bump into someone at a table behind him. Mrs. Coutt, he realized when he turned to apologize. She laid down the musical score she had been reading, removed her silver-rimmed granny glasses, and gestured to the empty seat across from her. Perhaps Rodney had mentioned that he was looking for Zachary's script and she had brought it along.

"You're that reviewer, aren't you," she said. "But promise you won't write anything about my playing tonight. I told Carol it's been too long since I've had a go at 'Mac the Knife,' but she insisted it was Zach's favourite piece, and so I'll have to mangle it as best I can. But then you can't write about music, can you, so that's all right."

"I beg your pardon," said Arthur, thrown off balance by her comment. "What do you mean, I can't write about music?"

"I read your review of our Friday night performance in Victoria. At the beginning you mention *The Mikado* is an operetta, and then you go on about characterization and themes and the director's vision. Sullivan might as well have stayed home and composed his music for the cats next door."

To his surprise, Arthur found himself warming to her voice; her broad Midlands accent could have come straight off the floor of a Nottingham shoe factory. Arthur had the odd feeling that he knew her well already. Instead of defending himself, he asked, "What should I have said, then?"

"Remember when Nanki-Poo calls himself 'A wandering minstrel . . . A thing of shreds and patches'? Well, that's Sullivan's operetta music: bits and pieces of this and that—marches and madrigals and romantic arias and sentimental ballads. Most directors are happy if their musicians can cope with this variety and stay true to Sullivan's basically Victorian instrumentation."

"And Zachary Smith?"

"Zachary, as you must know, was never happy leaving things alone. He encouraged me to give some of the key songs a modern musical inflection, to add the note of conflict he wanted to establish. Sometimes the effect is subtle, as in Ko-Ko's song about his 'little list.' You may not have noticed, but the phrasing is pure Kurt Weill."

"You've reminded me of a question I wanted to ask. Smith said if I came back to the theatre late Monday night, he would give me a copy of his new version of the 'list' song"—not exactly true, but close enough. "Obviously he didn't have the chance. Rodney suggested you might have put the play script away for safe keeping. Do you think I could borrow it long enough to copy the new words?"

"I see my reputation as a tidier-up has spread even to the newspapers! But I don't know anything about the script, I'm afraid. Zachary's play script was his holy book, and woe betide anyone who touched it." Mrs. Coutt paused, and Arthur realized that she was gazing at him with concern. "It must have been very disturbing to find Zachary's body. And now I've given you a lecture on music. I was forgetting we'd only just met. I hope you're not offended."

"No, I'm not." Strangely enough, it was true.

"Will you take your seats, please? We're ready to begin." Doc Johnson's voice came from a makeshift stage set up in a corner, where there was a microphone on a stand and a small speaker balanced precariously on a stack of plastic crates.

Seeing Rodney get up from Carol Smith's table, Arthur excused himself to Mrs. Coutt and edged his way toward the bar.

When the room quieted, Doc Johnson went on. "Carol asked me to be master of ceremonies for this occasion. As most of you know, an Irish wake isn't an evening of long, mournful speeches but a celebration of the life of the person who has died. So we will have a few words from Zach's immediate family and from his oldest friend, Larry Weston, and then we will get on with the wake, which is 'on the house.' So, let me call first upon Lavender."

Lavender was sitting toward the back of the room, at a table with Marlene and Sandra. She pushed back her chair and hurried to the stage, as though she might lose her nerve if she hesitated any longer. She stood gripping the microphone in silence for a moment, her breasts rising and falling, her long white skirt and blouse with sleeves like wings shimmering in the spotlight. An angel, Arthur thought, or a butterfly—

Her first words were barely a whisper. "My father was a brilliant man." She paused as if waiting for someone to contradict her, but the crowded room was silent, attentive. "Dad was a Gemini, and Geminis have to innovate or die. But they're caring people too. Geminis make great fathers. There was nothing Zach wouldn't do for Hendrix and me, nothing . . ."

Lavender gulped and her shoulders shook. Arthur was tempted to rush up to the stage and put his arms around her. Then she spoke again, her tone sharper.

"Lots of people don't understand Geminis, and so there's hostility." She paused, letting her gaze rest on each table of guests in turn. "You all think my dad's death was an accident. You should ask my stepmother what she knows about this so-called accident, ask her where she was when it happened. She looks so calm, but . . . but . . . just ask her, that's all . . . ." Her voice breaking, Lavender fled the stage and hurried toward the door.

Startled voices filled the room. Scattered phrases from Doc Johnson—"Let's please stay calm . . . let's respect the occasion . . ."—rang in Arthur's ears as he slid from his bar stool and followed Lavender into the night.

He caught up to her beside a battered Karmann Ghia, her head bowed as she hunted through her purse. In Arthur's eyes she had never looked more vulnerable or more beautiful. The moon made her thin white garments glow and tipped her hair with silver.

"Lavender," he said.

Her eyes remained fixed on her purse but her hand paused, waiting.

Arthur fumbled to find the right words. "About your father. I don't know if he was murdered, but I don't think his death was an accident."

Lavender straightened up angrily. "Are you saying my father committed suicide?"

Suicide? Oddly, he'd never considered that possibility, even after Thea mentioned it in Ruckle Park. But in the presence of a witness, who then took away the script? That didn't make sense.

"No."

The word hung in the silence between them while Lavender looked him over as though he was a Sunday roast at the butcher's. "What's your sign?"

"My sign?" Arthur was startled by the question. Then he remembered her reference to Geminis. "You mean my birth sign? My birthday's the middle of October. That's . . .that's Libra, isn't it?"

She didn't reply, and Arthur panicked. Was he born in the wrong month? Would she leave now? Had he blown it? Finally she said, her voice softer and less distant, "An air sign. Like my dad. I should have known." She hesitated. "Can we walk a bit?"

They strolled in silence downhill, toward the ferry dock. The water was silver all the way to Vancouver Island, except for a dark border below the opposite shore.

Moonlight shone, too, on Lavender, creating patches of shadow under her breasts. In the silence, Arthur was acutely aware of the body beneath the shimmering blouse and rippling skirt. Then she spoke again. "Tell me what happened on Monday night."

Arthur repeated the story he'd told the RCMP and Thea. He tried to hurry over the grisly details, but still he felt Lavender shudder beside him.

"You'd have to be stupid to kill yourself like that, and Dad isn't stupid—wasn't, I mean." Lavender choked over the verb. "The police say the safety peg must have been loose and fallen out. Dad would never have put his head in that machine without checking the safety peg. I know that. Hendrix would know it too if his brain was clear enough."

"It's hard to see how that peg could have been removed without your dad noticing," Arthur said. "Still, someone must have been standing close enough to leave those indentations in the blood, and someone must have taken the script."

"It has to be Carol," Lavender insisted. "She's a Capricorn, and Capricorns are ruthless. She could have waited until he put his head under the blade and then pretended to get his ponytail out of the way, or something like that, so she could take out the safety peg. Poor Dad. He would never believe me when I said she was evil."

Arthur struggled to separate what was plausible in this explanation from Lavender's animosity toward her stepmother. "If Carol killed your father, why would she take the script? Why would anyone take the script, for that matter."

They stopped short of the dock, where a lone foot passenger waited as the ferry lights drew closer. "It must have been Dad's satire. Sandra was telling me tonight how angry she'd been about a line in Dad's new version of the list song. He must have put in something really awful about Carol. And he'd never take it out. She must have gone back, and they argued, and that was the end for Dad."

Arthur struggled to remember the scene around the piano during Smith's song Monday night. Sandra had argued with Hendrix and stalked out, no question about that. And Lavender hadn't been there, because he'd looked. But Carol? He couldn't remember. Of course, even if she wasn't there, she might well have heard or seen Zach's words some other time.

"I can imagine your father and Carol arguing," he said cautiously. "But it's hard to imagine that she would kill him over a bit of satire."

"You don't know Carol. She as good as killed my mom, you know. Dad started giving her Mom's roles, and then having an affair with her, and the next thing we knew Mom was dead. Now Dad's giving Carol's roles to Sandra and she could see the handwriting on the wall. She killed him before he could dump her." Lavender's voice became warm, seductive, southern—Blanche Dubois in the Pacific Northwest. "I need a strong man to stand by me. A man who will write the truth and not be afraid. Can you help me?"

The speech was corny, and the accent was exaggerated to the point of parody, but Arthur's body responded. His mind, though, knew very well what his colleagues on the crime beat—not to mention the newspaper's lawyers—would think.

"Lavender," he sighed and started again. "I don't think my editors would publish anything without proof. But I really do want to help."

Lavender touched him on the forearm. "Libras are such sensitive people. Will you come with me to the police? If you say Dad was murdered, maybe they'll take me more seriously."

"Of course I'll come," Arthur said, happy to think that he was becoming important to her. "I can't say anything about Carol, you understand," he cautioned. "Nothing I saw points to anyone specific."

Her fingers, warm and slight, squeezed his hand. "You don't have to say anything about Carol. Hendrix and I are the only ones who know what she's really like, and he's too out of it to be any use."

"What's wrong with Hendrix?"

The ferry was nearing the dock. Lavender shrugged and released his hand. "I have to go. I'll pick you up on my way to the police station in the morning, say around eleven. You won't change your mind, will you?"

Arthur assured her he'd be waiting. Before he could screw up the courage to risk an embrace, Lavender set off up the hill. He hurried after her, his mind full of the next day's possibilities. When she said goodnight, she held his fingers for a moment through the car's open window.

As he stood watching the Karmann Ghia's tail lights recede, a voice spoke from the darkness. "What were you doing with my pretty sister, Mr. Newspaper Man?"

"Just talking." Arthur waited while Hendrix Smith levered himself out of his ancient MG.

"So what did you talk about, you and my pretty sister, my very pretty sister?" Hendrix's breath smelled strongly of beer.

"Mainly about your father. Why don't we go and sit inside?"

Hendrix swayed and then recovered. "Don't want to go in, hear everyone talking about my old man." He gestured toward the bench outside the garden wall. "Over there. Doesn't anyone else have a father? How 'bout you? You got a father? You get along?"

As he sat down, Arthur thought about the stern man who was already old and ill when he was a child. "I didn't have much to do with him."

"Maybe better that way. Better than him trying to make sure you followed in his footsteps. Good King Wencel—Wen-ces-las' footsteps. Page out of someone else's book. You know what I mean?"

"No."

"I thought reporters were smart people. You're a reporter, aren't you? Go on, ask me reporter questions. Ask me questions."

Hendrix was so seriously slurring his words that Arthur suspected questions would be futile. But here was his second suspect, inviting him to ask. "Hendrix, at the hospital the other night you kept saying, 'If only I'd gone back like Dad wanted.' You should have been there at eleven, long before I arrived. Where were you?"

To Arthur's surprise, Hendrix seemed to take his

question seriously. He half-closed his eyes, as though to bring back that evening. "Dad's van isn't working. So we take my car to town. After rehearsal he has errands . . . so he borrows my car and drops me off . . . near the White Whale. Supposed to meet him later."

"So you were at the White Whale on Monday night? With friends?"

"No, went . . . somewhere. Then walk to theatre. Late. Too late. Lights on, door open. Saw you and thought you'd died. But it was him, not you." Hendrix shot him a sharp look from under lowered eyebrows. "What about you? What did you see to report, Mr. Reporter?"

Suddenly Arthur had the odd feeling that he was the one being investigated. Was Hendrix not as drunk as he seemed? "Not much," he replied. "You heard what I told that constable. But maybe you can help me with the piece I'm writing on your dad. I wanted to use some of his original material for *The Mikado*, but no one seems to know what's happened to his play script. Do you have any idea?"

As he waited for an answer, his nerves taut, Arthur heard what sounded like a muffled sneeze from the other side of the garden wall. A smoker in the garden below, or someone on the stairs? Arthur strained to hear, but Hendrix was snapping his fingers and muttering. Then he broke off his muttering and stood up. "Screw the script," he said, and disappeared down the path and into the pub.

It took a moment for Arthur to register that Hendrix had been muttering: "I've got a little list, I've got a little list," over and over. Then a door clicked shut on the other side of the wall. Someone had been eavesdropping, he was sure of it. But who?

Arthur made his way inside and, avoiding the group gathering around Hendrix, headed for Larry Weston at the bar.

Weston clapped him on the shoulder. "You skipped out on my speech, but let me get you a beer anyway." Before Arthur could apologize, he went on. "Don't worry about it. After Lavender's fireworks, the whole thing was a shambles. Hendrix didn't show, Carol tried to carry on as though nothing had happened and broke down after two sentences, and I ditched my speech and proposed a toast to Zach. Sometimes drink is the better part of valour." He lifted his glass and swallowed a long draught.

"You had worked with him a long time—"

Weston emptied his glass and set it precisely in the middle of its mat. "Not tonight, Arthur. Ask me about Zach's career some other time and I'll be happy to tell you, but not tonight."

There it was again, the note of sadness beneath the genial exterior. Arthur mentally kicked himself for being so obtuse. He should have known he wouldn't get far with either his investigation or his review tonight, of all nights. He should find Thea and leave.

Before Arthur could make his escape, Weston said in a low voice, "It's none of my business, but there's something I think you ought to know."

Arthur leaned forward to catch the words over the surrounding babble.

"I noticed your face when you followed Lavender

outside," Weston continued. "More like Romeo than a reporter, if I'm not mistaken."

"What's that got to do . . ." stuttered Arthur.

"With me? Just that it's hard to tell a man who's fallen for an attractive young woman that she's a bit crazy."

"What do you mean, crazy? I'm not sure I want . . ."

Arthur felt Weston's large hand on his forearm, a gentle gesture.

"All I'm saying is that Lavender gets obsessions. Let me give you an example. About a year ago, our Company lost an arts grant that we'd been pretty sure we were going to get. Lavender became convinced that someone in authority hated her and her father and had joined up with Carol to put lead in their water supply. Carol was drinking the same water, but that didn't seem to get through to her. Anyway, the family lived on bottled water for months. Lavender's mother was manic-depressive, and Zach always worried that Lavender had inherited her mother's bad genes. I'm not telling you this to put you off—when she's not obsessed, Lavender's a radiant, sensitive young woman. . . ."

"So why are you telling me?" Arthur tapped his fingers impatiently on the table. "It's true; I like Lavender. And she seems to have no one who will listen to her. What's so wrong with being on her side?"

Weston leaned forward. "Zach's opera company was his dream, and I want the dream to live on. It's the best thing I can do for his memory. Lavender's accusations are ridiculous, and by next week she may well forget she ever made them. What worries me is that a rumour that Zach was murdered will get about, and that you will seem to be supporting it."

"Me?"

"Don't underestimate the power of the press, Arthur. This province is full of artists and ex-hippies, but the people who hand out the money are as conservative as you'll find anywhere. Any breath of scandal and you're out. No grants. No forgiving of rental fees. No sponsorships. Nada. So if a rumour like this spreads, Vesuvius Light Opera is in deep trouble." Weston paused and shrugged, as if to say he'd done his best. "I'm sure you're too smart to take what Lavender says at face value, Arthur. But I wanted to talk to you, just in case."

Before Arthur could reply, Thea poked her head around the corner. "There you are. I thought I saw you come in, and then you seemed to disappear. I'll just say goodbye to the Johnsons and then I'll be ready to go." She gestured toward the bar, where Doc Johnson was pouring drinks for a wispy-haired elderly man and a solidly built woman next to him—presumably his wife.

"Thanks, Thea. I'll meet you by your car." Taking his leave of Weston, Arthur headed toward the parking lot, his emotions in turmoil.

What should he do? Arthur stood alone by Thea's Honda, addressing his question to the night. But the moon sailed on in the sky, and the night offered him no answers.

# Chapter 16

"It's about time," Berwick said as Danutia entered the detachment the next morning. After a quick word to the duty constable, he motioned her back out the door. "Neighbour of mine runs a production studio. I've asked the Johnsons to meet us there. Bigger screen, sharper lens, the filmmaker on hand—it's our best chance."

"Score one for knowing people in the community." Danutia was surprised by Berwick's initiative. They'd run through the videotape three times last night without spotting anything out of the ordinary at the cove or around the clearing. A confused jumble of images inside the cabin, then a patch of wall or floor until the film ran out. The end, she had assumed.

"Anything else new?" she asked as she belted herself into the cruiser.

"Preliminary on the blood work. Or 's-e-r-i-o-l-g-y,'" he grumbled, tossing the papers he had been carrying into her lap. "Why can't people take the time to run a simple spell check?"

Danutia flipped to the conclusions. "Traces of alcohol on the clothes, but none in the bloodstream. The Jamieson's bottle must have been a plant. As for the hair samples from Mia—there's human blood mixed in, all right, some of it Bertolucci's, some not yet identified." Frowning, she glanced at Berwick. "There's no mention of Kelly's Band-Aid."

Berwick had turned onto a winding narrow road where houses large and small nestled among fir and cedar trees. He took the curves with practised ease, his hands easy on the wheel, his eyes straight ahead. "The fax said more to follow."

Disappointed not to have the matter settled, Danutia returned to the report. The next item cheered her up. "I knew it! The blood on the salal matches Bertolucci's, and the splatters show he was moving up the trail from the cove, toward the cabin. More splatters on the charred vegetation from the fire pit. He must have lost a lot of blood."

"Scalp wounds can be nasty." Berwick fingered a faint scar above his right eyebrow. "A guy caught me with his ring in a back alley after a barroom scuffle. Bled so much he ran away. I passed out and would have frozen to death if a cop hadn't found me." He chuckled. "That's when I decided to change sides."

There it was again, muted by thirty years in uniform, the restless energy she saw in young guys on both sides of the bars. Cops and criminals as flip sides of the same coin. Larocque. Bob Kelly, tense as a coiled spring. Maybe that's what attracted Marlene.

And what about me? Danutia wondered, conscious of Berwick's lanky form beside her, her breasts tingling as the sun's heat penetrated the windshield. She rolled down her window, glimpsing a flash of water as they sped past a hidden lake.

⋅◦⋅ ⋅◦⋅

Loco Productions occupied the lower floor of a split-level

house overlooking Cusheon Lake. Except for the grey in his long hair and beard, the producer, Marc Desmarais, reminded Danutia of the aspiring folksingers who used to flock around Alyne. While the two men discussed technical details, Danutia took in her surroundings.

An angled spotlight at the far end of the cavernous room revealed cabaret-style tables and a mini-stage where a cardboard skeleton clutched a microphone.

"That's Mabel," Marc said. "Make yourselves comfortable. She won't mind." He flicked a switch and a screen lit up behind the stage. Then a buzzer sounded and he headed back up the stairs, which were outlined in tiny lights like a runway.

Danutia thought about the endless nights she'd spent in front of her ancient 17-inch television. "Imagine watching *South Pacific* on a screen like that."

"I don't go in for musicals," Berwick said. "How about *Casablanca*?"

"I would have pegged you for a *Silence of the Lambs* type."

"Too much like work," he said, and for once Danutia agreed.

Shapes and voices descended the stairs. Danutia and Berwick rose to greet the Johnsons, and Marc settled them at an adjoining table.

"Mr. Demarais will run the tape in slow motion," Berwick said to Andy. "He'll pause every few seconds. Tell us what you see, and anything you remember that isn't in the film." He waved to Marc, seated at an elevated console behind them.

The lights dimmed. An image of lapping water filled the screen. Andy's voice from the darkness was thin as a ghost's.

Stuart Channel, the beach, the trail to the cabin with the giant Douglas firs dwarfing human presence, the arbutus trees ringing the clearing. He hadn't filmed the cabin yet; instead he'd taken the narrow path to the cove where Danutia had found the flashlight. And there it was, its rocky pools opening into the broad expanse of the channel.

"A couple of fishing boats were out," Andy was saying, "but I didn't film them. Too commercial. Seagulls circling overhead, like *Jonathan Livingston Seagull*—ever read that? Then the zoom shot in to the gull on the water—"

"That isn't a gull," Martha broke in. "It's a float."

"Nobody moors there," Andy snapped. "It's a gull, I tell you."

Danutia heard the scratch of Berwick's pen. "We'll come back to that," he said.

"Now we're heading back up the path. Those are salal and Oregon grape berries—they're really big this year. There's the cabin—" Andy faltered and fell silent. Finally he said, "It's my heart. I could have another attack."

Marc stopped the film and the lights came up. Berwick helped Andy to his feet. "I'll take you upstairs." To Martha, who was struggling into her windbreaker, he said, "I'll wait with him. You were at the cabin. I'd like you to watch the rest of the videotape. It's only a couple of minutes."

As Andy shuffled out of earshot, Martha whispered fiercely to Danutia, "You'll be the death of him yet."

"I hope not, Mrs. Johnson." She would have added, "I'm just doing my job," but that would comfort neither of them.

The lights went off and the film resumed. A thin sliver of blue poked out from behind the cabin.

"That must be Bob Kelly's truck," Martha said. "People wonder where he got the money for that new house. Rumour is he gets kickbacks from Ohara's contractors."

Danutia pricked up her ears. She had tried to check Marlene's story about an interest-free loan, only to discover that Ohara was again out of town. If the rumours were true, and Bertolucci had found evidence when he cleaned out the truck—

An artsy shot of the door frame, then cascading images of rough-hewn logs, the table, the floor as Andy stumbled over the body, then nothing. The lights came up.

"That black thing at the end," Martha said, clasping the front of her windbreaker. "It must have been the phone."

"That's as far as we got yesterday. You called 911. What did you notice while you waited for the ambulance?" Danutia asked, hoping to hear about a pack of Craven A's, flakes of red nail polish. Knowing she wouldn't be that lucky.

"Nothing," the potter said, her face sagging. "I had to keep my eyes closed to hold on. The smell. The dead man lying there. Andy bleeding and his pulse racing. It was like I sat there pouring my life into him, and if I moved, he'd die."

Danutia gave her a quick hug. "It must have been very

hard for you." While Martha laboured up the stairs, she thanked Marc and retrieved the video. Then she joined Berwick and the Johnsons at the top of the stairs. Martha's arm was linked through Andy's, and she was patting his hand.

"Andy told me yesterday about putting sand in the gas tank," she said. "Guess I should thank you for not charging him."

"He promised not to do it again," Berwick said. "You're sure that was a float off the cove?"

"No doubt about it," Martha said, and this time Andy didn't argue. "You saw how it bobbed up and down, straight and flat. Birds curve into the waves."

⋯ ⋯

"That float opens up a new possibility," Berwick mused when they were belted into the cruiser. "The first shot could have been fired from a boat."

"By a deranged kayaker?"

"I'm serious," Berwick said. "Listen. A float usually means one of two things: a mooring for a boat that's too big to beach, or a marker for crab pots or fishing nets. Most houses on the waterfront would have boat moorings, but no one lives on that stretch of coastline by the cabin. A float there is likely a marker, say for crab pots: Joe comes across somebody tampering with them, and the guy takes a potshot at him."

"And then this total stranger parks his boat somewhere, finds his way to the cabin, kills Bertolucci, and writes a suicide note referring to intimate details of his life."

"You're right," Berwick responded so quickly Danutia checked to see whether he was being ironic. She thought not; though his sunglasses hid his expression, his thumbs worried the steering wheel as though the answer he sought lay deep inside. "If you were merely handling someone else's lines," he went on, slowly at first, "you'd say your tiller got fouled up in the nets, or something like that. But if you were smuggling—"

"Smuggling? On Salt Spring?"

"Don't scoff. The Gulf Islands have a long history of it. There's a lot of money to be made bringing in cigarettes, booze, anything that's cheaper in the US. Or shipping out mary-jane. BC exports a quality product."

"The Drug Squad guy I flew over with says the pot growers have moved to the less populated islands."

"Doesn't have to be a big operation," Berwick said. "All you need is a few seeds, a greenhouse or an old barn, a generator—"

"Shouldn't be too many of those around," Danutia said.

"Are you kidding? The power goes out so often around here that a lot of people have a backup generator."

"Maybe that's where the money for the Kellys' new house came from. Martha mentioned rumours that he's getting kickbacks from Ohara's suppliers, but smuggling seems more his style. Travelling all over the islands like he does, he could run half a dozen grow-ops and ship the stuff from here."

"Forget about Kelly," Berwick said. "He was seen at the Dockside 'til around eleven."

"It could have been later. Bertolucci had his flash-light."

Berwick braked as an RV the size of an 18-wheeler lumbered onto the road in front of him, then followed the vacationing Californians at a sedate speed. "You've been assuming that Bertolucci was an innocent victim. I knew and respected the man, and I hope he wasn't involved in anything illegal. But think of the financial pressure he was under with Antonia's wedding. A two-week kayak trip, several nights at the Watermill, a week's sailing on a rented boat, who knows what else—where would the money come from? Not tending bar at the Dockside, I can tell you that. And not from a few days' work for Ohara. As soon as I read the suicide note, I figured he'd gotten himself into a financial mess and couldn't see a way out. When the focus shifted to murder, I lost touch with that gut reaction. But he could have accepted a job that was totally out of character because it would make a perfect cover."

"So you're suggesting Bertolucci was involved in smuggling, with a partner who knew him well enough to write the note."

"It's a possibility we have to investigate, at any rate."

"Where do we start?"

"We can eliminate Doc Johnson. He will scarcely get on a ferry, much less anything smaller. And Luigi, our Vancouver dark horse, is in the clear—the Vancouver police have confirmed that he left on a six-week trip to Italy long before the murder. None of the cast is likely to have had a boat out Thursday night—they rehearsed late and left early the next morning. But a couple might be able to give us a lead on that float. Emile Gaboune, the stage manager, is a mechanic for Pacific Marine, and Larry Weston runs fishing charters."

"I'll set up interviews," Danutia said, making a mental note to pin down the cast members' comings and goings while she was at it. Berwick might be right to eliminate them; he might also be prejudiced because they were people he knew.

Dust rose around them as the cruiser pulled into the gravel parking lot.

"Just to show I'm not totally pigheaded," Berwick said, "I'll check out those rumours about kickbacks. After I've talked to Lavender Smith. She accused her stepmother of murder at the wake last night. Now she probably wants me to lay charges."

"Does she have any evidence?"

"Last time she was in, she claimed someone was poisoning their well water. Time before that, she accused a boy up the road of putting a curse on her. I suspect her dad's death has unhinged her again."

"Look, I'm here because you asked Sergeant Lewis for help on the Bertolucci case, and Smith's death is none of my business. But I don't like it. Are you sure it was an accident?"

Berwick's hands tightened on the wheel. "I've been over that guillotine half a dozen times. There's no way someone could have tampered with the safety mechanism without Smith noticing. Dr. Moorhouse has been a community coroner for years. He examined the body and found no signs of foul play. So unless I get autopsy results that suggest otherwise, it's an accidental death."

Danutia stirred uneasily. He had been equally sure that Bertolucci had committed suicide.

⋅⋆⋅ ⋅⋆⋅

Emile Gaboune readily agreed to talk to Danutia during an early lunch break. Leaving behind the grease and clatter of Pacific Marine, the last in a line of rental and repair businesses huddled around the inner harbour, they made their way to the sun-warmed rocks by the water's edge.

Just beyond lay the White Whale, a handful of sailboats and motor cruisers bobbing alongside its private dock.

"Aren't you hot in those overalls?" Danutia asked as she readied the tape player.

"Ah, but feel the breeze," Emile said, raising a hand. "In Morocco, the old ones would bundle themselves up against the cold on a day like this."

To put Emile at ease, Danutia asked first about his friendship with Joe Bertolucci.

"Yes, Joe was my friend," Emile said in his warm, soft voice with its hint of a French accent. "Zachary—Zachary Smith—was my friend too, but not like Joe. Zachary and I work well together because I am the hammer in Zach's hand. I can make out of wood and paper and a bit of this and a bit of that what he sees in his mind's eye." He gazed for a moment at his hands, working the fingers as though he were handling tools. "It is not always pleasant to be a hammer," he said. "When the job

211

is finished, the hammer is tossed into the tool box until it is needed again."

Opening his lunchbox, Emile unwrapped a Subway sandwich loaded with deli meats and vegetables and chewed reflectively for a moment. His legs were crossed tailor fashion, as though he sat on feather cushions instead of rough sandstone. When he spoke again, his voice was tinged with sadness. "For Joe I am not a hammer. I am Columbus, I am Cortez, I am Vespucci. No, I exaggerate. But for Joe the Mediterranean was everything, and its waters were my home. And I speak a little Italian. I soak up languages like a—what is the English expression?"

"Sponge," Danutia said.

"That's it, like a sponge. Except that if you wring me, you don't get wet." The black eyes gazing at her were like Sharma's, revealing nothing. "You understand my meaning?"

Danutia nodded.

"Knowing this," Emile said, "Joe told me his story. His father was from a poor Sicilian fishing village. He brought his family to Canada after the war, when Joe was a small boy. The father went to work for one of the big canneries, thinking someday he would save enough money to return to Sicily and buy his own boat. In the meantime he fed Joe on the glories of the Mediterranean. So of course Joe wanted to be a fisherman like his father."

Emile took a small, neat bite from his sandwich, catching the dripping sauce with his tongue. In the harbour fishing charters came and went, their wake ruffling the water for three kayaks heading toward the open sea.

"His father would not allow it. 'Have I left behind everything I loved so that all your life you could be poor like me?' he said many times. Or so Joe told me. Like a good son Joe went to university, and there he discovered the Greek myths and the Roman myths—Ulysses, Aeneas, Icarus—all those tales of fathers and sons, and the fates that bind them together and tear them apart. As his son Gino was torn away from him, and now he is forever lost to Gino."

Danutia, sipping her lukewarm coffee, tried to call up an image of the young boy she'd seen with Antonia at the benefit. She remembered only the dazed look, as though he'd had the wind knocked out of him and hadn't recovered. Perhaps he never would.

Emile leaned forward, his voice dropping even lower as though he were imparting a secret. "Still, it is not Gino I worry about. He has lost only one father."

"What do you mean?"

"It is Hendrix Smith who worries me. First Joe, then Zachary. Joe was like a second father to Hendrix, you know. Or maybe you didn't. It was always Uncle Joe this and Uncle Joe that."

Emile popped the last of his sandwich into his mouth and chewed rapidly. "Zachary was a little bit jealous, I would say."

Danutia picked a stray bit of lettuce off the rock and tossed it toward a sea gull circling hungrily. "So would you say this was a source of conflict between the two men?"

Emile chuckled softly. "No, no, you are trying to trap

213

me. It was nothing like that. You see, Hendrix is like Zachary as a young man, even more talented but unfortunately less ambitious. Zachary wanted Hendrix to become the success he never was. Joe seemed to understand that what Zachary wanted for his son was not what his son wanted."

"Did Hendrix share Bertolucci's interest in sailing?" Danutia asked, trying to steer the conversation toward the mysterious float.

"I don't know. Joe did not talk to me about Hendrix. Only once he said something about Hendrix having a good head for business. But there," Emile said, "you are not interested in the dreams of young men. I watch the police shows, you know. When I saw Joe last, who would want to kill him, what I was doing the night he died—that is what you want to know. I am right, yes?"

Danutia nodded. "Start with when you saw him last."

"The Bloomsday party, June 16—Ah, you know about the unruly Mr. Kelly, I see. That night I asked Joe to help me check out a troublesome engine—the kind that hums like bees in the shop and then coughs and dies on the water. But it was not his fate." Emile's workboots scraped against the rock as he changed the cross of his legs. "The next morning Joe phoned. 'I'm disappearing into the wilderness for forty days,' he said. I remember the words because I did not understand."

"Jesus in the wilderness, fasting and praying and resisting the temptations of the Devil," Danutia said.

"So he explained to me. He said not to try to get in touch, he needed to be alone. Foolishly, I did as he asked."

"As far as we know," Danutia said, "Bertolucci was last seen alive on Wednesday evening. His body was found Saturday morning. We'd like to establish where all the members of the Vesuvius Company were during that period."

"Ah, the alibis," Emile said, his face lighting up. "I can assure you we were all much too busy to commit murder. And who among us would murder Joe? We were his friends. Still, you must ask."

His account of Wednesday night's rehearsal agreed with Marlene's.

"Thursday night was the same, at least at the beginning," Emile said. "About halfway through the first act Hendrix started missing cues. Zachary decided Kenneth Taylor, the understudy, should rehearse Nanki-Poo, so we took a break."

A tug approached, towing a monstrous yacht toward Pacific Marine. From the patio of the White Whale came whoops of laughter. "What's the matter, George?" someone called. "Run out of gas again?"

"Idiots." Emile's boyish face twisted in a scowl. "Trouble at sea is never an occasion for laughter. Where was I? Ah yes. The break. Everyone wanders in and out during breaks and when they're not required, to have a cigarette or make a phone call."

Danutia still hadn't determined where the last call to Bertolucci had originated. On a hunch she asked, "Is there a pay phone at the school? I don't remember seeing one when I was there for the benefit."

"It's in a corner near the dressing rooms," Emile said.

Danutia flipped through her notebook until she found her notes on the call. "You wouldn't know the number, would you?"

"But of course."

Danutia's excitement mounted as Emile rattled off the digits on the page before her. "Do you remember seeing anyone make a call that evening?"

"I didn't hear anything." Emile's left hand swept the air in a gesture of denial; the right held out a cookie, its chocolate coating melting in the heat. "Digestive biscuit?"

Danutia shook her head. "But you saw someone."

Polishing off the cookie in two quick bites, Emile bundled bits of garbage into his Subway wrapper and scrambled to his feet. "You must excuse me. My boss will fire me for chattering away when I should be working."

Danutia waited until his eyes met hers. "You honour the living by keeping their secrets," she said. "But do you honour the man who was murdered, the man who was your friend?"

Sinking back onto the rock, Emile crushed the sandwich wrapper until it was no bigger than his palm. Finally he said, "It was our Peep-Bo. Marlene Kelly."

No matter how often Berwick told her to forget about the Kellys, their names kept popping up, like the toy moles you whack with a stick at the fair. "Go on."

"She was standing there swaying a bit in her white pinafore, with her hand cupped around the mouthpiece, as though she didn't want anyone to hear."

"What time was that?" According to her notes, the incoming call was connected at 9:27 PM.

"Nine-thirty or so. We were about to run through the last act."

Emile must have seen something in her expression, for he hurried on. "Just because Marlene was talking to Joe—" He stopped abruptly. In the distance, crows cawed. A murder of crows.

"What made you think she was talking to Bertolucci?"

"She said, '*Ciao*,' and hung up, that's all."

"You knew they were lovers."

The muscles around Emile's eyes and mouth tightened. He scooped up a handful of small rocks and hurled them in the water one by one in short, angry bursts. When the last rock sank beneath the waves he said, "Marlene often talks to me when she is troubled in her mind."

"What time did she leave?"

"About ten-thirty, when the rehearsal ended." A faint smile crossed his face. "And now I remember. The alibi. I heard Ivy Coutt asking Marlene for a ride home."

"Did you see them drive off together?"

"No, but—"

"Never mind," Danutia said. "Did everyone leave then?"

"Not everyone." A wry smile played about his thin lips. "Zachary decided the backdrops were too conventional. 'No more cherry blossoms', he said. 'Let's give them the real goods about the imperialist western world.' So he sent Sandra Ohara to get some books on Japanese history while Lavender and I painted out the old sets and Zachary started the new ones. You were at the benefit performance. Did you notice that the tree trunks were twisted skeletons? And the clouds were atomic explosions? No? I told Zachary no one would notice."

"How long was Sandra gone?"

"Too long for Zachary—he was angry when she returned. Still, it couldn't have been long. She makes her little convertible fly."

Remembering the winding road to Welbury Bay, Danutia wondered that anyone could have driven there and back in so short a time, and at night. Sandra would know the road, that's true. Still there was something elusive about Ohara's daughter. The twitch in her father's eye. His concern over his business secrets becoming known. His emphatic denial that he'd told his daughter about hiring Bertolucci.

With Sandra's help, Emile went on to say, they had finished the sets about one in the morning. "Lavender went home with Sandra and Zachary threw a sleeping bag down on the stage. I offered to make a bed for him at my place, but he refused and I didn't insist. We had to load the truck by quarter to six to make the 6:20 AM ferry. By that time I could have killed Zachary with great pleasure. In the end he did it himself, like everything else. The Greeks call it 'hubris'—the pride that makes you insist on having everything your own way. Lavender is quite wrong to think differently, you know. Zachary was often quite careless, and without his hammer—"

"Why weren't you there that evening?" Danutia asked, knowing she shouldn't. Although she had told Berwick it was none of her business, she had a niggling feeling

Smith's death and his friend's were intertwined, as their lives had been.

Emile shrugged, his shoulders touching his ears and his eyebrows disappearing under a fringe of dark hair. "There wasn't anything to do. We had tested everything—the guillotine was working perfectly, the lighting was set. What I think is that Zachary wanted an excuse to be alone before the benefit performance, to say his own farewell to Joe."

"Did Bertolucci act with the company after he came here?"

"No, Zachary asked him many times, but always he refused. 'I have had enough of illusions,' he would say. But I think too he did not wish to be a puppet pulled by Zachary's strings."

Danutia glimpsed the two men caught in a shadowy dance, advancing and retreating. "Would you say Smith was deeply affected by Bertolucci's death?"

"We all were. Marlene tried to pretend Joe was no more than a casual friend, but her eyes—she had the blank stare of someone who's been tortured. Zachary shouted and swore at everyone. Without his anger the last two performances in Victoria would have been impossible." Again that rise and fall of shoulders. "We should have cancelled them both. And the benefit."

He picked up his lunch box. "If you ask me who would want to kill Zachary, I could give you half a dozen names, including my own. Being angry at Zachary was part of the excitement of working with him. But Joe? No one. I never saw bad feelings between him and anybody."

You're forgetting Bob Kelly, Danutia thought. Aloud she said, "Someone noticed a float off the cove about the time Bertolucci died. Do you have any idea what it might have been doing there?"

"I don't play around with hooks and lines and nets and traps," he said. "For that you should ask Larry Weston. If he isn't at home, he's probably out on the *Golden Reel*. The wharfinger's office could tell you."

Emile gestured across the harbour. "It's on the other side of Mouat Square."

Danutia scribbled her cellphone number on the back of her card. "If you think of anything else, call me."

As she watched Emile pick his way back over the rocks, Danutia thought about the ironies of fate. Joe Bertolucci, whom everyone liked, had been murdered and his death made to look like suicide. Zachary Smith, who had antagonized many, had accidentally killed himself. Or so it seemed.

Actors. Who better to play at death?

# Chapter 17
Salt Spring: Thursday, July 13

Free at last from his interminable breakfast meeting with Carol Smith, Arthur hurried back to the Tidewater, excited at the prospect of seeing Lavender. To his shock, he found his door unlocked and his room in chaos. The wardrobe was open, its drawers pulled out, his extra socks and underwear on the floor, papers shoved off the desk, the mattress half off the bed. Putting down his briefcase and laptop, he stepped into the bathroom. The lavatory tank top had been removed, 'Asshole' and 'Radicle Tarts' scrawled across the mirror in what looked to be bright red lipstick.

Some calm editor inside Arthur noticed the misspelling of 'radical'; the rest of him felt stunned, violated, angry, confused. Weston's warnings about Lavender's instability flashed through his mind. Had she done this? Had she arrived early, thought he was standing her up again, and trashed his room in anger?

Arthur checked to see if anything was missing. The change from his bedside table, his electric razor, and a packet of condoms. Nothing else, as far as he could tell. A couple of shirts he'd bought yesterday were still in their plastic wraps. Lucky he'd taken the laptop with him.

Surely Lavender wouldn't have taken the electric razor and condoms. Then who? 'Radical Tarts' sounded like a punk band. Punks. Cindy's friends at Jumpin' Java. One of them had sneered at his laptop, but they still might have broken in to take it; they certainly wouldn't have shared his taste in shirts.

Arthur straightened the mattress and threw himself on the bed, wondering whether to tidy up or leave things for the police.

"My god," Lavender said from the doorway. "Don't you know that messiness is really bad karma?" Then she must have seen his expression as he sat up. "You didn't do this?"

Arthur felt a wave of relief that Lavender had shown up, then guilt for doubting her. "No, it was like this when I got back a few minutes ago."

"Who would do this to you?" Lavender asked, parking herself on the bed beside him. The white blouse and skirt that had seemed so angelic on her last night were a bit bedraggled this morning, as though they had spent the night in a heap on the floor. Still, it was hard for Arthur to concentrate with her so close. Against the creamy paleness of her face and shoulders, the dreamy, slightly unfocused stare of her green eyes was appealing, but also disconcerting.

"Teenage vandals, I assume. I mean, not much has been taken . . ."

Lavender, gazing out the window now, didn't appear to have heard him. "Hendrix was in the parking lot last night when I left, wasn't he? Did you tell him you think Dad was murdered?"

Arthur wasn't about to admit that, as far as he was concerned, her brother was a suspect. "No, I just asked him about the script."

"What did he say?" Lavender's voice was sharp.

"Nothing really," he said hastily; then, to divert her attention, "I had the impression someone was eavesdropping."

"I knew it. Carol must have been spying." She leapt to her feet and paced around the room, stopping in front of the mirrored wardrobe. "Hendrix thought he saw a prowler outside the barn last night."

"But why come to my room? What could I have?"

"Dad's script, of course." Lavender contemplated her reflection, toyed with her hair. "I know! After Carol killed Dad, she couldn't find the script. Maybe Dad had a premonition and hid it. So she's still hunting for it."

"But what's that got to do with me talking to Hendrix?"

"Carol couldn't risk getting too close, so she didn't hear everything you said. She assumed that one of you had this missing script. Last night she tried to get into Hendrix's barn, and this morning she ransacked your room."

"But she couldn't have. The only time I've been out this morning was to have breakfast with her at the Blue Moon."

"You were with Carol this morning? Whose side are you on?" Lavender's green eyes were huge and accusing.

"We were talking about my article on your dad's career, that's all. I needed some material from her."

To his surprise, his response seemed to defuse Lavender's anger. She stopped pacing and when she spoke, it was so quietly Arthur could hardly hear her. "You mean you were with her all the time you weren't in your room?"

"Well no, Carol was nearly half an hour late." Not only

late but unapologetic. She'd rushed in, dumped a voluminous pile of programs and press cuttings on the table, and
insisted on going through them over breakfast. Then she'd
wearily run her fingers through her straggly blonde hair
and said, "I don't think I want to hear about Monday night
after all, and not because I killed Zach. It was a terrible
accident, and no one's to blame but Zach himself. As the
pop psychologists say, I have to 'put it all behind me' and
'get on with my life.'" She had smiled wanly as she got up
to leave. "I'm only thirty-five. Maybe I'll even have kids. As
you may have gathered, I wasn't a big hit with Zach's."

The truth of Carol's parting words rang in his ears as
Lavender triumphantly exclaimed, "There you are,
Arthur. The Blue Moon's only two minutes away. Carol
didn't have time to cover her tracks, so she scribbled messages on your mirror to make you blame teenagers. Come
on, let's go."

"But what about my room? Shouldn't I phone the
police?"

"You don't need to phone, because we're going to see
them, remember?"

On the short drive to the RCMP building, Lavender was
animated and impatient; once they were inside, her live-
liness vanished as swiftly as water down a drain. As they
waited for the receptionist to inform Sergeant Berwick of
their arrival, Lavender leaned over to whisper in his ear.
"This place has really bad vibes, Arthur. Last time I came
they didn't believe a word I said."

Remembering Larry Weston's story, Arthur wondered whether she'd taken her complaint about the water to the police. If so, would they consider him paranoid too?

Soon they were ushered into the office of the bald-headed man Arthur had seen at the benefit. Berwick laid a file on one of the stacks covering his desk and rose to greet them, less imposing in his uniform than he'd seemed before, a good two inches shorter and thirty pounds lighter than Arthur. The sergeant's grey eyes were kindly but appraising as he motioned them to be seated.

"Miss Smith, please accept my condolences on your father's death," he said. "We'll all miss Zachary but I know it's hardest for family."

Lavender kept her eyes downcast, as if she hadn't heard.

Berwick released his breath in a little annoyed puff and turned his attention to Arthur. "You found Zachary Smith's body, isn't that correct? You write for the *Post-Dispatch*."

"Yes, I'm their drama critic."

Berwick's lips moved a fraction, shaping a sardonic smile. "Ah yes. I appreciated your review of *Bullock's Folly*. Very tactful." The smile disappeared. "Now, I understand from Miss Smith's phone message that both of you have some concerns about her father's death."

"He was murdered!" Lavender burst out, without looking up.

Sergeant Berwick retrieved a notebook and pencil from the clutter. "You are both aware, aren't you, that the investigating officer and the attending physician agreed the case was one of accidental death? What makes you doubt that conclusion?"

Lavender was silent, so Arthur told his story yet again. Addressed to Berwick's impassive face, the details seemed to shrink in significance. With a growing sense of unease, Arthur went on to describe his ransacked room. When he came to Lavender's arrival, he stammered and stopped. No point in sounding like a complete idiot by repeating her theories.

"You were interviewed twice, Mr. Fairweather. Neither statement mentioned these suspicions."

"On Monday night I was in shock. When I talked to the same constable on Tuesday morning—French bloke, you know—he didn't seem the least bit interested in anything I said. So I shut up."

Letting out a tiny sigh of irritation, whether at him or at someone else Arthur couldn't tell, Berwick finished his notes and looked across at Lavender. "And now, Miss Smith?"

"It's Carol."

"You're referring to Carol Smith, your stepmother? Go on."

"Carol always plays Yum-Yum. This time Dad gave her Katisha. She hated playing an old woman. No one realizes how vain she is. I heard them arguing, lots of times. She'd kill rather than be humiliated. And that's—"

"Miss Smith," Berwick had raised his voice, and Lavender, startled, stopped in midstream.

"Miss Smith, if I understand you correctly, you have made a serious accusation. Will it satisfy you if I call Mrs.

226

Smith and ask about her whereabouts the evening of your father's death?"

"She's probably out," Lavender said, doubt in her eyes and voice. "I can give you the cellphone number." She clearly didn't know whether Berwick was taking her seriously or not. Arthur thought he knew the answer to that question; nevertheless, he was full of curiosity as Berwick dialed the number and explained the reason for his call.

Berwick made notes as he listened. A few minutes later he said thank you and put down the receiver. "Your stepmother has given me the names of people she was with on Monday evening from the time she left the rehearsal until she was informed of your father's death," he said, selecting a smooth agate from a small ceramic bowl of polished stones and calmly massaging it, as though reaffirming his allegiance to a world of hard facts.

Lavender spluttered in anger. "Of course she'd arrange an alibi. She's smart. She's . . ."

Berwick replaced the stone. "I'll verify her statements, of course. But from the names she's given me, the likelihood is that she's telling the truth. Now let me be clear. There's a set of procedures to be followed in case of any un-witnessed death. Those procedures have been followed. The police will continue to regard your father's death as accidental unless significant evidence to the contrary turns up. And you, young lady, must stop spreading malicious rumours."

Arthur, irritated by Berwick's attitude, asked, "What about my evidence?"

Berwick's eyebrows shot up at the word 'evidence.'

"Your statement this morning will go into the file along with the others. I'm sure you'd agree, Mr. Fairweather, that the issues you mentioned hardly justify launching an investigation."

"No, I don't agree. And what about my room?"

Berwick stood up. "You should fill out an Incident Report form; Betty has a supply at the front desk."

Emerging from Berwick's office, Arthur noticed the blond woman he'd seen in the White Whale, and again after Tuesday's *Mikado*, talking on the phone at a back desk. So he'd been right; she was a policewoman. The receptionist, whom he'd asked for an Incident Report form, gave him a dirty look when he remarked to Lavender, "Not much help, was he?"

Lavender's car keys dangled from her hand. "Arthur, do you believe Carol murdered my father?"

Arthur hesitated, knowing what Lavender wanted to hear. Then he found himself telling the truth. "Lavender, I think your father may have been murdered, but I can't be sure. And if he was murdered, I don't know who did it. All I can say is that I'm committed to finding out what happened."

Before he finished, he knew the truth was not enough for Lavender. She smiled sadly at him, turned away and hurried through the front door.

Like the small boy he had rescued on Tuesday, Arthur felt surrounded by a ring of hostile or indifferent people. Lavender refused to listen unless he agreed with her. And that slippery Sergeant Berwick proposed to file away their statements so they'd never see the light of day. But, so what? They could think what they liked. Until he found out the truth about Zachary Smith's death, he would stay on the case.

Tearing up the half-completed form, Arthur dropped the pieces into a wastebasket and marched out.

.. ..

The RCMP building sat at the top of a hill. As he thumped down the long flight of stairs into town, Arthur vowed to lose twenty pounds. Maybe even thirty. When he reached the park at the bottom, he dropped onto a shady bench near the playground, unsure what to do next.

At one end of the swings, a small blond girl in a bright red T-shirt whooped with delight as her father pushed her. Teenage smokers clustered at the other end, rucksacks piled around them like a protective wall. A Goth was talking to someone in a hooded sweatshirt. It could be Cindy; he couldn't tell.

The Goth must have noticed Arthur staring, because he detached himself from the group and sauntered over. Closer up, Arthur recognized him as Cindy's acned-faced friend who had sneered at the idea of a computer without *Deathwalk*. His curiously colourless eyes kept flicking back to his mates. "Got any spare change?"

Arthur's new paranoia about teens almost made him shout, "You took it all this morning." Instead he seized the chance to get information.

"I'll do a deal with you," he said. "Five bucks if you correctly answer a skill-testing question."

"Yeah, whatever." The boy started to roll his eyes, and then seemed to remember he wasn't talking to a parent. "Okay, what is it?"

Arthur watched the acned face closely as he asked, "Does the name Radical Tarts mean anything to you?"

"You mean the four chicks who think they're a heavy metal group?" The boy's eyes registered no guilt, but his contempt was unmistakable. "Even old guys like Metallica could blow them away. But they got the marketing. In two years time they'll be nothing." He shrugged and held out his hand.

"One more question," Arthur said. "I'm a newspaperman, you see, and I have to make sure my facts are right. How do you spell radical?"

The boy glanced around, as though hoping to find a cue card with the answer. "It's like, you know, in politics. I never was too good in English."

Arthur passed over a well-worn bill and the boy fled back to his mates.

So Radical Tarts is a band most teens would know about, and probably none of them could spell. If this one hadn't ransacked his room, some of his friends no doubt had. Not that Arthur could prove anything.

He was wondering where to find the closest beer when he noticed Mrs. Coutt slowly moving toward him, two heavy shopping bags making her a little unsteady on her feet. She smiled when she saw Arthur and set her bags down, seeming glad of an excuse to stop. "Mr. Fairweather. So this is what critics do with their mornings—sit about and enjoy the sunshine."

"On the contrary. My morning has had nothing but trouble in it."

Regarding him with motherly concern, Mrs. Coutt lowered herself onto the bench beside him. "So what's the matter with you then?"

"My room was broken into. Nothing much was stolen, but everything was messed up."

"Oh, you poor man. Did you talk to the police? Have they any idea who did it?"

"If they had, they weren't telling me. Teenagers is my best guess."

"Young people." Mrs. Coutt wrestled for a moment with a shopping bag that had fallen over at her feet. "These days they seem to do whatever they want, and often it's something criminal. It's because they cut themselves off from their parents." She paused and tried to smile. "I know I sound like an old nag. Young people aren't all the same. I shouldn't talk as if they were."

Arthur sensed an opening. "The young people in the Vesuvius Company are certainly different. Lavender seems to have worshipped her father, whereas I got the impression that Hendrix was always falling out with him. Do you have any idea why they didn't get along?"

"I'm not a gossip, Mr. Fairweather." Mrs. Coutt reached for her shopping bags.

"Call me Arthur. And I don't mean to pry."

Her principles established, Mrs. Coutt released her shopping bags and sat back again. "I was christened Valerie Ivy Gertrude, if you can believe that. But I've always gone by Ivy." There was a moment's silence, and

Arthur experienced again the odd feeling that he'd had at the wake, the feeling that he'd known Ivy Coutt for a long time. And, as at the wake, he sensed she felt this too.

"It's odd I'm going to tell you this, Arthur. Maybe your finding Zachary's body makes it feel like you're one of us. Anyway, please keep everything I say confidential. I'm sure Hendrix was under the influence of something in Victoria last Friday, because I heard Zachary threatening to drop him from the Company if he performed again in the state he was in. Zachary would have done it, too; he was at the end of his patience."

So I was right about the drugs, Arthur thought. If Hendrix had turned up stoned on Monday night, that could well have precipitated a deadly confrontation.

"Hendrix never talked to you about his father?"

"No, never. He seems to be one of those young people we were talking about. They put a wall up." Mrs. Coutt's voice went quiet, as if she were talking to herself. "Like my son, I sometimes think."

Arthur tried to probe as gently as possible. "I remember walking in on an argument between Rodney and Zachary. Zachary must have been a pretty difficult person to work with."

"Yes, once Zachary's mind was made up, that was it. But the quarrels weren't only one way. Rodney can be difficult too. But now I really must finish my shopping." Mrs. Coutt started to struggle to her feet.

Arthur wanted to ask her more, but sensed it would do no good to push. He took her arm to help her up. "Thanks for listening to me, Ivy. And I'd like to return the favour.

Anything you need to talk about, I'd be happy to listen. I know this is only the second time we've met but . . ."

To his surprise, Mrs. Coutt sat down again abruptly, her eyes misting up. "Don't mind me. The thing is, you're like my favourite nephew. You're so like him, it throws me off guard. When Rodney and I had all the trouble in England, William was the only person who would listen." She sighed. "I do need to talk to someone, someone more my son's age. I never thought I'd hear myself say I don't understand him, but I don't."

"What don't you understand?"

As Ivy Coutt turned to him, Arthur suddenly had the sense that, for her, they were back in England, talking in a cozy room they had talked in many times before.

"It's my silver, Arthur. My silver's missing. And it has to be Rodney taking it. But I should start at the beginning. I inherited a silver table service from my mother. It's the only thing of real value I own. My ex-husband took . . ." Her voice shook and recovered. "Anyway, everything is so informal in this country that I hardly ever use it, but now and then I get it out and give it a polish."

"My mother used to do that. She said polishing her fish knives and forks was the most peaceful thing she could find to do."

"It can be. But not the last time. A few weeks ago that was, when Rodney went off to this bank conference in Alberta. I was rattling around the house on my own so I decided to have a go at the whole collection. Most of it is packed away, you see; that's why I hadn't realized nearly all of it was gone. The boxes were full of wadded up newspaper. When Rodney came back I asked him what might have happened. He said he didn't know anything about it."

"But you didn't believe him?"

"I wanted to believe him, but who else could it have been? I started leaving my bedroom door open at night. I'm a light sleeper, always have been. I thought if I could catch Rodney in the act, he'd have to explain why he needed the money, and I could help him."

A cry of "Screw you!" drew Arthur's attention back to the group of teens. The Goth who'd bummed money shot a finger at his hooded friend, scooped up his rucksack and headed off. The rest went on smoking, paying no attention.

Nor did Mrs. Coutt, intent on her story. "A noise in the piano room woke me up around three this morning. The silver's stored in the cupboard there, so I went downstairs quiet as I could, without turning on the light. I had just reached the bottom of the stairs when—" she hesitated. "Anyway, when I turned on the light my musical scores were all over the floor but the silver cupboard was still locked. I'd moved the key, you see. I went back upstairs and Rodney's room was empty. It's got to be him who's taking things. Why should he steal from his own mother?"

Arthur put a reassuring hand on hers. "Maybe I can find out," he said.

"Well, I'm sure he's in some kind of trouble. He's got a good job in the bank and more than enough money for what he needs. But if he's stealing from me, who else might he be stealing from?" She paused. "Do you think it might be Rodney who ransacked your room?"

Arthur was wondering the same thing. "Did you see him this morning?"

She shook her head. "I was that upset I took a Valium. If he came back, I didn't know it."

Arthur didn't have to spell out the implications. "I'll have a talk with Rodney. I'll pretend I need to interview him again."

Mrs. Coutt sighed. "If you could find out why he's stealing, maybe he can stop before he does something worse. He's certainly not at all like himself these days. But please don't mention me." She struggled to her feet, wincing as she put weight on her left leg.

Arthur didn't remember her limping at the wake. "What's happened?"

"Just a bit of a sprain. I was so nervous I slipped on the stairs last night."

"Are you sure? Rodney didn't attack you, did he?"

"No, no, of course not," said Mrs. Coutt, gathering her bags. "Now I really must be going. My friend Mrs. Whitmore drove me into town, and we're meeting for lunch."

Watching Mrs. Coutt hobble away, Arthur wondered whether her story of slipping on the stairs was the whole truth. Rodney was an angry man, and she was a protective mother. Was she trying to cover up behaviour that she knew Arthur would judge more harshly than theft? Her revelations about Rodney certainly cast a new light on his role in the Vesuvius Company. He was treasurer—had he been stealing from the company? What if Zachary Smith had discovered it and refused to keep quiet? Or was the real conflict between Zachary and his son over drug use?

The teenagers were staring at him. Had he spoken aloud? He glared; they shrugged and turned away. He had the right to feel excited. Mrs. Coutt had given him possible motives for his two suspects. It was time to follow them up.

Thinking of Ivy Coutt's limp, he decided he would start with Rodney Coutt, pressure him to have dinner tonight. Forgetting entirely his desire for a beer, he set off in search of a phone.

# Chapter 18

At five forty-five Danutia settled herself on a bench overlooking Ganges harbour. According to the wharfinger, a freckle-faced young woman, Larry Weston's *Golden Reel* was due back at six o'clock. She'd added, laughing, "You can depend on that, too. Not a minute earlier and not a minute later." Danutia was taking no chances. Weston was the only lead she had left.

The sun had dropped behind Mount Maxwell, and a chill breeze blew off the water, bathing her in the scent of bruised peaches from the bright yellow gorse that rimmed the bank. The sounds of creaking swings and shrieking children floated over from the playground in Centennial Park. Nearer to hand, a couple of scruffy teenagers rocked back and forth on their skateboards, arguing about who would score a case of beer for them.

She had spent the afternoon trying to pin down the cast's movements after last Thursday's rehearsal, with little success. When she'd grumbled about message machines, Betty had suggested calling Rodney Coutt at the bank where he was a loan officer. None of the rest of the cast, it seemed, had a regular job. So, for lack of anything better to do, she had set off in the Blazer, stopping in at the school to check Emile's memory of the pay phone number and then going for a swim in Saint Mary Lake, its matchbook-sized public beach almost as difficult to find as Bertolucci's trailer. She was finishing off her mile with a lazy backstroke, telling herself to relax, to stop searching for answers, when she became aware of a thought hovering just beyond her closed eyelids. Her eyes popped open. Two black and white dragonflies zoomed past like drunken biplanes and disappeared from sight. That was it. According to Emile, someone had disappeared from Thursday night's rehearsal. But who?

So while she waited for the *Golden Reel*, she pulled out her tape recorder. Fastforwarding past Emile's account of his friendship with Bertolucci, reversing when she realized she had gone too far, at last she found the spot she was looking for.

". . . everyone in the cast was there, at least at the beginning," Emile was saying, his soft voice barely audible above raucous laughter. "About halfway through the first act Hendrix started missing his cues and Zachary decided Kenneth Taylor, the understudy, should rehearse Nanki-Poo." The hooting and shouting almost drowned out the last few words, then died away. Emile's voice again. "Idiots." Ah yes, the boat in trouble. Then Emile had mentioned phone calls, and she hadn't followed up the comment about Hendrix.

Did he stick around while the understudy rehearsed, or did he leave early? If only Berwick had nailed down everyone's movements when he talked to the cast on Monday. But on Monday, she reminded herself, he was still convinced Bertolucci had committed suicide and she was hot on the trail of Bob Kelly.

She thought of the enigmatic note Berwick had left propped against his bowl of polished stones for her:

PIRS=POTENTIALLY INTERESTING RESULTS: SMITH. MEET HERE 7:30. DINNER? Annoyed with his absence and game-playing—there were, after all, four Smiths involved in the case—she had shoved the message to the back of her mind. Now she wondered whether Berwick too had discovered something suspicious about the handsome young actor.

Startled by the low roar of an engine, Danutia glanced up. The black speck that had appeared at the entrance to the harbour only a few minutes ago had grown, taken form. A motorboat was nearing the dock, the name *Golden Reel* clearly visible on its side. Danutia packed up the tape recorder and strode down to the docks stretching into Ganges harbour like greedy fingers. There, amid the dank smells of fish and seaweed, gleaming yachts cast long shadows over weathered trawlers and patches of oil rode the waves like bruises.

The *Golden Reel* edged into its berth, its twin engines quietly humming. It was a larger, sleeker version of the kind of fishing boat her dad and uncles used. A Seaswirl 2300, the wharfinger had said, as though that would mean anything to Danutia. Four dark rods mounted behind the flat-topped sunroof thrust upwards like a comb, their gold-plated reels glowing in the setting sun. So that's where the name came from.

Antonia leaned against the railing, clutching a small silver box to her chest; her husband Marco stood beside her, rope in hand. Beneath the sunroof a large, weathered man gave instructions to Gino, who sat at the controls.

The twin motors coughed and died. Waves splashed against the dock, setting it rocking. Danutia grabbed hold of a piling to steady herself.

Marco flipped the bumpers overboard. "Catch," he said, tossing her the rope. She snubbed it around a cleat as she would tether a horse, while he scrambled past Antonia and leapt to tie up the bow.

"Have you arrested him yet?" Antonia asked.

What rumours had Antonia heard? So far the RCMP had successfully avoided media publicity. "Who?" Danutia asked.

"My father's murderer." Antonia's eyes, smoke-soft only a moment ago, turned hard as Berwick's obsidian as she read the answer in Danutia's silence. She rocked back and forth, as though to comfort herself, or the thing she held. "I knew it. Something wouldn't let me sprinkle Papa's ashes on the water. He can't be at rest until you catch his killer, and neither can I."

Weston came up behind Antonia and wrapped a protective arm around her. His face and neck were reddened and scored by wind and sun, his nose flat and slightly off center, as though it had been broken. In his blue chinos and striped knit shirt, he looked more like an aging football player than the imposing Mikado he had appeared in costume. Yet when he spoke, Danutia heard again the stern melancholy that had moved her during the benefit performance. "Couldn't this wait until tomorrow?"

"I'm afraid not," Danutia said, and introduced herself. "I'm actually here to talk to you, Mr. Weston." She turned to Antonia. "Dr. Einarsson asked me to tell you

Mia has settled down again. I'm sure you'd like to get her before the clinic closes."

Relief washed over Antonia's face. "I don't know what got into her this morning. We were going to take her with us, but she refused to go on the boat, and nipped me when I tried to carry her on. I guess she knew the time wasn't right." Standing on tiptoe, she gave Weston a light kiss on the cheek. "Thank you for taking us out."

Weston shook hands with Marco and helped Antonia onto the dock. Gino hung back. "When I'm eighteen, we'll sail to South America, right?"

"Just like your daddy promised." Weston wrapped the boy in a quick bear hug, then cuffed him on the shoulder. "Don't forget your big-time trophy catch."

Pulling open a bin under a rear seat, Weston scooped a still-wriggling fish into a plastic pail, sloshed in some water, snapped the lid on, and handed the pail to Gino.

"You give that to the chef at the Port House. Tell him Larry Weston said to cook it up for you."

Grinning shyly, the boy hefted the pail onto the dock and lugged it to where Antonia and Marco waited. They waved and headed up the stairs.

"Doesn't take much to make a kid happy," Weston said, steadying Danutia as she stepped aboard. His hand was huge and work-scarred, some welts still an angry red; yet his touch was surprisingly gentle. "Gino's a good boy, fallen among bad friends. Playing hooky, threatening to drop out of school. Joe made a deal with him. Said he'd work hard to buy a boat if Gino would work hard in school, and every three months they'd check to see how they were doing. When Gino graduated, they would sail to Tierra del Fuego."

"Mr. Bertolucci told you this?"

"Joe? No, Antonia. But when I talked to Gino, I acted like his dad told me so I could get him to keep his part of the bargain. Otherwise, he'd be in big trouble six months from now." His face darkened for a moment. "Something happens to a boy when his daddy dies." Then he smiled and the darkness seemed to lift. "Here I go rambling on, and I haven't even offered you a drink. What can I get you—coffee? Tea? A beer?"

Danutia shook her head. "Some questions have come up relating to Joe Bertolucci's death. Emile Gaboune said you were the person to ask."

"In that case, I'll put the boat to rights while we talk. I have to be at a rehearsal soon."

"Nice boat," she said. "Is it new?"

"Bought it from a guy in Victoria who went broke." Weston lifted a rod out of its holder and wiped it down with a cloth. "Most of this fancy equipment is just for show."

"Including the golden reels?"

"These babies?" In one fluid motion he mimicked a cast, a strike, a fierce battle, a triumphant reeling in of a gigantic fish. Danutia couldn't help but admire his evident love for and mastery of his trade.

"Yes and no." He gestured toward the next quay, where a small pigtailed girl was solemnly holding a fishing pole over the darkening water. "You can't land salmon or halibut with a bamboo pole and a safety pin. But these fancy dudes won't catch any more fish than a plain rod and reel. What they do catch," he said, returning the rod to its holder, "is guys with lots of money. The gold matches their Rolex watches. And they like playing with the electronic gadgets. They can pretend they're chasing submarines, firing heat-seeking missiles, shit like that. Excuse my language. But you aren't here about the charter business." Weston's smile didn't reach his eyes, swirls of green, brown, and gold as impenetrable as her brother's marbles.

"Someone spotted a float off the cove down from the Bittancourt cabin about the time Bertolucci was killed," she said. "We're checking to see what it was doing there, whether the person it belongs to might have seen anything. Do you know who fishes in that area?"

"Hard to say." Weston sloshed a bucket of water on the deck and went after it with a mop. "Commercial boats don't go in there much. Sports fishers try it during the salmon runs. Who did you say spotted the float? Did they get a close look?"

Danutia stepped aside as the mop approached. "Does it make a difference?"

"Most people put their name or their registration number on their gear, in case it gets washed overboard."

"I'm afraid we weren't that lucky," Danutia said, and immediately wished she'd bitten her tongue. Rule Number One: Don't give out information. Something in Weston's manner seemed to invite confidences.

"It probably wouldn't have helped," Weston said. "Gear gets lost or sold or stolen, and then the number's no use. I've lost two or three floats myself."

"Why would a float be anchored off that cove?"

"Crab pots, most likely," Weston said, stowing the mop and bucket. "You see floats like that all around the island."

So much for landlubbers, Danutia thought. Getting excited over nothing. Still, who knew what smugglers might try.

"Do you catch crabs?"

Weston laughed, a little uncomfortably. "I try my best not to."

Danutia could feel her cheeks redden. "That's not what I meant."

"Let me show you something." Again opening the bin, Weston hooked a fish through its gills. "Salmon," he said. "The only thing worth catching." The fish flicked its tail, spraying droplets of water. Danutia could feel the salt drying on her bare skin.

Weston filleted the fish and threw the entrails overboard. Seagulls materialized out of nowhere, shrieking and fighting over scraps of flesh.

"So you don't fish for crab?"

"Now and then, but not from this boat. Crab pots take up too much room. Joe usually ran the pots for me, out of my old trawler."

"Did you have any crab pots out last week?"

"No, I was too busy, what with the charters and the play. And Joe dropped out of sight after that business with Bob Kelly." Weston gathered up the knife and chunks of salmon and nodded toward the hatch. "Anything else you want to know, you'll have to come below while I grab a bite to eat."

Danutia hesitated. Another cramped, enclosed space, this one no doubt permeated with the smell of gasoline. She would much prefer to finish the interview here on deck. She glanced up as a ray of sunlight bathed the fishing rods in golden light. "Thy rod and thy staff, they comfort me," she murmured. Still, there was nothing for it. She would have to go below.

She paused on the last rung of the ladder and then, taking a deep breath, she squeezed behind the tabletop, where a cushioned bench doubled, she assumed, as a bed. Weston slid a single burner stove from under the corner sink, sliced salmon and vegetables while the water boiled for instant rice, and then stirfried them, his large hands moving effortlessly through a familiar ritual.

"Losing out on the crabbing business must have pinched, with all this equipment to pay for."

Weston spooned rice onto a plate. "Sure you won't have some?"

"Don't tempt me," she said.

"Your loss, my gain." Weston heaped fish and vegetables on top of the rice, doused everything with teriyaki sauce, and set to, wielding metal chopsticks with surprising delicacy and grace. "I get by," he said. "The crab business didn't bring in much after I paid expenses and a little something to Joe. It was more to help a friend, you know. Joe was always looking for ways to make money. What with Antonia's wedding and his promise to Gino about the boat . . ."

There it was again, the faintest suggestion Bertolucci might not have been the innocent victim she had presumed him to be. Tending Weston's crab pots would have been a perfect cover for smuggling. She'd heard of plastic-wrapped bundles of dope being dropped into the ocean, to be picked up by other boats.

"Who else might have been fishing in there?" Danutia pulled out her notebook.

Weston rattled off the names of half a dozen boats and their owners. "The wharfinger can give you their phone numbers," he said.

Danutia ran through the names with Weston to make sure she had them right. Then she said, with studied casualness, "I've heard rumours of smuggling on the island. Drugs maybe. Know anything about that?"

Weston laid his chopsticks in his plate. Not one grain of rice remained. "Not me. My days sitting on the floor and staring at the wallpaper are long gone."

"Know anybody who is into it?"

Weston rose and began washing up as quickly and methodically as he had cooked. "Now as I understand it, you're investigating a murder, the murder of my good friend Joe Bertolucci. So maybe I know a few people who smoke a joint now and then, or even pop a line. That doesn't mean they're murderers."

"Of course not. But there may be a drug connection, and we need whatever leads we can find." She moved along the bench so he could slide the burner back into place.

Weston was bent over, his head level with hers; his eyebrows, a fading gingery red, drew together in a frown. "I'd like to help you, Constable, but you know how it is—

when somebody's been like a son to you, you don't want to see them get into trouble."

Like a son. He couldn't mean Gino—from what he'd said, he hardly knew the boy before today. "Who are you referring to, Mr. Weston—who is getting into trouble?"

He straightened and turned away to rinse out the dish-cloth. "It's just a manner of speaking, that's all. Somebody got hurt during a performance in Victoria last week. We figured he messed up because he was stoned."

Missing cues during rehearsal. Messing up during a performance. There was only one person he could mean. "Hendrix Smith?"

"I didn't say that. Anyway, I can't believe Hendrix would get into really bad trouble. Though sometimes Zach wasn't so sure." Weston checked his watch. "And now if you'll excuse me, I have exactly seven minutes to get to the theatre."

As she clambered up the ladder, Danutia felt her excitement rise. One of the Smiths had turned up in the PIRS files. Hendrix had a drug habit. He had left the rehearsal early the night of the murder—

She'd forgotten to ask an important question.

"A formality, Mr. Weston, but we have to ask everyone at this point. Where were you on the night Joe Bertolucci was murdered?"

Weston closed and locked the cabin door behind him. "Of course you have to ask. I was at rehearsal, like every-body else in the cast. We broke up around ten-thirty. I was home by eleven, watching the late news from Seattle. I packed, went to bed at twelve-thirty. Got up at five thirty, showered, ate, drove to Fulford to catch the first ferry."

"Is there anyone who can vouch for your movements?"

"Afraid not," Weston said. "I live alone, and I like it that way."

"You seem very sure of your times and movements. Most people have to stop and think about what they did even the day before." Including me, she thought wryly, and for a moment felt a sudden yearning to live in such an immaculately ordered world.

Weston's gaze traveled over the *Golden Reel* from stem to stern. The deck was spotless, the gear neatly stowed. "Most people live sloppy lives."

# Chapter 19

"I realize that I said I'd cooperate," Rodney Coutt snapped as soon as the Highland Room's buxom hostess had seated them. "But really. We open in the new theatre tomorrow night, as you well know, and I have a million things to do. Isn't there someone else in the Company you can ask?"

Arthur sized up his dinner guest. Blue blazer, receding chin, toffy voice routed through his aquiline nose—the perfect caricature of an upper-class English twit. How can I gain this man's confidence, he wondered.

Aloud he said, "I am interviewing other people. Carol Smith has lent me her scrapbooks, and I've just come from talking to Sandra Ohara. But I'm interested in the future of Vesuvius Light Opera as well as its past. As acting director, you are in the best position to tell me."

"I see." Coutt, looking pleased in spite of himself, fussed with his menu. "I'll tell you what I can after we order. I have to be at the theatre soon. This is our first rehearsal in the new space, on top of everything else that's happened this week. I don't know how we'll manage to put on a decent performance tomorrow night."

Muttering something encouraging, Arthur glanced through the dismal list of stews, braised beef, and fish (baked, broiled, poached, or smoked), all served with mushy peas and oatcakes, no doubt. Laying the menu aside, he contemplated the Highland Room's panelled walls with their moth-eaten tartans and muddy-toned oil paintings of cowherds in kilts and bonneted women hastening toward picturesque cottages. The only other diners at this early hour—an elderly couple at a distant table—conversed in whispers. On Robbie Burns Day the place would be full, Arthur imagined, locals flocking in for haggis and other revolting dishes. What else could one expect? But the restaurant was Rodney Coutt's choice, and so he held his tongue and settled, on Coutt's recommendation, for the poached orange roughy.

"Now as to the future of the Company—" A look close to panic crossed Coutt's face as a muscular young man in a crisp white shirt and tartan trousers approached their table, waiter's pad in hand. He seemed vaguely familiar, and then Arthur noticed the gold watch. This was the school custodian who had been so insistent about locking up the school on Monday night. The man standing behind Coutt, outside the supposedly closed washroom. Well, well.

Coutt pulled out a handkerchief and dabbed at his forehead. "Dave, what are you doing here?"

"My new summer job. School authorities are fine with it, as long as it doesn't conflict with evening bookings. So what can I get you, gentlemen?"

They ordered, Coutt changing his mind several times before returning to the 'reliable' orange roughy. Getting impatient, despite his intentions, Arthur prompted, "So the future is . . ."

"What?" Coutt dabbed his forehead again, then frowned and hunched his shoulders as though trying to concentrate. "You said you talked to Sandra Ohara today. Did she mention her father?"

"Not a word. She hasn't been with the Company long enough to be of much use to me." He didn't add that she seemed intent on leaving it. She'd breezed into his hotel room and, ignoring his repeated comments about being on his way out, had quizzed him about his contacts in the film industry—reviewers, publicists, agents, directors—anyone in Vancouver or Hollywood who could possibly help her career. "Talent isn't enough any more," she had informed him, as though it had ever been. She had cited numerous cases of starlets given a chance only after they had created a buzz, one by charging a California politician with rape. "Anything to get out of this backwater," she had said. To Coutt he merely remarked, "She has big ambitions, young Ms. Ohara."

"If Ohara doesn't continue his support, the Company may not have a future," Coutt snapped. "When Sandra joined us, Zachary talked David Ohara into matching whatever we made in school honorariums or box office receipts. And still we barely got by. I'll have to talk with him after I see how we do at the box office this weekend." Coutt stared at Arthur over his glass of soda water. "This is not for publication, you understand. Zachary didn't tell anyone but me. Ohara doesn't want Sandra to think he bought her way into the Company."

"Of course not," Arthur said. "The rich always like to think they've earned their success."

Dave, the waiter, approached bearing a tray. "Gentlemen, your dinner." With a flourish, he set down their plates and three covered silver dishes with serving utensils as large as Scottish broadswords. Giving the two men a bow that seemed to Arthur distinctly satiric, he said, "Enjoy," and withdrew.

His worry having found another object, Rodney seemed hardly to notice. "Zachary could always come up with a grant here or a donation there," he said. "Since I lack his charisma, I'll have to find some other way to assure the Company's future."

And that, Arthur thought, is my cue. "I happened to meet up with your mother this morning," he said, raising the lid of the oblong serving dish. The fillets inside were neither orange nor rough, but, as he soon discovered, the most delicious fish he had ever tasted. The roast potatoes were heavenly, the mixed vegetables crisp and delicately seasoned. No sign of oatcakes or mushy peas. Not a bad choice old Rodney had made after all. He dragged his thoughts away from the food. "She didn't seem very happy."

Coutt ate methodically, giving no help with this line of conversation. Arthur was going to have to break his promise.

"She told me she's been losing her silver, bit by bit. I may not have any contacts in the film industry, but silver, that's a different matter. I said I could probably find out where it went."

Rodney stared coldly over a forkful of broccoli. "If Mother's silver is disappearing, then surely the police are the ones to investigate."

"Your mother won't go to the police." Arthur left a

pause for Coutt to register why. A sepulchral quiet descended upon the Highland Room. The two elderly diners had left; the hostess sat behind the cash register, reading a magazine; Dave folded napkins in a far corner. The only sound was the thump of a bass, steady as a heart-beat, rising from somewhere underneath Arthur's feet.

Rodney wiped his lips and dropped his napkin beside his empty plate. "I told you yesterday I would answer questions if and only if they pertained to Zachary and the Vesuvius Light Opera Company. Do I make myself clear?"

"Oh, this is about the Company all right," Arthur said. "'Money Rules.' Isn't that Pooh-Bah's motto? My guess is that lacking Smith's charisma, you've contributed your mother's silver to the company's finances. I can see how you might justify that—after all, the silver is no use to your mother and soon it would be yours anyway. But it leaves you with a guilty little secret, doesn't it?"

"My secret?" Rodney said, white-lipped. "That's what you've been after all this time, isn't it, you bastard. Here it is then: I'm homosexual."

Before Arthur could speak, Coutt held up his hand. "Yes, I know what you're going to say. This is Canada, in enlightened North America. What's the big deal? Well, you'd be right, if I chose wisely. A discreet partner my own age. Who's to know, or care? But I don't choose wisely. I choose young men. Like Dave over there." He nodded toward the young man folding napkins. "Greedy young men."

The expensive gold watch. "So that's why . . ."

"Yes," Rodney said, "my young flames want more than a middle-aged body and a modest salary can provide. So I have to find a way of raising money for . . . little luxuries. I stole from my father. I steal from my mother. Not very admirable behaviour, I must admit, but I can do without your admiration."

"It isn't just your stealing I don't admire. Your mother is limping. She says she slipped on the stairs last night. My guess is that she discovered you stealing, and you pushed her."

Rodney looked puzzled. "I wasn't in last night. One of my nights of good fortune, as I call them. When I stopped by for a change of clothes this morning, she was still in bed."

Arthur could feel his temper rising at Coutt's feigned innocence. "Why should I believe you? I've seen how angry you can get."

"Oh, now I understand," Rodney said. "This isn't about my mother at all, is it? Yesterday you were going on about how angry I was at Zachary, and here you go again. You don't want to accept that his death was an accident, do you? I saw you rushing after Lavender. Looking for a big story, and you don't care who gets hurt. Well, I have news for you. I'm angry because being a homosexual has made my life a misery. My mother is over-possessive and I wish I could live on my own, but she is also the only person who stood by me when my father disowned me and the local vicar told everyone in the village about my sinful behaviour."

Coutt's outburst had the ring of truth to it, but Arthur

wasn't about to give up his suspicions without a fight. "Did Smith know?"

Coutt rolled his eyes. "Zachary didn't care whether I buggered boys or sheep as long as he could use my opposition to sharpen his ideas. What you saw on Monday night was drama; we've played that scene many times."

"Then why wouldn't you tell me where you were on Monday night?"

Coutt sighed. "I was hoping to keep my private life private. But now that the RCMP knows, why not the newspapers as well?" He waved the waiter over. "Dave, that lady constable isn't the only one interested in my night life, it seems. Would you tell Mr. Fairweather where I've been every night this week?"

Dave grinned in a way that made Arthur feel foolish. "Has Lavender changed her mind, decided Rod here's the one killed her dad? Well let's see what we can do about that." He regarded Coutt thoughtfully, as though trying to dredge up a distant memory. "Last night you drove your old mum home from the wake like a good boy and then you came to my place. Barely left in time to keep from getting caught by that nosy Gaboune fellow that lives down the block. Tuesday night . . . that was the benefit. You and me sloped off afterwards, leaving your mum in the hands of good old Marlene."

Dave glanced toward the front; the hostess was beckoning him. "I'd better make this quick. Monday night, you took your mum home from the rehearsal and then picked me up at the White Whale, must have been around eight o'clock, and we went for a late dinner to that

Mexican place in Fulford. I was trying to work up the courage to tell you about this new job and drank too much tequila." He turned to Arthur. "I should have gone back to check on the school, but I was throwing up all over the place and I thought I could trust Smith to lock up. Rod took me home and put me to bed. Is that what you need to know?"

Arthur nodded and Dave, seeming not at all embarrassed, hurried toward the front. Soon he passed their table, heading for the kitchen with a white plastic bucket. A young couple and a teenage boy trailed behind him. Joe Bertolucci's son and daughter and the daughter's new husband, Arthur realized after a moment; Thea had pointed them out on Tuesday night.

Coutt pushed his chair back. Though he had tried to conceal his discomfort, he was clearly embarrassed by having his private life made public. "I must be off. I'm late for rehearsal."

Arthur had one last question. "Have you thought of applying for the Artistic Director position at the new theatre? If Vesuvius became the resident company, that would give it some security. That's what Smith intended, presumably."

Coutt shook his head, his watery blue eyes gleaming with malice. "Zachary had the temperament for it. I don't. Too many egos jostling for the limelight. I'll leave the job to Thea Roberts. She's good at bandaging wounded egos, from what I've heard."

Twit's revenge, Arthur thought, smarting from the jab. Then it struck him that Thea's application was supposedly a secret. "Did she tell you she'd applied?"

"I mentioned yesterday that I'd overhead Zachary arguing with someone Monday night. He was on his cell-phone. When he rang off, he muttered something about the bitch applying for the job he wanted, but she was dropping by later on and he'd put her straight."

Arthur was startled. "Did she meet him?"

"How would I know? I wasn't there."

As he settled the bill, Arthur stared thoughtfully at Coutt's departing back. Was he telling the truth? If so, why hadn't Thea mentioned the meeting?

Lost in thought, Arthur stepped from the restaurant into the lobby of the Port House and almost bumped into Thea, as though he had conjured her. She had traded her jeans and festival T-shirt for gauzy cotton pants and a hal-ter top that left her midriff bare. "Thea!" he shouted.

She dropped the hand of her companion, a straggly bearded man in his twenties, and waved him toward the steps leading to the downstairs bar. A gold medallion dangled against the man's black turtleneck. Booby prize, Arthur thought, hit by a strong and unexpected wave of jealousy.

"Who's the man?" Arthur asked, accusingly.

"Jeremy's the assistant puppeteer for *Peter's Political Puppet Theatre*. As you would have known if you'd stayed for the whole performance."

About to protest that he had seen quite enough of it, thank you, Arthur told himself, Don't get sidetracked. You're supposed to be investigating a murder, remember? He asked, more calmly, "Why didn't you tell me you saw

Zachary Smith late Monday night?"

"Because it didn't happen," she said as though to a not-too-bright-child. Then she relented. "I did call and arrange to see him, but I got tied up and couldn't make it." She took a few steps toward the stairs, her hips swaying in a way he hadn't seen in years, then glanced back. "So long, Arthur."

Was it his imagination, or had Thea had trouble meeting his eyes? Had she really not kept her appointment with Zachary Smith on Monday night?

Time for a beer. He'd unravelled some secrets, hadn't he? Time to celebrate. Celebrate or mourn, he wasn't sure which.

# Chapter 20
Salt Spring: Thursday evening, July 13

When Danutia arrived at the detachment, Berwick was sitting in his pickup, reading in the sun's last rays.

"Final blood report," he said, handing over the papers when she was belted in. "The blood on the dog wasn't Kelly's."

"Dammit," she said. "Lewis phoned this afternoon while you were out. If I don't have something solid by tomorrow, he's pulling me off the case. I have a couple of new leads, but I was counting on the blood report to buy some time."

"Mexican food? There's a great place in Fulford, if you don't mind a few flies." Berwick started the engine. "From the to-do list you left on my desk, your leads must have something to do with the Vesuvius cast."

Please God, tell me I didn't leave any embarrassing doodles, Danutia thought, grateful for the fading light. "I was checking alibis," she said. She told him about Marlene's call on Thursday night. "The number matches the incoming call to the cellphone. I stopped by the school this afternoon to make sure. And the times are right."

As she expected, Berwick's response was dismissive. "So she forgot Kelly had given Bertolucci the cellphone. Anything else?"

"Not much," she admitted. "Why can't these people have regular jobs? The only cast member I managed to reach, apart from Emile Gaboune and Larry Weston, was the banker with the voice like Henry Higgins."

"Rodney Coutt."

"That's the guy. Marlene gave his mother a ride home that night, all right, but he didn't know what time. His own alibi checks out. Seems he was shacked up with the school custodian. The woman downstairs was up all night with a sick baby. She saw them come in around eleven, heard them talking and moving around, saw Rodney leave about five forty-five Friday morning."

"Rodney's having it off with Dave? Guess I don't know everything that goes on around here after all."

The pickup slowed and Berwick eased it onto the gravel shoulder. The hills had opened out and the wooded slopes had given way to farmland. Barely audible above the rumble of the engine came Alanis Morrisette's plaintive voice singing, "All I Really Want." Then both voice and engine died.

"I have a little job to do," Berwick said, getting out of the cab. "It won't take a minute."

Danutia heard a clattering as Berwick took something out of the truckbed. In the gathering dusk she watched him carry a piece of metal to a FOR SALE sign at the edge of a field. When he stood back, hands empty, the sign proclaimed SOLD.

"The real estate agent would have done it," Berwick said as he clambered back into the cab, "but I said I was coming out this way anyway. What do you think?" He gestured toward the farm lying beyond Danutia's window. "Twenty acres of nearly perfect grape-growing land.

Sloping southern exposure, dry soil. A creek to channel the rain. See how the land drops off on the other side of the road? That means no frost pockets. I closed the deal today."

"I was trying to track down a murderer, and you were buying land?"

"Only took half an hour. The house comes with it."

The grey-green cedar split-level fit so neatly into the slope it was almost invisible.

"Now all you need is a wife and a couple of kids," Danutia said, trying not to sound bitter.

"In a couple of years," Berwick said, starting the engine. "When I close the door on the cop shop for good."

"Ironic," sang Morissette, her voice sharp-edged against the engine's hum.

An uneasy silence fell. As they neared Fulford, Danutia said, "Look, I'm sorry I snapped at you. I'm full of envy. You can have your career, retire with a nice pension, start a family. When I try to think about combining police work and children, my head swims. But if I'm going to do it, I can't wait 'til I'm fifty-five."

That much of the truth she could tell him. Not the part about liking older men. Not about the little thrill when she read his invitation to dinner. Not about sitting at his desk, fingering the rosy piece of quartz she'd plucked from his bowl of stones.

The sternness melted out of his face. "You'll manage," he said. "Look me up in ten years and tell me how you did it."

Disappointed, yet grateful for the gentle way he'd shut

that door, Danutia made a mental note to call Alyne. If she was going to get her head straight about men, she needed some help. Who better to give it than the bossy older sister who just happened to be a psychologist?

⋯ ⋯

They were passing the Black Swan Inn when Berwick's pager beeped. Berwick pulled into the parking lot. "Back in a minute."

Danutia fumbled in her backpack. "You can use my cellphone. I'll wait outside."

"No need, it's business," he said, taking the phone and punching in a number. He identified himself and listened intently. "Lock the doors and stay inside. I'll send a constable right away. Yes, of course I'll come, but it will take me twenty minutes to get there."

"What's up?"

"Intruder at the Smith place." He radioed the constable on patrol with instructions as he turned the truck around. "I'll tell you on the way."

He didn't, though, not at first. The early-evening traffic was too heavy. Berwick kept his attention on the road, passing when he could, and a couple of times when Danutia wished he hadn't. But then he knew the road and she didn't. The truck's headlights flashed across the SOLD sign on the sergeant's new property, but he sped past without a glance. She wondered why the call had come directly to him. After-hours calls, he had explained to her at their first meeting, were routed through the dispatcher outside Victoria.

The truck topped a rise and the road ahead was miraculously empty, as though the cars they'd been tailing had vanished into another dimension. Berwick's hands loosened on the steering wheel.

"That was Lavender Smith calling," he said. "This morning she wanted me to charge her stepmother with murder. Tonight she says she and Carol are being stalked."

"Aren't they at a rehearsal?"

"Not any more. Carol got hysterical and Lavender drove her home. As she turned into the driveway, she saw a man disappear around the corner of the barn. The barn's been converted into living quarters for Hendrix, as I understand it. It could be Lavender's overheated imagination at work again. On the other hand, when I dropped by this afternoon to talk to Hendrix—didn't find him, by the way—Carol said Hendrix had heard a prowler last night. I gave her my card, told her to call me direct if anything else happened. I don't want any more sloppy police work, and I don't want another mysterious death."

"A prowler at the Smiths—was that what your note was about?"

"No, I only heard about that later. The retrieval system turned up a Customs report on Hendrix. He was searched in the Vancouver airport in May on his way back from Seattle. They found traces of marijuana, but not enough to charge him."

They were nearing Ganges and traffic had picked up again. Berwick turned north, avoiding the centre of town, then east onto a road Danutia found vaguely familiar. The truck's headlights swept over a two-storey house with a barn across from it and a small greenhouse at the back. Then she remembered. She'd passed the place on her way to meet the Johnsons.

An RCMP cruiser was parked in the drive, its lights flashing. A constable came around the barn, his flashlight sweeping the ground as he walked toward them.

"Find anything?" Berwick called, slamming his door.

"Footprints, but no sign of a break-in," said the constable. Newfie accent—McTavish, it would be. He waved the flashlight along a diagonal from the barn to a tangled mass of trees and undergrowth. "There's a side road about fifty metres on. That's where he must have parked. Footprints come this way through the vegetable garden. Traces of mud beside the cherry tree and around the barn door, then it peters out. The prints are fresh. Ms. Smith says she turned off the water as they were leaving for the rehearsal."

As though on cue, a figure in white materialized beside Berwick. "Fee, fie, foe, fum," Lavender said in a slow, heavy voice. "I smell the blood of a police-mun." Her white cotton shift could have been a dress or a nightgown, the tangled mass of ebony hair uncombed or artfully arranged. But even in the dusky twilight there was no mistaking the dark circles under the eyes or the feverish light shining from them.

"Didn't catch him, did you?" She cackled like a wicked witch. "Flat-feet with empty hands. You wouldn't even have come if Carol hadn't seen him too. That murdering bitch."

"Ms. Smith," Berwick said patiently, "The couple that

your stepmother said she was with last night have confirmed her whereabouts at the time of your father's death."

"She could have taken out the safety bar before she left."

"May I speak to Carol? I'd like her permission to look around inside the barn. There's no sign of forced entry, but it's still possible the intruder got inside."

"You mean he may have trashed it, like Arthur's room?" She wrinkled her nose, which was thin and sharply pointed. "Hendrix lives in there, you know," she whispered to Danutia. "Carol wanted to give voice lessons, so she turned his room into a studio. You should hear the way she yells at the little brats—"

"Could I talk to her?" Berwick cut in.

Lavender shrugged, her thin shoulders rising like a bird's wings. "I gave her one of my sleeping pills. She's probably out of it by now." Suddenly she whirled away. "I'll get you a key."

Theatre people, Danutia thought. Takes a little drama to get them moving.

While they waited, they examined the footprints as well as they could by flashlight. Boots with a heel, they guessed; they'd need a mould to determine the size. McTavish covered the best prints with a tarp and went back to his rounds, with instructions to circle by every half hour.

Lavender sauntered up and handed Berwick a key with an exaggerated shudder. "Better turn the light on before you go in. Gives the rats time to clear out. Switch is on the right inside the door. Don't call if you need me."

Danutia followed Berwick through the barn door and

into the half-forgotten smells of the country: the mustiness of dusty rafters and rotting hay, the sharp prick of ammonia.

"Whew, I wouldn't want to live out here," she said.

"It's clean enough," Berwick said. "And it hasn't been trashed."

He was right about that, though for a moment it was hard to tell for the clutter everywhere. Clothes were strewn over a rat-chewed sofa and matching chair, CDs across an old drop-leaf table, which also held a CD player, a hot plate and an electric kettle, all plugged into an extension cord leading to the single outlet. A second extension cord carried an overhead light, a reading lamp, and a long cord strung up to the loft.

"It's a wonder the place hasn't burned down," Danutia said, examining the rat-chewed cords.

"Give the rats some credit," Berwick said. "They're keeping Lavender out of our hair while we nose around."

"Yeah, maybe we'll stumble across some hallucinating rodents."

The sleeping loft yielded their only discovery. Tucked under the mattress were well-thumbed copies of *Forbes*, *Fortune 500*, and the current *Wall Street Journal*.

"I can understand hiding *Playboy* or *Hustler*," Danutia said, passing the *Forbes* to Berwick. "But why would anyone hide these?"

"Maybe he isn't. Maybe he's just protecting them from the rats."

"Hold on," said Danutia, pulling out a folded sheet of paper from the *Fortune 500* she'd been thumbing through. A transaction record from Funds for Social Change. "This is the company Bertolucci invested with. Somebody's been running a fair bit of money through this account. Almost fifty-thousand dollars." She took down the account number and transaction dates, replaced the paper, and tucked the magazines under the mattress. "I'll see what I can find out."

"The stock market's not a bad place to launder drug money," Berwick said.

Danutia followed his bald head down the ladder. "Do we have enough for a search warrant?"

Berwick motioned her out the door and turned to lock it behind him. "Afraid not. I'll see what I can do after you've tracked down that company."

Danutia heard a rustling sound from the nearby cherry tree. "RCMP," she said. "Come down at once."

The lower branches of the tree shook as Lavender half-raised herself, her white shift a soft shimmer against the darkness. "'Do you play croquet with the Queen today?'"

"What?"

"It's a quote," Lavender said. "You know, the Cheshire Cat. It's my favourite part." The branch she was lying on, Danutia could see now, was part of what must once have been an elaborate tree house, its floorboards fitted between the lowest branches, its roof barely visible. "'We're all mad here.'"

"I'm inclined to agree with you." Danutia was about to follow Berwick to his truck when Lavender spoke again.

"'This time it vanished quite slowly,'" she said, sliding one leg off the branch, "'beginning with the end of the tail, and ending with the grin, which remained some time after the rest of it had gone.'" Slowly she drew back her arms and head, grinning grotesquely, and stood upright.

With a wrenching sound, one of the boards gave way. Lavender shrieked and grabbed wildly for a branch. Leaves and twigs came tumbling down, and then something heavy landed beside her with a thud.

"Are you all right?" Danutia asked.

Lavender's voice trembled. "Yes, but you'd better come up here. It looks like a body."

Danutia helped the girl down and then climbed into the tree. The bundle she handed to Berwick, who'd come running when he heard the commotion, was almost as tall as she was, but by no means a body. Carrying it into the barn while Berwick escorted Lavender to the house, Danutia removed the outer wrappings, a tarp and a tattered blanket. Inside was a heavy plastic bag sealed with duct tape.

"I bagged some dirt from the outer creases of the tarp," Danutia said when Berwick rejoined her. "It was moist, so it didn't come from the tree." She sliced the tape with her pocket knife and reached inside. Something hard, wrapped in faded blue towels. Danutia unwound the towels. A .303 Winchester with an elaborately carved stock. She looked up at Berwick.

He bent over to examine the rifle, careful not to touch it. Three initials had been cut into the stock like a running brand: RBKRBKRBK.

"I guess we aren't through with Bob after all," he said.

# Chapter 21

Danutia and Berwick returned to Ganges expecting to find Hendrix still at the rehearsal. Instead the theatre was dark. The truck headlights flashed over Emile, checking the back exit. As Danutia hopped out, his soft voice came floating through the warm summer night. "Don't shoot. I surrender."

Danutia was in no mood for games. "There was an intruder at the Smiths' place tonight—"

"A peeking Tom? Is someone stalking Lavender? She is a very beautiful young woman—"

Danutia cut short the fantasies. "We're trying to get in touch with Hendrix."

Emile spread his hands and shook his head. "Unfortunately I cannot help. Half an hour ago or so, Rodney threw down his gloves and told everyone to go home. I was putting away the props when I heard Hendrix and Sandra bickering backstage. When I returned, they were gone."

Now there were two men to track down. At the detachment Berwick set the hunt for Bob Kelly in motion, while Danutia focused on Hendrix Smith.

First she called the Oharas. Sandra wasn't in, according to the housekeeper, and if she were, Hendrix certainly wouldn't be with her. "Mr. Ohara won't allow it," she said. Ohara had seemed uneasy about his daughter when Danutia first interviewed him. Now she wondered whether he had good reason.

The other cast members either weren't home or disclaimed any knowledge of Hendrix's movements after the rehearsal. Finally Danutia phoned the Smiths' residence; perhaps Hendrix had returned home without notifying them, despite Lavender's assurance that she would have him call.

"Why are you badgering me? Don't I have enough problems?" Lavender asked. "His car's in the shop, so he must be with a friend." Reluctantly she gave Danutia a list of Hendrix's friends and their phone numbers.

At the third try Danutia found herself talking to Hendrix's sharp-tongued grade three teacher. An honest mistake on Lavender's part? Mischief? Or a deliberate attempt to protect her brother? Danutia wondered as she shredded the list. By then it was close to eleven. She rang the Oharas anyway. This time the housekeeper, sounding cross, said Sandra had popped in to use the photocopier and had gone out again. She had asked the girl to call the RCMP, hadn't she?

Rubbing her stiff neck, Danutia walked into Berwick's office. He was busy on another line and motioned for her to wait. She paced back and forth beside the window. A moon as lopsided as Zachary Smith's grin stared back at her from the night sky.

"Marlene Kelly," he said when he hung up. "Just got home after stopping for a drink at the country club. Bob is supposed to pick their boys up from the grandparents in Courtenay tomorrow. She thinks he may have decided to go up early. His truck was spotted on the Crofton ferry this evening, so that fits. I'll get the Courtenay detachment on to it."

"I need to move," Danutia said. "Do you have any photos of the Vesuvius Company? I want to go around to the restaurants and bars, see if I can find Hendrix that way. I might at least run into Sandra Ohara or someone else in the cast."

"Good idea. The two night patrols are tied up with a traffic accident. But why the photos? There aren't more than half a dozen places open this late, and Hendrix is well known."

"You and your tight little island," Danutia said, aware she was being unfair even as she said it. "Everyone else on Salt Spring may know Hendrix Smith, but I don't—I've only seen him in costume and face paint. Him and half the others."

"Point taken," Berwick said. Two minutes later he had found what she wanted.

"Publicity stills at the theatre," he said, hanging up the phone. "Thea Roberts, the Arts Festival Director, will meet you there."

This time when Danutia approached the theatre, the foyer lights were on and someone was moving around inside. A dark-haired woman in Indian cotton pants and halter top removed the last of the thumbtacks and handed Danutia a stack of glossy 8x10s. The name Hendrix Smith was scrawled across the top one. It showed a handsome face, with regular features and a wide, slightly false smile. A face not yet strongly marked by experience or tragedy.

"Sergeant Berwick mentioned someone prowling around the Smith place. It's more than that, isn't it?"

Danutia looked up to find the Festival Director gazing at her with shrewd dark eyes.

"Otherwise he wouldn't have asked me to keep quiet about it, and he wouldn't be sending—"

"I'm in charge of this investigation," Danutia said, and immediately wished she hadn't. She couldn't seem to keep her mouth shut tonight. Nerves. She had to put together a case for Sergeant Lewis by tomorrow.

"Just so," Thea Roberts said, holding open the foyer door.

⸱⸱⸱ ⸱⸱⸱

At Bouzouki, where a few late diners lingered over wine and baklava, Dimitrios waved away her credentials. Of course he remembered Len's good friend, the one who didn't like retsina. The poor Smith family, so much tragedy and now this. Hendrix had not been in that evening, nor had his lovely girlfriend, but the moment Dimitrios laid eyes on the young people, he would insist they contact the RCMP.

The White Whale was jammed with people waiting for tables, drinks in hand. From the patio Danutia could hear voices arguing about the merits of *Bullock's Folly*.

"What a bloody farce!" The British newspaperman. She inched closer. No one from the Vesuvius cast was with him, as far as she could tell. She moved back toward the entrance as the overworked hostess clicked toward her, shuffling menus. No help there.

Across the road, the Port House dining room was closed for the night. The Porthole pub at the back was a different story. From its open doors the steady thump of an electric bass and the crash and rattle of drums spilled into the night. At the front a five-piece band in Day-Glo tank tops moved their lips, their voices drowned out by their instruments. Fishing nets hung from the walls and ceiling, and the young crowd milled about like brightly coloured shoals of fish. Danutia squeezed through to the bar.

Lavender, her arm around the waist of the whippet-thin young man at her side, was leaning against the bar rail, sipping a tall drink through a straw. Still wearing the white shift, she had tidied her hair and donned a beaded green necklace that matched her eyes.

"Shouldn't you be home with your stepmother?" Danutia asked.

"She's no mother to me," Lavender said. "Anyway, it was too spooky there by myself. Jeremy here says he'll protect me from evil spirits." She fingered the bronze amulet that hung on a leather thong against his black turtleneck. His beard was scruffy, his blond hair straggly. Danutia was wondering what Lavender saw in him when he smiled lazily, a smile rather like the Cheshire Cat's. Maybe that was it, Danutia thought as they drifted away.

The barman grumbled that he hadn't seen Hendrix in a week or so, as he'd already told Lavender.

And that was that for the nightspots of Ganges. She could also cross the Black Swan at Fulford off her list, she learned when she checked in with Berwick: McTavish had finished with the traffic accident and stopped in there.

No Hendrix. So, adrenaline fighting with fatigue, Danutia headed north to Vesuvius.

It was past closing time at the Dockside, the last stragglers wandering out to their cars.

Doc Johnson was in his office but not alone. He gestured toward the fox-faced man with the brandy glass. "You know Ed Fidelman, I believe. We're just having a nightcap. As my namesake so rightly said, 'Claret is the liquor for boys; port for men; but he who aspires to be a hero must drink brandy.' Won't you join us?"

Danutia hesitated. Her headaches, and her mother's Baptist strictures, meant that she rarely indulged. Drinking was something her dad did with the other men at the raucous Ukrainian gatherings her mother so strongly disapproved of. Still, the day had been long and frustrating; she could use a little comfort, even from a bottle. She fell back on a safe line of defence.

"Not when I'm on duty," she said, coughing a little to mask her temptation. "Open a window, would you? I'd like to breathe a few more years."

"About the autopsy," Fidelman said, stubbing his cigarette and pulling another chair forward. "Sorry I didn't get back to you. My grandfather, who's in his nineties and healthy as a horse, had another of his near-death experiences and the whole family rallied around, as usual. It's the excitement that keeps him alive, I think."

Doc Johnson banged at the window frame until it opened an inch or so, then eased himself back into his leather chair. "Berwick called a couple of hours ago. Bob Kelly hasn't been in tonight, if that's what you want to know."

"No, I'm here on another matter," Danutia said, gazing thoughtfully at the doctor.

He set down his glass and half-rose from his chair. "If you'd like me to leave—"

"No need," Danutia said. He had gone along with her from the beginning; she stood to lose more than she would gain by trying to exclude him now. Briefly she explained about the intruder. "Any idea where I might find Hendrix? Or any of the rest of the cast?"

Fidelman gave her a sharp glance, as though wondering why she was concerning herself with such a minor matter.

Doc Johnson chortled, and two thin wisps of smoke escaped upwards. "The Dockside isn't exactly Hendrix's idea of a good time, I'm afraid. Rodney Coutt and his mother were in with Mary Jackson, who played Katisha last year. They left about an hour ago. I understand Mary's taking over for Carol tomorrow night."

Fidelman emptied his brandy glass. "Doc was just telling me about Zachary. That's two bizarre deaths in the last week. You examined the scene?"

"I was in Victoria."

"Berwick then. He would have been doubly careful after that fake suicide," Fidelman said.

KEEP YOUR MOUTH SHUT! rang in Danutia's ears even as she found herself admitting, "He wasn't at the scene either."

"Oh no, let me guess," Fidelman said. "Larocque was on duty and tried to handle it all by himself. Who else would be so idiotic?"

Danutia didn't contradict him.

"And of course he called Moorhouse, didn't he?" Fidelman turned to Doc Johnson. "Moorhouse sure as hell wouldn't have noticed anything—he's blind as a bat and usually two sheets under. Not a problem if you're examining old ladies who die in their beds, or kids fished out of the water. But a beheading!" He gave Danutia a long appraising look. "Even that drunken sod might have been suspicious if you'd said from the beginning that Bertolucci had been murdered."

Danutia felt the red creep up her neck and into her face. Why hadn't she sent Fidelman away when she had the chance? Then she caught herself. What was more important, saving face or finding a killer? She took a deep breath and felt her embarrassment recede. Fidelman might be tactless and abrasive, but he too was after the truth.

"Maybe there's a chance yet," Fidelman said. "Do you have the autopsy results on Zachary?"

"No, Berwick didn't have any grounds for requesting priority."

"Zachary was a strong man, and nobody's fool. If he was killed, he must have been unconscious. Tell the medical examiner to look for a thumb-sized bruise just behind the ear."

Danutia was silent for a moment. The two deaths had seemed so dissimilar. Gunshot wounds in a remote cabin and a faked suicide note. An equipment failure amongst the comings and goings of a temperamental theatre company. If they were both murders—and here she cautioned herself against being carried away by Fidelman's conviction—what they shared was a sense of improvisation, of opportunistic crimes committed by a creative but ruthless person. Was that person Hendrix Smith? Suddenly her task seemed much more complex.

Doc Johnson's leather chair creaked as he leaned forward to knock the ashes from his pipe. His brow was furrowed, his eyes troubled, as though he had followed her thoughts to some grim place. He laid his pipe aside and picked up the brandy bottle.

"Do have a drink, Constable," he said, nodding toward the bewigged portrait on the wall behind him. "As the good doctor said, 'Life is a pill which none of us can bear to swallow without gilding.'"

With a sly grin Fidelman offered a brandy snifter. Danutia stretched out her hand.

# Chapter 22
## Salt Spring: Friday morning, July 14

Stumbling back from the bathroom after too many beers and not enough sleep, Arthur found himself staring at a manila envelope propped up on his desk. Had someone come in . . . ? No, he remembered now. He'd found the envelope shoved halfway under the door when he'd staggered in during the wee hours. Assuming it contained more documents from Carol Smith, he hadn't bothered to open it.

The writing didn't look much like Carol's, though. He pushed back the curtains, wincing a little at the bright sunlight, slit open the envelope, and pulled out two sheets of paper. On top was a handwritten note on thick ivory bond:

Dear Arthur:

I'm onto a story hotter than that Hollywood scandal I was telling you about. None of that boring history of the Vesuvius Company you're so keen on. You'll never believe who's involved! I'll give you the material, you write it, and we'll both be celebrities. Enclosed is my insurance policy. Publish it if I miss Friday's performance. But I know I won't.

Your friend,
Sandra Ohara

Sandra Ohara! He'd talked to her twice and now she

was calling him her friend and telling him he wrote boring pieces. What cheek!

Turning to the second sheet, Arthur stared at it blankly for a moment, and then with mounting excitement. This was the page he had been looking for, or, more precisely, a barely legible photocopy of it: the score for Ko-Ko's 'list' song with the words of the middle verse crossed out and new lines substituted, presumably by Zachary Smith.

His excitement waned as he recalled Sandra's reference to the song as her 'insurance policy.' Insurance against what? Did the song in fact identify Smith's murderer, as Lavender had insisted? If so, then his room must have been ransacked, and Mrs. Coutt's music room searched, in a vain hunt for the script. Arthur shuddered at the thought. Now Sandra's note hinted that she planned to confront the culprit. Stupid, stupid, stupid. It was obviously too late to stop her. If she was in danger, the best thing Arthur could do—the only thing he could do at the moment—was to try to figure out whom she suspected.

Reluctantly Arthur settled himself at his desk and struggled to decipher the director's tiny, crabbed writing, strangely at odds with his ebullient personality. Eventually he pieced together the new verse:

> There are men who act like women and suddenly erupt,
> They surely won't be missed—they surely won't be missed!
> And dopers building business here, there's nothing so corrupt,

I've got them on my list—I've got them on
   my list!
The tortoise with his neck stuck out, no good
   at catching crabs;
And all the scheming actresses, their talents
   up for grabs,
And pontificating pub men of an eighteenth-
   century kind,
And wily Orientals with development in
   mind,
And that singular anomaly, the quiet environmentalist,
I don't think he'll be missed—I'm sure he
   won't be missed!

.•- -•.

If Arthur had expected the identity of Smith's murderer to
leap out at him, he couldn't have been more wrong.

The last few references seemed the most obvious.
'Pontificating pub men,' 'wily Orientals' and 'the quiet
environmentalist' surely pointed to Doc Johnson, David
Ohara, and the group Thea had told him about, Save Salt
Spring History, or "sssh!" Except for the racial stereotyp-
ing, the lines seemed fairly harmless. It was hard to imagine them leading to murder.

Just a minute, he thought. Only the people at the
rehearsal heard the song, so I can rule out Ohara and the
environmentalists. Doc Johnson was there, but he com-
plained about Smith's lines disappearing from Tuesday's
performance, so he can hardly be a suspect. That means

the killer has to be a member of the Vesuvius Light Opera Company.

If so, who? Sandra had been visibly upset at the rehearsal, presumably by the line about 'scheming actresses' who allow themselves to be 'grabbed' to further their careers. A nasty jab, all right. Still, he could cross her off his list; after all, she had passed along the song to him. What about Carol? If she had once been a 'scheming actress,' as Lavender charged, surely that was old history. Nothing in the song suggested a guilty secret that Carol might try to protect, and Berwick seemed satisfied by her alibi.

'Men who act like women and suddenly erupt' —that had to be Smith making fun both of Rodney Coutt's sexual orientation and of his temper. The man certainly would not be happy to have his homosexuality broadcast to an audience, and his claim that he and Smith argued with each other for dramatic effect still seemed dubious.

But there were also strong pointers to Hendrix Smith. No wonder he had bolted when Arthur asked him about the script. Both Ivy Coutt's speculations and Arthur's own observations suggested conflict between father and son over Hendrix's drug use. The line about 'dopers building business here' put this conflict in a stronger and more dangerous light. Maybe Hendrix had built a business on the drug trade that he would kill to protect, even if the threat came from his own father. And that half-line about sticking his neck out—had Hendrix deliberately allowed Zachary's sword to hit him, to create the impression that he was the one in danger, not his father? Arthur didn't know what to make of the rest of the line—'no good at catching crabs.' Maybe it was an old family joke.

If it was an old family joke, Sandra Ohara would know it. No wonder she seemed so unconcerned about her own safety—she wouldn't expect harm from her lover. She must be planning to make a name for herself by getting Hendrix to confess. Knowing that Arthur was looking for the missing script—he'd told enough people—she had entrusted the page to him because he would understand what she was up to.

Hold on, Arthur told himself. This is all speculation. There's still no firm evidence that Smith was murdered. The whole thing could be a publicity stunt Sandra has concocted. Anything to create a buzz, like that Hollywood starlet she'd talked about.

He looked longingly at his bed. Surely there was nothing to do but wait until the performance, as Sandra requested. He wasn't reviewing until noon. Another couple of hours sleep would cure his hangover, make him feel better.

Except that, as Arthur moved toward his bed, he didn't feel better. He felt as he had when he'd been tempted to flee the island: that he had good reasons to avoid getting involved, but none that were good enough. He sighed. What could he do?

The obvious answer was to go to the RCMP. But did he have anything more concrete to offer them than last time? He didn't. If his original observations counted for nothing with Sergeant Berwick, then Sandra's letter and the photocopy would surely count for less than nothing, just more melodrama from the artsy fartsy crowd.

Still, what if Sandra didn't turn up for tonight's performance? He needed a contingency plan. But what?

The bedsprings creaked as Arthur plopped down. He had to rest his aching head for a few minutes. He stretched out and closed his eyes, his mind still racing. To act or not to act. To be or not to be. Shakespeare's *Hamlet*. He had played an overweight Claudius in a student production, disappointed because he thought he'd had a chance at the starring role opposite a waif-like Ophelia who set his head spinning. Arthur tried to drag his thoughts back to the problem at hand, but memories of *Hamlet* kept returning.

Not Ophelia, though: the play within a play. A travelling theatre company arrives at Elsinore, ready to perform, and Hamlet turns their play into a trap. He alters a scene so that it echoes the way he believes his uncle Claudius killed the king, Hamlet's father. And, indeed, when Claudius witnesses the scene, he springs from his seat and rushes out.

Altering the lines . . . How could he do that with *The Mikado*? A few minutes thought and he had the changes mapped out in his mind. It was a really wild plan. The question was, would it work? A pity Thea wasn't here to advise him. It now seemed astonishing that yesterday he had been suspicious of her. Why didn't he just call her?

As if in answer to his thoughts, someone knocked sharply. Arthur slipped into his trousers and flung open the door. There stood Thea, scowling, back in her working uniform of jeans and T-shirt. "Thea, come in. I'm so glad—"

"Glad to see me?" She marched in and stood glowering at him like a lion tamer facing an unruly big cat. "I wonder why, when you seem intent on destroying my Festival?"

Feeling the need for some sort of protection, Arthur grabbed up the shirt he'd worn the night before. "Destroying your Festival? I don't understand."

"One," Thea said, counting off the charges on her fingers, "Rodney Coutt says you seem to be blaming him for Zachary Smith's death. He's finding it very difficult to put together a show under that kind of pressure."

"But Thea—"

"Two, you promised to get your article on the new theatre into this morning's paper. Is it there? No, and yet tonight's opening performance would be the perfect opportunity to raise money. Three—I won't even mention how insulted I was last night when you accused me—"

"Look Thea, I apologize, but I haven't had time—"

"You haven't had time? Listen, Arthur—"

"No, you listen. You encouraged me to investigate Smith's death. That's what I've been doing."

Thea fixed him with her look of patient martyrdom. "I assumed you'd soon realize Zachary had died in a freak accident and get on with your job. I want that Artistic Director's position, Arthur. Do you think I'll get it if I can't deliver on publicity and the opening performance is a shambles? At least stop pestering people. Including me."

Thea marched out. The door closed behind her with a click of finality. The end.

The click reverberated somewhere deep inside

Arthur's chest, at first with a hollow, empty sound as of a prison door clanging shut, and then quickening into the clickety-click of a train picking up speed. Yes, he and Thea shared interests, and yes, she was supportive, and yes, if he got in the way of her career, she'd do her best to run right over him. This was why they had separated, and nothing had changed.

But maybe recognizing this changes something for me, thought Arthur. Maybe I don't need Thea's approval, or Lavender's, or any other woman's to justify what I'm doing. Maybe I should go ahead and try my plan.

But how? His only ally in the light opera company was Ivy Coutt. Luckily she was the pianist. But he also needed one of the singers.

Could he persuade Larry Weston? Weston was Zachary Smith's best friend, but Arthur couldn't imagine him doing anything that would disrupt the performance. His only other possibility was Rodney Coutt. He would hate the idea as much as Weston, but from what Arthur had seen, his mother could keep him in line. And what if he was the murderer? Arthur would have to take the gamble.

Casting a longing look at his pillow, Arthur reached for the telephone.

# Chapter 23
## Salt Spring: Friday, July 14

It was midmorning before the first break came. Danutia had spent her few hours in bed tossing and turning. Should she discuss Fidelman's hunch with Berwick? What if he told her Smith's death was none of her business? Finally at six in the morning she'd phoned Sharma to ask him to press Krahn for a quick autopsy on Zachary Smith. Sleepy-voiced, he'd asked, "Why me?"

"Because you won't piss him off," she'd answered.

She went into the detachment early to catch McTavish as he went off shift. All had been quiet during his periodic checks of the Smith place, he reported. He had spotted a passenger in Lavender's Karmann Ghia on Rainbow Road about 3:23 AM and pulled the car over. The passenger was not Hendrix but a scruffy-bearded artsy type—"Ah yes, Jeremy," Danutia said, "still protecting her from evil spirits."

She could use some protection from evil spirits herself, Danutia thought ruefully. Not that Sergeant Lewis was an evil spirit, exactly. Yesterday he had given her an ultimatum: if there were no significant developments in the case—"big developments," he'd emphasized—he expected her to report for reassignment by four o'clock this afternoon.

So it was with a growing sense of frustration and panic that Danutia was trolling the Internet, trying to track down Funds for Social Change, when Berwick sauntered into the mailroom, rubbing his bald spot with an air of satisfaction.

"The stakeout in Courtenay paid off," he said.

"About time," Danutia snapped, exiting the program.

Berwick went on as though she hadn't spoken. "Kelly came whistling up the sidewalk of his parents' place about ten minutes ago with a new soccer ball for the boys. A little red-eyed, but spruced up for the occasion. A constable is driving him down." He glanced at his watch. "If they hit the Crofton ferry right, they should be here by one o'clock."

Danutia knew she should apologize, but she didn't. To make amends, she asked, "What about the boys?"

"The grandparents are bringing them. Any leads on that investment fund?"

Danutia shook her head and wished she hadn't. Punishment for accepting Doc Johnson's brandy. "Nothing so far."

⋯ ⋯

Ferries being what they are, it was 2:35 PM before Bob Kelly was escorted into the detachment. After four hours in the muggy heat, his dark hair was matted, his blue denim shirt sweat-stained, his cotton slacks rumpled. Danutia regarded him with a mixture of hope and despair. She still hadn't heard from Sharma, and now it was too late for her to be in Victoria by Lewis's deadline. This had better pay off, she thought as she took her last two Aspirins.

Following Kelly up the stairs, Danutia noted that his

black workboots were identical to the pair Marlene had handed over to Berwick this morning. As they climbed, the heat rose too, releasing ancient odours of dust and smoke. This time Danutia entered the identifying information on the tape while Berwick faced Kelly across the narrow table. He'd been following up on the rumours; Kelly was his man now.

"What's going on?" Kelly asked. "Don't I rate the Victoria hotshot any more?"

Ignoring the question, Berwick said, "Time to come clean, Bob. A rifle was found at the Smiths' last night. We can prove it's yours. We can prove you put it there. What we want to know is why."

"I don't know what you're talking about," Kelly muttered.

"Cut the crap. We have a photo of you with the rifle, and a pair of boots identical to those—" Berwick pointed at the boot Kelly had propped across his left knee—"fit the footprints in the vegetable garden."

Kelly's eyes darted to his boots. They had obviously been cleaned and polished, but even so Danutia could see mud clinging between the treads. Kelly must have seen it too. He dropped his foot to the floor and leaned forward, staring accusingly at Danutia.

"That fuckin' rifle. First Marlene, and now you. 'Do you want your boys to get their heads blown off? Sell the damn thing,' she said. Easy enough for her to say. It wasn't her grandpa did the carving. My twelfth birthday, that's when he give it to me. To be passed down to my son on his twelfth birthday. But she don't see it like that.

So it's nag, nag, until I says okay, I'll get rid of it, and the Glock too."

"But you didn't," Berwick said encouragingly. "You wanted your son to have his legacy."

Kelly turned back to Berwick. "Damn right. Marlene never rides in the company truck, so I stuck them under the seat and more or less forgot about them until the night—" He gazed up at the ceiling as though it had suddenly gone dark, and then nodded in Danutia's direction.

"So when you asked about the rifle the other night I could have shit bricks. I figured something must have happened that I didn't know about. So the next morning I wrapped the rifle up good and dug a hole for it in the woods. But it didn't seem right just to leave it there. Then I thought why don't I take it up to Courtenay with me, ask my old man to keep it. So I dug it up again and put it back in the PD truck.

"Then when I come in to supper I find there's a message from the fuckin' RCMP on the machine and a note from the wife on the fridge. 'Hi, dear, there's no fuckin' dinner again tonight because I've gone to Victoria to buy an expensive dress for the fuckin' reception tomorrow night, and then I'm going straight to the fuckin' theatre.' Or words to that effect. So I had a couple beer and headed out.

"So then I'm passing the Smith place and thinkin' it's all their fault, them and their fuckin' opera company. If it wasn't for them, my wife would be home where she belongs. Joe was their fuckin' friend. Hell, they'd probably been out to the cabin. Let them explain how they come to have my rifle."

The rest was much as they had surmised. Kelly had parked on the side road and made his way through the garden. When he heard a dog barking inside the house, he decided to leave the rifle in the barn, which turned out to be locked. While he was trying to decide what to do, headlights turned in. He shinnied up the cherry tree and wedged the rifle in its branches. When the coast was clear, he hightailed it for the ferry.

"That's the truth," Kelly said, "and no harm done." He patted the shirt pocket where his smokes should have been, shrugged when nothing was there.

"Harm was done," Danutia said. "You terrified two women. They're still struggling with the shock of Zachary Smith's death, and now they're afraid that someone is stalking them. What were you doing snooping around there Wednesday night?"

"Wednesday night? After you'd been accusing me of murder? That would've been pretty stupid, wouldn't it." Kelly leaned forward to appeal to Berwick. "I wouldn't hurt a fly, would I, Sarge?"

Kelly stared stubbornly at the floor.

Instead of answering, Berwick said mildly, "That's quite a house you built, Bob. A lot of people wonder where the money came from. Marlene told Constable Dranchuk here you'd had an interest-free loan from Ohara. I was up island yesterday afternoon and heard some different stories. Talk of kickbacks from contractors. Hush money from grow-ops on Ohara's undeveloped properties. Maybe hush money wasn't enough any more, you wanted a bigger piece of the action. That cove's a drug runner's dream. A perfect little operation. Then Bertolucci came along. You tried to buy him off, threatened him, and things got out of hand. Is that what happened?"

"I didn't shoot nobody," Kelly muttered.

Suddenly Danutia knew what had happened. "You shot at Mia."

"The fuckin' dog kept coming at me. Wouldn't leave me alone."

"Tell us about it." Berwick tossed a pack of Craven A's and matches on the table. "Take your time."

Kelly grabbed the package, shook out a cigarette and lit it. After a couple of long drags, he began. "Here's what happened, swear to God. When I got to the cabin—"

"What time was that?"

"Eleven, eleven-thirty, something like that. The cabin was dark, but the door was open, so I figured Joe had gone for a walk. I moseyed over to the truck, aimin' to get the guns and be gone before he came back. Then something came crashing into my legs."

"Mia."

"I didn't know that at the time, did I. It could have been a cougar or a wild dog, who knows what. So I kicked out, trying to make it let go my pants leg. Finally I got the cab door open and hauled out the rifle and gave the thing a good smack. It went yelping off toward the sea. That's when I saw the white markings, and knew it was Joe's dog. Like I said, that dog never did like me. I was fuckin' mad, you know what I mean? So I jumped in my pickup and fired off a couple of rounds after it, and then I got out of there."

"Did you see Bertolucci at any time during all this?"

"No, I swear it. I figured he was somewhere out there in the dark, laughing at me."

Or lying wounded by a stray bullet, his blood soaking into the sand, mingling with the waves. And the spent cartridges? When she passed the Kellys' house on Wednesday morning, there was a red Dodge pickup among the vehicles in the driveway. When she stopped back by to talk to Marlene, it was gone. "The red Dodge?" she asked. "Where is it now?"

Kelly answered without taking his eyes off Berwick. "At home. I took the PD truck to Courtenay. If you're after the cartridges, though, you're out of luck. I threw them out."

Berwick shook his head. "You may be the one out of luck, Bob, after all the lies you've told us—"

"Wait. Somebody was there after me. It slipped my mind, like, what with all that's been going on. A guy in a three-quarter ton pickup. He was coming around that sharp curve just up from the beach—"

"Maybe that's where he was going, the beach," Berwick said.

"At that time of night?" Kelly took a long drag on his cigarette and exhaled. The cut on the back of his hand was healing, Danutia noted. And it wasn't his blood on Mia. The ash was about to fall. Hardly registering what she was doing, she dug out her empty Aspirin bottle and shoved it toward him.

"Thanks," Kelly said, startled. "Anyway, I didn't get a look at the guy, but my headlights caught a logo on the cab door—something tall, a crane or something."

"Okay, Bob," Berwick said. "Don't leave the island. And you better hope we find a truck with that logo."

.•. .•.

It was now 3:45 PM. While Berwick set the duty constable to phoning Salt Spring construction companies, Danutia tried again to reach Sharma. Put on hold, she went over Kelly's latest story and had to admit that this time she believed him. Kelly had trusted Berwick and so he had told the truth. He hadn't trusted Danutia and so he'd lied. What had Sharma said? The more she could free herself of prejudices and preconceptions, the more likely she was to discover the truth. She'd have to tell him he'd been right.

A voice came on the line. Constable Sharma was in court. Would she like to leave a message?

"No, that's all right," she said. "Give me Sergeant Lewis." Hearing Lewis's gruff voice, she took a deep breath. She had no big developments to report. Maybe next week she would be back in uniform.

# Chapter 24
Salt Spring: Friday, July 14

The second break came an hour after Lewis put her on leave without pay and ordered her to return to Victoria. Danutia was sitting in Berwick's cruiser, waiting for the Fulford ferry, when her cellphone rang.

It was Betty. Dimitrios had just called from Bouzouki. He had been lighting his outdoor grill when he glimpsed Hendrix Smith on the balcony of a townhouse opposite the restaurant, stretching in the late afternoon sun. He wasn't sure which balcony.

Danutia agreed to pass on the message to Berwick. "But why didn't you page him instead of phoning me? I might have been on the ferry by now."

"I didn't want you to miss out," Betty said.

While Berwick headed back to Ganges at unseemly speed, Danutia bullied a yawning Lavender into giving her the information they needed. Ten minutes later Berwick pulled into an illegal parking spot in Mouat Square and they hurried toward the row of pink townhouses that stretched like a bunker to the end of Grace Point. At Number 5 Danutia pressed the doorbell, and again.

No sound from inside.

Danutia punched in the number Lavender had given her. A phone rang beyond the closed door. Turning to give Berwick a thumbs-up, she caught a glimpse of something sparkling on the water beyond the Bouzouki. It was Larry Weston's *Golden Reel* riding at anchor at the government wharf, fishing rods glinting like golden wands.

When the answering machine picked up, Danutia said, "RCMP on your doorstep. We need—"

The door swung open. Hendrix stood in the entranceway, one hand on the doorknob, the other clutching a bath towel around his waist. Water dripped from his long dark hair, glistened on his bare torso, gathered in pools around his feet. His face was pinched and unfriendly. Danutia wasn't sure she would have recognized him as the cocky young man of the publicity photo.

"What's happened now?" he asked.

"Constable Dranchuk, from General Investigations, Victoria. I believe you know Sergeant Berwick. We're investigating reports of a prowler at your place on Rainbow Road."

"Oh that. Can't it wait? I've got to be at the theatre soon." He shivered in the chill of a sudden breeze.

"No, it can't," Danutia said. "May we come in?"

"At least let me get some clothes on." He ushered them into the living room and padded toward the stairs, leaving a trail of moist footprints on the tile.

The small living room was furnished in black leather and chrome, elegant if you liked that sort of thing, which Danutia didn't. Leaving Berwick in front of a CD cabinet, she wandered into the kitchen-dining area, which reeked of stale beer. Several dozen Corona and Dos Equis bottles, some half-full, stood on the table and countertop. Drugs and booze, she thought, and then stopped.

Nothing substantial linked Hendrix to Bertolucci's death or to Zachary Smith's, she reminded herself, only a web of possibilities, coincidences, and rumours, but the presence of the bottles disturbed her.

Hearing thumps on the stairs, Danutia returned to the living room and seated herself on one of the loveseats flanking the gas fireplace. A moment later Hendrix entered, dressed in black shorts and a grey Simon Fraser University T-shirt. He dropped the sandals he was carrying and began towelling his hair.

"About this prowler," Danutia began.

"Don't pay any attention to Lavender." Hendrix dropped the wet towel onto the tile floor and slumped onto the loveseat across from Danutia. "She makes a big production out of everything. I was bombed Wednesday night. Seeing ghosts everywhere."

"I'm not talking about Wednesday. Last night when your sister and stepmother arrived home, they surprised an intruder near the barn."

Hendrix pulled his wet hair back into a ponytail and wound a rubber band around it. "So now they're seeing ghosts too."

"What they saw was no ghost. There were no signs of a break-in," Danutia said, skirting around their search through Hendrix's living quarters, "but there were footprints and a rifle—"

"At our place? You must be joking. I was never allowed to have a water pistol, much less a BB gun. Maybe it belongs to one of Lavender's crazy friends."

Danutia watched the young man closely. "We've

identified the rifle," she said. "It belongs to Bob Kelly."

"That sleazebag? Why would he leave it at our place?"

His ignorance appeared genuine, Danutia thought, but his free and easy attitude bothered her. The bottles in the kitchen suggested a different story. Whatever it was, she was getting nowhere. She gave Berwick a nod.

"According to the police information service," he said, "you were searched by Customs on May twenty-second and found to be in possession of marijuana."

Hendrix picked up a glossy brochure from the piles on the glass-topped coffee table in front of him and glanced through it, seemingly unconcerned. "A few shreds in a jacket I hadn't worn in months. Man, you'd find more Mary Jane on half the people on this island."

"Furthermore," Berwick went on, "you were injured during a performance last week. The rumour is that you were on drugs."

Hendrix threw down the brochure. "First rifles, and now drugs. What is this anyway?"

Berwick moved closer. "Joe Bertolucci was murdered at the Bittancourt cabin. We have reason to believe some-one was using the cove there to smuggle drugs."

The anger drained from Hendrix's face, leaving him ashen. He dropped his head into his hands and hunched his shoulders, and a tremor ran through his body. When he finally looked up, the cocky, self-absorbed young man had seemingly disappeared, leaving in his place someone older.

"I should have believed Antonia," he said, his voice deeper. "I thought she was like Lavender—you know, they get an idea in their heads and won't let go. But if Joe was murdered . . ." He spread his hands, as though to indicate that the world had changed and he had no choice but to change with it. "Look, there was nothing sinister about what happened in Victoria. My timing was off, that's all."

Berwick's tone was neutral. "Because you were on drugs?"

Hendrix gave a dry, tight laugh. "Drugs are a mug's game. I gave them up before I was out of my teens. Believe it or not, I'd been up all night doing stock market research."

"Stock market research," Berwick repeated, his tone skeptical.

"Surprised? The irony is, I'm working on ethical investments. If only I could have told Dad about it. . . ." The corners of his mouth turned downward, but Danutia didn't sense any feeling behind his words.

"Why did everyone assume you were doing drugs?" She asked.

"Suppose your father stopped talking to you when you switched university majors from Arts to Business. Suppose you still wanted his approval." A smile flitted across Hendrix's face. "I'm not a bad actor, you know. I decided to play the part of the dopehead son. Dad could deal with that, he'd been one himself. Much better than soiling yourself with filthy lucre. It was a great cover."

Berwick looked around the room. "Speaking of covers," he said, "no one seemed to know your whereabouts last night."

"You mean what am I doing here? This is a holiday place for my economics prof at SFU," Hendrix said. "I keep an eye on it when he's not here, look after the plants, that sort of thing. In return he lets me use a spare room as an office."

Before Berwick could respond, his pager beeped. Danutia handed him her cellphone and he stepped outside.

Danutia weighed this new image of Hendrix as a young business type and found she didn't trust it. She had the disturbing feeling that he could be either an egotistic young man speaking the exact truth, or a psychopath presenting a wall she would never penetrate until it was too late.

As though he sensed her doubts, Hendrix suddenly said, "Here, I'll show you," and led her upstairs to a small room furnished with an unmade daybed, a rickety bookcase, a battered filing cabinet, and a makeshift table holding a desktop computer and printer, scattered with papers. No problem with rats here, obviously.

"You wouldn't believe how much research it takes," Hendrix said, picking up a sheet of paper. "Look at this list. These are companies working for positive social change—like heritage seed companies, and worker-owned steel mills with good labour practices."

The list was printed on Funds for Social Change letterhead.

"Just a minute," said Danutia. "I spent all morning trying to track down Funds for Social Change. Nobody's ever heard of it."

"That's because it doesn't exist yet," Hendrix said, "but it will. Now that I can prove you can make a reasonable return. Joe was my guinea pig. He pretended to invest the fifteen thousand dollars he spent on Antonia's wedding and honeymoon. We'd get together every few days to review the portfolio, make some changes. If it had been real, he would have made a tidy profit."

What if it was real, Danutia thought, and the money is in your pocket?

"The night Joe Bertolucci died," she said. "There was a rehearsal. I understand you left early. Where did you go?"

"I came here. The play was eating up my time. Professor Cohen got me a grant to develop this fund. I have to have something to show him by the end of August."

Danutia asked more questions. Had Hendrix discussed Bertolucci's portfolio with the professor? Had he discussed his project with anyone else at all? Lavender? Sandra?

As Hendrix repeatedly answered no, Danutia's doubts grew. She was taking down Professor Cohen's telephone number when Berwick appeared in the doorway, asking her to join him downstairs.

"What's up?" she asked when they were in the kitchen, out of earshot.

"Betty asked me to call David Ohara. It seems that someone claiming to be Ohara phoned the theatre box office earlier this afternoon, saying he was flying Sandra to Vancouver for a screen test with a visiting Japanese director and she likely wouldn't be back for the evening performance. Ohara heard about it ten minutes ago when he dropped by to pick up some tickets for tonight."

Danutia had felt troubled by Ohara's comments about his daughter, but had never followed up properly. Brushing aside the stirrings of guilt, she said, "Maybe the screen test is for real, but her father didn't arrange it."

"That's possible," Berwick said. "I've asked Betty to check out the film companies in Vancouver, and sent a constable around to the ferry operators to find out if she's been seen leaving the island. Ohara's worried because her bed hasn't been slept in."

That wasn't his only reason for worry, as they both well knew.

Danutia thought back to her hunt for Hendrix. "Emile saw her arguing with Hendrix after the rehearsal, around nine o'clock. According to Ohara's housekeeper, she used the photocopier about ten-thirty and went out again. No one else reported seeing her."

The printer in the office above them clattered into action. They glanced up at the ceiling, and then without another word mounted the stairs.

Berwick planted himself in the doorway of the small office; Danutia crossed to stand in front of the open balcony door, only a few feet from where Hendrix sat at the computer. "David Ohara phoned. He's concerned about Sandra. Apparently she didn't come home last night. We thought you would know where she is."

Hendrix kept his eyes glued to the computer screen. "Ohara?" he said absently. "I thought he was away on business."

"That's hardly the point. The question is, where is Sandra?"

"How would I know?" Hendrix double-clicked his mouse.

"Turn off the computer and pay attention," Danutia said. "You were seen arguing with her at the end of the rehearsal last night. What do you know of her whereabouts after that?"

"Nothing, I tell you." A series of clicks. "She's a grown woman. She can sleep where she likes. What business is it of mine?"

"So she wasn't here with you."

The computer whined as it closed down. "I was working all night."

"And you aren't worried that something might have happened to her."

Hendrix swung around in his chair and glared up at Danutia. "Look, this happens all the time. We argue; she stalks off; she comes back the next day. Always the same story."

Except that this time she's not back, Danutia thought. She had been inclined to believe that his apparent callousness about the deaths of his father and Joe Bertolucci was the egotism of youth. Now his lack of concern for Sandra was changing her mind. Egotism could become so all-encompassing that no one else mattered, even killing them didn't matter. Aloud, she said. "What were you arguing about last night?"

Hendrix's gaze faltered and he reached for the sheets he had printed out, his face for a moment turned away. Danutia waited for the lie she sensed was coming.

"Nothing, really. She'd stolen a song out of Dad's script after the rehearsal Monday."

Before or after Smith died, she wondered. "Why would she steal the song? Presumably everyone had a copy of the script."

"Dad had rewritten the song, putting in a lot of local references. Sandra was angry because of something he'd said about her. She didn't want him singing the song in public."

Danutia reached over and took the papers Hendrix had been fiddling with. "What did that have to do with your argument?"

Hendrix stared bleakly at her. Finally he said, "She wanted me to help her figure out Dad's writing."

"And you wouldn't? Why was that?"

"She kept going on and on about Lavender's new theory that Dad was killed because of that song, and we could figure out who had killed him. Crap, all of it. Dad wasn't killed. It was an accident. That's what I kept telling her. An accident. Don't get dragged into this by my crazy sister. Tear up the song and forget about it."

"And did she?" Danutia asked, knowing the answer, knowing too in a flash of understanding why Ohara had tried to keep secrets from his daughter, and that he had failed.

"No," Hendrix said, "she just got angrier. Larry came along about then and I asked him to talk some sense into her, but in a few minutes she was back, saying I was never any help and she would figure things out without me. Then she left. As I said, we've done the same scene with different words more times than I can count. I didn't think anything of it."

"Do you think anything of it now?"

"Well, of course I'm a bit worried if you say she's missing. But she's tough and she does what she wants. She'll turn up, you wait and see—she couldn't bear to miss opening night." He gave Danutia a half smile. "And now I really must get to the theatre, or they'll be sending the police to look for me."

"Wait here," she instructed.

When she and Berwick were again in the kitchen, she said, "I don't trust him."

Berwick picked up an empty beer bottle. Danutia couldn't keep her eyes off the label. Dos Equis. Two X's. Two lives crossed out. Would there be a third?

"I'm not so sure," Berwick said, setting the bottle down. "The newspaperman who found the body was with Lavender when she came to see me yesterday. Neither of them said anything about a song, but Fairweather did mention that Zachary's script was missing, and that he'd noticed indentations in the pool of blood. Lavender's accusations against Carol were clearly groundless, and he seemed to be supporting them, so I didn't follow up. Now I wonder. What Hendrix said about Sandra stealing the song could be true."

"He could also have known the song pointed to him, and kidnapped her to keep her from revealing it. I'll check out Ohara's photocopier," Danutia said. "It's a long shot, but maybe she's left us a clue."

# Chapter 25
Salt Spring: Friday evening, July 14

Rodney seemed on the verge of hysteria. He'd already called in a panic this afternoon, and now, as well as Arthur could make out, there was another crisis involving Sandra.

As soon as Rodney hung up, Arthur dressed for the evening and hurried down to the new theatre, where chaos seemed to reign. Carol Smith, looking close to tears, sat on the edge of the stage clutching her water bottle; Thea bent over her, talking quietly. Behind them, Larry Weston, in his Mikado costume, paced the stage alongside an older woman whom Arthur had not seen before, discussing the blocking for the performance due to start in—Arthur checked his watch—fifty minutes.

Then his arm was grabbed from behind. Rodney Coutt and his mother shepherded him into a small, unfinished workshop at the back of the building.

"What kept you?" Rodney's garish 'Money Rules' T-shirt contrasted with his strained expression.

"Why did you call me to come down?" Arthur was indignant. "I thought we'd already agreed to scrap my plan, since Sandra has gone off for a screen test."

"A hoax—" Rodney spluttered.

Mrs. Coutt calmed her son and then explained that she'd run into David Ohara at the box office and learned that he knew nothing about Sandra's alleged screen test. "He must have got straight on the phone to the police," she said. "They interviewed every last one of us, and only left a few minutes ago."

"Did you tell them about my plan?" Arthur asked.

"I didn't," Mrs. Coutt said. "I just thought Sandra would walk through the door any minute."

"You have to tell them about Sandra's note." Rodney was emphatic. "This isn't play-acting. There may be a murderer on stage tonight, and you won't even tell us who you suspect."

"I know this is serious," Arthur said. "But I don't believe going to the police will help. I bet they didn't discover anything about Sandra's whereabouts from the cast, did they?"

"Not as far as we know," said Rodney, cautiously.

"You see, they have no understanding of art. I'm sure they think all actors are liars." For a moment Arthur had a vivid memory of Sergeant Berwick's appraising grey eyes. "So it's impossible for them to tell when one of the company actually is lying."

"Maybe. I don't know . . ." Rodney let out a sigh.

Arthur pressed on. "If we tell the police right now, we'll lose our one chance to flush out the murderer. I think we need to try my plan. After all, it has the advantage of surprise. The question is whether you both have the nerve to carry on."

Mrs. Coutt, who had been listening intently, said, "He's right, you know, Rodney." She tugged at her skirt, as if preparing for battle. "I'm nervous too. But it's worth trying."

"What about you, Rodney?"

"Goodness knows what the audience will think. All right, I'll do it. As long as you promise to turn Sandra's letter over to the police right after the performance."

"I will," Arthur said, relieved. "I'll be happy to leave the rest to the police. And who knows? Sandra may still turn up."

···· ····

She didn't, though.

And so shortly after the performance began, Danutia stood impatiently ringing the after-hours buzzer at the detachment.

Berwick opened the heavy metal door, spilling light into the darkness. "Find anything?" he asked, staring past her as though the missing girl might materialize from the shadows.

"I don't know," she said. As she stepped inside her cellphone rang. Dennis, she thought, then knew it couldn't be. It must be Sharma, whose call she had been so desperate to receive a few hours ago, in hopes of pacifying Lewis. Now she prayed he'd discovered something, anything, that would help them find the girl. She pressed the button and listened. When she hung up, she told Berwick, "Krahn had a quick look at Smith's body. There's a definite contusion around the left carotid artery."

"Enough to make him black out?" Berwick asked.

Danutia nodded. "Same as Bertolucci's."

The lines in Berwick's face hardened and set, like clay drying. He ran a hand across his bald spot, not gleefully

307

this time, but slowly, as though his fingers searched for something he'd lost. He didn't try to explain or excuse his handling of Smith's death, and for that Danutia was grateful.

Opening her backpack, Danutia took out a plastic bag and handed it to Berwick. "Four sheets of crumpled paper from the wastepaper basket beside the copier. But they're too faint to read."

Berwick held a sheet up to the light and squinted. "Maybe we can bring it up."

Danutia followed him to the photocopier behind Betty's desk. While they waited for the machine to warm up, she asked, "Anything from the door-to-door downtown?"

"Sandra was in the liquor store around nine-thirty last night, buying two bottles of sake instead of her usual Chardonnay. When the clerk asked about it, she said the sake was for her dad's guests. Ohara says he didn't arrive until two o'clock this afternoon, and he keeps his liquor cabinet well stocked."

The photocopier's green light came on. The first three sheets remained illegible, though Danutia set the control for darker, darker still. On her second try with the last sheet, faint pencil markings appeared between the lines of the printed score. Even with a magnifying glass she couldn't make out the words.

"It's no use," she said finally. "Maybe this is a wild goose chase. Nearly everyone in the cast said Sandra would do anything to advance her career. She could have cooked up this disappearing act for the publicity."

"If this is an act," Berwick said, "it's a damn convincing one."

Of course it's convincing, she wanted to say, they're all actors, it's their job to be convincing. She pushed the thought away. "Okay," she said wearily, "if there is a killer, it has to be someone in the Vesuvius Company. That's the only way all the pieces fit together—the fake suicide note, the fake accident, the fake phone call to Ohara. Hendrix Smith is still our best bet."

"How can you say that? Everything he's said holds up so far. I talked to Professor Cohen. He corroborated their arrangement and says if we want to go over the condo, we'll have to get a search warrant. McTavish had a good look around at the Smith place and didn't find anything suspicious—no sign of Sandra or her convertible, no tampering with the power line, nothing in the greenhouse except tomato plants."

She and Berwick had questioned all the other cast members when they brought Hendrix to the theatre. Danutia thought back to their responses. "What about the British banker, Rodney Coutt? He seemed nervous as hell."

"They're all nervous," Berwick said. "Think what they've been through this week."

Protecting his islanders again. They'd never get anywhere this way. Danutia glanced at her watch. "I'd better get over to the theatre. Is everything set there?"

"Betty phoned just before you arrived," Berwick said. "The cast is accounted for, except Sandra of course. So are the others—Bob Kelly, Doc Johnson with Andy and

Martha, Thea Roberts and the newspaperman, Ohara and his business associates. Constables outside front and back."

Berwick had taken care of everything, it seemed. Only one question niggled at her. "Where's Larocque?"

Berwick shrugged. "He's coming off a double shift, so I couldn't put him on the road. He's watching the back of the theatre 'til you get there."

"Then I'd better get there quick." As she picked up her backpack, her cellphone rang again.

"This is Emile," said a soft voice. "You said I should phone if I remembered anything else about last Thursday night."

Trying to control the excitement in her voice, Danutia said, "Yes, go on."

"A few minutes ago I was standing in the wings, ready to open the curtain for the second act, when I noticed one of the flats was out of place. Quickly I adjusted it—"

Get to the point, Danutia wanted to say but didn't, afraid he would lose his train of thought.

"—and then I started thinking about the night we painted out the cherry trees while we waited for Sandra to bring books on Japanese history. She was gone a long time, as I told you, and Zachary was angry. 'Don't blame me,' she said, 'I had to drive all the way home.' The thing was, you see, she had gone somewhere closer for the books first. . . ."

One little scrap of information, and a new pattern formed.

# Chapter 26
Salt Spring: Friday evening, July 14

'Leave it to the police' indeed, Arthur thought as *The Mikado* neared its end. When he'd concocted his plan, he'd had a vague image of the murderer attempting to bolt, guilt written all over his face, only to be captured by the police, who would congratulate Arthur and his accomplices for their enterprise. The problem was, there weren't any police, as far as he could tell. Not a single uniform visible in the whole auditorium. Where were they? Looking for Sandra, presumably. Not knowing what Arthur knew, the police had no particular reason to be at the theatre.

As the cast grouped for the finale, Arthur held his breath. Mrs. Coutt switched into the opening chords for Ko-Ko's 'I've Got a Little List' song, as they had arranged. Amidst murmurs from the audience, Rodney stepped forward and Arthur waited for the opening notes. To his horror, Coutt motioned for the piano to be quiet and announced that as a tribute to the director's memory, he would sing Zachary Smith's last piece of original songwriting.

You idiot, thought Arthur. There went the element of surprise. Nevertheless, he watched Hendrix Smith carefully as Coutt sang the strange lines. As the song ended, Arthur sensed rather than saw a tremor of agitation somewhere in the cast, though not in Hendrix, who looked merely puzzled. A tremor, but that was all; no one fled.

Then the audience was standing and applauding, and continued to applaud through the finale.

At last people started to make their way toward the exits and Arthur moved with them, feeling empty and deflated. Then he saw Thea fighting her way toward him, face like a thundercloud. Not wanting to face her anger at his 'interfering', Arthur plunged into the crowd. Taking the first door marked Exit, he found himself in a long dark corridor ending in a metal door. He opened it and stepped into the sharp night air, a tonic after the stuffiness of the theatre. Looking around, he realized he had emerged onto the staff parking lot.

He was congratulating himself on his escape when a large pickup truck pulled out of a parking place, catching him in its headlights. Suddenly the truck swung toward him, engine roaring.

⸺ ⸺

Later than she'd planned to be, Danutia backed the Blazer into a narrow space in the as-yet-unpaved staff lot and marched toward Larocque's cruiser. He'd just that minute dozed off, he protested when she reamed him out. No one had left, he was sure of that, he had an unobstructed view of the back exit.

Except, she had learned from Emile, there were three rear exits. She ordered Larocque to move his cruiser where he could observe the door to the gallery wing. She would cover the two giving onto the staff lot, where the cast had agreed to park. Her windows open to the cool night air, she settled in to wait.

Abruptly the exit door closest to her was flung open and a bulky figure appeared in the doorway, silhouetted against the light. The height was about right, but the posture . . .

Somewhere to her left an engine sputtered into life. Larocque? If he scared the suspect off . . . she craned her head. No headlights, no movement visible in the paved lot. The sound must have carried from the street beyond.

A large truck roared into motion. Instead of heading left, past Larocque, it swerved close to the figure in the doorway, bounced over the curb and shot off into the night.

Danutia gunned her engine and pulled up beside the fallen man. "Are you hurt?" she yelled. "If not, get in."

"The bloody bastard," said an aggrieved British voice. Scrambling to his feet, he patted his arms and legs. "He's ripped my new shirt."

"Get in! He could have done worse."

"Well, forgive me for living." He clambered in. "It's not my fault—"

"Can it," she said, reaching for the hand mike. The radio crackled. "Dranchuk to Berwick. Suspect's truck just left the theatre at high speed, going toward the centre of town. Almost ran down the newspaperman—"

"Fairweather. Arthur Fairweather."

"No injuries," she said, ignoring his dirty look. "Now, get this. As the truck crossed my headlights, I saw the logo. It wasn't a crane Kelly saw. It was a fishing rod. A rod with a golden reel."

"Keep on him," the radio crackled back. "I'm at the

wharf. I'll stay here until we know where he's headed."

"He's just turned left. I'll give you the street in a second. Here we are. Rainbow Road."

"You'll come to a Y intersection in about five kliks. If he's heading toward his place, he'll turn right. McTavish just radioed from there. I'll send some backup."

"What's all this about, anyway," the querulous voice beside her demanded. "It's like a scene out of a bad movie—"

"It's no movie," Danutia snapped, her eyes fixed on the taillights ahead. They were into the countryside now, no traffic, no lights except the ones receding in front of them as the truck picked up speed.

"Who would try to run me over?" Fairweather grumbled beside her. "And why?"

"The truck belongs to Larry Weston," Danutia said. *And I don't know how he got past Larocque,* she fumed silently.

"Weston! Surely not. He's such a nice chap, and a great Mikado. He invited me to go out on his boat—"

"He's a suspect in two cases of murder. For some reason he seems to have added you to his list. I picked you up to find out why."

Danutia heard a thud and a muttered, "Bloody hell," as her passenger tried to straighten his legs. "You think Weston murdered Zachary Smith and that other bloke?" he asked, rubbing first one knee, then the other. "And kidnapped Sandra?"

"That's what the evidence suggests."

"And I'm on his list?" Fairweather fell into a welcome

silence. Moist night air flowed through, laden with the scent of earth and pine. An owl floated across the road in front of them. Danutia imagined the silent descent, the talons tearing through quivering flesh.

"My plan worked after all, it seems," Fairweather said, sounding pleased with himself. "I just had the wrong man."

"What plan?" The truck's taillights disappeared over a rise. Danutia pressed a little harder on the accelerator. She mustn't lose him, not now. There was still a chance Sandra was alive.

Fairweather stirred on the seat beside her. "It's like the play-within-a-play in *Hamlet*—you know, 'the play's the thing to catch the conscience of the king.'"

Catching his glance, Danutia scowled.

"Well anyway," he hurried on, "Zachary had written new words to the Lord High Executioner's song—you know, 'I've Got a Little List.' I heard them at the rehearsal Monday, and when he was murdered I knew bloody well the song had something to do with it, but the words were lost, or stolen, and you people wouldn't listen, so when Sandra passed them on to me last night—"

"Let me get this straight. Sandra gave you evidence that you strongly suspected was linked to Smith's death and you didn't get in touch with the police?"

"Wait a minute," he said. "She didn't exactly give it to me. She put it under my door . . ." Danutia waited for the half-truth, or outright lie, she had learned to expect when people knew they had acted stupidly.

"I was already asleep, you see, and anyway her note

didn't say much, just that she wanted me to have the 'list' song in case she didn't turn up for the performance tonight."

"She said that? She was clearly putting herself in danger of some kind, and you didn't notify us?"

He shifted uneasily. "I thought I knew who the murderer was, and I didn't think he'd harm her. So after Ohara phoned—except it wasn't Ohara—"

"Yes, we know all about the fake call."

"Anyway, I convinced Rodney and his mother—she's the accompanist, a real musician—to do Smith's version of the song right before the finale."

No wonder they seemed nervous. They'd withheld vital information.

"I guess I expected the murderer to look guilty and rush away, as Claudius does in *Hamlet*. When that didn't happen, I thought I'd ruined the opening night performance for nothing, so I ducked outside. But I guess my plan worked after all."

"What do you mean it worked. You tipped off our suspect, you almost got yourself killed, and you may have signed Sandra Ohara's death warrant."

"If anybody in the bloody RCMP had paid attention on Monday night, or yesterday morning—"

"Damn!" Danutia exclaimed. Weston's taillights had winked out for a moment, and when she picked them up again, they were running into the darkness to the west.

She flicked on the radio. "Berwick, are you there? Weston turned left instead of right at the Y, toward the Kellys' place. Are they still at the theatre?"

"Betty says everyone except Weston and Fairweather

are still at the reception, swigging champagne."

"There has to be an accomplice. If it isn't one of the Kellys, who is it?"

"If Weston's heading for the cabin, he may have a boat waiting. The cove would be an obvious pickup point if his partner doesn't know the waters around here. There aren't any other roads out, but there are a lot of trails through the woods. If Weston abandons the truck, try to keep him pinned down until my men are in position."

Now the Blazer too was heading west, the forest closing in on both sides. Danutia pushed the accelerator harder.

"I'll drop you at the Kellys' house," Danutia said to the angry silence beside her.

"You'll have to drag me out," Fairweather said. "And I don't think you want to waste your time on that. I vowed I'd find Smith's killer, and I'm not quitting now."

"You're not a cop, and you'll do as I say," Danutia retorted, her fingers gripping the wheel.

"You have no backup. I'll be your backup."

"And do what? Recite Shakespeare?"

"I could at least create a diversion, help you stall for time until the cavalry rides over the hill."

"I don't need you messing up the evidence."

"You don't have to worry about that," Fairweather snorted. "You cops will manage that for yourselves."

Danutia winced. "Okay, you can fill Berwick in when he arrives." Shifting to the offensive again, she added, "At least we were zeroing in on the right man. From the sound of it, you had someone else in mind. Who was it?"

"I'm not telling." Then he must have thought better of it. "Hendrix Smith."

"Not a bad guess," Danutia admitted. After all, she had thought the same until Emile's phone call. Emile had remembered that on the night of Bertolucci's murder, Sandra had gone first to Weston's to borrow books on Japanese history. Not finding him home, she'd made the longer trip to Welbury Bay. Weston had assured Danutia he had been home alone all evening, and she, so easily taken in by older men, had believed him.

Fairweather settled his jacket and straightened his tie.

The headlights they were pursuing swept over Kelly's bulldozer and disappeared into the darkness ahead.

Danutia tried to get Berwick on the radio. No response, and she was slipping farther behind. If only it was Sharma in the seat next to her, someone she could trust with the details while she concentrated on the winding road, which soon, she remembered, would make a sharp turn and drop to the beach.

When she hit gravel she braked, but not quite enough, and the Blazer skidded toward the murky blackness where the creek tumbled. Then the tires gripped and she eased back onto the road.

Below lay the beach where she had met the Johnsons only two days ago. Moonlight glinted off water, and farther off, the faint red and green of a boat's running lights.

The parking lot was empty; the gate across the drive was shut. Weston might have set up an ambush there. She parked beside the road and tried again to reach Berwick. This time he answered.

"Weston must have headed for the cabin," she said. "Maybe that's where he's holding Sandra. I'm leaving Fairweather with the Blazer near the beach parking lot. There's a boat offshore. Could be Weston's pal."

"McTavish and O'Connell should be there in ten minutes. I'll try to get a copter or a Coast Guard cutter to check out the boat, then I'm on my way."

"I'll head up to the cabin. Send a couple of guys up the drive to join me and a couple along the beach, past the point with the huge boulder. We have to cut off Weston's rendezvous." She signed off.

Switching off the dome light—if Weston was waiting at the gate, she didn't want to be an easy target—Danutia opened her door and climbed out.

She unholstered her pistol. Looking down, she saw the reassuring soft green glow of the tritium night sights. She gave Fairweather firm instructions to stay put and then, pistol in hand, she set off for the cabin where Joe Bertolucci had died.

# Chapter 27

Arthur fumed with guilt and anger. What if the bloody copper was right and he had endangered Sandra Ohara's life by not going to the police? If so, he wasn't about to sit quietly and do nothing.

He scrambled out of the Blazer, his knee aching from where he'd banged it against the theatre door. To the north a sprinkling of golden lights like fallen stars marked the hamlet of Vesuvius. He scanned the dark waters of the channel, looking for the craft Dranchuk had mentioned to Berwick. Yes, there were lights out in the channel: a white masthead light and lower down, a red port light on a sleek dark shape Arthur guessed was a motor cruiser. It was still at a distance, but coming closer. Was that Weston's accomplice? If so, how long before he reached the rendezvous? Ten minutes? Fifteen? There was no sign of Berwick's men.

Like it or not, the snippy constable would have to accept his help.

Ignoring the radio, which crackled out an indecipherable message, Arthur set off across the moonlit beach. Dranchuk had told Berwick to send a couple of men to the cove beyond the rocky point he could see jutting out some half-mile away. So all he had to do to find the cove was keep to the shoreline.

He hadn't reckoned on an incoming tide, and apparently neither had Dranchuk. The thin strip of beach had already all but disappeared. Soon scrambling over slimy boulders, under a sheer cliff that cut out any helpful moonlight, Arthur kept himself going only by the thought of what he owed Sandra Ohara. He was closest to giving up when a great vertical boulder—the keystone of the point, he guessed—forced him to climb upwards through a tangle of tree roots into a trackless mass of dark fir forest with thick underbrush. Just when he thought he could go no farther, he found a narrow path, hardly wider than a deer trail, that led him directly to a small cove wholly enclosed by the keystone boulder on his right and a rock almost as big on his left. Without the path he would have missed it.

At the edge of the cliff he halted. Below, near the keystone boulder, a dark mass took form against the glitter of the cove's shell beach. An overturned rowboat. The motor cruiser was probably hovering in deeper water, waiting for Weston to row out. If he acted quickly, he could put an end to that plan.

Rough steps had been cut into the cliff. Arthur scrambled down. At its base, he found a rock the size of a soccer ball. Wishing he didn't have to make so much noise, he brought the rock down hard. The night reverberated with the sound of splintering wood.

From the cliff above came Weston's deep bass. "What the hell do you think you're doing?"

Arthur could make out only one dark shape with an odd voluminous look to it. The Mikado's kimono, Arthur suddenly realized. Weston was still wearing it. Where was Sandra? A muffled cry and flying shadows told him she was trying to free herself. A blade glinted and the struggling figure grew still.

"Bastard," Arthur said, lunging toward the steps. "Turn the girl loose."

"Oh, it's you. Stop right there, Fairweather. I've got a knife at the young lady's throat. If you make another move, I'll use it."

Arthur halted, the rock still in his hands.

"You won't be needing the rock," Weston said. "Put it down, and then you can sit on it while we wait." Arthur was about to drop the rock in front of the steps when Weston said, "Not there, beside the rowboat."

Arthur did as he was told. When he looked up again, Weston had settled himself on the top step, with Sandra wedged between his knees and one arm around her shoulder. Sitting in the moonlight with the shadowed kimono above him, Arthur had the strange feeling that he was still in the theatre.

"Chased me up the road, did you? And now you're trying to cut off my escape route, is that right?" Weston asked, imitating Arthur's Manchester accent perfectly. No doubt he had been equally good at imitating Ohara. The man's own voice, when he spoke again, had a harder edge than Arthur remembered. "Too bad I didn't manage to run you over outside the theatre."

"Too bloody bad you're stuck here," Arthur said, gesturing toward the smashed rowboat.

"You don't think I'd rely on something so flimsy, do you? That thing hasn't been used in years." The kimono billowed like a sail as Weston gestured toward the sea.

"My partner should be along any minute now, unfortunately for you. You and your solitary heroics."

"What makes you think I'd do this alone? I told the police everything."

"Where are they, then?"

Arthur was wondering the same thing.

⋅⊷ ⊶⋅

While Arthur was scrambling over the wet rocks, Danutia was racing toward the Bittencourt cabin. At the edge of the clearing she stopped to catch her breath. Except for Weston's truck pulled up close to the porch, she might have been inside a fairy tale. Bright moonlight silvered the towering firs and the tiny weather-beaten cabin, where glimmers of golden light seeped through the cracks.

Either Weston hadn't noticed he was being followed, or she'd made better time than he expected. Two days ago her steps had been slowed by Andy Johnson's laboured breathing. Tonight, once past the gate with its drooping banners, she'd holstered her pistol and raced up the dim tunnel between the trees, gambling that Weston would make straight for his hostage. And it seemed he'd done just that.

Wait for reinforcements, Berwick had said, and she knew that he was right, that this was no time for solitary heroics. Could she keep Weston pinned down for the twenty minutes or so it would take Berwick and his men to arrive? If she circled around to the path to the cove, she could cut off an escape by water, but then he could hustle Sandra into the truck and take to the back roads.

Danutia eyed the old Ford. The golden reels gleamed on the door panel, unmistakable now. Keeping her body low, she darted into the truck's shadow. From the cabin came the murmur of voices, Weston's low rumble and a light soprano that had to be Sandra Ohara's. She breathed a sigh of relief. At least the girl was alive.

Bending down, she removed the dust cap from the back tire and squeezed the valve with her fingernail, then made her way to the others. As the air whooshed out she felt a guilty thrill and wondered whether Andy Johnson had felt the same.

She was straightening up when she was startled by high-pitched laughter from inside the cabin.

Why would Sandra be laughing? Hendrix said she'd do anything to advance her career. Perhaps she and Weston had cooked up the scheme and drawn the newspaperman into it. What a fool Danutia would look if Berwick arrived to find the whole thing had been a hoax, a publicity stunt. She'd better have a look.

When the voices rose again Danutia doubled over and sprinted around the end of the porch, then flattened herself against the splintered wall. Earthy smells rose up around her, the must of decaying timber and decaying vegetation, and a lingering sickly sweetness from the decaying body that lay inside scarcely a week ago. No sound except the soft hoot of an owl from deep in the woods and the murmur of voices from inside. Pistol in her right hand, left arm extended to brush away cobwebs and brambles, she inched up to the window's soft golden glow. The plastic sheeting diffused and distorted the shapes inside as though they were underwater.

She would have to risk moving into the open.

Slowly she backed away and to the right, her eyes glued to the window, her ears straining for any change in the rhythm of the voices.

One dark shape snapped into focus. Weston's samurai wig, its whorls and topknot throwing grotesque shadows against the plastic screen. Sandra must be sitting against the wall.

The voices stopped. Danutia froze, waiting for a sound, a movement. Silence, then a click. Readying her pistol, she slipped into the shadows where she could watch both window and door.

Nothing moved, but from the cabin came a familiar *Top 40* voice.

Puzzled, Danutia crept to the porch and, pistol extended, flung open the cabin door.

For a moment, relief washed through her. No body, no blood, no sign of violence. Still, Sandra had clearly been held here: the rope tied to the chair, the crumpled tape on the floor, the scattered bits of food attested to that.

First relief, and then a flood of anger at her own stupidity.

A flashlight was propped against a boom box, its beam playing over the Mikado's wig.

She'd fallen for the trick every police force recommends for discouraging intruders. Leave a light on and a radio or TV playing. Or a tape recorder like her own, Danutia thought angrily, as Alanis Morrisette again sang "Ironic" into the moonlit night.

She should have known Weston would go in for theatrics. When Sandra confronted him last night—for that was surely what she had done—he must have surreptitiously recorded part of their conversation over the music that was playing. *Jagged Little Pill* indeed. Danutia had let him slip through her fingers, taking his hostage with him.

Danutia raced out of the cabin and around the truck, grazing her leg on the front bumper. She cut through the scattered remains of the fire pit to where the path to the cove should be. A cloud had drifted across the moon, and she had to cast back and forth before she found the break in the thick undergrowth. She'd only gone a few steps on the hard-packed earth when a distant crash like splintering wood broke the stillness.

A falling tree? Or Weston's escape boat cracking up? The strait hadn't looked rough, to her unpractised eye, but what did she know of tides and currents? More likely, the tide had picked up the old rowboat she'd noticed and smashed it against the rocks.

Silence settled over the woods again. Moonlight filtered weakly through treetops and glistened on the undergrowth, making the path a bright ribbon unwinding ahead of her. Danutia raced toward the cove, scarcely noticing when brambles snagged her trousers and branches scored her arm, careful only of the tree roots that threatened to trip her up.

A rustling in the bushes ahead.

Danutia dropped into a squat and drew her pistol. The grip was sweaty in her hand. A mosquito whined maddeningly around her head, attracted by the smell of sweat and the night sight's greenish glow. The air was cooler now, the rich scent of cedar and fir undercut by the salty tang of the sea. In the moonlight ahead, an arbutus leaf settled slowly to the ground. Arbutus trees overlooked the cove. She must be nearing the end of the path.

The rustling subsided. Wiping her sweaty palms on her trousers, Danutia advanced, cautiously now, conscious of leaves crackling underfoot and in the distance, the dull slap of waves.

A puff of wind brought Weston's low rumble floating toward her, then the murmur of a different male voice. One of Berwick's constables? Or Weston's accomplice? She crept forward until the accent stopped her.

Fairweather! What was he doing here?

# Chapter 28

With the menacing figure of the Mikado looming down at him from the cliff top, Arthur could think of nothing to say. Where *were* the police, he wondered for the second time tonight, though this time fear gripped him. Had something happened to Constable Dranchuk on her way to the cabin?

"Just as I thought," Weston said. "Your forte is words, not action. Though it was you who put Rodney up to that tribute to our dearly departed, wasn't it? Sandra told me she'd given you a copy of Zachary's little masterpiece. When I took the script, I didn't think to make sure the song was still there. That was careless of me. But now everything's going according to plan again. Clever of you to figure out about the smuggling."

"I don't know anything about smuggling."

"Then you're not half as clever as I gave you credit for. Who else would he mean by 'dopers building business here' and that comment about crabs? He knew about my grow-ops, and he knew how I was getting the stuff out."

Arthur felt a tide of anger rising up in him. "You killed him because he might have blown your cover? How could you do that? Smith was your friend."

"You have no idea what my relationship with Zachary Smith was like." Weston's deep voice shook. Prudence told Arthur to back off, but he found he couldn't.

"He invited you into the country he'd adopted and the

328

company he'd formed, he regarded you as his closest friend, and you killed him."

"That's a tidy plot line, Mr. Theatre Critic." Weston's voice was scathing. "But rather simplistic, don't you think? Is that all a sophisticated critic can offer?"

"Who cares about complicated plot lines—"

"You should, Fairweather." Weston's arm moved and again metal glinted. Arthur felt fear seize his throat, but Weston went on speaking. "I'm guessing we have five minutes. While we're waiting I'll tell you about my new play. You didn't know I wrote plays, did you?"

"No, and I don't—"

"It's about a theatre director and his friend."

A cold wind was blowing off the water again and Arthur shivered. "I'm listening."

"As I said, the play is about a theatre director—let's give him a good biblical name. How about Ezekiel? Zeke for short. And his friend—Wes. Now, as the play starts, Wes has become disillusioned by his service in Vietnam and the chaos of life in America, so he's gone AWOL and sneaked across the border into Canada to stay with his draft dodger friend Zeke. Wes is a man who craves solitude, you understand. He wants to go to Japan to train as a Noh actor and live a very disciplined life. But he doesn't have any money, and, as Zeke points out, Wes's fugitive status would be revealed if he tried to leave the country. So Wes goes into the fishing business and acts in the director's plays."

Hearing a clank behind him, Arthur glanced over his shoulder. The motor cruiser was at the mouth of the cove now, dipping and rising in the swell. A man was kneeling at the back, untying a dinghy. Arthur scanned the cliff top. No sign of help.

"I see you're not very interested in my play, Mr. Theatre Critic." Weston's tone was icy. "Perhaps you're ready for the next stage in the evening's entertainment."

Arthur imagined the knife slicing open Sandra's throat, and then his own. "Sorry. I'm listening."

"Are you sure? I wouldn't want to bore you."

Weston was toying with him. Had he already killed Dranchuk? Is that why he was so calm? Or did he actually believe Arthur had come here alone? Arthur had offered to be Dranchuk's backup, and he'd been no help at all. The only thing he could do now was to keep Weston talking.

"Your play has definite possibilities."

"Come, come, we have no conflict as yet," Weston said. "And conflict, as you know, is the essence of drama. First, there's internal conflict. Wes has befriended an influential Japanese-Canadian businessman, who will arrange for him to be admitted to Japan with no awkward questions being asked. But still Wes has no money, and as a point of honour, he cannot accept money from his patron. Then an old acquaintance from his army days gets in touch, offering him a way to make all the money he needs."

"Smuggling dope," Arthur said.

"Brilliant. But here's Wes's inner conflict: the criminal life he is being offered is the opposite of the disciplined life he seeks. He struggles to find a way out of this dilemma, to no avail. So which does he choose?"

"Obviously for Wes the end justifies the means."

"I'm afraid so. Like so many of us, he takes the expedient path, setting the tragedy in motion. End of act one."

Why was Weston telling him all this? He sensed the man had a need for order, a need to justify what he'd done by making it part of a story. A story in which, right now, Arthur could only play a minor role, the theatre critic trying to keep himself and Sandra Ohara alive as long as possible. Aloud he said: "And so Act Two: the external conflict."

"You'll make a dramatist yet, Fairweather. Scene 1: Wes receives a call from his partner. There's been a spot of trouble in the remote location where the shipments are transferred. The partner's been forced to shoot an onlooker, doesn't know whether the man's dead or not. Scene 2: Wes is forced to complete the job an itchy trigger finger started. He is reluctant—still internally conflicted, you see—but the wounded man could identify him. He cleverly sets up the death to look like suicide."

"So that's why you killed the man in the cabin . . ."

"In the play," Weston's tone was icy again, "this unpleasant event ends the second act, and leads to the third."

In his mind's eye Arthur saw again the pool of dried blood, and the head. "The third act," he said, "where the director dies." Not to mention the theatre critic. He cast a surreptitious glance behind him. The dinghy was wallowing in the tidal swells, which had already engulfed most of the beach. If the police didn't arrive soon, Weston wouldn't have to kill him—he'd be swept out to sea.

"Where the director dies," Weston agreed, a current of sadness in his voice now. Real or feigned, Arthur wondered, as the deep voice rolled on. "Somehow Zeke finds out about the smuggling—I haven't decided who tells him, maybe a snoopy young actress—and proposes that his old friend make regular 'contributions'—under a different name, of course—to his struggling theatre company. Wes is not surprised by this proposal; Zeke, like his favourite character Ko-Ko, is a modern man, struggling to survive at any price, and Wes figures he can spare a bit for his buddy. That was his first mistake."

There was movement above as Weston adjusted his hold on Sandra. Had she been trying to break free? Arthur wondered.

Settled again, Weston continued. "You know all about tragic flaws, Mr. Theatre Critic. Well, I guess you could say Wes's tragic flaw is his desire to please people. Kind of like the Mikado, you know, pleasing Katisha by saying she can marry his son without asking young Nanki-Poo his views on the matter. So first he gives Zeke money. Then his smuggling partner runs into a spot of trouble, and he tries to fix it. But when Zeke learns there's been an apparent suicide at that isolated spot, he puts two and two together. You see Wes's dilemma."

"And so he decides to kill the director."

"Not so fast, Mr. Theatre Critic. I told you to beware of simple plots. Wes and Zeke have been friends a long time, and at first Wes thinks that if he makes bigger contributions, his friend won't betray him. He discovers how wrong he is when Zeke makes veiled references to his criminal activities in a song. The guy that died was also a good friend of Zeke's, you see, and so Zeke isn't so happy about keeping Wes's secret any more. Later that evening Wes pleads with Zeke to withdraw the song, to give him just a little time to settle his affairs and get out of the country. As he has for so much of their lives, Zeke taunts him about being slow as a tortoise. Only this time something snaps in Wes, and before he knows what he's done, Zeke's blood is spilling onto the stage. This is how the play ends: with Wes's realization that one death simply leads to another. A grim ending, don't you agree?"

"Grim not just for you," Arthur burst out. "How could you sacrifice lives in the way you've done?"

"And how can I go on sacrificing them? Isn't that a more pressing question? This snoopy bitch—" a muffled cry from Sandra— "is worth more to me alive than dead, until I've reached my destination." He rose, pulling Sandra up with him. "Come on, my dear," he said. "Our ride is approaching. But don't forget my 'Snickersnee.'" The knife blade flashed.

The breeze picked up the loose folds of Weston's kimono, and the towering figure again reminded Arthur of the Mikado's electrifying presence.

"You are not part of my plans, I'm afraid," Weston said. "We've had one 'suicide,' one 'accident.' I've run out of tricks. This time there'll be no doubt it's murder."

Suddenly Arthur understood what Zachary Smith must have known about his friend: the ruthlessness beneath the genial exterior. Known, but known too late.

"Got your gun?" Weston boomed out to the man in

the dinghy, now barely thirty feet away. Arthur watched with horror as the man held onto the rudder with one hand, reached down and pulled up a rifle with the other. He'd stalled as long as he could.

"Good," Weston said. "If our friend here makes a move, shoot him."

Arthur was thinking furiously. What could he do? Maybe wait until Weston was near the bottom of the steps, then knock Sandra aside and try to wrestle Weston to the ground. In the confusion of the struggle, it would be hard for the accomplice to shoot accurately.

As Sandra fumbled her way down the shadowy steps, Arthur coiled himself to spring.

# Chapter 29
Salt Spring: Friday night, July 14

Why hadn't Fairweather stayed in the cruiser as he'd agreed, Danutia fumed. If he'd let himself get taken hostage . . .

Creeping closer to the voices that floated in and out like a late-night radio station, she caught the words "Act Two: the external conflict."

Anger as cold as ice surged through her. Weston and Fairweather, calmly talking about the theatre. So the whole thing was a hoax, and the newspaperman was part of it. What was her role—the cavalry riding over the hill? Or the patsy with egg on her face? She'd throw them both in jail, and the girl too. But if it was a hoax, why wasn't Sandra joining in the conversation?

Then she remembered Weston's truck swerving toward the man in the doorway, Fairweather's frightened look when he scrambled in beside her.

Hard to believe that was in the script.

She crept forward. When she came to a sharp left turn in the path, she could hear Weston's deep rumble again. This was where she'd found the first blood-splattered salal leaf. From here it was about twenty metres to where the path opened up, and then a three or four-metre drop to the beach via rough-hewn steps.

Leaving the path, she dropped to her belly and elbowed her way forward through thinning undergrowth toward the arbutus trees overhanging the cliff edge, pausing often to listen for any telltale change in the murmur of voices. Words, phrases took shape in the night air and dissolved again, like the shifting colours of a kaleidoscope.

". . . the director dies . . . snoopy young actress . . . tragic flaw . . ."

The two men, talking. Sandra silent.

While part of her mind tried to fit the words together, another guided her over moonlit tree roots and stony out-croppings to the cliff's edge. A moist breeze whispered past, cooling her face and throat. She grasped a low-lying arbutus branch and peered over the thinning salal.

The cliff's edge hid the beach below. All she could see was the two boulders standing like sentinels at the mouth of the cove and the waves shimmering like a sequined dress.

No rescue boat. Yet. For that much she could be thankful.

The voices were louder now, though most of the words still indistinct. But where were they coming from?

Danutia brought her legs under her and edged upwards.

One end of the old rowboat was bobbing in the waves.

The beach route she'd so confidently told Berwick about would be underwater by now. Berwick and his men would have to cover two sides of the triangle, as she had.

She'd have to find some way to stall.

Against the lighter patches of rock and water Danutia could see two dark shapes, one on the beach, one at the top of the cliff. If she hadn't been here before, she would think they were boulders. Which was Weston, which

Fairweather? The voices were no help. The trickster wind blew them about until they hovered in the air, disembodied.

The beach figure flung out an arm, and Fairweather's voice burst out. "How could you sacrifice lives—?" He must have come by the beach route and reached the cove before Weston. Maybe the theatre talk had been his way of stalling. Danutia was mentally congratulating him when she saw a dinghy rising and sinking in the waves. A larger boat must be moored farther out.

From the cliff came a muffled cry and flurry of movement, then the massive figure of the Mikado rose against the paler sky, the sleeves of his kimono billowing in a stiffening breeze. Ahead of and slightly below him stood a slighter figure, head bowed.

Sandra and Fairweather were trapped between Weston and his accomplice.

Weston shouted, "If our friend here makes a move, shoot him," and gave Sandra a shove that sent her stumbling a few steps down the cliff, her head a blacker ball against the darkness of the night. She paused and looked around, then nodded almost imperceptibly. Had she heard scuffling sounds the men had been too preoccupied to notice? Caught a glimmer from Danutia's pistol?

Two more steps and the girl would be out of Weston's reach.

Keeping the arbutus between her and the man with the rifle, Danutia edged back toward the path until she had a clear line of fire. She saw Sandra hesitate a moment, then fling herself toward Fairweather.

Danutia seized the moment. "Police," she yelled. "Freeze."

Weston whipped around into a knife-fighter's crouch, his blade flashing as he peered into the darkness. They both seemed to be waiting for the rifle shot that didn't come.

From the water a twangy American voice shouted, "Fuck you, Weston! I didn't bargain on killin' no cops." The dinghy's small engine putt-putted as it came about and headed out of the cove.

"It's no use, Weston," she said. "Drop the knife."

"We can't let our little play end so lamely," he boomed out. Whipping his kimono around him, he rolled backward down the steps and onto the sand.

While Weston struggled to disentangle himself from the folds of his kimono, Danutia ran toward the steps, scanning the beach for the two hostages. Their heads popped over the edge of the rowboat, only a few metres from Weston.

"Stay down!" she yelled.

She had to get between them and Weston before they tried something foolish.

As she neared the steps her body took over, her muscles gathering and releasing, flinging her forward and down until she landed near the rowboat with a soft thud, her gun hand steady, her brain ignoring the pain from her ankle.

Weston was scarcely a body's length away, his arms outstretched as when he had sung 'My object all sublime.' Only now water was lapping at his feet and she could see the thin blade of a filleting knife glisten in his right hand.

"Drop the knife or I'll shoot," Danutia said.

"Would you now," Weston mused. "And here I had you pegged as a good little Prairie girl, church on Sundays, no sex without marriage, or at least the prospect of a trip down the aisle." He gazed after the retreating dinghy, then down at the water rising around him. "Whatever happened to 'Thou shalt not kill'? To turning the other cheek?"

"You should have thought of that before you started killing innocent people. On the count of three. One—"

"Not so fast, Constable. What makes you think these were innocent people? Not Sandra, there. She's still alive, but she certainly isn't innocent. Know what she figured my life was worth? Half a million dollars. If I didn't happen to have that much stashed away, too bad. And what about good old Zachary? So he screwed around on his crazy wife and she committed suicide. Her choice, right? So he criticized and ridiculed and bullied everybody around him. They could turn the other cheek, right? And when they did, he ridiculed them for it. Or Joe now, ruining his wife's life, his kids' lives, with his drinking. You call them innocent? There's no such thing as innocent people. You should know that. Original sin."

"They were imperfect, like the rest of us. That doesn't mean they deserved to die."

"We all die, Ms. RCMP Constable, whether we deserve to or not. My government taught me that real early. All that matters is achieving our objective. Taking out that sniper. Holding that hill. Killing anyone that stands between us and our objective. It doesn't always work, but that's the best we can do. Your objective is to do a good job, please your bosses, climb a step up the career ladder. If you have to kill me, so be it. That's what doing your duty comes down to in the end, isn't it?"

Don't listen to him, Danutia told herself. The incoming tide nibbled at her boots. Behind her she could hear scrabbling as the tide forced the two onlookers away from the little shelter the rowboat afforded, back toward the steps. Weston might try to pick one of them off—

"You needn't worry about me," Weston said, as though reading her thoughts. His voice was tinged with the melancholy she had understood almost too late. "There is only one path now, the path of the samurai warrior." In a twinkling he reversed the knife. Its handle pointed toward Danutia, seemingly harmless. A knife-thrower's tactic.

"Two . . ."

Weston's hand whipped downward.

Danutia squeezed the trigger.

The knife was not hurtling toward her or the others behind her. It was making a slow circuit of Weston's abdomen. He was already falling, his robe settling on the incoming tide like a black curtain.

# Epilogue
## Victoria: Friday, August 11

Danutia Dranchuk stripped off her sweaty slacks and shirt, put on shorts and the thinnest T-shirt she could find, and carried the mail into the cool air of her balcony. Ignoring the bills, she opened the envelope marked *Victoria Post-Dispatch*, and pulled out a scrawled note attached to a press clipping.

> Dear Ms. Dranchuk:
>
> Or should I call you Constable? I was sorry I couldn't come to Ohara's event last Sunday. Given my finances, I have to review when there's reviewing to be done. Alastair Graham, the editor of the *Gulf Island Gazette*, sent me this editorial about the occasion from Wednesday's paper. Alastair's a pompous so-and-so, and his editorial sounds like the Sermon on the Mount, but I thought you might like to see it. We 'plucky young people' have to stick together!
>
> Enjoy!
> Arthur

Danutia found herself smiling. Fairweather's handwriting was like him, large and ungainly, but with something likeable about it. She moved on to the newspaper clipping.

# GOOD NEWS AT RAINBOW COVE

Last month, Rainbow Cove, down from the old Bittancourt cabin, witnessed some of the most dramatic events ever seen on Salt Spring Island: a man since charged with two murders and the kidnapping of Sandra Ohara was apprehended by two plucky young people.

Since that day in July we have been waiting for the other part of this drama to unfold. What would Mr. David Ohara do with this property, once rumoured to become a multi-million-dollar golf resort?

That wait ended on Sunday, August sixth, at the peace vigil commemorating the fiftieth anniversary of the bombing of Hiroshima. Although the atomic bombs that devastated Hiroshima and Nagasaki were deployed by order of US President Harry Truman, Canada too must accept responsibility for their use. For by our treatment of the Japanese among us—citizens and recent immigrants alike—Canadians of European descent demonstrated our readiness to inflict unbearable suffering on civilians who had done us no harm.

Mr. Ohara chose this day of infamy for a supreme act of generosity and forgiveness. He started his short speech by expressing regret that his business dealings had become a means of avenging the losses suffered by his parents, once-prosperous market gardeners on Salt Spring who died in the internment camps. For this heartless pursuit of material success, he went on to say, he has been punished by almost losing what he holds most precious, his daughter. He concluded by announcing the donation of the Mt. Erskine property to Save Salt Spring History, to be held in perpetuity as a public park.

In accepting this magnificent gift, Martha Johnson, founder of SSSH, made a surprise announcement of her own. When she learned of Mr. Ohara's intentions, she approached the elderly owners of the farmland once held by Mr. Ohara's parents. Though the details are yet to be worked out, they have agreed in principle to leave their property to SSSH, which will create a museum and Japanese garden there as a memorial to the Salt Spring residents who were dispossessed and forced into the interior.

If only our world leaders were capable of such honesty and mutual respect, we might all learn to live together in peace.


Danutia remembered the bitterness in Ohara's voice when he'd pointed out his parents' resident alien cards to her, and his choked silence when Martha Johnson made her surprise announcement. If the murders of two islanders had opened gaps in some lives, they had also allowed a great rift in the community to be bridged. She would call Arthur, thank him for the clipping.

As she reached for the phone, it rang.

"Lewis here," said the gravelly voice on the other end. "I've got a case for you."

# Acknowledgements

This is a work of fiction. While we have tried to capture the spirit of Salt Spring Island and its history, we have taken a few liberties, particularly in inventing the cabin of Manoel Bittancourt, an early settler about whom little is known. The characters and events are purely imaginary.

Many things have changed on Salt Spring since we began this book: the theatre has been finished; the RCMP detachment has moved into new quarters; a vineyard now exists where we imagined one; businesses have come and gone. Above all, the pace of development has quickened. A determined group of Islanders, with the help of The Land Conservancy of British Columbia, saved a large tract of land from logging; new housing developments are now transforming the landscape and culture of Salt Spring. In recognition of the complementary forces of stability and change, we will donate a portion of the proceeds of this book to the Artspring Theatre and to The Land Conservancy.

Our inspiration for this book came from watching a spirited performance of *The Mikado* put on by the Alberta Opera Company. We would like to thank the former director, Derril Butler, and the current director, Garner Butler, for their advice.

We would also like to thank the many other people who shared their time and expertise, among them Jim Ainsley, Carlin Bennett, Don Boyes, John McAstocker, Paul Minvielle, Patricia Nobile, Marilyn Strongitharm, Larry Thompson, Bob Wilson, and the librarians of Salt

Spring Library. We are especially grateful for the assistance we received from members of the RCMP: Constable Robert Doyle, who explained the workings of the Salt Spring detachment; Constable A.J. Voth, firearms expert at the Edmonton forensics lab, who read an early draft and saved us from making some embarrassing mistakes; and Constable Melissa Brown, Community Policing Section, West Shore detachment, who answered many questions. Any errors in the book are ours and not theirs.

For the history of Salt Spring, we found these sources particularly useful: Bea Hamilton, *Salt Spring Island* (Vancouver: Mitchell Press, 1969); Beth Hill et al, *Times Past: Salt Spring Island Houses and History before the Turn of the Century* (Community Arts Council, 1983); Charles Kahn, *Salt Spring: The Story of an Island* (Madeira Park, BC: Harbour Publishing, 1998); and Anne Smart, *All about Salt Spring: A Visitor's Guide* (1994 ed.). We consulted these works on the history of Japanese Canadians: Ken Adachi, *The Enemy that Never Was: A History of the Japanese Canadians* (Toronto: McClelland and Stewart, 1976); Barry Broadfoot, *Years of Sorrow, Years of Shame: The Story of Japanese Canadians in World War II* (Toronto: Doubleday, 1977); Toyo Takata, *Nikkei Legacy: The Story of Japanese Canadians from Settlement to Today* (Toronto: NC Press, 1983); and Charles H. Young and Helen R.Y. Reid, *The Japanese Canadians* (Toronto: University of Toronto Press, 1938). The story of the samurai follower is recounted in *Legends of the Samurai*, trans. Hiroaki Sato (Woodstock, NY: Overlook Press, 1995).

We also thank those who read the manuscript, in part

or in whole. Caterina Edwards and Sandra Mallett offered both unwavering encouragement and helpful comments on several drafts. Donna Askin, Chris Beck, Kathy Crandall, James Hawkins, Robin Hedley-Smith, Glen Huser, Bonnie Moro, Greg Randall, Helen Rosta, Fred Schloessinger, Kathleen Keating Schloessinger, and Betty Wilson also gave useful feedback. Marilyn Bowering taught us how to craft scenes; Peter Robinson inspired; Sean Stewart not only set a good example but also gave friendly filial advice. We appreciated the good humour with which Lynne van Luven, our editor for NeWest Press, pointed out weaknesses and trusted us to fix them. Without all of those sharp minds and sharp eyes, this would have been a lesser book.

Kay Stewart
Chris Bullock
September 2005

**more great mysteries**
from NeWest Press . . .

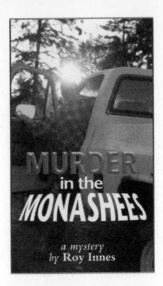

# Murder in the Monashees

### ROY INNES

RCMP Corporal Paul Blakemore is jolted from his mundane policing duties in the small Monashee Mountain village of Bear Creek by the discovery of a frozen corpse on a snowy slope just outside of town. There are no signs indicating how the body got there—no footprints or drag marks—nothing. It's as if the victim has fallen from the sky. The discovery that the victim is a well-known environmental extremist brings the Vancouver Homicide Unit in to take over the case, creating turmoil in the sleepy mountain town. What they find is a disturbing trail of clues that stretches the breadth of British Columbia. A killer has come to Bear Creek and only time will tell who the next victim will be.

ISBN 10: 1-896300-89-8 PB • ISBN 13: 978-1-896300-89-4 PB

$10.95 CDN • $7.95 US

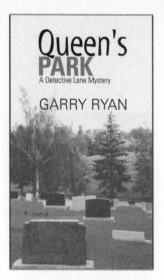

## Queen's Park
### A Detective Lane Mystery

**GARRY RYAN**

Detective Lane has a knack for discovering the whereabouts of missing persons. But the city's latest case has disappeared without a trace. After a brutal attack on his young nephew, ex-mayor Bob Swatsky has gone missing with 13 million dollars of tax-payers' money. Is he on the run with the cash, or is it something more sinister? A zany cast of characters, including a love doll, and a chain-smoking grandma with an oxygen tank, lead Detective Lane on a thrilling romp through the streets of Calgary. The chase is on, and alone, Lane must uncover the truth before someone ends up visiting Queen's Park cemetery . . . permanently.

Look for Detective Lane in *The Lucky Elephant Restaurant* coming Spring 2006.

ISBN 10: 1-896300-84-7 PB • ISBN 13: 978-1-896300-84-9
$10.95 CDN • $7.95 US

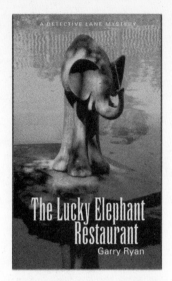

# The Lucky Elephant Restaurant
## A Detective Lane Mystery

### GARRY RYAN

Detectective Lane is back, tracking down trouble on the streets of Calgary with his sharp-eyed partner Harper in tow. The duo must find the missing daughter of local radio celebrity Bobbie Reddie before it's too late. But is Bobbie really as saintly as her fans believe? Lane must uncover the truth or this time the danger will hit much closer to home.

"A first-rate gem of a detective story."

—Rick Mofina, *The Dying Hour*

ISBN 10: 1-896300-97-9 PB • ISBN 13: 978-1-896300-97.9
$10.95 CDN • $7.95 US

KAY STEWART was born in Texas, and CHRIS BULLOCK in Cheshire, England. Stewart has a BA in English with honours from Texas Tech University, and an MA and PhD in English from the University of Oregon. Bullock has a BA and a PhD in English from the University of Leeds in Yorkshire. They met while teaching at the University of Alberta in Edmonton. Well-established as writers and editors, they moved in 2000 to a rural property near Nanaimo on Vancouver Island, where they spend their time writing, supporting environmental causes, and enjoying the spectacular West Coast nature around them. Stewart is also an enthusiastic novice gardener and Bullock runs a poetry study group for the C.G. Jung Society of Victoria. *A Deadly Little List* is their first novel.